For Rod and Herr Baedeker.

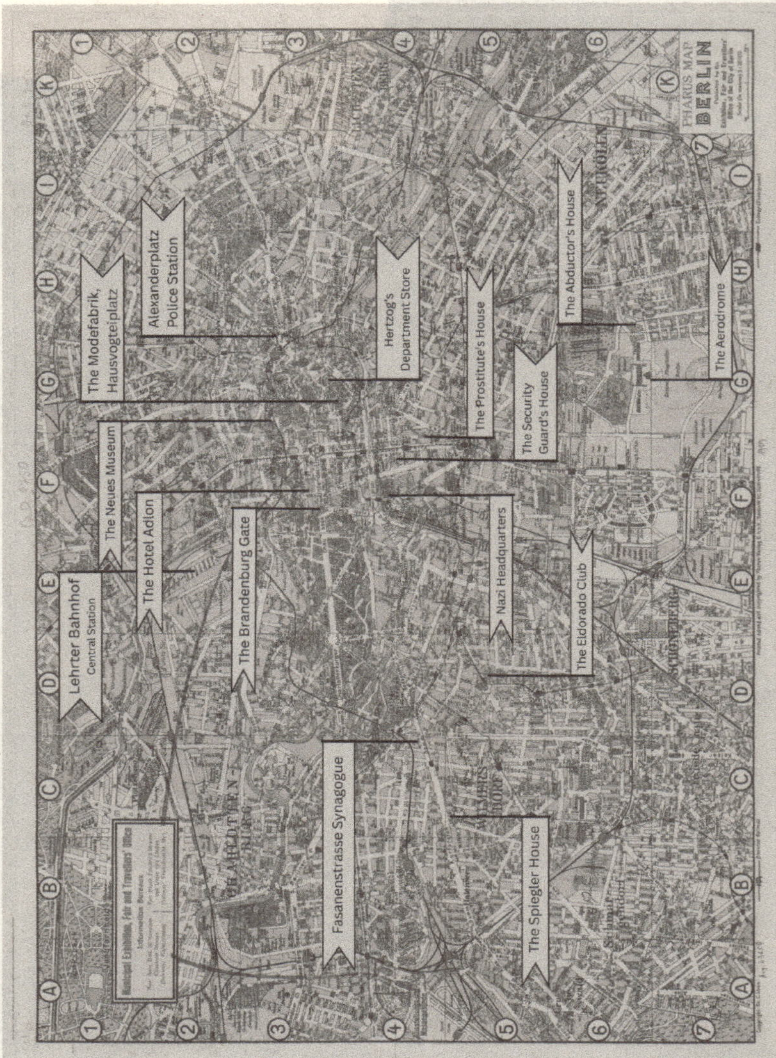
Lehrter Bahnhof
Central Station
The Neues Museum
The Hotel Adlon
The Modefabrik, Hausvogteiplatz
Alexanderplatz Police Station
The Brandenburg Gate
Hertzog's Department Store
The Prostitute's House
The Security Guard's House
The Abductor's House
Nazi Headquarters
The Eldorado Club
The Aerodrome
Fasanenstrasse Synagogue
The Spiegler House
PHARUS MAP
BERLIN

Berlin, 1930

THE BERLIN MURDERS

Also By Fiona Veitch Smith

The Miss Clara Vale Mystery Series

1. *The Picture House Murders*
2. *The Pantomime Murders*
3. *The Pyramid Murders*
4. *The Penford Manor Murders*
5. *The Berlin Murders*

The Poppy Denby Investigates Series

1. *A Front-Page Murder*
2. *Murder at the Old Vic Theatre*
3. *Murder on Lexington Avenue*
4. *Murder at Winterton Hall*
5. *Murder at the Art Gallery*
6. *Murder of an Oxford Scientist*

THE BERLIN MURDERS

FIONA VEITCH SMITH

embla books

First published in the UK in 2026 by

embla books

An imprint of Bonnier Books UK
5th Floor, HYLO, 105 Bunhill Row,
London, EC1Y 8LZ

A CIP catalogue record for this book is available from the British Library.

ISBN: 9781471417573

Also available as an ebook and an audiobook

1

Typeset by IDSUK (Data Connection) Ltd
Printed and bound by CPI (UK) LTD, Croydon CR0 4YY

FSC
www.fsc.org
MIX
Paper | Supporting responsible forestry
FSC® C013604

The authorised representative in the EEA is Bonnier Books UK (Ireland) Limited.
Registered office address: Block B, The Crescent Building, Northwood, Santry, Dublin 9, D09 C6X8 Ireland
compliance@bonnierbooks.ie
www.bonnierbooks.co.uk

Chapter 1

1st September 1930, Newcastle upon Tyne, England

The sewing room of Levine's Costumes was a sea of silk and chiffon. The colours of the season were shades of blue and green, with cloth draped over furniture and swirled on the wooden floor like tidal pools at the seaside. Paper patterns and calico toiles were pinned to dressmakers' dummies, while every inch of wall was covered with sketches of dresses and skirts, trousers and blouses and torn-out pages from French magazines. In the midst of it all, with pins in her mouth and hair like the snakes of a Medusa, stood Juju Levine – costume designer extraordinaire.

Miss Clara Vale, the lady detective who occupied the office space above Levine's Costumes, had popped in for a cup of tea. 'Is this a good time, Juju, or are you too busy?' asked Clara, edging her way between two dummies and resisting the urge to apologise to them.

'Oh, Clara!' cried Juju, taking the pins from her mouth. 'Of course I don't have time, but I'll always make time for you!'

'Should I put the kettle on?'

'Yes, please,' said Juju and cleared a bolt of fabric from a table to make room for the tea tray.

Clara relocated an alarmingly combustible swatch of gauze from the vicinity of the primus stove before lighting the flame and popping the kettle on top. She ought to have a word with Jonny – Juju's more sensible sibling and business partner – to remind his sister of fire safety measures. It was pointless talking to Juju now, she was far too consumed with preparing for the show in Berlin next week.

'Will Jonny be joining us too?' asked Clara as the kettle began to bubble and hiss.

'No, no,' said Juju. 'He's with Andrew the accountant.' And then she caught her breath. 'Oh golly, Clara, I'm sorry, I shouldn't have mentioned him.'

Clara smiled at her friend and took the kettle off the flame. 'Don't worry about it. Andrew and I are fine. He's still my accountant. We're still friends and have a very good professional relationship.'

'But no hope of rekindling the romance?'

Clara shook her head. 'None at all.'

Juju's eyebrow twitched mischievously. 'Ah, it's because of the handsome police inspector, isn't it?'

'Juju! You're incorrigible!' Clara laughed.

Juju sighed and swooned into a chair. 'I'm just a hopeless romantic. So,' she said, refusing to let Clara off the hook, 'is it the inspector? I heard you were seen twirling the dance floor with him at the Policemen's Summer Ball.'

'Guilty as charged,' said Clara, stirring tea leaves into the pot. 'But we shan't be doing much more twirling, I'm afraid. Thanks to the Penford Manor murder case, he's been offered a promotion . . . in Manchester.'

Juju's face fell. 'Oh, Clara! And to think he wouldn't have solved that case without you. You've shot yourself in the foot!'

Clara chuckled. 'It's not that bad, Juju. I'm very fond of Inspector Hawkes but the last thing I want right now, with the agency doing so well, is to be tied down . . . to a man.' Although, she thought to herself, if she were to be tied down to anyone, then Sandy Hawkes was a very good candidate. She hoped that perhaps one day their paths might cross again. However, for now, she would keep that vision to herself.

Juju accepted a cup of tea from Clara. 'Your uncle would be very proud of how well you are doing, Clara. He always knew you'd make a good detective. Have you any new cases on the go?'

Clara nodded. 'A small one. A woman has hired us to find out which of her domestic staff has stolen some jewellery. Bella's out on the job right now.'

'Oh,' said Juju. 'That's disappointing.'

Clara gave her a quizzical look. 'Why disappointing? I know it's not as exciting as mass murder and blackmail, but frankly, I'm pleased for a quieter spell. Four huge cases in twelve months has been a baptism of fire for me. I've had enough jam for a while, time to work on some bread-and-butter business.'

Juju took a sip of tea. 'Not disappointing for you, Clara, I know. But it is for me.'

'Why's that?'

'Because,' she said, gesturing around her, 'I was planning to ask you to come to Berlin with me.'

'Whatever would I do in Berlin?'

Juju threw her hands in the air. 'Be my muse! My model! Ever since I designed that Nefertiti dress for you, Clara, you have become my inspiration. Unless I'm specifically commissioned to design for someone, it is always the imaginary "you" that I design for. You're the perfect build, the perfect height and – with your Louise Brooks looks – the perfect Hollywood face.'

Clara was startled. 'Good grief, Juju, that's a bit much.'

Juju gave a dramatic sigh. 'I know, I know, but it's true. I can use some models from the department store when I get there, but I'll have to adjust the fit on everything. But if you were to come with me . . .'

Oh, I could never do that! thought Clara. But she didn't want to disappoint her friend. 'I'm sorry, Juju. I would if I could. But I really don't have the time, I have a case on the go.'

Juju leaned forward. 'And if you didn't have the case? Would you come? It would mean the world to me if you did. You know this is my big chance, Clara. My first opportunity to take part in an international show. I don't want to make costumes for the theatre forever. You've still got age on your side, but I'm turning fifty next month. I'm not getting any younger. I want to see my designs on the runways of Paris and New York. And now, I have a chance in Berlin . . .'

'And I'm delighted for you,' said Clara. 'You'll be fine without me. More than fine. You're such a gifted designer. You're going to shine in Berlin, mark my words.'

Clara smiled encouragingly at her friend. Just then, the door of the sewing room opened and a tall ginger-haired woman wearing a bright yellow hat and an even brighter smile stepped in. It was Bella Cuddy, Clara's assistant.

'Oh, there you are, Miss Vale. I thought you might be having a cuppa with Miss Levine.'

'Do you want one?' asked Juju.

'Aye,' said Bella, taking off her hat and putting it on one of the dummies. 'I could murder a cup o' tea. But let me tell you the good news first.'

'What's that?' asked Clara, as Bella sat down.

'I've solved the case, miss! It was the woman's husband, not the servants. He nicked his wife's jewels and pawned them to pay for a gambling debt. And I've got the evidence to prove it.'

Juju beamed. 'So, does that mean it's case closed?'

'Aye, Miss Levine, I think it is.'

'Oh, Bella,' said Juju, clapping her hands. 'We are *so* pleased to hear that! Aren't we, Clara?'

'Hmmm,' said Clara, and she took a long sip of tea.

Chapter 2

4th September 1930, Ijmuiden, Port of Amsterdam

The Queen Wilhelmina steamer slowed down as she approached the Dutch coast. To the delight of the passengers, dolphins accompanied her into the mouth of the river IJ, joyfully leaping back and forth over the ship's wake. It had been a relatively still crossing of the North Sea from Newcastle's Port of Tyne, and Clara and her friends had slept easy in their cabins. They were now tucking into a hearty on-board breakfast.

Bella was on her second helping of eggs and bacon. 'Young Sophie won't know what she missed!' she said, ladling some marmalade onto her toast.

Jonny Levine, a short, bald, modest man with a neat little moustache, nodded and sipped his strong Dutch coffee. 'Yes, the weather's been good, but it could just as easily have been as bad as she feared.'

'It's quite an understandable fear,' agreed Clara. 'Particularly if she's never been on a boat before.'

Juju pursed her lips. 'Well, she could at least have tried! She put me in a difficult spot, cancelling like that at the last minute. I'm just grateful Bella agreed to come in her stead.'

Bella, whose first trip abroad had been to Cairo earlier in the year, had jumped at the opportunity when Sophie, Juju's apprentice, had backed out. Bella was getting quite an appetite for foreign travel, thought Clara. However, Clara was a little put out that she had to close the office for a week as no one would be there to man – or woman – it. That had been one of the main reasons she'd hired Bella in the first place: to look after the office when she was away. But as she saw the excitement on Bella's face when she, Jonny and Juju were talking about their trip to Berlin, Clara had given in and agreed that she could come too.

'I suppose we could just put a note on the door saying when we'll be back,' she'd said. 'And to leave any messages with Sophie downstairs.' Sophie had been told that if there was anything she felt couldn't wait, she was to send a telegram to an address in Berlin where Clara would receive it. And with Clara's friend Dr Charlie Malone put in charge of feeding the cat, the collective members of Vale Investigations and Levine Costumes set sail for Amsterdam.

There they would meet up with two other groups: one from Paris, another from New York, and together they would all catch the overnight train to Berlin.

She turned to Juju who had attempted – but failed – to tame her corkscrew curls with a paisley silk scarf. Juju's flamboyant personal style was in stark contrast to her more conservative twin brother, but Clara knew that the siblings were the perfect business partners. She the creative genius, he the astute businessman. Clara suspected Jonny had more to do on this trip than just cheer for his sister at the fashion show.

'So, tell me more about these people we're meeting, Juju. You said they are also designers.'

Juju swallowed a mouthful of pancake, drizzled with honey and cinnamon.

'Hugo Treves and Danny Cohen – or Danyl Kohan as we knew him when we first met. A Russian émigré. He was a student back then. The summer of 1913. Jonny and I were visiting our cousin Jakob. Jakob worked in Hertzog's Department Store and got us holiday jobs in the men's and women's wear departments. And that's where we met Hugo. He's French and came to Hertzog's to do his apprenticeship in design while he studied at Universität der Künste Berlin – the university of the arts. We all got on like a house on fire. Particularly Hugo and Jonny.'

She winked at her brother.

He flashed her a warning look. Clara noted it but didn't probe. Instead, she asked: 'And Danny? What was he studying?'

Juju returned her attention to Clara. 'Oh, something to do with the business side of fashion. He was always more of a manager than an artist. Although he did – and does – dabble in design. But then the war started in 1914 and we had to leave Germany. We didn't meet again until after Armistice. Jonny and I went back to Berlin in 1920. We didn't realise that Hugo and Danny were in town again too, until we bumped into them at a cabaret club. That one on the Kurfürstendamm I think, wasn't it, Jonny? The night we saw Anita Berber perform.' She turned to Clara and Bella. 'I don't know if you've seen any of her films, but she was huge in Germany. Sadly, I heard she died a couple of years ago. Drug overdose, I believe.'

'Tuberculosis,' corrected Jonny.

Juju rolled her eyes. 'Well, that was the official report.'

'How long did you all stay in Berlin?' asked Clara.

'We considered staying there permanently,' said Jonny. 'I was going to go into partnership with my cousin Jakob.

But then inflation started getting out of control and it was no longer a safe investment for me. And the whole country was on the brink of a revolution in 1923. So we went back to England.'

'And Danny and Hugo?'

Jonny waved to the waiter to pour him another cup of coffee. 'Danny moved to America. I don't think the changes in Russia appealed to him.'

'You mean the Bolshevik Revolution?'

Juju nodded. 'That's right. He thought for a while he might be a Bolshevik, didn't he, Jonny? But then he realised he liked the fine things in life too much. He moved to America, started a fashion business and converted to capitalism. And that's how Danyl Kohan became Danny Cohen.'

'And Hugo?' asked Clara.

'Hugo went back to Paris,' said Jonny, quietly.

There was an awkward pause. Juju looked to her brother, but when he didn't say more she turned back to Clara.

'He's a fabulous designer,' she said. 'Very gifted. Just not much of a businessman. He always needed someone else to look after that part of things. We thought for a while that he and Danny might go into business together. But then they had a falling-out.'

'What about?' asked Bella.

'Creative differences,' said Jonny.

'More like creative similarities,' said Juju.

'What do you mean?' asked Bella.

Juju leaned forward to share her gossip. 'Well, you see, there was a dress that Hugo designed . . .'

'Leave it, Juju. It's all forgiven and forgotten now,' Jonny snapped at his sister.

Juju gave a little snort. 'Hardly! Hugo is the master of holding grudges. As are you.'

'I said *leave it.*'

Juju huffed. 'Oh, all right.'

'Well,' said Clara, looking from Juju to Jonny, 'I look forward to meeting them both.'

And then the captain's voice spoke over the Tannoy, first in English and then in Dutch: 'Ladies and gentlemen, welcome to the Netherlands . . .'

'Eeee,' said Bella, in a broad Geordie accent. 'We're gannin' on a new adventure!'

* * *

Clara, Bella and Juju spent a glorious day in sunny Amsterdam while Jonny attended a series of business meetings. The exact nature of Jonny's business, beyond the costume shop in Newcastle, was quite opaque, but Clara had caught hints that it was to do with imports of fabric from the colonies and its distribution around Europe and over to America. Juju appeared uninterested in her brother's entrepreneurial affairs and was delighted to accompany Clara and Bella around the Dutch city. It was Clara's first time in Amsterdam, and she was charmed.

It was as busy as London, with just as many motor cars and trams, but bicycles – wave after wave of them – were the main mode of transport. Clara and Bella were nearly run down twice trying to cross Stationplein – the great cobbled square outside the

Central Railway Station – which was criss-crossed by trams, taxis and bicycles coming from the opposite direction from which they expected. After pulling her two friends back from yet another near-death experience, Juju explained that in Amsterdam, like the rest of Europe, vehicles drove on the right of the road, not the left. She then insisted on taking Bella and Clara's hands – like little schoolgirls – to guide them across the roads. Clara considered it a humiliation worth paying in order to stay alive.

But once she got the hang of the road layout, she began to relax and appreciate the beauty of the city. Unlike London, which has just one river running through it, Amsterdam was criss-crossed with canals and waterways, with brightly painted wooden barges moored to stone walls. Lines of elm trees – with their leaves turning from green to early autumn yellow – were reflected in the canals on one side, while casting cool shadows over the cobbled streets on the other. Tall, skinny buildings, of five or six storeys, topped with traditional Dutch gables, overlooked the canals, their facades as brightly coloured as the bobbing boats below.

Juju led them from one city island to another, over picturesque bridges, with flower vendors and puppeteers gathered at each end. She threw money into a hat and the three women were charmed by a performance of clog-wearing dolls dancing to the music of an organ grinder. Lunch was bought and eaten by a canal, their legs hanging over the side, and then mid-afternoon coffee, accompanied by a puff-pastry stuffed with almond paste and drizzled in honey, crowned their wonderful day. As the shadows grew longer and the Amsterdamers climbed on their bicycles, it was time for the English ladies to catch the overnight train to Berlin.

Chapter 3

Jonny was waiting with their luggage in the first-class lounge at Amsterdam station. He had already supervised the loading of the two enormous trunks that contained Juju's collection onto the freight carriage. The four suitcases at his feet were the personal items of the travelling party.

He looked pointedly at his watch as the three ladies entered, smiling and refreshed after their day in the city. Juju gave a mock tut. 'We're on time, Jonny boy. Don't worry.'

'Hmmm,' said her brother. 'Did you have a good day?'

'Oh, it was grand!' said Bella. 'But hard to understand what anyone said!'

Jonny chuckled. 'I think they'd find it hard to understand you too!'

'Fortunately, Juju's Dutch is excellent,' said Clara. 'I didn't know she was so multi-lingual! I have some French and a bit more German, but nowhere near as fluent as Juju.'

Jonny smiled warmly. 'Indeed. My sister is a woman of many talents. It does help to have family on the continent. The Levines originally came from Eastern Europe, but we've got relatives all over the place now. The Jewish community is very close-knit – no matter where in the world we end up. And speaking of which . . . here's Danny!'

A large, round-faced man wearing a smart pin-stripe suit and a stylish fedora filled the doorway of the waiting room. He opened his arms wide when he spotted the Levine twins. 'Jonny!

Juju! Come to Danny!' He had a pronounced New York accent, but Clara could still hear hints of Russian. Juju squealed with delight and stepped into his embrace. Jonny offered his hand. Danny bellowed a laugh and shook hands so vigorously Clara thought Jonny might be lifted from his feet.

Danny then stepped aside and gestured to two much slimmer people behind him. A tall, statuesque blonde woman in her thirties, wearing an impeccably cut travelling suit of sage-green tweed with bottle-green velvet trim and matching hat, and a younger man in his twenties, straining under the weight of three suitcases.

'May I present Miss Hilda Markwald – my model – and young Benji Finkelstein, my assistant.'

Jonny reciprocated the introductions by describing Clara as Juju's model, and Bella as the assistant.

The blonde woman's eyes narrowed and she pursed her lips.

Hmmm, thought Clara. *What's that about?*

But the young man managed a friendly smile and a slightly out-of-breath greeting with a pronounced New York accent.

Jonny looked at his watch. 'So, we're just waiting for Hugo . . .'

'Wait no more, *mon ami*!'

The most elegant man Clara had ever seen posed in the doorway. *Posed*, she thought, *was just the right word for it.* Hugo Treves's long legs, in maroon flannel trousers, were positioned as though he were just about to step onto a dance floor. And he held his hands, with pink silk cuffs peeking out of the sleeves of his maroon jacket, as though he were presenting a fine Ming vase at an auction.

'Hugo!' Juju pirouetted from Danny's gorilla-sized arms to be caught in the Frenchman's embrace. He held her shoulders and kissed her extravagantly on both cheeks.

'*Mon petit* Juju! You look younger than ever! Dreary old England hasn't dampened you one bit!'

'Oh, you old charmer!' said Juju, warming the entire room with her smile.

'And where is Jonny?'

'I'm here, Hugo,' said Jonny, stepping quietly forward, but staying out of kissing distance.

Hugo's voice lowered as he took a cautious step towards Jonny. 'It has been too long, old friend.'

Clara watched as the two men's eyes met, the air charged with something unspoken. The longing emanating from Hugo was almost palpable. But it was met with cool caution. Clara remembered what Juju had said on the steamer this morning about Jonny and Hugo getting on particularly well when they first met. She wondered what had happened between them to create this odd tension. She knew of Jonny's forbidden passions. Had they been . . . lovers?

But before she could wonder any further, Hugo pulled his eyes away and scanned the room. Introductions were made of the various assistants and models. Accompanying Hugo was a waif-like girl of eighteen or nineteen with hair as dark as Clara's. But where Clara's skin was pale as porcelain, the girl's was warm and brown. She reminded Clara of some of the women she had recently seen in Egypt, and she guessed that the young model might have parentage from French North Africa: Algeria, Tunisia or Morocco. She was introduced as Merlette – no surname given.

Next to Merlette was a man in his early forties who would have been handsome but for the severe scarring on one side of his face. Clara had seen injuries like his before: he had likely been a soldier in the war and exposed to mustard gas. The man was introduced as Pierre Dreyfus. Hugo described him as his 'business partner'.

'Pierre's far better with figures than I am,' he said. Then with a playful wink, 'The numerical kind, that is.' Pierre greeted everyone in passable English, but Merlette only spoke French.

A moment later and the first-class conductor for the Mitteleuropa train to Berlin entered the lounge and announced that it was time to board.

* * *

The Mitropa Schlafwagen, like its sister company Wagon-Lits that ran the Orient Express, was famed for its luxurious, modern accommodation. The operators proudly provided each passenger with a brochure extolling the virtues of the sumptuous locomotive. The compartments were designed by the renowned Bauhaus creator Walter Gropius, with sleek geometric lines and highly polished chrome surfaces. There were fold-down beds decked with the finest linen, a basin with running water and a table where tea – or something stronger – could be enjoyed in privacy. Flushing lavatories were shared – two per coach – but for those reluctant to venture too far to spend a penny (or a pfennig) each compartment had its own commode.

There was a communal dining car serviced by a fully-fitted electric kitchen overseen by a Michelin-approved chef, and a small army of waiters. A smoking lounge and bar were attached to the dining car, where passengers could enjoy a communal drink while getting to know their fellow travellers.

Juju had insisted that she and Jonny would be covering all Clara and Bella's expenses, and despite the women saying they would be happy to share a compartment, Juju had booked them adjoining berths – with a connecting door between them.

'Eee, this is nowt like the trains back home, Miss Vale!' Bella said as she flopped down on Clara's bunk.

Clara smiled. 'No, it isn't. And they even expect us to change for dinner, so we'd best put on our nicest frocks.' Clara stripped down to her bandeau and camiknickers then sat down on the cabin chair and slipped off her stockings. She opened her suitcase and found a clean pair, sliding them on and clipping them to her silk garters. 'I think a cocktail dress will do,' she said, unfolding a blue crêpe silk dress, cut on the bias with a godet skirt, tied with a hip sash, and long sleeves with musketeer cuffs. It was from the 1929 Jean Patou collection, and she'd last worn it at a dinner party in London in February. 'What are you going to wear?' she asked Bella.

Bella screwed up her nose. 'Don't worry, miss, you won't have to go looking in the lost-and-found frocks for me this time. Miss Levine made sure I have some suitable options.' She jumped up and went through the connecting door to her own compartment and returned a few moments later holding an emerald-green crêpe georgette sleeveless dress with a calf-length handkerchief hem. The dress had the new hip skimming lines of the 1930 season and the draped cowl neckline.

Clara gasped. 'Oh, Bella! That's beautiful! Juju has done you proud. It matches your eyes and sets off your hair to a T. And it makes my old frock look positively old fashioned!'

Bella smiled at her employer. 'You will never be old fashioned, Miss Vale, you're the most modern woman I know. And the most beautiful. You'd look good in a sack!'

Clara laughed. 'Well, let's hope I won't have to resort to that!'

* * *

At almost seven o'clock the train was travelling east, away from the setting sun. But there was still enough light to see the passing Dutch countryside. They had left Amsterdam behind, travelling south-east through the suburbs with their charming gabled houses and neat front gardens. The train was now chugging through the North Holland countryside, with black-and-white Friesian cows grazing in the shadow of windmills. It was like a picture postcard.

Clara and Bella made their way to the dining car, following the sound of a jazz record. Clara wondered how a gramophone would perform with the jolting of the train carriages, but so far so good. Perhaps on such a modern train, she thought, the disruption would be minimal.

The ladies were met at the door of the dining car by a waiter in a white coat. He greeted them with a polite bow and ushered them inside.

The jazz music welcomed them with seductive chords. It was a Hoagy Carmichael record – 'Georgia on my Mind'. Clara had heard it in her friend Charlie Malone's extensive music collection.

Bella, beside her, who had a good musical ear, smiled and started gently humming. But it was the hubbub of conversation in the dinner car that dominated the soundscape. The other passengers were already seated and dressed to the nines: the women dripping jewels and the men in black tie and tuxedos. White-coated waiters fluttered between the tables, pouring wine and taking orders. Juju waved to Clara and Bella. She and Jonny were already seated at a table for four along with Hugo and Danny. 'I hope you don't mind sitting over there, ladies,' she said, gesturing, 'but we thought we'd take some time to catch up with our old friends.'

'Over there' was a table set for six with four people already seated: Hilda Markwald, Benji Finkelstein, Pierre Dreyfus and Merlette – the respective assistants, business partners and models of the group Clara was coming to think of as *the Berlin Four*. Pierre and Benji both stood, Pierre giving a gallant bow and Benji a wide smile. 'Good evening, Miss Vale, Miss Cuddy,' he said, pulling out a chair as Pierre did the same, catching Clara's eye. Clara nodded to the Frenchman and slipped into the seat beside him, leaving Bella to take up the hospitality of the young New Yorker.

'I see you are wearing a Patou,' said Hilda, her voice as cool as her eyes.

Clara nodded to the American model.

'It's not *this* season though, is it?' Hilda's eyes ranged from the hem to the neckline to the statement cuffs.

'Of course not,' said Clara, with a tight smile. 'What serious woman would waste her money on buying designer frocks every single season?'

Benji laughed. 'Well, hopefully there are a few of them, Miss Vale, or we'll all be out of business!'

'This isn't Miss Vale's usual business,' said Bella to Benji, and then frowned at Hilda.

'Yes, I can tell,' replied Hilda, flashing her teeth in what might have been meant as a smile but was more of a snarl.

'I once modelled for Patou,' said Merlette in French.

'Really?' answered Clara in the same tongue. 'Do tell us about it, *mademoiselle*.'

Hilda rolled her eyes and said in English, 'I think the word "modelled" might have been lost in translation here.'

'That's enough!' snapped Pierre in French. Then in English: 'Please do try to be pleasant, Hilda. Or you'll ruin the evening for everyone.'

Hilda pursed her lips and narrowed her eyes, but she held her tongue.

'So, what is your usual business, Miss Vale?' asked Benji.

Clara smiled at him. 'I run an enquiry agency. And Miss Cuddy here is my assistant.'

Benji's eyes opened wide. 'You mean you're a PI? Like Philo Vance? The detective fella in the movies?'

Clara chuckled. 'A little like that. But with fewer damsels in distress.'

Bella tutted. 'That's not quite true, Miss Vale. You've helped quite a few damsels in distress. And a few gents too!'

Benji's face was alight with excitement. 'Gee, ladies, that's just swell! So, tell us about your most exciting case.'

'Well,' said Bella, twinkling with pride, 'that would probably be the one that took us to Cairo. We flew in an aeroplane over the pyramids and hunted down a murderer in the desert!'

'Gee whiz! Were there mummies and curses and ancient tombs?'

'Oh yes, Mr Finkelstein, all of that, and more!'

But before Bella could continue, Clara interjected. 'Perhaps we should save the stories for later, Bella. I'd like to know what to expect when we get to Berlin. And who better to tell us than these experts?' She directed her last comment towards Hilda.

'I believe you are an experienced model, Miss Markwald. I hope you can guide us a little.' Clara smiled, hoping to break through the veil of animosity with a hint of flattery. Her tactic appeared to work.

'Well,' said Hilda, softening a little, 'I *am* very experienced.'

'Do tell . . .' said Clara.

Pierre rolled his eyes. Hilda gave him a pointed look and then turned to Clara. 'Well, I have modelled in Paris, London and New York.'

'And now Berlin,' said Clara.

'Oh, of course Berlin. Many times. But Berlin is not on the same level as the other three.'

'And yet here you are . . .' muttered Pierre in French.

Merlette gave a little chuckle but was quickly silenced by a glare from Hilda.

'Tell me about Berlin, though,' said Clara. 'As you have astutely observed, this is very new to me. Miss Cuddy and I are only here as a favour to Juju. Her assistant dropped out at the last minute and her model . . . well, I think she said she would use a model in Berlin, but as she had used me as a template for her designs, it was easier for her if I came.'

'But you have no modelling experience,' said Hilda.

Clara flapped her hands in mock surrender. 'Absolutely none at all.'

'You have the look of a model,' said Pierre in English.

'*Oui*,' said Merlette in agreement.

Clara quickly returned to Hilda, sensing that she would not appreciate any suggestion of rivalry. 'Perhaps. But I am an amateur. I have a lot to learn. What can I expect in Berlin, Miss Markwald?'

Hilda gave a condescending smile as she lit a cigarette. She pulled on it, exhaled slowly then said: 'Well, we'll be based at Hertzog's.'

'One of the biggest department stores in Berlin,' added Benji.

'I've heard about that,' said Clara. 'That's where Juju, Jonny, Hugo and Danny met before the war.'

'That's right,' continued Hilda. 'Hertzog's was at the forefront of German ready-to-wear – or, as we call it in America, off-the-peg – fashion. During the war, access to Paris was limited, so other countries were forced to come up with their own fashion lines. Still influenced, mostly, by Paris. They would send designers there to sketch what was on the runway from the top houses: Worth, Poiret, Vionnet . . .' she nodded at Clara's dress '. . . Patou and, more recently, Chanel, and then recreate them to be sold – far cheaper – either in the department stores or through catalogues. In America we have Sears, in England I believe you have Littlewoods.'

'Oooh, Littlewoods!' interjected Bella. 'I love their dresses!'

Hilda pursed her lips around her cigarette but did not reply.

Clara frowned. 'So, the designs are stolen?'

'Not stolen,' said Pierre, 'merely inspired.'

'You are French, *Monsieur*, and you still think that?' asked Clara.

Pierre shrugged and then replied in French. 'It is business. I am Hugo's business partner. He is the creative. His inspiration is his business.'

'Monsieur Hugo is always original,' said Merlette, in French.

Hilda snorted. 'Hardly, my dear.' Then in English, 'Hugo's designs aren't *always* original.'

'Well, Miss Levine's are!' said Bella.

'Yes, they are,' agreed Clara, but she couldn't help thinking about the Parisian magazines she had seen on Juju's workshop wall.

Benji Finkelstein, suddenly serious and sounding older than his years, added sagely, 'There's a fine line between imitation and inspiration.'

'Indeed, there is,' agreed Clara. 'Does Mr Cohen do his own designs?'

Hilda sucked on her cigarette and shrugged. 'He claims to.'

Benji was just about to say something when Hilda pinned him with her eyes.

Interesting, thought Clara. She smiled at Hilda. 'Thank you, this helps me to get a clearer picture. So, what is the purpose of this fashion exhibition in Berlin?'

'It is part of the new Berlin Fashion Week,' said Hilda. 'It's Berlin's attempt to set itself apart from Paris, London and New York.'

Clara raised an eyebrow. 'Yet they're inviting people from Paris, London and New York. Well, Newcastle at least.' She caught Bella's smile and wrinkled her nose in reply.

'Yes,' said Hilda, 'but they all have connections to Berlin. They all worked or studied there. And there are other designers too. Ones who still live in Germany. We are just here to give it an international flavour, yet still to keep it within the family.'

'The family?' asked Clara.

Hilda shrugged and tapped some ash into an ashtray. 'I speak metaphorically, Miss Vale. But by family, I mean those known to Hertzog and his artistic director Jakob Spiegler. And of course, most of them are Jewish . . .'

She wafted her hand dismissively. Pierre frowned, Benji lowered his eyes and cleared his throat.

'And that's a problem?' asked Clara directly.

'No, no, not at all.' Hilda gave an insincere smile and called over the waiter. 'We're ready to order.'

Chapter 4

Clara woke with a heavy feeling in her bladder. She lay on her bunk for a few minutes, trying to decide whether to hold it in until morning or get up. The luminescent dials on her travel clock told her it was one o'clock. She doubted she could hold it for another five hours. So, reluctantly, she pulled back the covers and got up. She considered using the commode but decided instead to use the proper toilet further down the carriage. She pulled on a silk dressing gown and opened her compartment door and immediately heard the murmur of voices. At the end of the carriage was a blonde woman in a scarlet kimono talking quietly to someone near the connecting doorway to the next carriage: it was Hilda Markwald. But Clara could not make out who she was talking to. The timbre of voice – too low to hear the words clearly – suggested a man. Hilda's voice was higher pitched and more distinct, and Clara caught snatches of what was being said.

'It's too soon . . . wait till we get to Berlin . . . don't want to reveal our hand . . . too much suspicion . . .'

The man's reply was muffled, but whatever he said seemed to irk Hilda who retorted with something like, 'Don't be stupid, man! You'll give the game away . . .'

Before Clara could hear any more, a door opened between Clara's compartment and the whispering couple, and another man stepped into the corridor.

Hilda turned at the noise and Clara saw her interlocutor slip into the other carriage.

Hilda and Clara recognised the second man at the same time, but only Hilda spoke.

'Hugo! You're up late.'

'As are you, Hilda.'

Hugo peered past her. 'Who was that you were talking to?'

'Just the guard. I was asking for some cocoa. I couldn't sleep.'

'You could have just rung your bell,' observed Hugo.

'And you could have just stayed in your own compartment,' sneered Hilda. 'Were you looking for cocoa too?'

'I was not. I heard Merlette crying out. I was just checking on her.'

Hilda sniffed. 'And how is she?'

'She is settled. She just had a bad dream. Good night, Hilda.' And with that the French designer opened the door next to Merlette's and went back to his own compartment.

Clara, unseen, decided she'd use her commode after all.

* * *

A few hours later, Clara awoke to a soft knock on the door. 'Breakfast in fifteen minutes, Miss Vale.' She looked at her watch and saw it was a quarter to six. The train was due into Berlin at seven fifteen. She pulled up the blind on her window to see it was pre-dawn but there was enough light to see that the bucolic Dutch countryside had given way to a semi-industrial area, hugging the railway line and bridging rivers. Between the towns the topography was hillier than the Netherlands and Clara could make out the shadow of a forest or woodland.

She mentally considered the map of Germany in her *Baedeker's Travel Guide* and thought they must be halfway between Magdeburg and Potsdam. She got up and knocked on Bella's door, to find Bella was already awake and nearly dressed.

'Morning, Miss Vale! I heard you up and about during the night. What was that all about?'

Clara smiled at her assistant. 'I'll tell you at breakfast. Give me five minutes and I'll be ready.'

* * *

Clara and Bella were shown to a table for two. They were greeted enthusiastically by Juju at the next table who was having breakfast with her brother.

'Did you sleep well, ladies?' asked Jonny.

'We did,' lied Clara with a smile.

'Spiffing!' said Juju. 'There's nothing like the rocking of a train to lull you to sleep. I slept like a baby! Which is just as well because we've got a big day ahead. Our cousin Jakob will be meeting us at the station, we'll drop our luggage at his house in Charlottenburg, then we'll register our arrival at the police station. After that, I'm sorry to say, we'll be straight to work! So, tuck in,' she said, nodding at the plates of omelette and sausage the waiter was placing in front of them, 'you'll need your strength.'

'You didn't sleep well, did you?' whispered Bella.

'No, I didn't,' said Clara quietly, and proceeded to tell her companion what she'd seen and heard during the night.

Clara looked over at Hilda Markwald who was sitting at a table with Benji Finkelstein and Danny Cohen. The model was perfectly made up, wearing a pink silk blouse over fashionable wide-leg trousers in bold purple, and looked as if she hadn't missed a wink of sleep. All three Americans appeared in a relaxed mood, conversing easily.

This was in stark contrast to the French table. Hugo was speaking sharply to Pierre, while Merlette poked unenthusiastically at her omelette. Clara wondered what Hugo had been doing in her compartment last night. Was it, as he said, that she had been having a bad dream, or was it something . . . well, something more unsavoury, as Hilda had suggested. Clara would be surprised if it were. She had the strong impression that Hugo was attracted to men, not women, but one never knew. Some people were attracted to both sexes.

If that was the case, she hoped that Merlette had been a willing participant. But, she knew, it would be difficult to say no to her employer. Clara's heart went out to the poor girl, who had seemed ill at ease since she'd met her. Although, she reminded herself, it really was none of her business. It was also none of her business that Pierre Dreyfus looked completely washed out, his hands quivering as he raised the coffee cup to his lips. His pupils, she noted, were suspiciously dilated. Clara knew these to be possible signs of morphine addiction. With the scarring to his face, suggesting mustard gas burns, Clara would not be surprised if he used morphine to dull the pain. While it was well over a decade since he would have sustained his injuries, the pain, she had heard, never quite went away. And even if it did, the amount of morphine he would have taken when first injured could quite easily have led him down the path of addiction. Her heart went out to him too.

She wondered what Hugo was berating him about, but she couldn't quite hear . . .

'So, who was Hilda talking to last night, do you think?' asked Bella.

Clara returned her attention to her assistant. 'I have no idea. But I don't believe for a minute that it was a guard, or that she was asking for cocoa. It's not really my business, of course, but if this were a case we were working on, I'd be very suspicious.'

Bella laughed. 'Aye, me too. But as there's been no crime, there's nowt to be suspicious about.'

Clara chuckled. 'Very true. We're not on the job, Bella, but it's hard not to think like a detective.'

Bella nodded. 'Aye, it is.' She raised her glass of orange juice in mock salute. 'Once a detective, always a detective.

'I'll drink to that,' said Clara, and raised her glass in return.

Chapter 5

Friday 5th September 1930, Berlin

Arrival in Berlin: Railway Stations
*A policeman, posted at the exit from each railway station, hands the traveller a metal ticket with the number of a cab, on his stating whether he wishes a motor-cab ('*Auto*') a horse-drawn cab ('*Droschke*') or a luggage-cab ('*Gepäck-Droschke*'). Cab and luggage fares see p.10. –* **from *Baedeker's Berlin and its Environs*, 1929**

It was rush hour at Lehrter Bahnhof, the main station in Berlin. Commuters, dressed for the office, rushed to catch their trains on the Stadtbahn, Ringbahn, S-Bahn or U-Bahn, all linking into the central station like a spiderweb. The Berliners ignored the out-of-town travellers disembarking from the sleeper train, looking around, peering at signage and wondering where to go next. Fortunately for Clara and Bella, Juju and Jonny knew exactly what to do. They bade farewell to the other travellers visiting for Fashion Week, who were taking care of their own accommodation, and then the ladies waited on the platform while Jonny arranged for a luggage cab.

It was then that something caught Clara's eye. A few carriages further down the platform, a man got off the sleeper train, carrying a suitcase in one hand and a rolled-up newspaper in the other. It was too far to see clearly, and his face was shadowed by a wide-brimmed fedora, but there was something about him that was familiar. As Clara tried to place him, she saw him raise his newspaper and wave to someone. And that someone, leaving the platform with the American group – Danny Cohen and Benji Finkelstein – was Hilda Markwald. Clara could see that Hilda had seen the man, but she pointedly turned without acknowledging him and walked away. He then turned briskly on his heel and walked in the other direction. Annoyingly, Clara still could not place him, but she filed it at the back of her mind – along with the snippets of conversation she had overheard last night – before turning her attention back to her friends.

Five minutes later and the three ladies were squeezed into the back of a taxi while Jonny climbed in the front. He had just supervised the transfer of the large trunks to a luggage van that would take them to Spiegler's Modefabrik, where they would have their base before later moving to Hertzog Department Store. He explained to Clara and Bella that Hertzog's was in the east of the city, on Spree Island, but they would be staying at their cousin's residence in the west, in Charlottenburg. 'Not to worry, there are plenty of trains around the city. And cousin Jakob has a motor.'

'And why isn't Jakob meeting us now?' asked Juju, sounding peeved. 'He said he would.'

'I know,' said Jonny. 'Apparently something came up, to do with Fashion Week. He said it couldn't wait. At least he sent a telegram to inform us on arrival. It's not such a bother to get a taxi.'

'I suppose not,' Juju huffed. 'At least now I can play tour guide.'

Clara smiled at Juju, whose plump thighs were comfortably pressing against Clara and Bella's legs on either side. 'I'm sure you'll be a splendid tour guide.'

Along with Juju's cheerful commentary, Clara was struck by the beauty of the city. The wide avenues, lined with shady linden, maple and oak trees, were watched over by regal buildings in classical style. Austere and militaristic statues were dotted along the central axis of the avenues, in honour of the kaisers, generals and imperial leaders of yore. Like Amsterdam, the city was criss-crossed by waterways, with each bit of land linked to the other by bridges. The combination of greenery and rivers cooled the city and there was a freshness to the air that Clara missed in London, yet the sun seemed warmer. It was a pleasing combination.

The taxi took them first past the Reichstag, the German parliament, where Jonny pointed out the government of the Weimar Republic was preparing for federal elections next week. The neo-renaissance facade reminded Clara a little of the British Museum with its columns and triangular apex, but its crowning glory was a spectacular dome, visible for miles around.

They then drove past the imposing Brandenburger Tor – the giant neoclassical gateway between west and east Berlin – with six columns topped by a statue of Victoria, the goddess of victory, in a chariot pulled by four horses. Clara and Bella craned their necks to see her in her magnificence.

'Is that our old Queen Vic?' asked Bella.

Juju chuckled. 'No. Just the same name. Although Queen Vic *was* related to the German royal family.'

'Aye, so I heard,' said Bella. 'Funny how we went to war then, isn't it?'

'Funny and sad,' agreed Clara.

The taxi then skirted the Tiergarten, the vast green park in the middle of Berlin, adjacent to the Zoological Gardens where lions and elephants dwelled. As they turned onto Potsdamer Straße, Juju pointed out that the funny letter on the street sign that looked like a capital B was pronounced 'ss' – like in hiss.

'So, Potsdamer Strasse,' Clara clarified for Bella's benefit. 'And *strasse* means street.'

The taxi continued through the Friday morning traffic until it turned onto the broad tree-lined boulevard of Kurfürstendamm. 'This is like our Oxford Street in London,' gushed Juju. 'Where the well-heeled Berliners come to shop.' She indicated left and right at sparkling shop windows showcasing luxury goods. 'The leading designers all have boutiques here.'

'Hard to believe there's an economic depression, isn't it?' said Jonny.

The taxi driver next to him gave a disdainful grunt, the first indication he'd given that he understood the English chatter of his passengers.

Jonny turned to him and conversed in German, while Juju kept up her patter, pointing out this or that shop and remembering what she'd bought there.

Clara heard the odd word in German from the men in front and wished Juju would pipe down a little so she could listen in. 'Depression'; 'inflation'; 'unemployment' and 'desperate times' were a few of the words she picked up. And then 'elections' and 'National Socialists'. Jonny spat out the word 'Nazi', making it sound like an expletive. She strained to hear more, but the conversation came to a halt as the taxi driver turned off the main boulevard, down a genteel side street and onto Lietzenburger Strasse. Clara looked up to see ladies watering plants on their apartment balconies while below them customers from cafés spilled out onto the pavement, sipping coffee, smoking and reading their newspapers. If there was an economic depression in Berlin, the comfortable suburbs of Charlottenburg and Wilmersdorf hid it well.

Soon Lietzenburger became Olivaer Platz, with four- to six-storey town houses and apartment buildings overlooking a leafy square. The architecture was close to what in England would be described as 'Georgian style', and there was a certain similarity to Clara's parents' house in Kensington.

The taxi slowed as an old man crossed the road with his dog, heading for a central park where small children played with a ball, while their nannies and mothers chatted nearby. The gentleman raised his hat in thanks.

The taxi finally stopped at a tall, white town house with red geraniums cascading from window boxes, and, as if to match, a brightly painted red front door.

'Look, Jonny,' said Juju, 'it hasn't changed a bit! Oh, it's wonderful to be back!'

The red door opened to reveal a tall, slim woman in her late fifties. Her dark hair, streaked with silver, was pulled back into a bun. Her demeanour was at first glance severe, but as Clara drew closer, she could see laughter lines around her dark eyes and a mouth that spread easily into a smile.

'Juju!' exclaimed the woman as her short, plump, English cousin enveloped her in an embrace. Then Jonny trotted up the steps and kissed her on both cheeks.

Juju turned and beckoned Clara and Bella forward. 'Ladies, this is my cousin's wife, Frau Estelle Spiegler – we call her Stella. And Stella, these are my friends, Miss Clara Vale and Miss Bella Cuddy, who will be working with me this week. Miss Vale here speaks some German, but Miss Cuddy does not.'

Stella shook hands warmly with the two newcomers. 'Welcome, ladies,' she said in strongly accented but reasonably fluent English. 'We will do our best to speak and understand.'

'Yes, we will,' said Clara in German. 'Your English is very good, Frau Spiegler. Better I think than my German.'

'I think you are too kind, Fräulein Vale,' said the German woman in her own tongue. 'And please, call me Stella.' Then in English, 'Welcome Miss Cuddy. Do not worry, everyone in this house – apart from the servants – speaks some English. Now,' she said, peering at Bella, 'have you eaten? Are you hungry?'

Bella looked at Clara. They had both eaten. *What should we say?* was the unspoken question between them.

Fortunately, they were saved by Juju. 'Well, I can't speak for these two, but I'm absolutely famished.'

Jonny chuckled. 'Nothing wrong with a second breakfast, that's what I always say!'

They all laughed, and Stella led them into the house.

* * *

After being shown to their rooms on the second floor and then using the ablution facilities, Clara and Bella joined the Levines and Spieglers for breakfast. The father of the house, Jakob, was at work already, but Clara and Bella were introduced to the

Spiegler children: Karl, a young man in his early twenties, who was tall and slim like his mother, and Mitzi, a stocky girl in her late teens, sporting a fashionably short haircut, and wearing what looked like a man's suit, complete with tie and waistcoat.

Clara had heard that the androgenous look was all the mode in Berlin, but she had not seen it for herself. She approved of its practicality.

The table was spread with cold meats, boiled eggs, toast and fruit, and a maid brought in a fresh pot of coffee.

'Wouldn't our guests prefer tea?' asked Mitzi. 'The English love their tea!'

'Is that what your Mr Isherwood tells you?' asked Karl.

Mitzi scowled at her brother. 'He's not *my* Mr Isherwood.'

'Now, now, you two. Stop the squabbles,' said their mother. 'Mr Isherwood is Mitzi's English tutor,' she added in explanation. 'And he sometimes escorts her to social events. You will meet him in due course. But Mitzi is right. Would you like tea instead of coffee?'

'I'd love a cup of tea, *danke schön*,' said Bella, to everyone's surprise. Her face lit up with pride. 'I've been practising.'

Chapter 6

Police:
HEAD POLICE OFFICE (Polizei-Präsidium), Alexander-Platz. The Passport Office *entrance is in Alexander-Str. (1st floor, open 9–1; from No. 153 for foreigners). All foreigners arriving in Berlin must report personally at the police station within 24 hrs. with their passports and separate photos.* – **from *Baedeker's Berlin and its Environs,* 1929**

After breakfast, and with apologies from Juju that there was no time to rest, the English party, accompanied by Karl Spiegler, headed back east across the city. They needed to get to the passport office at the Alexanderplatz Police Station before it shut at one o'clock. Karl guided them to catch the S-Bahn train at Savignyplatz Station, a fifteen-minute walk which took them past a large Reform synagogue on Fasanenstrasse.

'We used to attend synagogue here back in the early twenties,' explained Jonny. 'It's a Reform one. Quite liberal.'

'Will you go again during this visit?' asked Clara, knowing that Juju and Jonny were not very observant Jews and rarely attended the Orthodox synagogue in Newcastle as it was far too conservative for them.

'If there's time. There'll be an Erev Shabbat service this evening. That's the Friday night service to mark the beginning of our sabbath. But I expect Stella will be hosting a meal at home,' he said, looking to his young cousin.

'She will,' confirmed Karl.

As they walked past the synagogue, Juju gasped and pointed. On the outside wall someone had painted in large red letters: *Juden aus!*

'What does it say?' asked Bella.

'Jews out,' whispered Clara.

Karl sighed. 'It's happening more and more. We'd just got the last lot cleaned off. In fact, that's why my father couldn't meet you off the train today. Something similar has happened at our factory and he needs to get it cleaned up. But come,' he said, ushering the English visitors past the graffiti, 'we need to hurry, or we'll miss the train.'

* * *

The Alexanderplatz Police Station – known to locals as the Red Castle due to its red-brick facade – loomed over the Alexanderplatz public square. According to Clara's *Baedeker*, the square was named after Tsar Alexander I and was now home to Tietz and Wertheim department stores. While shoppers scurried across the square like ants, behind the myriad windows of the Castle, police officers investigated crimes and checked foreigners' luggage for smuggled sausage and wine.

Clara, Bella, Juju and Jonny waited on chairs in the corridor for their turn in the passport and customs office. Clara watched, curiously, as uniformed and non-uniformed officers walked past. It was a busy police station, and Clara wondered what crimes were currently under investigation. As she looked to the end of the corridor she caught her breath. *There was that man again! The man from the train station!*

'I'll be back in a minute,' she muttered to her friends and without further explanation, strode down the corridor.

The man, with his back to her, was talking to another man. As she approached, she heard him say in German:

'It's all in the file. Let me know if you have any questions.' And as she heard him speak, she knew she had not been mistaken. She *knew* this man.

'Flight Lieutenant Winter?' she asked in English.

The man stiffened and turned. He was an attractive blond man in his thirties who had an air of Lawrence of Arabia about him.

It was Larry Winter! The American pilot she had met on the way to Cairo and the man who had been so helpful in wrapping up what she referred to as the Pyramid Murder Case.

His eyes widened in surprise. 'Miss Clara Vale! What are you doing here?'

'I was going to ask you the same. I saw you get off the train from Amsterdam this morning.'

'You were on that train too?' he asked.

'Yes. What a pity we didn't meet. You weren't in the dining car.'

He smiled. 'I wasn't in first class.'

That was a surprise. As far as Clara knew, Larry came from a very wealthy family. He owned a number of aircrafts and, when in Egypt, had stayed at the most expensive hotel. But perhaps he had taken a hit from the Wall Street crash . . . She was too polite to think of mentioning it.

'Ah, that would explain it,' she said, keeping her voice light. 'Although you did pay first class a brief visit . . .'

His face looked blank. 'Meaning?'

'You were chatting to Hilda Markwald in the early hours. In the first-class carriage. Around one o'clock, I think it was.'

Larry shook his head. 'I'm afraid you are mistaken, Miss Vale. That wasn't me.' He grinned. 'I do not know a Miss Markwald and I was tucked up nice and cosy in my second-class cabin all night.'

'Oh?' she said, remembering him waving to Hilda this morning on the platform. But she kept her face straight. 'Sorry, my mistake. I thought it was you.'

He smiled in return. 'No. That wasn't me. But if I'd known you were in that carriage I might very well have asked for an upgrade. It's swell to meet you again, Miss Vale. And is that Miss Cuddy I see down there?'

'It is,' said Clara. 'And my friends from Newcastle, Juju and Jonny Levine.'

The German man beside Larry cleared his throat.

'Sorry,' said Larry in German. 'I met this lady in Cairo. I don't know if she speaks German . . .'

'I do,' said Clara in that language. 'Not particularly well. But I can get along.'

'You never said!' Larry exclaimed.

Clara smiled. 'You never asked.'

The German man's eyes twinkled behind wire-rimmed spectacles. 'You should introduce us, Winter.' He pronounced Larry's surname the German way, with a V.

Before Larry could do so, Clara announced in German, 'I am Miss Clara Vale. From England.'

'And I am Detective Inspector Strauss,' replied the German man in English.

Larry chuckled. 'I didn't know you spoke English, Strauss.'

'You didn't ask,' replied Strauss.

They all laughed.

Strauss gave a curt little bow. 'Welcome to Berlin, Miss Vale. Are you here for business or pleasure?'

'Oh, pure pleasure,' said Clara. Then nodded to her friends at the end of the corridor. 'But my friends are here on business. Berlin Fashion Week. I am just helping out.'

'In what way?' asked Larry.

Clara was suddenly embarrassed. She felt out of her depth moonlighting as a fashion model.

'I – well – I will be wearing some of Miss Levine's designs.'

The two men exchanged an appreciative glance. 'I'm sure you will wear them very well,' said Strauss.

Clara flushed. Then cleared her throat. 'Yes, well, it was all very last minute . . . and Miss Levine was desperate and if I hadn't agreed she would have been in a pickle and . . .'

'Clara!' Juju was hailing her from the end of the corridor. 'We're up next!'

Clara smiled at Larry and Strauss. 'If you'll excuse me, gentlemen . . .'

They both inclined their heads.

'Where are you staying?' asked Larry.

'With the Levines' cousins. I'm not sure of the address offhand . . . Olivaer Platz something or other . . .'

Larry nodded. 'Not to worry, I'll find you.'

'Clara!'

Clara gave an apologetic shrug.

'Excuse me, I really must go.' Clara hurried back along the corridor, wondering how Larry would find her – but wondering even more about why he had lied to her.

Chapter 7

Clara and her friends emerged from the underground U-Bahn station onto the Hausvogteiplatz square in the Mitte district of Berlin. Karl had told them on the short journey from Alexanderplatz that the area was the hub of the Berlin garment and fashion industry. Of the 2,700 businesses with offices or premises on the square the vast majority were owned by Jewish people. Behind the elegant eighteenth- and nineteenth- century facades were tailors' workshops, design studios, dressmaking factories and the offices of fabric importers and textile wholesalers.

Karl led them to a tall six-storey building with a brass plaque declaring this was the home of Spieglers Modefabrik – Spieglers Fashion Factory. On the limestone wall to the right of it was a red smear, which two young women in aprons were scrubbing furiously. Karl greeted them in German but didn't ask what they were doing. Clara suspected they were removing the anti-Jewish slurs Karl had mentioned earlier.

'I see it's just Spiegler,' observed Jonny. 'Not Hertzog & Spiegler.'

'That's right,' said Karl. 'My father still works with Hertzog, as their fashion director, but he set up his own business in twenty-five, a year or two after you went back to England.'

'Yes, he mentioned that, but I still thought he'd gone into partnership.'

Karl shook his head. 'No. He and Hertzog do not see eye to eye on some things. For Hertzog, the fashion side of the business was always just that – a sideline. He has an entire department store to run and isn't completely focused on fashion. My father is. He has his own vision. He wants to innovate. And so do I. The economic slump has slowed us down but once we're through this – perhaps by thirty-two or thirty-three – I think Spieglers is going to become a leading player in the Berlin fashion industry. It was our idea to take part in the *Modewoche* – the Fashion Week – and although it will be based at Hertzog's department store, after a gala opening elsewhere, we are the ones who are organising it. So, Cousin Juju, you and your friends from Paris and New York will be based here.' He pushed open the door. 'Let me show you to your workshop.'

The factory was not the type of hard industry factory that Clara associated with the word. But, as the root Latin word *factorium* suggested, it was a place of makers. And what they were all making or designing or selling was clothing. Over four floors there were workshops filled with sewing machines, cutting tables, design studios and offices. In the basement there was a storage space with a large garage-style door which opened onto the back street for deliveries. Clara and her friends were eventually shown to a workshop space where they found Juju's large trunks waiting for them. They had customs labels pasted on them declaring them *genemicht* – approved. But when Juju opened them, she gasped: 'What a mess!'

The customs officer had done a thorough search and just tossed all the garments, shoes, accessories and sewing supplies into a bundle and shoved it back in. 'We'll need to get this all straightened out. Can you help me, Bella, please?'

'Of course, Miss Levine. That's what I'm here for.'

'Do you need me to help too?' asked Clara.

Juju smiled at her. 'Not now. Go get yourself a cup of tea. I'll be needing you once this is all in order.'

'And I'll go make some phone calls, if that's all right,' said Jonny. 'I've got a few deals on the go that I need to finalise.'

'That's fine. I'd rather not have too many hands to supervise,' said Juju.

Karl nodded to Jonny. 'You can use the telephone in my father's office. He won't be long. His secretary said he's gone to collect the French and American teams from the Hotel Adlon. And, Miss Vale, perhaps instead of that cup of tea you would like to see my laboratory . . .'

Clara caught her breath. 'You have a laboratory?'

'I do. I believe you studied chemistry at Oxford.'

'That's correct,' said Clara.

The young man preened. 'Well, I too am a chemistry graduate, Miss Vale. In fact, I am working towards my PhD at the Humboldt University of Berlin. And I am applying my research right here. Would you like to see it?'

'Oh yes,' said Clara. 'I'd love to!'

* * *

Karl Spiegler's laboratory was housed in the attic. 'In case I blow us all up,' he said wryly. 'If I'm up here only the roof will go.'

Clara was pleased to see the lab, although not very big, was well equipped with the most modern of technology. She looked longingly at an almost brand-new microscope and the sparkling rows of beakers and flasks. And then she gasped. In the corner, with a chimney pipe feeding through a skylight in the roof, was a metal cabinet, a little like an oven. 'Is that a fume hood?'

Karl grinned. 'It is. It just arrived last week.'

'I hadn't realised they were commercially available yet. I've only ever seen them in university labs.'

'They're just on the market. Not cheap but essential, I believe, for the work I do here.' He grinned again. 'In other words, worth the money to keep me alive.'

'And what is the work you do here? Something that produces noxious fumes – or you wouldn't need the hood – but what specifically?'

Karl gestured to a clothes railing hung with strips of fabric. 'I am working on developing hybrid rayon fabric. Specifically, a rayon linen hybrid. So, the fume hood is mainly used to protect me from carbon disulphide and hydrogen sulphide emissions.'

'Very wise to use it then,' observed Clara. 'Carbon disulphide can cause serious cardiovascular problems with continued exposure.'

'Yes,' agreed Karl, 'and hydrogen sulphide can cause olfactory paralysis and sudden loss of consciousness in high concentrations – even just short exposure. Worst-case scenario,' he added with an affected melodramatic shiver, 'convulsions then death.'

Clara patted the fume hood. 'Better safe than sorry!'

Karl chuckled. 'Indeed.' He passed her a swatch of silky material. 'This is rayon silk. You'll probably be aware that it's been commercially available for quite a few years now. But no one has yet developed a commercially viable rayon linen.'

Clara allowed the fabric to run through her fingers like liquid. 'Hmmm,' she said, 'it feels wonderful. But . . .' She frowned.

'I think I *have* encountered rayon linen before. A case I was working on earlier in the year involving the wrappings of a mummy. Turns out it was rayon pretending to be linen.'

Karl nodded. 'Yes, there are rayon linen mixes used for bandages. But they are crude. Not suitable for high-quality clothing.' He passed her another swatch of fabric. 'That's pure, natural linen, suitable for summer trousers. See how soft it is? See how it drapes? You wouldn't have got that with the bandages. They would have been coarse. I'm hoping to approximate the look and feel of this.'

Clara stroked the fabric with her fingertips. 'Yes, the bandages were coarse. So, you're looking to make something more refined then. What benefits would you get from that?'

'Fine linen is very expensive. It's made from fibres from the stem of the flax plant. The finest quality flax is grown in China. But with the political upheaval there – the battles between the communists and the nationalists – trade is frequently interrupted. We can't guarantee a steady supply into Europe and that affects the price. If we can develop a high-quality rayon linen hybrid, that will cut the price of production and allow us to make more with less. The top haute couture fashion houses will still use pure linen, but factories like ours produce good-quality clothing for less. The ready-to-wear market has burgeoned with rayon silk; we want to do the same with linen.'

Clara nodded her understanding. 'So,' she said, looking around the lab, 'how far have you got?'

'I thought you'd never ask! Have a look at this . . .'

He unpegged a swatch of white cloth from the rail and gave it to Clara. 'What do you think?'

She rubbed it between her fingers, draped it over her arm, compared it to the previous fabric and then said: 'It's almost indistinguishable!'

He grinned. 'That's what I'd hope you'd say. Now, let me show you how I reached this point . . .'

Half an hour later and Clara had microscopically viewed fibres, examined formulae, asked challenging questions and come to the conclusion that the young man in front of her was a chemical genius. 'This is incredible, Karl. What does your PhD supervisor say?'

Karl let out a long breath. 'He hasn't seen these latest formulae. I'm going to present it to him after Fashion Week. So, for now, you and I are the only people who know about it.'

'What about your father?'

'Well, yes, him too. But no one else. A few other people know I'm working on something; that's not a secret. But no one knows the exact formulation.' He closed his notebook and tied it shut with a thong. He then unlocked the bottom drawer of his desk, placed the notebook inside and locked it again. He pocketed the key and smiled at Clara.

'Thank you for your encouragement, Miss Vale. I suspected I'd got something unique here, but your affirmation has confirmed it. Now I'm far less anxious about what my supervisor will say.'

Clara gave the young man a warm smile. 'I'm sure he'll be very impressed.'

There was a knock on the door and a woman entered. 'Herr Spiegler,' she said in German, 'your father is here with the other guests. He asks that you and Miss Vale come down to the studio.'

Chapter 8

The woman led the way down to the studio workshop where Clara had left Juju and Bella. Now the Americans and French had joined them, each to their own corner, and the workshop was a flurry of fabric and flounces. The assistants were steaming and ironing garments while the designers were pinning sketches to work boards. The models – Hilda and Merlette – waited to be summoned. Merlette was paging through a fashion magazine while Hilda, her long legs crossed, was smoking a cigarette. Both women wore silk dressing gowns. Merlette looked up and waved at Clara. Hilda blew out a plume of smoke.

'There you are!' said Juju, pinning the last of her sketches to the board then picking up a pink gown and offering it to Clara. 'Could you take off your clothes and put this on please?'

'Here?' asked Clara.

'Of course!' said Juju. 'There's a changing screen over there.' She pointed to the makeshift dressing room created by a folding room divider, a chair and a full-length mirror. 'No time for shyness now, Clara.' Then she chuckled. 'But you *can* keep your underwear on.'

'That's a relief,' muttered Clara.

Before she slipped behind the screen she was hailed by Jonny Levine and a slim, middle-aged man. 'Miss Vale!' said Jonny. 'May I introduce my cousin Jakob Spiegler.'

'Good day to you, Miss Vale,' said Jakob warmly in English. 'My cousins speak most highly of you.'

'Good day, Herr Spiegler,' said Clara in German. And then in English: 'Well, that is heartening to hear but they have yet to see my modelling skills.'

Jakob crinkled his eyes in amusement. 'Oh, you'll learn quickly. There's really not that much to it. You walk and look elegant. Both skills you already appear to have. And for any finer points, I'm sure the other ladies will be only too happy to advise. Isn't that right, Miss Markwald?' he asked the blonde American.

'I'm not here to train amateurs,' snapped Hilda then took a long draw on her cigarette.

'Well show us how it's done then,' said Danny Cohen. 'Here, put this on. We need to check the fit when you walk.' He had a mauve-coloured silk crêpe garment draped over his arm. He held it up, allowing the ankle-length skirt to fall to the floor. It was an afternoon dress to be accompanied by a small bolero for the shoulders. Clara noted that the waistline was higher than the natural waist – a shift from the drop-waist style of the previous decade – and that the skirt would skim and accentuate the belly, the hips and the derrière, rather than hiding them. A woman would need to be confident about her body to wear it. But Hilda was nothing if not confident.

'Ooh la la!' said Hugo in French. 'I hope you've packed your corset, Hilda!'

Hilda scowled. 'And why do I need a corset?' she asked in English.

'Because,' he answered in French, flicking the magazine from Merlette's hands, then running his fingers down a column of text until he found the place, 'it says here, in *Chic Parisien*, no less that "*The year 1930 brings a fundamental change in fashion with the new silhouette. But not every woman has a naturally even body line with narrow hips, which is necessary to wear the new tightly fitted dresses. The new fashion demands a slim line, which makes bodices, corsets and hip belts indispensable again.*"' He smirked and gave the magazine back to his young model.

Hilda gasped. 'You're an impudent little man, Hugo!'

Clara caught her breath, waiting for Hugo to respond, but Jakob Spiegler stepped between them. 'That's enough,' he said in German. 'Fräulein Markwald is right, Hugo, that was impudent. Now, please apologise, and I expect that to be the last I hear of this. I brought you all here as professionals. I expect you to act like it.'

'Pwah!' said Hugo. 'I will not apologise to her. But I will apologise to everyone else for creating a scene. And to you, Jakob. I will not do it again.'

Jakob let out a long sigh. 'You had better not, Hugo. Now,' he said, switching to English and including everyone in the room, 'you have to the end of today to ready your outfits. Tomorrow we will move everything to the Neus Museum in anticipation of the gala opening tomorrow night. We will meet the other German designers and their models there. Do not take your entire collections tomorrow, just what will be shown at the gala. The rest will go to Hertzog's for the remainder of Fashion Week. So, gala at the museum then the rest of the week at the department store. That's where the buyers will do most of their business. Any questions?'

There were lots of questions from Juju, Jonny, Hugo and Danny. And while they talked, Clara slipped behind the divider and changed out of her day clothes. Wearing only her underwear she considered her body in the full-length mirror.

She certainly didn't have a flawless figure. What would she look like in the figure-hugging gowns that were coming back into fashion? She'd thought she might carry them well – better than the boxy 1920s – but Hugo's catty comments to Hilda caused her to think twice. But then she shrugged. There was nothing she could do about her natural shape. And Juju had been dressing her for over a year now. She knew what she was getting.

As Clara was trying her gown, Hilda appeared behind the screen, the mauve dress over her arm. Clara smiled at her. 'I'm sorry Hugo was so unkind to you. And undeservedly so. I'm sure you'll carry that dress off beautifully.'

'Of course I will,' said Hilda, shooing away Clara's sympathy with a flick of her hand. 'Hugo is just jealous. He wanted me to model for him, you know, but I went with Danny instead. And then he had to get that Moorish mare Merlette instead. Who is nothing compared to me! Nothing!'

Clara was gobsmacked. She opened and then closed her mouth, unable to utter the words she wanted to say. To her relief, Juju popped her head around the divider.

'Are you ready to try something on, Clara?'

The words sent a chill down her spine. *Why on earth did I ever agree to this?* But she quelled her anxiety and smiled at her friend. 'As ready as I'll ever be, I suppose.'

* * *

'Imagine you're walking down an esplanade on the Riviera!'

Clara nodded to Juju and tried to imagine herself in the south of France – or, as Bella jokingly suggested, the promenade in

Whitley Bay. The beach pyjamas she was wearing were surprisingly comfortable, and she enjoyed the feel of the wide-legged trousers swishing around her ankles as she walked. She had been relieved that her first outfit was loose fitting and made of linen: not the silky, slinky gown that Hilda was flaunting. Although, a quick glimpse at Juju's garment rail showed there were a couple of slinkies to come. For now, she appreciated being able to practise her walk in a less revealing, but still flattering, ensemble. She had never worn beach pyjamas before, but Juju had shown her a magazine photograph of the German actress Marlene Dietrich wearing them while taking a break on the set of her new film, *The Blue Angel*. Clara had to agree with Juju that Fräulein Dietrich looked both comfortable and stylish.

Juju's version was sage green with a forest green trim on the nautical collar of the tunic blouse. As Clara walked, under Juju's direction, she wondered how the outfit would feel if made from Karl Spiegler's new rayon linen mix. It would, she understood, make the commercial manufacture of the outfit considerably cheaper. Might that make it more attractive to the buyers attending Fashion Week? It was, of course, too late for this Fashion Week, but if Karl's formula could be approved and put into production, a model could be wearing it next year.

It looked like Karl was discussing that very thing with his father, Jonny, Hugo and Hugo's business partner, Pierre. The men were looking at her and making her feel very uncomfortable, but they were clearly talking about her outfit, not her.

'How does it feel?' asked Juju.

'A little too snug around the waist, if I'm honest, but everything else feels fine.'

Clara came to a stop in front of Juju who lifted the tunic top to examine the waistband. 'Not a problem,' said Juju, 'I can let that out an inch. This is why we like our girls to walk in the clothes in advance of the show, isn't it, Danny?'

'It sure is,' said Danny Cohen, watching his own 'girl' walking in the slinky silk gown. Despite Hugo's catty remark, it appeared to be a perfect fit on Hilda's perfect body.

'How does it feel, Hilda?'

The blonde woman shrugged. 'Fine.'

'Good,' said Danny, then to his young assistant. 'Benji, get the next dress.'

Meanwhile, Merlette emerged from the makeshift dressing room. Everybody stopped what they were doing and turned to watch her. She wore a black evening dress in crêpe georgette with bias cut panels cascading to a flounced hem which swept the floor. The scooped cowl neckline fell in loose folds from diamanté-encrusted straps, revealing the flawless flesh of the young woman's chest. At the back, the dress plunged to her waistline, making it very clear that she was not wearing a brassiere. With all eyes on her, the young French model glided down the walkway. Her movement was effortless, her limbs swaying like the stems of an exquisite orchid in the gentlest breeze. *A black orchid*, thought Clara, *rare and very beautiful, with the delicate fabric suggesting ethereal petals.*

Merlette turned at the end of the room and returned up the walkway, all eyes still on her. *There was something very special about the young woman*, thought Clara. While Hilda looked like she'd just stepped off the cover of a fashion magazine, Merlette looked like she'd just stepped out of a dream. And by the look of young Karl Spiegler, she would be in his dreams for a long time to come. Clara smiled to herself, then frowned as Hilda deliberately cut across Merlette's walk; bumping into her and making her stumble.

'Watch where you're going,' snapped Hilda.

Karl rushed forward and caught Merlette's arm, steadying her. She smiled at Karl and the young man looked as though he would melt.

'How does it feel, *ma cherie*?' asked Hugo in French.

'It is perfect,' she answered in her soft, quiet voice.

'Too perfect!' barked Danny.

'What do you mean?' asked Pierre.

'I mean this!' The American strode to a clothes rack and extracted a dress. Everyone, apart from Hugo, gasped. The dress was almost identical to Merlette's. The only difference was that it was midnight blue, not black.

'Where did you get that dress?' asked Pierre.

'I made it,' said Danny.

'From which design?' asked the Frenchman.

'An original.'

'Nonsense,' said Hugo. 'It is I who created this design. Your assistant must have copied it when he visited Paris earlier in the year.'

'I did no such thing!' said Benji.

'Then where did you get the design, Danny?' asked Hugo, his voice dripping with sarcasm. 'We know everyone steals French ideas. You Americans, English and Germans,' he said, taking in the rest of the room, 'do not have an original bone in your bodies!'

'I beg your pardon!' Juju launched herself into the argument.

But before it could get out of hand, Jakob Spiegler intervened. 'That's enough! All of you! Danny and Hugo come to my office please and we can discuss this in private. Bring your original designs if you have them.'

The two designers stared daggers at one another but, as guests of Jakob Spiegler, they eventually complied.

'Bleedin' heck,' muttered Bella as the men left the room, leaving Merlette weeping and Karl trying to console her, while Pierre, Hilda and Benji launched into their own argument. 'And this is just day one.'

Jonny caught Clara's eye and together they let out a mutual sigh.

'What are we going to do now?' asked Bella.

'Well,' said Juju with forced jollity, 'shall we try on the next dress?'

Chapter 9

At the Spiegler home on Olivaer Platz, it was sundown. The lights were dimmed as the family and their guests gathered around the table for the Friday evening Shabbat meal. The men – Jakob, Karl and Jonny, who were all wearing yamakas – had recently returned from temple at the synagogue on Fasanenstrasse, while the women of the family would attend on Saturday morning. The table was set with a selection of meze dishes: pickled herring, chickpeas, grated cabbage and carrots, and something called *baba ganoush* – aubergine mashed up with lemon and oil. Clara had never had aubergine in England. The centrepiece of the table was a large, braided loaf – that Juju told Clara was called the *challah* – covered in a cloth. Stella Spiegler, as the mother of the house, lit the ceremonial candles, called *licht bentschen* and intoned a prayer, while Juju whispered a translation to Clara and Bella:

'Blessed are You, Lord our God, Ruler of the Universe, who has sanctified us with commandments, and commanded us to light Shabbat candles.'

Then it was the turn of Jakob, as the father of the house, to say a prayer for the wine, known as the *kiddush*. 'Blessed are You, Adonai our God, Sovereign of all, Creator of the fruit of the vine. Blessed are You, Adonai our God, Sovereign of all, who, finding favour with us, sanctified us with *mitzvot*. In love and favour, You made the holy Shabbat our heritage as a reminder of the work of Creation.'

At that point the cloth was lifted from *challah*, another prayer was uttered, and the meal began.

Apart from the extended rituals at the beginning of the meal and some unfamiliar names of dishes, it was, to Clara, a dinner party like any other. The meze was followed by a clear chicken broth with *matzhah* balls. On closer inspection these turned out to be a kind of dumpling. And very tasty too. Clara and Bella were on more familiar culinary ground when the soup was followed by a roast chicken and accompanying roast vegetables. It was during this course that Stella mentioned her husband looked tired. He explained that it had been a very long day, starting with the anti-Jewish graffiti and culminating in the blazing row between Danny and Hugo. He went on to report that neither man could prove which of them first came up with the disputed design as neither of them had their original sketches with them.

'Perhaps neither of them did,' observed his daughter, Mitzi, who had discarded the man's suit she'd worn this morning for a more conservative dress. 'Perhaps they both stole it from another designer.'

Juju shook her head. 'I think "stole" might be too strong a word, Mizti. They might have just been inspired by the same design, as I was inspired by Marlene Dietrich's beach pyjamas.'

'Yes,' agreed Jonny, 'but you used that as a starting point and created your own work from it. You didn't just copy it. Another designer, with the same inspiration, would have made something different. Danny and Hugo's dresses were identical, apart from the colour – and even that was very similar.'

'So, what are they going to do?' asked Karl. 'Will one of them not show their dress? And if so, which one? Poor Mademoiselle Merlette is quite shaken by it all.'

'And who is Mademoiselle Merlette?' asked his mother.

Karl flushed red. 'She is Hugo's model.'

'Is she very beautiful?' asked Mitzi, mischievously.

'She is,' said Karl, trying to sound nonchalant, but failing miserably.

Mitzi laughed. 'Oooh, Karly boy is in love!'

'I am not!' Karl snapped. 'But if I were, it would have nothing to do with you! At least I am looking for a spouse and don't wander around the cabaret dives of Berlin on the arms of strange men.'

Mitzi bristled. 'Mr Isherwood – singular – is one man, not men. And he is *not* strange. Is he, Father? You like him, don't you?'

Jakob sipped his wine carefully then said, 'Mr Isherwood is a good tutor. And a safe gentleman to accompany you on social occasions.'

'Not a glowing endorsement of a potential husband,' sniped Karl.

'That's enough,' said his father in German. Then to his daughter: 'When are you next seeing him?'

She jutted her chin. 'Tonight. We are going to a new cabaret club. Miss Vale, Miss Cuddy, perhaps you would like to join us? The famous Josephine Baker will be making an appearance.'

Clara smiled at her. 'Ordinarily, Miss Spiegler, I think we would have – Miss Cuddy particularly enjoys a good show – but we have had a long day and tomorrow will be an even longer one, I think. So, it will be early to bed for us tonight.'

Mitzi looked disappointed, but the nod of approval from the Spiegler parents confirmed to Clara she had made the correct decision – for political reasons. However, Clara had heard of Josephine Baker and would love to see her. 'Perhaps sometime next week?' she added.

Mitzi brightened immediately. 'That will be splendid!'

'No need to wait that long,' said Jakob. 'I believe she is performing at the Adlon tomorrow night too. We have booked the ballroom for a Fashion Week party after the gala event. So,' he added, looking pointedly at his daughter, 'if the only reason you are going out tonight is to see Miss Baker, then you could wait until tomorrow, Mitzi, and save Mr Isherwood some money.'

She smiled sweetly at her father. 'Thank you for your concern for Mr Isherwood's financial wellbeing, father, but I think we'll be going out tonight anyway.'

Jakob shook his head. 'Whatever are we going to do with you . . .' he muttered, before Stella interjected, wanting to know what Mitzi was going to be wearing.

Meanwhile, Karl had started a conversation with Jonny and Juju about synthetic linen.

'Those beach pyjamas Miss Vale was wearing today would be the perfect outfit to trial it on. We could make them for at least a third cheaper than if we used pure linen. Isn't that right, Father?'

'It is,' said Jakob. 'I think Herr Hertzog would be interested in stocking them in his off-the-peg range.'

'Do you really think so?' asked Juju.

'I do,' said Jakob, and raised a glass.

Juju's eyes sparkled. Clara was delighted for her. This, she knew, was her dream, to design clothes that could be stocked in department stores around the world. Clara put aside all her misgivings about being out of her depth as an amateur fashion model and realised she had made the right decision to help her friend.

'Are you expecting any trouble tomorrow night?' asked Jonny.

'Trouble?' asked Jakob.

Jonny swirled the wine in his glass. 'Of the anti-Semitic kind. I heard that last year some Nazi thugs harassed people as they arrived.'

Jakob nodded. 'Yes, they did. But we're ready for them this year. I have spoken to the police and they will have a presence there.'

Jonny looked surprised. 'Really? I had heard that the police frequently turn a blind eye to National Socialist thuggery. Particularly since that Hitler fellow and half-a-dozen goons were elected to the Reichstag in twenty-eight.'

'It was a full dozen, unfortunately,' said Stella.

'It was,' agreed her husband. 'But still a tiny minority. And that's how they'll stay. No sensible German will vote for them.'

'It's not the sensible ones I'm worried about,' said Stella, and she stabbed her fork into a chicken wing.

Jakob gave her a gentle smile. 'Don't worry, my dear, it's all bluster and it will soon blow over. Once we get through this economic downturn things will settle. Mark my words. But to get back to Cousin Jonny's question: there's nothing to worry about. I have a contact in the Berlin police – by the name of Strauss – and he has assured me there won't be any trouble.'

'Strauss? Detective Inspector Strauss?' asked Clara.

Jakob looked surprised. 'Indeed, Miss Vale. How do you know him?'

'I just met him today!' She went on to tell Jakob about seeing her old acquaintance, Larry Winter, at the Alexanderplatz police station and her introduction to Strauss.

Mitzi perked up at the mention that Larry Winter was a pilot and that he, Clara and Bella had been in Cairo together.

'Cairo? How exciting! Oh, do tell us what happened there, Miss Vale. I've heard rumours about mummies and priceless jewels. Is it true?'

'Oh aye, it is!' said Bella. And the rest of the dinner was spent recounting Clara and Bella's grand adventures in Egypt.

Chapter 10

Saturday 6th September 1930

The New Museum, Museum Island:
Admission: 9 am–3 pm. Sun; Tue; Fri – free. Mon – closed. Owing to the fluctuation of the mark, it has been found impossible to give the fees of admission for the intermittent days. The ground floor is occupied by the Egyptian Museum, one of the most important collections of the kind [. . .] founded in 1828. [. . .] The acquisitions and German excavations of more recent times have enriched the museum to such an extent that many of the objects have been stored away for the present. [. . .] By the back wall: statuette of Queen Nefertete (limestone). Perhaps the most lifelike portrait of all Egyptian art. – **from *Baedeker's Berlin and its Environs*, 1929**

The bust was only nineteen inches high. But what it lacked in height it made up for in beauty. Clara had heard of the famed bust of Queen Nefertiti, unearthed in a dig in Egypt in 1910, and read newspaper articles of its allure. But press reports were often exaggerated, so Clara had been prepared to be disappointed. However, like the mask of Tutankhamun she'd seen earlier in the year in Cairo, the visage of this Egyptian royal lived up to its reputation. Made of painted limestone, it lacked the bejewelled lustre of the Tutankhamun mask, but the simplicity of the lifelike features – the exquisite neck and jaw – were far superior in Clara's mind. It was a pity the queen had lost an eye, but the one that remained bored into Clara's soul.

'She's breathtaking, isn't she?' said someone with an American accent.

Clara was startled and turned to see Larry Winter, dressed in white tie and tails, standing at her left shoulder.

'She certainly is,' said Clara and then circled the queen's pedestal so she was facing Larry. 'I didn't know you were coming to the gala show.'

Larry smiled. 'I'm here with a delegation from the American embassy. I wasn't intending on coming, but when you mentioned yesterday that you would be performing at the Fashion Week, I changed my mind.'

'Well, I'm hardly *performing*, Lieutenant Winter. I'm just walking up and down a ramp.'

Larry's eyes twinkled. 'Then I look forward to seeing you walk. And please, Clara, after all we've been through together in Egypt, I thought we were on first-name terms now.' He lowered his voice. 'At least in private.'

Clara looked around them. There were half a dozen people in the Nefertiti gallery. She lowered her voice too. 'Well, we're not in private, are we?'

Larry gave a curt nod. 'No, we're not, Miss Vale. My apologies. I am suitably chastised.'

She chuckled. 'And so you should be.'

Bella entered the gallery, waved to her, then tapped her watch.

'Oh dear, it's time to go.'

'Oh dear? You don't sound very enthusiastic about all this, Cla—sorry, Miss Vale.'

Clara sighed. 'I'm a bit out of my depth, really. I only did it as a favour to my friend Juju. What she didn't tell me is that all the other models are professionals.'

Larry gave a sympathetic smile. 'I understand you're nervous, but you need to know that everyone else – and I mean everyone – thinks you are just as beautiful as any model – or,' he said, nodding to Nefertiti, 'Egyptian queen.'

Clara knew this was just flattery, but she appreciated his attempts to calm her. 'Thank you. Can you believe it, I'm far more scared than I was flying for the first time!'

He chuckled and held out his arm. 'Well, that, Miss Vale, was because you were in the hands of a professional.'

'Exactly! And that's what I'm not!'

He sighed. 'Oh, Clara. You'll be fine. Whenever I'm nervous about doing something new I think about something I know I'm good at – like flying – and carry that attitude with me. So—' he grinned '—just imagine that everyone in the room is a potential murder suspect and you are about to reveal the killer. That should make you feel better.'

'Murder suspects?' Clara laughed and slipped her arm through his. 'Not quite the tone Juju might want, but all right, I'll do it. Lady detective style.'

* * *

The gala opening of Fashion Week was being held in the Colonnade Courts of the New Museum, made up of two intersecting courtyards: the Egyptian Courtyard, designed like an Egyptian temple, and the Greek Courtyard, surrounded by stone friezes, depicting the fall of Pompeii. The two courtyards – once open to the elements – had recently been covered by a glass roof, creating a year-round exhibition space. The guests, including Berlin celebrities of stage and screen, politicians, diplomats and members of the press, were gathered in the Egyptian Courtyard, sipping champagne and German Riesling. After a short speech by Herman Hertzog, the financial backer of the show, they were ushered to their seats in the Greek Courtyard next door. Above them, members of the press – with their cameras – were positioned on a mezzanine floor, and when the rich and famous made their entry, light bulbs flashed like fireworks.

Clara and the eleven other models were in an anteroom off the Greek Courtyard, waiting for their turn to walk. Juju and Bella were fussing around her: Bella touching up her makeup and Juju straightening the pleats of the ice-blue gown in which Clara would open the show. Appropriate to the setting, Juju had told her that while exotic Egyptian style had influenced the 1920s fashion scene, a more classical Greek influence was the inspiration for the gowns of 1930. The blue chiffon cascaded in a myriad of pleats from an Empire line bodice, falling to the floor like fluting in one long Ionic column, while the little puff shoulder sleeves were structured like the spiral volutes on top of a pillar. Although Clara was still nervous, she had to admit that the dress was stunning and perfectly suited her figure.

'You look smashing, Miss Vale,' said Bella. 'Absolutely smashing.'

There were tears in Juju's eyes as she stepped back to appreciate her handiwork.

'It's a beautiful gown,' said Clara. 'And I hope I do you proud.'

Juju clasped Clara to her then released her, swallowing hard. 'Oh, you already have, Clara. Thank you for doing this. Are you ready?'

Clara nodded, remembering what Larry had said about focusing on what she was good at – not what she wasn't. 'Lady detective in the house,' she whispered.

'What's that, pet?' asked Juju.

'Nothing,' said Clara. Then, as Jonny ushered her forward, she took his hand and climbed the few steps onto the runway.

'Off you go,' he said.

And so she went.

Clara did not look to left or right as she walked, focusing instead on a statue of Achilles at the end of the runway, but she was aware of a collective intake of breath as she moved. She hoped it was a gasp of appreciation for Juju's beautiful gown, rather than of shock for her amateur presentation, and was surprised when she got to the end of her walk to be rewarded with warm applause.

'You were splendid!' said Jonny as he helped her back down the steps.

Clara felt immense relief.

As the evening progressed, Clara relaxed and began to almost enjoy the backstage buzz, while front of house her successive walks became less stressful. Hilda, Merlette and the other models didn't appear to be nervous at all, and sweet Merlette even took time to speak to Clara, telling her how well she was doing.

Hilda ignored her, but Clara didn't take it personally. Hilda ignored everyone.

Until, that is, Merlette's final walk.

Jonny had told Clara that Jakob had brokered a gentleman's agreement between Hugo and Danny that neither of them would show their version of the disputed gown. When Hilda wore a cream silk dress for her final walk, it showed that Danny was keeping up his side of the agreement. But then, in the very final walk of the evening, Merlette, not meeting anyone's eye, hurried to the walkway wearing the sensational black crêpe georgette. Hugo grabbed her arm and manhandled her up the steps, before anyone in the anteroom could stop her. On the other side of the curtain, gasps of admiration and exuberant applause greeted Merlette as she walked. Clara wasn't surprised, both Merlette and the gown were stunning, but there was shocked silence backstage. As Merlette returned, Hilda pounced on the young model, tearing the dress from her delicate body. Clara and Bella grabbed Hilda and pulled her away, while Benji, Pierre and Jonny held Danny back from Hugo. Merlette's sobs were drowned out by the audience's cheers.

'I'll kill you!' bellowed Danny.

Hugo smirked. 'Oh, I'd like to see you try.'

Chapter 11

Unter den Linden

The handsomest and busiest part of Berlin, which likewise comprises the most interesting historical associations, is the line of streets extending from the Brandenburg Gate to the former Royal Palace [. . .] Unter den Linden (the Linden) derives its name from the lime trees (interspersed with chestnuts) with which it is planted, resembles the Boulevards of Paris. [. . .] The Linden is to Berlin what Bond Street and Picadilly are to London. [. . .] Unter den Linden, 1. The Hotel Adlon. 300 rooms. (150 with baths). Lunch from midday. Dinner from 6 o'clock. Entertainment until late . . . **– from *Baedeker's Berlin and its Environs*, 1929**

The taxi pulled up outside the grand facade of the Hotel Adlon, its lights bathing the Pariser Platz in the historic centre of Berlin. The Platz was also home to the American and French embassies, within a stone's throw of the imperial Brandenburg Gate. And just over the park was Berlin's Academy of Arts. Representatives from both embassies, as well as the British, had attended the fashion show and now most of them were spilling out of taxis and piling into the Adlon for an after-party.

Bella was squeezed into the back seat with Clara and Juju, while Jonny sat in front with the taxi driver. In the two cars behind them were the French and American designer groups. Bella hoped the catfight from the New Museum would not spill over to the after-party. If it hadn't been for her and Miss Vale, that poor little lass Merlette might have been floored. That old hag Hilda was a real piece of work! Still, the French fella had been out of line showing that frock when they'd agreed not to.

A pack of press photographers were snapping and flashing as each taxi emptied. Bella gasped as two elegant couples stepped out of the car in front of them.

'Eee, that isn't Charlie Chaplin, is it?'

Clara and Juju craned their necks to see.

'It is!' said Juju. 'And that looks like Miss Louise Brooks on his arm! Oh, she does look like you, Clara.'

'And that's Mary Pickford, isn't it?' asked Bella, star-struck.

'Yes! With Douglas Fairbanks!' gushed Juju.

'Did you see any of them in the audience, Miss Vale?' asked Bella.

Clara shook her head. 'No. I didn't focus on anyone. I just looked at the statue of Achilles. I was terrified I was going to fall and make a fool of myself!'

Bella smiled warmly at her employer. 'Oh, you didn't make a fool of yourself, miss. You did a grand job. Didn't she, Miss Levine?'

Juju took Clara's hand and squeezed it tightly. 'You certainly did. I couldn't have asked for a better model, Clara. Thank you for doing this. And all the shows next week.'

'Will they be as fancy as tonight?' asked Bella.

Juju shook her head. 'No. They'll be at Hertzog's department store. For shoppers and fashion buyers from abroad. But that's where the real business is done. Tonight was just to give the press something to talk about.'

Clara frowned. 'And it looks like they're all here now. Do you think we can get past them?'

Jonny chuckled. 'Don't worry, the Hollywood crowd will distract them. Besides—' he turned his head and smiled at Clara '—your dashing pilot is here to escort you.'

Larry's handsome face appeared in the window. Bella sensed Clara tense beside her. Was it out of excitement? Bella had thought there might have been a romantic connection between them in Cairo, but it was too soon after Clara's romance with the accountant had ended. And now would it be too soon after the flutter of romance with the policeman? *Poor Miss Vale,* thought Bella, *timing is never on her side.* And then Bella gasped. Another face appeared next to Larry's: the archaeologist Rudy Werner. The last time Bella had seen him was when she and Miss Vale had been working on a case that involved the smuggling of ancient Egyptian artefacts – and trying to outwit a serial killer! But before that, she and Rudy had spent a few very romantic days on a cruise ship. Bella had always wondered what might have happened if their romance hadn't become derailed by murderous matters. And now here he was in Berlin. Was she being given a second chance? She bit her lip in anticipation. *Crikey, I'm in luck!*

* * *

Clara had to admit that Josephine Baker, the exotic dancer and singer from America, was as sensational – and scandalous – as everyone had said she would be. She was credited with dancing the first ever Charleston in Berlin, back in 1924, and had been a frequent visitor to the city ever since. Clara heard Miss Baker now lived in Paris because in her home country there were venues that would not allow a black person to perform. Berlin seemed to have no problem with the colour of her skin. Clara wondered how Miss Baker would fare in England. She expected most London venues would object more to the lady's risqué costumes than her race. Bella was certainly surprised. 'Eee, Miss Vale, she's wearing next to nowt!' But Bella, and the rest of the audience, were soon won over by the delightful Miss Baker's joyful performance.

Clara and Bella were seated at a large round table set for nine. There were the Levines, Clara and Bella, Larry Winter, Rudy Werner, and the French group: Hugo, Pierre and Merlette. The Americans were two tables over, seated with the Spiegler family and a young gentleman next to Mitzi – *I wonder if that's the much talked about Mr Isherwood?* Then Clara caught Hilda's eye – and quickly looked away. *If looks could kill . . .*

Fortunately, at her own table no one seemed to want to kill anyone. There was a warm buzz of conversation as friends, old and new, chatted and laughed. Clara noted with some interest that Jonny and Hugo were quietly talking as two old friends would. Or, as she'd first thought when she'd seen them together at the train station in Amsterdam: two old lovers. Speaking of lovers, Bella was basking in the attention of Rudy Werner. Clara had been very pleased to see him too, and had had a few moments to catch up with his news.

When they'd last met in Cairo, Rudy had told her he was struggling to get his doctoral thesis finished. That, after all the intrigue at the pyramids, had now been completed. So, Rudy was now Dr Rudolf Werner, PhD, archaeologist and Egyptologist. As such, he'd been promoted to assistant director of Egyptian antiquities at the New Museum and had been there to see the fashion show. He was also a close friend of Larry Winter and the two men – who had attempted to wine and dine Clara and Bella in Cairo – appeared to be picking up where they'd left off.

But Clara was watchful. Firstly, she was reluctant to spin out of the arms of one man and into those of another. Things had not progressed too far with Inspector Sandy Hawkes before he had been transferred out of town – just a kiss or two – but she had to admit if he'd stayed in Newcastle things might have become more serious. He was very attractive, and they got on well, but . . . as always, she was reluctant to allow her relationships to go too far. She didn't want to get married. Certainly not yet. So, if that was where the man wanted to go . . . was it fair to continue? But did that mean she was destined to be romantically unattached for the rest of her life? That was something she wasn't prepared to commit to, either. Why were things always so complicated?

But that wasn't the only problem with Larry Winter. She still didn't know why he had lied to her about Hilda Markwald. And why he had so blatantly denied meeting Hilda or visiting the first-class carriage when she'd spoken to him at the police station. She'd let it ride as she was hoping that Larry would come clean about it, as they say in those American pictures, but as yet he had not. She had been planning to ask Hilda at the fashion show if she knew him. If Hilda denied it, it would be obvious that they were both hiding something.

But if she admitted knowing him, it would only be Larry that was being evasive, for reasons she still had to figure out. However, after the kerfuffle, where Clara and Bella had physically yanked Hilda off Merlette, she doubted the American woman would ever talk to her again. She needed to pursue her suspicions about Larry another way. So, when Larry left the table to go to the bar, she took the chance to speak to Rudy.

'Did Larry tell you that I saw him on the train from Amsterdam to Berlin?' she asked.

Rudy nodded. 'He did. He said if he'd known you and Miss Cuddy were in the first-class carriage he would have arranged to move.'

'Do you know why he wasn't in first class in the first place?' she asked.

Rudy shrugged. 'Larry is not fussy. He has been known to sleep in tents or under the stars in the desert. He would not need the comfort of first class unless—' his blue eyes twinkled '—there was someone he wanted to spend time with.'

Clara smiled. 'It seemed like he wanted to spend time with Hilda Markwald. Do you know her?'

Rudy cocked his head to the side. 'You're not jealous, are you, Miss Vale? There is really no need to be.'

Startled, Clara cleared her throat and ran her thumbnail along the crease of her napkin. 'Of course I'm not jealous. I was just surprised to see them together, and for him to deny that he knew her. Does he know her?'

'I expect he does. Miss Markwald is well known both in America and in Berlin.'

'Do *you* know her? I mean, beyond knowing who she is?'

Rudy looked at Clara curiously. 'Why all these questions, Miss Vale? Are you investigating something?'

Clara shrugged. 'No. Not really. As I say, I was just surprised that he denied he had spoken to her when I saw them together and I was wondering why.'

Rudy smiled. 'Perhaps it was to avoid all this.'

Clara frowned. 'All this?'

'Well, perhaps he didn't want you thinking that he and Miss Markwald were romantically involved in any way. Perhaps he wants it to be known that he's . . . how should I put it . . . available?'

Clara was taken aback. She had not for a minute considered that Larry and Hilda could be romantically involved. It had not seemed like that sort of conversation. There was something . . . oh, she couldn't put her finger on it . . . something less *benign* about their encounter.

'So, he does know her then.'

Rudy nodded. 'He does. As do I. Miss Markwald and I are members of the same organisation.'

'And what organisation is that?' asked Clara and took a sip of her wine.

'The National Socialists.'

'The *Nazis*?' Clara spluttered.

'Indeed. Have you heard of us?'

Clara thought about the graffiti on the synagogue and the Spiegler factory. 'Yes, I have. In fact, I saw the handiwork of your members within a few hours of arriving in Berlin. Not a good introduction.' She went on to tell him about the anti-Jewish slurs.

He carefully sipped his wine then put down the glass, keeping his fingers on the stem. He twirled it as he spoke. 'How do you know it was National Socialists who did that?'

'That's what the Spieglers told me.'

'The Jewish Spieglers.'

Clara's eyes narrowed. 'Yes. My hosts.' She lowered her voice. 'And there are Jewish people at this table too. Not too far below you for you to enjoy their hospitality this evening, are they?'

Rudy stopped his twirling. 'Miss Vale. You misunderstand me. I personally have nothing against Jewish people. Jews are well represented in the museum world I work in – and I get along with all of my colleagues, Jewish and non-Jewish. But you need to understand that there is a feeling among the ordinary people of Germany that Jews are *over*-represented in so many areas. In banking, in finance, in the press, in industry . . .' He gestured around them. 'Including the fashion industry. And so many shops are owned by Jews. The department stores are mainly Jewish. Need I go on? They are eating the cream when ordinary Germans can't afford bread.'

Clara looked around her. 'You are telling me that the majority of people in this hotel are Jewish? The majority of people who can afford to eat and drink at a place like this? Not just tonight, but any night? That Jews make up the majority of the wealthy people in Berlin?'

Rudy shook his head. 'No, not the majority. But – and you must understand that it's not my view, but the understandable view of others – that there are just *too many of them*.'

'Too many? How many Jews are in Germany?' asked Clara. 'What percentage of the population?'

Rudy shrugged. 'I do not know. Perhaps twenty-five per cent.'

Clara laughed, coldly. 'Well, I do know. My good friend Jonny here – that Jewish gentleman on the other side of the table – told me that Jews make up less than one per cent of people in Germany. In Berlin, that is a bit higher, around three per cent. But still far from *too many.*'

Rudy shook his head. 'But don't you see, Miss Vale, that's the point. If they're not so many, how do they manage to be so influential? To have so much money? To get the best jobs? It's not seen as *fair*, Miss Vale. Not by *real* Germans. And while I do not approve of the thuggery we're seeing on the streets – including the graffiti you saw – I do understand it. And the National Socialists are going to do something about it.'

Clara lowered her voice again. 'Meaning?'

Rudy pursed his lips. 'Meaning we – if we get more seats in the Reichstag in the election next week – will make policies to favour *real* Germans.'

Clara worked hard to keep her voice low. 'You keep saying *real* Germans,' she whispered. 'Aren't the Spieglers *real* Germans?'

But before he could answer, Bella, who had been chatting to Merlette while Rudy and Clara were in serious conversation, chipped in. 'Sorry to interrupt, Miss Vale, but I think the dancing's about to start. And I'd love a dance . . .'

Rudy pushed back his chair and stood up. 'Excuse me, Miss Vale. It's been a pleasure speaking with you. But Miss Cuddy is right. It's time to dance.' He extended his hand to Bella. 'Will you do me the honour?'

'Aye, I will!' said Bella, flushed with excitement.

Clara watched them walk to the dance floor along with couples from all over the room.

But the joy had gone out of the evening.

Chapter 12

Sunday 7th September 1930

The next morning, Clara had to coax Bella out of bed. Clara had got home not long after midnight. She and Juju had caught a lift with the senior Spieglers, but Bella had stayed on longer at the hotel, dancing with Rudy. Jonny had also stayed on. He was trying to negotiate a rapprochement between his old friends Danny and Hugo. The younger Spieglers were occupied with romance – Mitzi with her Mr Isherwood and Karl with Merlette. Although Larry had tried to convince her otherwise, Clara was not overly interested in dancing or romance. Besides, she knew she had a long day ahead.

Despite being a Sunday, the design teams were all planning on working to prepare for the opening of Fashion Week at the Hertzog Department Store on Monday. They would first go to the Spiegler Factory and then transport everything to Hertzog's.

Bella declined breakfast and asked for two aspirin instead, but was still ready to leave with Clara, Juju and Karl. Jakob had left earlier and was going to travel by train, leaving Karl to bring the ladies in the motor car. Clara assumed Jonny was with Jakob.

Karl, who had had hardly any sleep, was remarkably chipper. *The constitution of youth*, thought Clara. He also appeared very pleased with himself. Clara wondered if it was to do with Merlette, but was too polite to ask. Juju had no such qualms.

'Did you see Mademoiselle Merlette back to her hotel room last night?' asked Juju mischievously.

'Of course, Cousin Juju. A gentleman would see a lady to her door.'

'Just to her door?'

Karl blushed.

Juju chortled.

Clara dug Juju in the ribs.

'She seems like a very nice young lady,' said Clara, quickly.

'She is,' said Karl.

'How long has she worked for Hugo?' asked Clara, hoping to prevent Juju from jumping in and teasing her young cousin further.

'I'm not too sure. He might have hired her in anticipation of coming to Berlin.'

'When Hilda Markwald turned him down?' asked Clara.

'Who told you that?' asked Juju, suddenly serious.

Clara shrugged. 'Hilda mentioned it. She said Hugo had asked her to model for him but she decided to work with Danny instead.'

'Utter nonsense!' declared Juju, flapping her hands.

'Oh?' asked Clara, suddenly genuinely interested in the conversation.

'Yes. That's total poppycock. Hilda just wants people to think she can pick and choose who she wants to work with. That she's the one in charge. But she's not. Hugo stopped working with Hilda years ago. They had a spectacular fall-out – back in twenty-five, I think – and he swore then never to work with her again.'

'What caused the fall-out?' asked Bella, stirring from her near slumber in the front passenger seat.

Juju's eyes lit up. 'Well, it's not for me to spread gossip . . . but . . . let me just say that they were romantically involved for a while but then Hugo tired of her and found another lover.'

'Another woman?' asked Bella.

Juju cleared her throat. 'Well, no, it was another man.'

'Eeee, really?' asked Bella.

'Really,' said Juju.

So, thought Clara, *my suspicions about Hugo were correct.* But he was bi-sexual, as they described it in psychological circles, not homosexual. 'I expect Hilda would not take well to being spurned for a woman or a man,' observed Clara.

'Not one bit!' continued Juju. 'She took a pair of cutting shears to Hugo's spring collection. Pierre was the one who told me about it. They nearly lost the entire business. Pierre was furious.'

'I'd be furious at her too,' said Clara.

Juju nodded. 'And not just at Hilda. Hugo as well. Pierre said Hugo had provoked her.'

'Was it Pierre who was the man in question?' asked Karl as he drove past the Kaiser Wilhelm Memorial Church at the top of Kurfürstendamm, then waited at a crossing while some Berliners, carrying picnic baskets, headed towards the Zoological Gardens.

Juju shook her head. 'No. There's nothing going on like that between Hugo and Pierre.'

'They're a funny pair though,' said Bella, as Karl continued driving. 'Can't figure them out. That Pierre seems like a nice fella. What's he doing working with Hugo? Like chalk and cheese they are.'

'They are,' said Juju. Then smiled. 'A bit like me and Jonny, I suppose.'

'Aye,' said Bella. 'But you're brother and sister. There's a reason for you to be together.'

'I heard it's because Hugo saved Pierre's life during the war,' contributed Karl, turning onto Budapester Strasse. 'Is that true, Cousin Juju?'

'I believe so,' said Juju. 'Hugo doesn't talk much about it, but I heard he found Pierre in a trench. Near to death. And carried him to a hospital tent.'

'Eeee, that was a brave thing to do,' said Bella.

Juju pursed her lips. 'Yes, it was. Hugo is not all bad, you know. He's a bit of a handful, and has got what they call an artistic temperament, but he's a good man at the bottom of him.'

Clara was glad to hear that. She had been wondering what Jonny had seen in him. But unlike her travelling companions, she did not want to pry. Jonny and Hugo's business was their own.

* * *

'Would you mind coming with me to the laboratory?' asked Karl of Clara as they arrived at the Spiegler Modefabrik. 'I left my new fabric soaking in a solution overnight – as an experiment – and I'd like to see the results. I thought you might be interested. That's if Cousin Juju can spare you.'

'Not a problem,' said Juju. 'Bella and I can get everything packed. But I'll need you when we go to Hertzog's, Clara.'

'Of course,' said Clara. They turned to walk up the stairs and were greeted by Danny and his assistant Benji, heading to the workroom. Both men looked tired. Benji yawned.

'Sorry, Miss Vale.'

'Late night?' asked Clara, smiling at the young man.

'It sure was that,' said Benji. 'But a good one.' He grinned.

'Time to get to work now though,' said Danny, giving his assistant a pointed look. 'I'm all for painting the town red, and I did a lot of that when I was a young fella, but we've got a lot to do, son.' Then to Clara: 'Good morning, Miss Vale. Will you be joining us in the workshop?'

'Shortly,' said Clara. 'Karl just has something to show me first. Something scientific.'

'You're a clever young fella, aren't you?' said Danny. 'Your father must be very proud of you.'

'Oh, I am,' said Jakob as he came around the corner, accompanied by Jonny. 'But don't be long, son. We'll need Fräulein Vale at Hertzog's.'

'We won't be long, Father,' said Karl and then ushered Clara towards the stairs.

Five minutes later, they were on the top floor and Karl took out a key to unlock the laboratory door. But the door was already unlocked. Karl looked surprised. 'I'm sure I locked it.'

Clara sniffed and recoiled. 'Hydrogen sulphide! That's strong! Is your fume hood not working?'

'It was yesterday,' said Karl, then gagged at the putrid smell. He pulled his coat jacket over his nose. 'Stay here, Miss Vale, I'll go and open a window. You might want to close the door, or we'll stink out the whole building.'

Clara shut the door behind Karl but a moment later he flung it open, his face ashen. A gas mask dangled from his hand. Then he slammed the door behind him.

'What is it?' asked Clara.

'It's . . . it's . . . Oh, Miss Vale! There's a dead body in there!' And then he fell to the floor in a faint.

Clara knelt beside him and checked his pulse and his breathing. Both seemed steady, but she still needed to get the young man medical help. First though, she should check that the 'dead body' was really dead. By the smell of it, there was a high saturation of hydrogen sulphide in the laboratory. It was toxic, but the poor person might still be alive. She picked up the gas mask from the floor, put it on, flung the door open and stormed in. She ran first to the window and opened it wide – then turned to the fume hood. With his head inside the cabinet, bent at the waist and with his legs dangling to the floor, was a man in a tuxedo suit. Clara reached into the cabinet and grabbed his shoulders, intending to pull him out. But he wouldn't budge. She felt around until she found his neck and tried to find a pulse. There was nothing. She pressed her ear to his back to see if she could detect any breathing. Again nothing. It was not looking good for him. She needed to find the gas and shut it off before she could do anything more. She felt around inside the cabinet again until her hand found something metal and cylindrical – she pulled it out and to her relief saw 'H2S' on a label. She twisted the valve shut. Then she tried again to dislodge the man. This time she found his arms and felt along them. They were wrapped around the extractor pipe and . . . *My God, are those handcuffs?* She would only be able to tell if she stuck her head in and had a look. But she needed to wait for more gas to dissipate – her gas mask could become dislodged if she wiggled her head to get it into the cabinet.

She ran back outside the laboratory to check on Karl. He was beginning to stir. 'Are you all right?' she asked in German.

'I . . . I think so. The man, is he . . .'

Clara nodded. 'I think he's dead. I've shut off the gas and opened the window. It will be stinky in there for a while, but it should soon be at safe levels. Then we can check it out properly. How do you feel?'

Karl moved his head gently from side to side. 'A little dizzy but I think I'm fine.'

'Were you wearing the gas mask in there?' asked Clara.

'Yes,' said Karl. 'I keep them on a shelf beside the door. I put it on immediately. But a little bit must still have got through.' He rose to his knees then leaned forward and coughed. Clara patted him on the back until he recovered.

Both Clara and Karl knew that a 'little bit' of hydrogen sulphide would not have been enough to overcome him. And as Clara had just discovered, the gas mask was working perfectly well. *He fainted from shock*, thought Clara. But she didn't want to embarrass him further.

'Yes,' she said gently, 'a little bit must still have got through. How are you feeling now?'

'All right, I think,' he said, and started to regain his feet.

'Good,' said Clara. 'I need you to call the police and the fire brigade. Tell them there's been a chemical incident. Excessive hydrogen sulphide. But it's been cut off at source. I doubt they'll need to evacuate the building. However, you will need to tell them someone is dead. Then go find your father. Only tell him about it. And Jonny, if he's there. But no one else. The last thing I need is hysterical people traipsing over a crime scene.'

'A crime scene?' asked Karl, his eyes widening in shock. 'I know someone has broken in. But the dead man . . . is he the burglar? Or someone else? And . . . well, what happened to him . . . are you sure it wasn't just an accident?'

Clara thought of the poor man handcuffed to the extractor pipe. 'I have no idea yet what happened in there, but one thing I do know: it definitely wasn't just an accident.'

Chapter 13

Detective Inspector Strauss watched through his wire-rimmed spectacles as the police photographer took shots of the man with his head in the cabinet under the fume hood. Thereafter he instructed his sergeant to dust the cabinet for fingerprints which were, in turn, photographed. It was only after that had been done that he gave permission for his sergeant – wearing a gas mask as a precaution – to stick his head into the cabinet with a pair of bolt cutters to release the victim from his handcuffs.

Clara appreciated the detective inspector's forensic thoroughness. She also appreciated that he had allowed her to stay in the laboratory while the preliminary investigation took place. It seems he had been informed by the German Embassy in Cairo of what a sterling job she had done on the case there, resulting in the exoneration of one of their citizens who had been framed for attempted murder.

Strauss helped ease the man out of the cabinet and lay him on the floor. Clara gasped.

'Do you know him, Fräulein?'

Clara stared into the bloated and discoloured face. It was still recognisable.

'Yes,' said Clara. 'That is Hugo Treves. A French fashion designer. We arrived together from Amsterdam on Friday. He is here – like all of us – for Berlin Fashion Week.'

'And when did you last see Monsieur Treves?'

'Alive? That would have been last night at the Hotel Adlon. There was a cabaret. Josephine Baker was performing. All of the fashion teams attended after the gala event at the New Museum.'

Strauss nodded. 'Can you put a time on it? When you last saw him?'

Clara nodded. 'It was half past eleven. The party was still going but I decided to leave early, along with the designer Juju Levine, and our hosts: Herr Spiegler, who owns this factory, and his wife, Stella. I said good night to Monsieur Treves as I left the table.'

'And who was he with at the table?'

Clara thought a moment as Strauss opened a notebook. 'His business partner, Pierre Dreyfus, Jonny Levine, the business partner and brother of Juju, my assistant, Miss Bella Cuddy, the archaeologist Dr Rudy Werner from the New Museum, and our mutual friend Flight Lieutenant Larry Winter.'

Strauss perked up at the last name. 'Winter was there? Good. I'll speak to him. He's usually very observant.'

Then he gestured around him. 'The young man who runs this laboratory. The one who called us in.'

'Karl Spiegler. Jakob Spiegler's son.'

'Was he there last night too?'

Clara nodded. 'He was. When I left, he was dancing with the model, Merlette. I'm afraid I don't know her surname.'

Strauss nodded and made some notes. 'You said you are staying with the Spieglers?'

'I am.'

'And does young Karl still live with his parents?'

'He does.'

'Can you confirm what time he got home last night?'

Clara shook her head. 'I'm afraid not. I was in bed by half past twelve and asleep no later than one. He wasn't home by then. But he was home this morning. We had breakfast together.'

'Who else wasn't home by the time you went to bed?'

'Miss Cuddy, Karl's sister Mitzi and Jonny Levine. But again, all were home this morning, so they must have got in some time, I just wasn't awake to make note of it. You should ask the Spiegler servants. Or whomever is responsible for locking up.'

Strauss' eyes twinkled. 'Thank you for that advice, Miss Vale, I think I know how to conduct an investigation.'

Clara was chastened. 'My apologies.'

'Not at all,' said Strauss. But Clara was under no illusions that he would tolerate her overstepping the mark in the investigation. She was here at his discretion. She made a note to tread carefully.

'So, tell me what happened when you arrived at the laboratory,' he asked, turning to a fresh page in his notebook.

Clara explained exactly what had happened and – when the question was raised – why she was qualified to identify the toxic chemical that was used.

Strauss looked impressed. 'A scientist, a detective *and* a fashion model. No wonder Winter is so taken with you, Miss Vale.'

'I am not really a model,' she said. 'I am only doing it as a favour for my friend. But yes, I am a scientist and a detective.'

'A *private* detective though. With no official jurisdiction.' His eyes narrowed shrewdly.

There it was again. The gentle reminder to stay in her lane.

'That's correct, Detective Inspector. I am happy to be of assistance if you need it. But only if you need it.' She endeavoured to keep her tone respectful but still professional. She wanted Strauss to know that she would comply but not grovel. It was essential that respect between them was mutual or she would not get what she needed from the relationship.

To her relief, Strauss nodded, seemingly assured that she understood the pecking order. 'Well, you've been very helpful so far, Miss Vale. Thank you. Perhaps a few more questions—'

There was a knock at the door. The sergeant opened it to reveal a man carrying a doctor's bag, followed by two assistants with a stretcher between them.

'Ah! Herr Doctor Ritter. I have an interesting customer for you today.'

'Herr Detective Inspector. I hope it will be worth missing my Sunday dinner over.'

Strauss gave a tight smile. 'May I introduce Fräulein Vale. She is a detective from England and will be helping us with our investigation.'

Ritter snapped his heels together and gave a curt bow. *A military man*, thought Clara. She noted too that Strauss had not qualified her status as 'amateur' or 'private', even to waylay any surprise that she was a woman. She appreciated that.

'Fräulein Vale is also a scientist so should be able to answer your questions about the chemicals used.'

'Herr Spiegler could do that too. In fact, he probably should. It's his laboratory,' said Clara.

Strauss nodded. 'Yes, we will be speaking with him. But until his whereabouts last night have been verified, his – how should we say – his *objectivity* cannot be guaranteed.'

'You mean he's a potential suspect,' said Clara.

Strauss shrugged. Then said in English: 'Your words, not mine, Miss Vale. Would you mind assisting Dr Ritter? I have more evidence to gather. And the sergeant will need your fingerprints to eliminate them from the crime scene. I'm sure you understand.'

Clara nodded. 'Yes. Of course.' Then she turned to Dr Ritter and said in German: 'I will help as much as I can. But ultimately Karl Spiegler will be the man to speak to. This is his laboratory.'

Ritter made a guttural sound. Clara wasn't sure if it was a growl of displeasure or a grunt of assent. He was a large man with a round, red face. It looked like he hadn't missed too many Sunday dinners in his time.

She worried for his stability as he lowered himself to his knees, but he managed it without assistance. She knelt beside him.

'Strauss said you know about the chemicals used. Tell me,' he said brusquely, as he proceeded to examine the body.

Clara told him what she knew.

The doctor grunted again. 'Do you know the emission rate for the canister?'

'I don't,' said Clara, 'but I see why you ask. It would be good to know how much time had elapsed before I turned it off.'

Another grunt.

'It was not open to its full capacity,' continued Clara. 'I can tell you that. But enough for a slow emission. How slow, I do not know.'

'Could you find out?' he asked.

'I could do a controlled experiment will a full canister with a properly functioning fume hood, yes.'

'This one is not properly functioning?' he asked, nodding to the cabinet.

Clara shook her head. 'No. But it was on Friday when I saw it. And Karl Spiegler said it was working as it should yesterday too.'

Ritter grunted then finished his brief examination. 'The marks on his wrists show restraint – while he was still alive – but I see no external injuries that could have caused death. I will have to open him up to find out more. The gas is the most likely cause, but there is a chance it could have been released post-mortem. That's why I need to know emission rates. It will also help narrow down the time of death.'

'What would you normally do if you needed help with a scientific investigation?' asked Clara.

'I would ask someone at the university science department. But I believe young Spiegler is a student there. That might cause problems with the credibility of witnesses – until he is cleared as a suspect. I will still ask them, but if you, Fräulein, could also do a test first we will have a benchmark.'

'Of course. But I will still need an operational fume hood, and I have no idea why this one isn't working. Do you mind if I have a look?'

'Be my guest,' said Ritter. 'Strauss? The Fräulein wants to look in the cabinet. All right?'

The detective looked up from his position behind Karl Spiegler's desk. 'Yes, but only if it is safe to do so, and try not to touch anything.'

Clara smiled at him. 'I know how to conduct an investigation, Detective Inspector.'

'Touché, Miss Vale, touché.' He pushed his spectacles up the bridge of his nose and knelt down to examine the desk drawers.

By now the gas had dissipated out of the window. Clara knew it was safe to stick her head in the cabinet under the hood. But she put on the gas mask anyway, to allay the policeman's concerns.

Then she put on a pair of rubber gloves, found a small footstool and positioned it in front of the cabinet. As she did, she spotted a cufflink on the floor. *A clue?* she wondered. She picked it up and passed it to the sergeant standing nearby. He slipped it into an evidence bag. 'Now, do you have a torch?' asked Clara.

He passed her one. 'Do you need me to hold the stool for you, Fräulein?'

She shook her head. 'No, thank you.'

A moment later, she had her head in the cabinet. It was about a metre in width and height and seventy centimetres deep. Her body blocked the natural light from the laboratory but when she turned the torch on she could see that it was almost empty, except for a large wadge of fabric that had been shoved into the mouth of the extraction pipe that went through the hood. She pulled at the fabric until it was dislodged then backed out of the cabinet.

With her feet back on the ground, she showed it to the sergeant.

'What's that?' he asked.

She wasn't sure, but she had an uneasy feeling she had seen it before. She shook it out and a long midnight blue dress unfurled. The very one Danny had designed for Hilda.

Chapter 14

The workshop that had on Friday been a hubbub of strutting fashion and feisty rivalries was morosely silent. The national groupings were not huddled in their corners, but mixed. Danny Cohen was sitting with the Levine twins. The usually composed Jonny was slumped with his head in his hands, while Danny patted his shoulder. Jonny looked up when Clara and Strauss came in, his face fraught with worry. As was Merlette's as she sat with Pierre, his arm around her.

Benji Finkelstein and Bella were sitting quietly in a corner while Jakob and his son were standing at a window in quiet but earnest conversation. Only Hilda was alone, furiously sucking on a cigarette. A uniformed police officer stood at the door, not menacingly, but with enough authority to make it clear that no one there was free to leave. He stepped aside as Strauss and Clara entered.

'Is it him?' asked Jakob, striding across the floor. 'Is it Hugo? What happened, Inspector?'

Strauss raised his hand to quieten Jakob, then pushed his spectacles onto the bridge of his nose. 'Thank you for waiting, ladies and gentlemen. You will have heard that a body has been found in Herr Spiegler's laboratory. I regret to inform you that upon examination it has been identified as your colleague, Monsieur Hugo Treves.'

Merlette burst into tears.

'Oh God, no!' gasped Jonny and clutched his sister's hand.

Hilda shrugged and gestured around the room with her cigarette. 'No surprise there. He's the only one who isn't here.'

'Do you have any clues as to what happened to him, Detective Inspector?' asked Jakob, his voice taut.

Strauss nodded. 'We are gathering evidence. And the police doctor is examining him now. The body will be transported to the mortuary where further investigations will take place. We cannot confirm cause of death until that happens.'

'The gas was the cause of death,' murmured Karl.

'That might be so, or it might not,' said Strauss. 'We must wait for the official report. In the meantime, I will need to speak to everyone in this room, starting first with you, Herr Spiegler Junior, and followed by the young lady. Sorry, mademoiselle, I do not know your surname.'

'She does not speak German,' said Pierre.

'Ah,' said Strauss, 'and I do not speak French. A difficulty.'

'I speak some French,' said Clara. 'It's not as good as my German, but I can do my best to translate for you. If that will be useful.'

Strauss turned to her with the now-familiar twinkle in his eyes. 'That will be most useful, Fräulein Vale. Most useful indeed.'

* * *

Jakob Spiegler had allocated an office on the floor below the laboratory in which Strauss could conduct his interviews. Merlette waited on a chair outside, her fingers nervously pleating and unpleating the fabric of her skirt. Clara was ready to sit with her, but Strauss asked her to come into the office. 'Just in case he tries to bamboozle me with science,' he whispered.

She very much doubted Karl would do any bamboozling and was concerned that Strauss was so suspicious of the young man. Jakob Spiegler was concerned too and said he would be calling a lawyer.

'You can certainly do that, Herr Spiegler,' said Strauss, 'but I am not interviewing your son under caution. I am just trying to get a clearer picture of what happened. But if you would like to wait for your lawyer, then of course we will. However, the sooner we speak to everyone the sooner everyone can go home.'

'It's all right, Father,' said Karl. 'I have nothing to hide. I'll be pleased to help the inspector in whatever way I can.'

'Good man,' said Strauss, and ushered him and Clara into the office, while Jakob kept Merlette company.

Strauss sat behind the desk with his notebook open. Clara took a seat in front of the desk beside Karl.

'So,' said Strauss, 'tell me what happened when you arrived at the laboratory. I know you explained this when I first arrived, but I did not get all the details as I had not yet seen the crime scene.'

Karl went on to explain what happened when they got to the laboratory. As far as Clara could tell his account was almost exactly the same as the one she had given to Strauss. *Good,* she thought, *nothing suspicious or untoward.*

Strauss nodded as he took notes. 'You said the door of the laboratory was unlocked.'

'That's correct,' said Karl.

'And had you left it unlocked?' asked Strauss.

Karl shook his head. 'I didn't think I had. I always lock the door when I leave. There are dangerous chemicals and expensive equipment in the laboratory. I don't even let the cleaner in without my supervision.'

'And when did you last lock it?'

'Saturday afternoon. About three o'clock.'

'Does anyone else have keys?'

'There is an extra set in my father's office in case I leave mine at home. Have you checked that they are still there?'

Strauss gave a tight smile. 'I have not as I have only just heard of it. But I will certainly check with your father. And keys for the factory itself? Are there spare keys in your father's office too?'

'Yes, there are.'

'Who normally opens up here?'

'My father does.'

'At what time?'

'He's usually here around seven. So the security guard who is the night watchman can get home to bed.'

'You have a night watchman? What's his name?'

'Lederman.'

'And where does this Lederman live?'

Karl shrugged. 'I don't know. My father will.'

'Thank you,' said Strauss, noting this all down. 'You are Jewish,' he suddenly added, looking pointedly at Karl.

'I am.'

'You do not observe your Sabbath? You were working on a Saturday before sundown?'

'I'm not strictly observant. No one in my family is. I came in to prepare an experiment. I needed to soak some fabric overnight in a chemical solution. I was going to show Fräulein Vale the results of my experiment today. That's why I took her with me to the laboratory.'

'And what chemicals did you use?'

'Sodium hydroxide and lanolin.'

Strauss looked at Clara. 'Are they known to you, Fräulein Vale?'

'They are,' said Clara. 'Sodium hydroxide is used to create viscose – or rayon as it is sometimes called. That's a type of fabric. And lanolin is derived from sheep's wool. What was the experiment, Karl?'

'I was trying to see if I could replicate the gabardine effect on my linen rayon hybrid.'

Clara nodded her understanding. 'You were trying to waterproof it.'

'Yes, I soaked some fabric overnight.'

Strauss looked from Clara to Karl. 'Is that the gas from the cylinder?'

Both Clara and Karl shook their heads. 'No,' said Karl. 'The sodium hydroxide was in powder form. I mixed it with lanolin oil. If you allow me into the laboratory, I can show you . . .'

Strauss raised his hand. 'No one is going into the laboratory just yet. Fräulein Vale, does what Herr Spiegler say make sense?'

'Yes, it does. He would not need the hydrogen sulphide for this experiment.'

'Hydrogen sulphide? That is what was in the canister?'

Clara and Karl nodded. 'Yes,' said Karl, 'It is a by-product of the process by which viscose is made. But the chemical itself can be used to make dye. I have a few canisters in the laboratory.'

Strauss quirked an eyebrow in Clara's direction. She nodded her agreement.

'So,' said Strauss, making notes, 'you were not actually using this hydrogen sulphide in your experiment yesterday?'

Karl shook his head. 'No. It was a benign experiment. Using powder and oil. Both of them are used in washing detergents. Nothing dangerous in small quantities. Although prolonged contact with the skin can cause burns.'

'Did you use the fume hood?'

Karl nodded. 'Yes, but just to get rid of any smell. The amount of chemical used was not hazardous.'

'And the fume hood was working yesterday?'

Again, Karl nodded.

'And the canister that was used today? Where was that usually kept?'

'In my store cupboard.'

'Locked?'

Karl shook his head. 'No, it's enough that the laboratory door is locked. And as I said, no one goes in there without me. Not even the cleaner.'

Strauss cocked his head to the side. 'And yet you locked your desk drawer.'

'Yes. For added security. Just to clarify, Inspector, I *do* keep the cupboard locked where the legally proscribed poisons are contained, as is the law, but other chemicals that are hazardous but not necessarily lethal unless used in large quantities, I keep in the store cupboard.'

'Is that how things are normally done in laboratories, Miss Vale?'

'It is, Inspector. As far as I can see Herr Spiegler has used the normal safety precautions. It is a well-ordered laboratory.'

Strauss snorted. 'So,' he said, and turned to Karl, 'you do *not* keep potentially dangerous chemicals under lock and key, but you *do* secure a drawer? What is in the drawer that is so important?'

Clara remembered Karl locking the drawer after he'd placed his notebook in it. The notebook with the formula to his new fabric.

'Notes of my experiments,' said Karl. 'I keep the book in that drawer.'

'And your experiments are that important?' asked Strauss.

'One of them is. The one that has created my new fabric. If I can ramp it up to production, it could be very important indeed.'

'Important enough to kill for?'

Karl gasped. 'What are you saying? What has Hugo Treves's death got to do with my fabric?'

Strauss shrugged. 'I have no idea. But there is some connection. That locked drawer has been forced open. And you say you placed a notebook in there. I saw no notebook.'

Karl stood up and headed for the door. 'Where are you going?' demanded Strauss.

'My notebook! My formula! Someone's stolen it!'

'Sit down!'

The young man froze.

'I said sit down!'

A quivering Karl returned to his chair.

'Don't worry,' said Clara, trying to soothe him. 'I'm sure Detective Inspector Strauss will do everything in his power to retrieve your notebook. Do you have it written down anywhere else?'

'No, but it's all in here,' he said, tapping his head.

'Then all is not lost,' said Clara gently. Then to Strauss: 'Are you finished questioning him now? You said yourself he's not under caution. And, quite clearly, he had no need to steal his own formula.'

Strauss shook his head. 'No. I am not yet finished. But you can leave now, Fräulein, my questions are no longer about the laboratory.'

'I'd prefer she stayed,' said Karl, his voice cracking. 'Will you stay?' His eyes implored Clara's.

'Yes,' said Clara. 'If that's all right with Detective Inspector Strauss.'

Strauss sighed. 'Well, it's not necessary,' he said in English. 'But I'll allow it. I must warn you though, Miss Vale, your expertise is not needed for this part of the interview, so I expect you not to interject. Is that understood?'

'It is,' said Clara and gave Karl a reassuring smile.

'All right then,' said Strauss, switching to German and turning his attention to a very nervous Karl. The young man's face was deathly pale. His eyes like a rabbit's in its last moments of life.

Strauss's voice softened – a little. 'Now, there's no need to be frightened, Herr Spiegler, I'm just trying to sketch as full a picture as possible as to Monsieur Treves's last hours. I'll be asking everyone at the Adlon and more besides. So do not feel that everything is focused on you. It is not. But I do need you to answer as truthfully and accurately as you can. Because if there are any contradictions in your account, they will soon come to light. Is that clear?'

Karl swallowed and then nodded.

'Good,' said Strauss, his pen poised over his notebook. 'Then let us begin. Fräulein Vale has told me that she left the hotel at around half past eleven. When she left, she said she saw you and Mademoiselle Merlette dancing. Is that correct?'

'It is.'

'And what was Mademoiselle Merlette wearing?'

'Wearing?'

'Yes. Am I not speaking clearly enough? Do you recall what dress she was wearing?'

Karl flashed a look at Clara. She gave him a reassuring smile but didn't speak.

'It was a red dress. Silk. Cut on the bias. An Empire line bust and string straps.'

'Thank you for that detail. Are you sure it was red?'

'Quite sure.'

Strauss looked at Clara. She nodded her agreement.

'All right,' said Strauss. 'Do you know when she changed out of the black dress she wore at the end of the fashion show at the New Museum?'

'Straightaway, I think. I don't specifically recall. But it wouldn't have been permitted for her to wear it away from the show. I expect Hugo – Monsieur Treves – would have wanted to close Fashion Week with it.'

'But you did not see her change out of it?'

'I did not. It is not my habit to ogle models as they undress. She would have changed behind a screen.'

'Did you see it?' Strauss suddenly asked Clara.

'No. As Herr Spiegler said, she changed behind a screen. But I can confirm that at the Adlon she wore the red dress already described.'

'And did either of you see what happened to Fräulein Markwald's blue dress? The one, I believe, looks almost identical to the one Mademoiselle Merlette was wearing apart from the colour? The one the argument was about?'

'How do you know about that?' asked Karl.

'Miss Vale told me about it.'

Clara had indeed told him about it. As soon as she found the dress. She wondered why the dress was in the laboratory. Was Hugo – or his killer – trying to destroy it? Or was the dress placed there in an attempt to frame Hilda? Clara would love to be a fly on the wall when Strauss interviewed Hilda, but she very much doubted she'd be invited. However, she *would* be present for Merlette's interview. Strauss may also consider that Merlette had been trying to destroy the blue dress, out of jealousy or pique. That she was in the laboratory last night, so angry with Hugo for setting her up to be attacked by Hilda at the museum that she turned on her employer. It was certainly possible, but didn't seem likely. Clara considered the physique of the young woman. Surely, she was not strong enough to have dragged Hugo Treves into the fume hood cabinet? But she might have had an accomplice . . . It seemed that that was the line of enquiry Strauss was following too. That perhaps Karl and Merlette were in it together.

'Now, Herr Spiegler. Where was Monsieur Treves while you were dancing with Mademoiselle Merlette.'

Karl thought a moment and said: 'I'm not entirely sure. I saw him talking to Jonny Levine for a while. Around the time Fräulein Vale left. But I don't recall much beyond that.'

'How would you describe their demeanour, Monsieur Treves and Mr Levine? Was it animated? Angry? . . . *Intimate?*

Karl bit his lip. 'I don't honestly know. I didn't pay much attention to them. I was focused on my dance partner. But I don't recall any histrionics. They were just talking. I can't say more than that.'

'All right,' said Strauss, 'thank you. Now, can you recall what time you left the Adlon?'

Karl shook his head. 'I don't recall.'

'Come now,' said Strauss, 'I don't need an exact time. But was it around twelve? One? Two? You must know that. Unless you were too drunk to remember?'

Karl shook his head vigorously. 'I was not too drunk to remember. I had been drinking. But not excessively. I still had my full faculties. As to when I left, it must have been around two o'clock.'

'Are you sure?'

'I . . . I think so.'

'You think so? You're not sure?'

Karl shook his head.

Strauss smiled. But there was no warmth in it. 'Well, not to worry,' he continued, making notes. 'I will be speaking to the hotel staff. The lobby staff will remember. As will the taxi driver who took you home. Did you take a taxi home?'

'I did.'

'Alone?'

'Yes.'

'Not with Mr Levine?'

'No. I do not know where Jonny was. I lost track of him.'

'When did you last see him?'

Karl shrugged. 'I don't recall. The last time I remember seeing him was when Fräulein Vale left. Whatever time that was. But beyond that, I do not remember seeing him.'

'All right, thank you. Fräulein Vale said she left around half past eleven . And you say you left around two o'clock. Two and a half hours later, during which time you do not recall seeing him. Was he at home when you arrived?'

Karl shrugged. 'I do not know. He might have been already in his bedroom. You should ask him.'

'Oh, I will,' said Strauss and made a note.

Clara's eyes narrowed. What was Strauss implying about Jonny? Surely he couldn't think . . . but, as she'd agreed, she held her tongue. For now. The rest of the interview with Karl consisted of him trying to avoid admitting that he and Merlette had left the ballroom around midnight and spent some time together – alone – in her room. Strauss did not press him to describe what had gone on behind closed doors. It was enough that the young man had – with some embarrassment – admitted to his whereabouts, and why he had not seen Jonny or Hugo after Clara left. And with that, the interview was over. Karl was free to leave and Merlette was invited to take his place.

Chapter 15

The 'little blackbird' made herself as small as possible. With her shoulders hunched, and her chin on her chest, Clara was sure that if she'd had wings like her namesake, they would have been wrapped around her delicate frame.

'What is your surname, Fräulein?' asked Strauss.

Clara, as she was to do for the rest of the conversation, translated, struggling at times to find the correct French word, but managing, mostly, to make herself understood. When she replied to Strauss it was in English. Having to receive in French, translate into her own head in English then having to translate again into German was just too confusing for her limited language skills. The detective inspector realised this very quickly, and so asked his questions in English.

'Your surname, miss, what is it?'

'It is Hassan.'

'Arab?'

'My mother is from Tunisia.'

'And your father?'

'I did not know my father.'

'So, Hassan is your mother's name. And where is your mother now?'

'She died when I was fourteen.'

'In Tunisia?'

Merlette shook her head. 'No. Paris. My mother came first to Marseilles. She was then offered work in Paris.'

'Work as . . .'

'A seamstress.'

'With Monsieur Treves?'

'Yes.'

'And you accompanied her?'

'Yes.'

'You say your mother died when you were fourteen. How old are you now?'

'Nineteen.'

'And who looked after you after your mother died?'

'Monsieur Treves.'

'In his house?'

'Yes.'

Strauss and Clara exchanged a brief look. Clara recalled the night on the train when Hilda encountered Hugo coming out of Merlette's compartment in the middle of the night. But Strauss did not press the girl to discuss the nature of her relationship with her employer. *Perhaps he might later*, Clara thought. For now, he focused on the events of the previous evening and the whereabouts of the blue dress. Merlette confirmed that she had worn the black dress – at Hugo's behest – but she had not seen Hilda's blue dress.

'All right,' said Strauss, 'where did *your* dress go? Is it still at the museum now?'

Merlette shook her head. 'No. Monsieur Treves and Monsieur Dreyfus packed everything up and brought it back here to the workshop in the factory. Today we would do any repairs needed to it and steam it clean again, before taking it and the other clothes to the next venue at the department store.'

'Monsieur Dreyfus?'

'Pierre Dreyfus,' interjected Clara without translating. 'Hugo's business partner.'

'Ah yes. And was he at the Adlon last night?' he asked in English.

'Yes,' said Clara, as she recalled when she'd last seen him. 'He was talking to Larry Winter. About the war, I think. He was injured in a gas attack. That's how he got the scarring on his face. And I heard, just this morning, that it was Hugo who saved his life.'

'Did he now?' asked Strauss, making a note. 'Well, thank you for that information. Now, shall we continue with Miss Hassan?'

Clara nodded and continued her role as translator.

'So,' said Strauss, 'do you think Mademoiselle Markwald's blue dress will be downstairs in the workroom? Have you seen it this morning, Mademoiselle Hassan?'

Merlette shrugged. 'I don't know. I haven't looked at my own clothes yet, and certainly not Mademoiselle Markwald's. I just arrived when news came of . . . of . . . poor Monsieur Treves.'

Strauss nodded. 'All right. Back to last night. Who did you travel with to the hotel?' asked Strauss.

'On the way there I was in a taxi with Monsieur Spiegler's daughter Mitzi and an English gentleman.'

'His name?'

'Ish—Ish something.'

'Isherwood,' Clara provided. 'Mitzi Spiegler's English tutor.'

Strauss nodded. 'And on the way home from the hotel?'

'There was no need for a taxi,' answered Merlette. 'I am staying at the hotel.'

'Ah,' said Strauss. Clara saw his eyes narrowing as he homed in on his prey. She hoped his next shot wouldn't hurt the little bird too much.

'And what time did you retire to your room?'

'A little after midnight.'

'Alone?'

'Of course.'

'Are you sure?'

Silence.

'Come now, Mademoiselle Hassan. We know you were not alone. And if you lie to us about this, we will wonder if you are lying to us about other things. Things that could really get you into trouble. Spending some time with a gentleman in your room will not get you into trouble with the police. Being part of a murder will.'

Merlette was now visibly shaking. Clara reached out and held her hand. 'Come,' she said quietly, 'the inspector is right. It is better you tell the truth before you get yourself – or the person you were with – into further trouble. Because in a murder investigation the police need to know where everyone was. And at what time. Who were you with, Merlette?'

Strauss did not reprimand Clara for this intervention but leaned forward to hear Merlette's answer.

'It was the young Monsieur Spiegler. Karl. He came into my room.'

Strauss nodded his approval. 'Thank you. And what time did he leave?'

Merlette sighed. 'I do not know, I fell asleep. He was gone when I awoke.'

'And what time was that?'

'Just before dawn. I slept well.'

So, thought Clara, Karl's departure time from the hotel was not yet confirmed. She glanced at Strauss; his face was inscrutable. Then he refocused his attention on the little bird.

'Were you at breakfast at the hotel, Mademoiselle?'

Merlette nodded.

'And who from the fashion party was there? Who of the people in the workshop downstairs were there for breakfast?'

Merlette thought a moment and then shook her head. 'No one. I did not see anyone there. Perhaps they ate before or after me. I breakfasted alone.'

'Did you leave for the factory straight after breakfast?'

'Not long after. I went to my room first to freshen up and collect my coat.'

'But straight after that?'

Merlette nodded. 'Yes, we left straightaway.'

'What time was that? And who is *we*? You said you breakfasted alone.'

'I did. I joined some gentlemen who were in the foyer, heading to Spiegler's. We left around half past eight and got here a little before nine o'clock, I think. I didn't check the time.'

Strauss noted the times. As did Clara. She had got to the factory around twenty past nine.

Strauss continued his questioning. 'With whom did you travel, Miss Hassan?'

'Monsieur Cohen and Monsieur Dreyfus. We travelled in a taxi together.'

'And Mademoiselle Markwald and the young American man?'

'Benji Finkelstein,' added Clara.

'Yes,' said Strauss, 'Finkelstein. Did you see him or Miss Markwald before you left the hotel?'

'I did not.'

'And you say you did not see any of them at breakfast.'

'That is correct. I did not see them.'

'And Cohen and Dreyfus? Where did you first see them this morning? They may not have been at breakfast, but perhaps you saw them elsewhere? In the corridor perhaps?'

'No, only in the hotel lobby as we were about to leave. Monsieur Dreyfus was waiting for me. He did not mention Monsieur Treves's whereabouts. And Monsieur Cohen then asked if he could share the taxi as he was alone. At least that's what I think was said. They spoke English.'

'And they didn't say where the others were?'

Merlette shook her head. 'But Mademoiselle Markwald and Benji were already here when we arrived.'

Strauss made some notes and then asked: 'Did you see Spiegler senior and Jonny Levine at all?'

'Monsieur Levine?'

'Yes. The Englishman.'

Merlette nodded. 'I did. They were already here when we arrived. All of them. The only one who wasn't was . . .' she looked to her right in the direction of the laboratory '. . . Monsieur Treves.'

Chapter 16

Detective Inspector Strauss spent the next three hours interviewing everyone in the workroom – but unfortunately for Clara, she was not permitted to sit in. All the interviewees spoke either German or English as a first or second language, and Strauss was fluent in both. As each interview was concluded, the interviewee was permitted to leave the premises.

'Oh, it's just so frustrating that I can't hear the rest of it!' Clara told Bella as the two of them sat at a coffee house across the square from the factory on Hausvogteiplatz. 'What did he ask you?' she probed, as Bella tucked into an *apfelstrudel* drenched in condensed milk.

Bella answered between bites. 'He was interested in who was talking to who at the Adlon. And also about the big argument at the New Museum. I think he's cottoned on to the tensions between Danny and Hugo about the dress. Also, he wanted me to confirm if I'd heard Danny threatening to kill Hugo.'

Clara stirred a sugar cube into her coffee. 'Does he mean Danny's outburst at the museum?'

'Aye, that's the one. I told him I did, but as far as I could tell it was what anyone would say when they're upset. I told me little sisters countless times I'd kill 'em but they're still walking happily on God's good earth.'

Clara nodded then sipped her coffee. 'Yes, it was an understandable outburst. But if you had threatened to kill your sisters then the next day one of them turned up dead it would be seen in a different light. Did Strauss ask you anything else about Danny?'

'What time he left the party last night.'

'Which was?'

'Around one o'clock.'

Clara nodded and then told Bella that Merlette had said he travelled in with her and Pierre this morning. 'That, I believe, was around nine o'clock. But it doesn't account for his whereabouts between one and nine.'

'Aye,' said Bella. 'Someone was here before nine o'clock killing old Hugo. Do you know what time he died?'

Clara shook her head. 'That's hard to say. The body was beginning to stiffen a little when I found it, but it was still moveable. It takes around eight hours for a body to become fully stiff. But it was just slightly stiff. The face was frozen – that happens around two hours – and it had just started in the limbs. So I can only approximate, and it's just that, I'm afraid, as no matter what they say in detective novels, determining time of death is a very inexact science. There are all sorts of variables: the room temperature, the size and physical condition of the body, whether the victim had been taking any medication, and so on. But with all that said, it's still useful to *try* to determine the potential time frame of death. So, I would guess for Hugo that was three to five hours before we found him. The doctor will know more when he conducts a proper autopsy – and I am going to try my hardest to get in on that.'

'Oh, aye? How are you going to wangle that one?'

Clara smiled. 'I have some leverage. The doctor has asked for my help to do an experiment on the time it takes for a gas canister to empty. I will do that for him this afternoon. But I intend to make it conditional upon me being able to observe the autopsy. I've already helped them translating from French, so I think they owe me. I'll have to be careful how I approach it though.' She looked at her watch. 'Rigor will now have fully set in, so the doctor has to wait for the body to relax again. That will take at least twelve hours from now. I doubt he'll be doing the post-mortem in the middle of the night, so I expect it will be tomorrow morning. I'll speak to the inspector about it after he's conducted his interviews.'

Bella finished her strudel, her appetite completely unaffected by the gruesome discussion. She wiped away her moustache of condensed milk then said: 'So, working with the three to five hours then. You found him at half past nine, is that right?'

Clara nodded. 'Yes. Give or take a few minutes.'

Bella counted on her fingers. 'Well, me sums are not that good, but as far as I can tell he could have been killed as late as half past six or as early as half past four. Is that right?'

Clara smiled at her assistant. 'Your sums are spot on, Bella. And I like your train of thought. Yes, that's the time frame I believe we're looking at. The information about the gas will help narrow it down too.'

'Do you think the inspector is also working with those times in mind?'

'Yes, I do. He seems like he's a very experienced investigator. So that's why he's trying to figure out who was where when. I expect the next thing he'll be doing is going to the hotel to confirm people's whereabouts between the time they left the party and this morning. Those who were booked into the hotel and those at the Spiegler house.'

Bella's eyes widened. 'You mean us?'

Clara smiled. 'Yes, us. And the Spieglers and Juju and Jonny.'

Bella bit her lip.

'What's wrong?'

She shrugged. 'Oh, I'm sure it's nowt, Miss Vale, but I don't think Jonny came home at all last night.'

'How do you know that?'

'Well, Rudy – Dr Werner – dropped me off at around three o'clock. And the servant – the poor fella looking after the door – asked me if Mr Levine was still coming because he wanted to get to bed.'

Clara leaned forward. 'Just Mr Levine? He didn't ask about anyone else?'

Bella shook her head. 'No. Just him. I think everyone else was in. Karl and Mitzi had got home before me, the fella said. So, it was just Jonny.'

Clara nodded thoughtfully. 'Yes, I'll speak to the servant – and I'm sure Strauss will too – but I think your assumption is probably correct. Everyone else was home. But how do you know Jonny didn't come home at all? After three o'clock?'

Bella folded her napkin and put it on her tea plate. 'Because I was up at six to go to the lavatory. On my way back to bed, I passed his room and the door was slightly ajar – his bed hadn't been slept in.'

Clara felt her stomach tighten. 'Oh dear. That's not going to look very good for Jonny.'

Bella looked around the café, then lowered her voice. 'Oh, Miss Vale,' she whispered. 'You don't think he did it, do you? Not Mr Levine!'

Clara leaned forward and lowered her voice to match Bella's. 'Of course I don't think that. But I worry that the inspector will. He was already asking about Jonny earlier – when interviewing Karl and Merlette. And me. Jonny was the last person I saw with Hugo last night. I've already told the inspector that. Did you see them together after I left, Bella?'

'Mr Levine and Hugo?'

'Yes.'

Bella bit her lip again. 'Aye, I did. After you left, they were talking for a while. Then Mr Levine went to the bar. That's when Hilda moved in.'

Clara cocked her head. 'What do you mean, moved in?'

'She was a bit tipsy. She wanted Hugo to dance with her. She wouldn't take no for an answer.'

'And did he dance with her?'

'Aye. Eventually. He didn't seem keen at first but once they got on the dance floor he loosened up. And they stayed there for a good few dances. He's a dab hand at the foxtrot. Mr Twinkle Toes, he was.'

'And Jonny? What did he do?'

Bella shrugged. 'He just sat and waited at the table.'

'Happily?'

'Not really.'

'How long did he wait?'

'I don't know,' said Bella, the frustration rising in her voice. 'I wasn't taking that much notice. And I'd had a good few drinks by then.' She sighed. 'I'm sorry, Miss Vale, I didn't know I'd have a murder investigation to deal with.'

Clara smiled gently. 'That's all right. Neither did I. But let's try to remember as much as we can. So, Jonny was waiting at the table. Did Hugo come back to join him?'

Bella shook her head. 'No. He and Hilda sat down together at another table. After a bit, Mr Levine went to join them. Hilda told him to get lost. At least that's what it looked like from where me and Rudy were sitting. I couldn't hear, but I could see their body language. It looked like Mr Levine expected Hugo to contradict her, but he didn't. Mr Levine looked humiliated, poor fella. Then he left.'

'On his own?'

'Aye. And he didn't look happy about it. But before you ask, I don't know what time it was for sure. Maybe one o'clock?'

'But he didn't come home then. I wonder where he went?' Clara's stomach tightened even further. Surely Jonny couldn't have . . . no, it was unthinkable. But she was sure Detective Inspector Strauss wouldn't consider it unthinkable. She turned her attention back to Bella. 'What happened after that? With Hilda and Hugo?'

Bella swallowed hard and looked around the café again. 'Oh, Miss Vale. I wish I'd never said anything now. And I wish I could tell you Hugo and Hilda stayed together and left together, but they didn't. The truth is, Hugo left a few minutes later.'

'On his own?'

'Aye. I think he might have been trying to catch up with Mr Levine.'

'Why do you say that?'

'Because when Mr Levine left, Hugo kept looking after him. And Hilda didn't like it. They looked like they might have had a row about it. Then Hugo got up and left.'

'To follow Jonny?'

Bella bit her lip. 'I can't say for sure. But that's what it looked like to me.'

Clara felt a cold shiver down her spine. 'And you told the inspector this?'

Bella swallowed hard. 'Aye, miss, I did.'

Chapter 17

It was two o'clock by the time Strauss concluded his interviews. Everyone, other than Clara, was instructed to go home or to their hotel. They would be contacted later if further questioning was required. Clara was desperate to speak to Jonny Levine, but as soon as she arrived back from the café, she was ushered upstairs to the laboratory by a police sergeant. Neither Strauss nor Dr Ritter were there, but the sergeant told her that Ritter had asked her to conduct the experiment and report her findings as soon as possible.

The sergeant watched nervously as she put on a white lab coat, goggles and gloves.

'Is it safe?'

Clara nodded. 'As long as I take safety precautions, yes.'

'And me?'

Clara suggested he wait outside. Relieved, he retreated and shut the door. Clara was pleased to be alone. The surfaces of the laboratory were covered in black dust – graphite powder, used to reveal fingerprints. If this had been Clara's investigation she would have photographed the prints and used them in her detection process. But alas it was not her investigation, nor did she have a camera. Unless . . . she searched the cupboards and drawers and found what she was looking for. A portable box camera.

'Perfect!' A few minutes later she had located a stock of film and flash bulbs then set about photographing the dusted prints on the fume hood, the H2S canister – which had been left on a bench for her attention – and the bottom drawer of the desk. She then put the camera in her bag. She would need to find somewhere to develop the film. She'd ask Karl when she got back to the house.

She then turned her attention to the canister.

She had spoken to Karl earlier and he had told her where to find a full canister for comparison – and where he kept his manufacturer's receipts, equipment operating instructions and his notes on stock levels. The files were in an ordinary filing cabinet. First, she found the fume hood instructions and familiarised herself with the details. She had used one, but that was around a decade ago. Then she turned to the hydrogen sulphide listing. Karl had replenished his stock with three one-litre canisters six weeks earlier. Of the two canisters in the cupboard, one had already been used, and one was still full, its valve sealed. She placed the canister that had been used to kill Hugo on a scale, weighed it and determined only a third had been used. That surprised her. If Hugo had been dead for a minimum of three hours before she found him, as the onset of rigor suggested, she would have thought the canister would be almost empty. She snipped the wire seal on the new canister, attached a brass control valve and pressure gauge, placed it in the fume hood cabinet and set the clock on her experiment.

While she waited she read through Karl's notes – in German – on the various procedures he conducted in his laboratory. Two hours later, Clara knew more than she would ever need to about the chemistry of textiles, and her German reading skills had vastly improved. However, more importantly, with the new H2S canister emptied by thirty per cent, she determined that if full when opened, the gas used to kill Hugo had only been released around half past seven in the morning. By the state of rigor mortis, the Frenchman had been dead at least an hour before that. Of course, her estimate of rigor mortis by visual clues and touch were not forensically exact, and she could have been wrong, but she would be surprised if she was. It was more likely that he had died *before* half past six, not after.

But there was also a chance the canister had not been full when it was opened. In which case her calculations would be off again. Had it been full? She examined the seal that she had snipped off the new canister. It was aluminium wire with a red tag, stamped with the manufacturer's crest. What had happened to the other seal? The police had searched the laboratory and taken some things away, but would they have removed a wire seal? Would they have known what it was if they found it?

She looked around, but there was no sign of a second cut tag. She checked the rubbish bin – there were a few discarded items, but no tag. Had the police emptied it? Possibly, but why would they take the tag and not leave it for her with the canister? And, if they didn't know what it was . . . well, they would have left it in the bin.

She got down on her knees and searched the floor. Again, she found nothing. But then, just as she was about to pull herself up, something caught her eye. Under the bench, right at the back against the skirting board . . . something red. She reached under and clawed it towards her. In the process her fingers rolled over something else . . . and when she retrieved both items she confirmed that one of them was indeed the tag from the canister, which meant it very likely had been full when it was first opened. This was corroborated by Karl's records where he had noted only one out of the three canisters had been used.

So, if the canister had only been open for two hours before she entered the laboratory, and Hugo was already dead, who had opened the canister at half past seven, and why? And if Hugo had not died of excessive hydrogen sulphide inhalation, what had he died of? She would hopefully find out at the post-mortem in the morning.

She then turned her attention to the second item she'd found under the bench. It was a glass vial which looked as though it would hold about twenty millilitres of liquid. She had seen these vials before. Near the end of the war, as an enthusiastic eighteen-year-old, she had volunteered in a pharmacy that processed medical supplies for a military hospital. She found a cotton bud and scraped inside the glass. There was a residue of pale green liquid. Yes, it was as she suspected: the vial had contained liquid morphine. It was enough to put someone to sleep but not to kill them.

But why put them to sleep handcuffed inside a fume cupboard? Had the killer subdued Hugo with the morphine and then released the gas later? But why the time delay? Why wait? And why do it when Hugo was already dead? And what did this have to do with the theft of Karl's notebook? Had Hugo walked in on a burglary? And if so, what was he doing here in the early hours of the morning? And what did Hilda's dress have to do with any of it? She didn't know the answer to any of these questions – yet – but the glass vial had given her a clue. She would of course hand it over to Detective Inspector Strauss and Dr Ritter, but, before she did, there was someone else she needed to talk to. And she needed to speak to them before they talked to the police.

Chapter 18

Clara informed the police sergeant that her experiment was completed and requested that he let Detective Inspector Strauss know that she would attend the police station in the morning to explain her findings. She then asked permission to use a telephone. After escorting her to Jakob Spiegler's office, the sergeant gave her some privacy as she first telephoned the Spieglers and spoke to Bella. She then put through a call to the Hotel Adlon and asked to speak to Larry Winter. When he came to the phone, she invited him to meet her for an early dinner at the hotel, which he agreed to, wholeheartedly. But as she headed to the door of Jakob's office, she caught sight of herself in a full-length mirror – her day dress was crumpled, her stockings laddered and there was a splodge of black fingerprint dust on one of her shoes. *Blimey, I can't go in this!*

A few minutes later, Clara had opened one of Juju's trunks and found what she was looking for: a floaty sea-green confection in chiffon and silk with a matching silk scarf. Juju had embroidered shell motifs on the bodice and along the hemline, as well as on the scarf. As she pulled on a fresh pair of stockings and slipped into the slinky cocktail dress, she checked her reflection in the mirror. *I look like a mermaid!* But her hair was like seaweed. She ran a comb through it, but after hours in the laboratory wearing a mask and goggles, it really needed a good wash and style, which she didn't have time for. So instead, she tied the scarf around her head to make a turban, allowing the tasselled ends to dangle over her shoulders. She had seen the look in Juju's fashion magazines. Now she looked like a Hollywood vamp! But it would do.

Concerned that the scarf might slip, she searched the haberdashery box and found a couple of jewelled safety pins. She was just about to close it when something caught her eye: a jet cufflink. Clara caught her breath. The item gleaming at her from the trunk was identical to the one she had found earlier today, on the floor in front of the fume hood cabinet. If she recalled, both Hugo's cufflinks were accounted for, although one cuff was not properly buttoned, so it wasn't his . . . Did the cufflink belong to the killer? If so, why was its mate in Juju's haberdashery box? With no more time to ponder, she slipped the cufflink into an evening bag she had found in the trunk, then put that bag into her satchel – which already held the camera she had borrowed from the laboratory. The bulky satchel was hardly cocktail attire; she would check it into the hotel cloakroom.

* * *

Clara was relieved that only a handful of tables at the Hotel Adlon restaurant were occupied – and none by anyone involved in Fashion Week. It was only six o'clock and most guests would dine later. The bar, however, was full and Clara put her head down as she walked past, reluctant to engage in conversation with anyone she might know. In fact, she'd been so reluctant that she had wanted to suggest she and Larry meet somewhere else, but as her knowledge of Berlin was limited, she'd decided that the hotel was the best option. Besides, she could also question some of the staff about what they'd seen of the comings and goings of various guests the previous evening. She expected Detective Inspector Strauss had already done that, but she doubted very much he would share his findings with her. She was not officially on the case.

She was, however, dressed for cocktails. She hoped Juju wouldn't mind her borrowing one of the show items. Clara did not know if Fashion Week would now go ahead. The last she had heard Jakob Spiegler was in discussions with the various teams, the management of Hertzog's Department Store and the police. Buyers were already in town and tickets to the shows had already been sold. It was Spiegler's Modefabrik that was the crime scene, not the department store. And more specifically than that, the laboratory at the *fabrik*. Clara expected the police to give the go-ahead, but until they did the collections remained in the workroom.

Larry was already at the table, in black tie. He was smoking a Lucky Strike cigarette – just like she remembered him doing in Cairo. He looked her up and down appreciatively. 'Do you want to go to a cocktail bar instead? Or perhaps a jazz club?'

Clara smiled. 'I was limited for choice with what to wear.'

Larry's eyes twinkled. 'Well, you look spiffing, as the Brits would say.' He pulled out her chair and she sat down.

Larry waited until the waiter poured their wine then said: 'What gives me the feeling this is not just a social engagement?'

Clara smiled. 'Can't a girl just want a pleasant meal with a pleasant companion?'

He chuckled. 'At six o'clock on a Sunday? After the "girl" has been helping in a murder investigation all afternoon? Probably not. What can I do for you, Clara?'

Clara took a sip of her wine. A perfectly chilled Riesling. It would go well with fish. 'So, you heard about the murder then?'

'Of course. It's all anyone in the hotel is talking about.'

'And have you spoken to Detective Inspector Strauss yet?'

Larry shook his head. 'Not yet. But he sent word that he'd like to speak to me in the morning. He's been busy all afternoon interviewing hotel staff.'

Clara was relieved to hear that. She had hoped to speak to Larry first. She did not want Strauss warning him not to speak to her.

'Good,' she said, then paused to order an asparagus soup starter and a seabass for main from the hovering waiter. Larry chose shellfish bisque for his entrée and pork chops for his main course.

'So, what happened?' asked Larry.

Clara gave him a brief account of the discovery of the body and the initial suggestion that Hugo had been gassed. She did not tell him that her subsequent investigation in the laboratory cast doubt that gas had been the cause of death. She had not even told Dr Ritter that. She would do so in the morning.

'Golly,' said Larry, seriously taken aback. 'That sounds like a complicated method of murder. Handcuffs? Who would have those? And who had access to the factory and the laboratory? And who would know what to do in the laboratory and which gas to use? And who would even want to do it in the first place?'

'Indeed,' said Clara, buttering some bread, 'those are all questions DI Strauss is asking. Means, motive and opportunity.

Those are the three key avenues of all murder investigations. Strauss is currently concentrating on the opportunity.'

'And you? What are you focusing on?'

'At the moment I'm assisting the police pathologist, a Dr Ritter, to determine the means. That's why he asked me to help him with testing the gas canister.'

'And motive? Is anyone asking about that?'

'Oh yes,' said Clara, 'that's in everyone's mind. Particularly with the controversial dress being found at the crime scene. But for now, the suspect list needs to be narrowed down to who was actually able to commit the murder. Who does and does not have an alibi. Someone may very well have wanted Hugo dead, but if half the staff of the hotel Adlon swore that person did not leave the premises the entire night, then they are not likely to be the killer.'

'Not likely, but still possible?'

'Indeed,' said Clara, putting down her butter knife. 'Alibis are sometimes fabricated. Or bought . . . But for now, that's what Strauss will be focusing on. Who was where, when. And I expect that's what he'll be asking you tomorrow. For instance, I believe you spent much of last night after I left talking to Pierre Dreyfus. Is that correct?'

Clara had to wait for a reply as the waiter placed soup plates in front of them.

When they were alone again, Larry picked up his spoon, ready to dip into his bisque. 'Dreyfus is a suspect?'

Clara shrugged. 'No more than anyone else. But I just want to check a few things, if you don't mind.'

'Not at all. I'll do whatever I can to help. As I always do, Clara.' His pale blue eyes drank her in.

It did not make Clara uncomfortable. There was an undeniable attraction between the two of them. And, if circumstances had been different that night in Casablanca . . . with the sound of the surf and the room bathed in moonlight . . . well, best not to dwell on that. After Casablanca there had been Cairo – and Larry had been a great help in her investigation there. But her faith in him had been tarnished recently when he lied to her about meeting Hilda Markwald on the train. She still needed to get to the bottom of the why and wherefores of that. But for now, she had more important things to ask him.

She waited until the waiter removed their soup plates then asked: 'Do you recall what cufflinks Pierre was wearing last night?'

Larry looked amused. 'Not in the slightest. I can't say I spent much time looking at his wrists.'

Clara smiled. 'All right, I thought I'd ask.'

'The cufflinks are a clue?'

Clara shrugged. 'Possibly. But let's focus on what you can remember. What time did Pierre leave the party last night?'

Larry thought a moment and then replied: 'Around one o'clock, I think.'

'Did he leave alone?'

'Yes and no.'

'Meaning?'

'Meaning he followed Hugo after he left. And Hugo left just after Jonny.'

'How do you know he was following Hugo? He could just have decided to leave around the same time.'

Larry took a sip of wine, then answered, 'Because he told me that's what he was doing. He said that he was worried

Hugo was going to gamble. It's a problem Hugo has, apparently. Pierre said that he sometimes used the fashion house as collateral in card games. They nearly lost the house – literally – last year. Pierre had to take out bank loans to pay off Hugo's debt and save the business. He was furious with Hugo about it.' His eyes opened wide. 'Do you think that would qualify as a motive?'

Clara nodded. 'It might. But it's still too early in the investigation to say for sure. What does make me wonder though, is why Pierre was so chatty about this with you. Are you friends? Have you met before?'

Larry shook his head. 'No, last night was the first time we'd met. But Rudy, who *has* met Pierre before, introduced us. He thought we might get along as we were both on the Western Front during the war. On the same side—' he grimaced '—which, at that time, Rudy and I weren't.'

'But you are now,' observed Clara.

'Of course!' Larry laughed. 'You saw us both in Cairo. We work together on archaeological digs. His team has hired me as a pilot many times. So, when I heard you were going to be appearing at the museum last night, I gave him a ring and asked for him to arrange a ticket for me.' He grinned. 'I told you last night I was there with the American Embassy, but I just said that to pretend I was there accidentally. I wanted to keep things casual.' He lowered his voice. 'But it was no accident, Clara, it was very intentional. I *wanted* to see you.'

His eyes filled with desire.

Clara felt her body respond in kind. But she cleared her throat and brought her seductive thoughts under control.

'So,' she said, 'you were explaining about how you ended up at the museum last night . . .'

He laughed. 'Back to business, eh, Clara? All right. So, as I said, I was officially Rudy's plus one. But as you and the lovely Miss Cuddy were both there, we soon split up to, how should I put it, pursue our separate interests.' He gave Clara another meaningful look.

She shrugged it off and had a sip of wine, before continuing her questioning. 'Right then, back to Pierre. How did you and he start talking?'

'Well, you left early and Rudy – thoughtful guy that he is – hooked me up with Pierre while he was dancing with Bella.' Larry raised an eyebrow playfully. 'Does that all meet your approval, Miss Vale? Are there any holes in my story?'

Plenty, thought Clara, *but not about last night . . .*

'Righty-ho,' she said, instead. 'So, you spoke about the war, did you?'

'Mainly.'

'That's what I thought. And why I wanted to talk to you.'

He mimed stabbing himself in the heart. 'Oh, Clara. So you confirm it's not because of my charm.'

She chuckled. 'I'm afraid not. But if you'll indulge me . . .'

He smiled. 'How could I not? What do you want to know?'

'Well, I believe he was gassed in the trenches. That's what caused his scarring.'

'Yes, that's what he told me. Mustard gas.'

'And did he tell you that Hugo had been the one to save him?'

Larry snorted. 'Well, that's one way of putting it.'

'What do you mean?'

'According to Pierre, Hugo was trying to make up for his mistakes.'

'Meaning?'

'Well, he said Hugo had been his senior officer. He said the officers knew the Germans were releasing mustard gas. He said they did not provide the men with enough gas masks. And that he, and some of the other men, thought they should have retreated until they were better supplied.'

'So, he blames Hugo for this?'

Larry shrugged. 'Not just him. But he was one of the officer corps. The gas came. Pierre, who was a corporal at the time, had a mask. But he gave it to one of the young privates. A kid who had only arrived at the front the day before. So Pierre was gassed, the kid wasn't.'

'He saved the boy's life?'

Larry lowered his eyes and poked at the half-eaten chop on his plate. 'He saved it that day. But a week later the kid was shot in no-man's-land. He died anyway.'

'I'm very sorry to hear that,' said Clara, quietly. Then, as an air of sadness settled around them, she asked: 'Where was Pierre at the time?'

Larry sighed, as if acknowledging the ever-near spectres of war before he resumed the conversation. His voice was brisk, matter of fact. 'He said he was in the field hospital. That's where Hugo took him. As you've already heard, Hugo came to the trench – wearing a gas mask – and saved him.'

He stopped poking the chop and put down his fork. He looked up at her, his eyes startled, his face pale. 'Is it just my florid imagination, or does this sound like it might be linked to what happened in the laboratory? A distorted version of it, perhaps?'

Clara put down her own fork, suddenly having lost all appetite. She knew exactly what Larry was thinking. The same thoughts had crossed her mind. But she resisted the urge to allow a fabricated scenario to become an established theory too soon. She had done that in her previous case and had become so wedded to one theory, and one suspect, that it had almost derailed the investigation. So, she kept her voice neutral and said: 'There is some similarity, yes, but there are a lot of differences too.'

'But it could mean Pierre did it?'

Clara shook her head. 'No, it doesn't mean that. It's just one very tenuous possibility. We'll need a lot more evidence than a bizarre theory about the re-enactment of a wartime trauma before we start pointing fingers at anyone. And remember, other people knew about the gassing too. It's not something only Pierre knows.'

Larry looked at both of their plates. It was clear that no more food would be consumed. 'Do you want to go to a club? Or for a drink?'

Clara thought about this a moment and nodded. 'Yes, I would. But a very specific club.'

'And which club is that?'

Clara pushed back her chair. 'I'll tell you after I speak to the hotel staff.'

Chapter 19

Despite Larry's best efforts to convince her to let him join her, Clara insisted he wait in the bar while she set about interviewing the hotel staff about last night's – and this morning's – comings and goings of the Fashion Week guests. He was playfully petulant, but complied.

She started at the reception desk, an island of teak in a vast marble hall. In the centre of the hall was a bubbling fountain spouting from six black marble elephants. Clara had heard that it had been a present from an Indian maharaja who stayed at the Adlon when in town. The nearby bar, where she had left Larry, was called the Elephant Bar in its honour. The marble elephants watched as bellboys and porters pushed trolleys of luggage back and forth across the foyer like pack animals, serving the guests as they arrived and left.

Clara approached the reception desk, overhung by an extravagant chandelier with a hundred glittering light bulbs. She introduced herself as Fräulein Vale, a detective from England, who was working on behalf of the organisers of the Fashion Week – the people who were paying the bill for the guests who were staying there. This was a bit of a stretch, but she reckoned she could convince Jakob Spiegler to back up her story. And who knew, perhaps he might be persuaded to formally hire her. She was currently pursuing the investigation out of a combination of curiosity and concern that the Berlin police had it in mind that Jonny was the killer. She wanted to clear her friend as soon as possible. But if she could get paid to do it, all the better! Her business would not survive long if she did everything for free.

But the receptionist did not have to know this. He was a middle-aged gentleman whose moustache might once have been a rival to the old kaiser's; it had somehow survived the modernisation of the Weimar Republic. She hoped he was not as conservative and disapproving as his facial hair suggested. She summoned up her best German and in her most authoritative voice asked if he could confirm the whereabouts of the Fashion Week guests last night. As her employers were paying the bill, she stressed, they had a right to know. She hoped the implication that her 'employer' might stop paying the bill at the hotel was understood. Again, this was something of which she would need to retro-inform Jakob, but it was a chance she needed to take.

The receptionist cleared his throat. 'I was on duty last night, yes, but the police have already asked this.'

Clara nodded. 'Yes, I know. Detective Inspector Strauss and I have spoken.'

She managed to maintain a guileless expression, even though she knew Strauss would be furious if he knew she was using him to pursue her own ends. However, if his ends and her ends coalesced in the identification of the murderer, she hoped he would, eventually, forgive her.

The receptionist's moustache twitched. Clara waited. The moustache twitched again. But just as she was about to rephrase her question, contemplating if a 'tip' might spur things along, he said: 'All right, what do you want to know?'

Relieved, she nodded her approval. She did not smile, not wanting him to think her too frivolous and friendly. Men like him, she knew, responded better to a woman who considered herself socially superior, than one who resorted to sweet-talk.

'Let's start with Fräulein Hassan. Merlette Hassan. What time did she go up to her room after the party and what time did she come down to breakfast?'

The receptionist confirmed Merlette's story and timings. He also confirmed, after an embarrassed pause, that he had been told that a young gentleman had accompanied her to her room and left at two o'clock.

'I called a taxi for him,' the receptionist explained.

So, thought Clara, *that is Karl's story confirmed too.*

She wanted to probe Pierre, Hugo and Jonny's timings, but there were other guests that she needed to find out about first, as no one she had spoken to so far – including Bella, Larry, Karl or Merlette – had managed to pin them down other than to say where they were in the morning.

'Can you tell me about Fräulein Markwald? What time did she leave the party?'

'Around half past one.'

'Alone?'

'I believe the older American gentleman, Herr Cohen, saw her to her room.'

'And then?' Clara raised an eyebrow and waited for him to confirm whether Danny went into the room with Hilda.

'I was not informed what happened after that,' he said flatly. 'I was at the desk all night.'

Clara nodded. 'All right. Can you tell me if either Fräulein Markwald or Herr Cohen left the hotel after they went to their rooms?'

'They did not.'

'Is this the only exit?' She pointed to the main entrance, a rotating door intermittently releasing ladies in furs and gentlemen in top hats and overcoats, guarded on each side by liveried footmen.

The receptionist shook his head. 'No. There are other exits and entrances. But this is the only one used by guests.'

'But they could have used another exit?'

He frowned. 'They could have, Fräulein, but why would they?'

Indeed, why would they? That was another question. But one the receptionist couldn't answer.

'What of the young American? Herr Finkelstein. Did you see him last night?'

The receptionist nodded. 'I did. He left the party moments after Fräulein Hassan and her gentleman companion. I saw him watch them go up in the lift. Then he went up too.'

'In the same lift?'

'No. He waited for them to go then took the next one.'

'Where did he go after that? To his room?'

The receptionist cleared his throat. 'I was informed he waited outside the Fräulein's room for about half an hour. Then went to his room. I thought he had retired to bed but then he came down here at about a quarter to two, wearing his hat and coat.'

'Did you call a taxi for him too?'

'I did not. He left on foot.'

'And what time did he return?'

'Around seven o'clock. Just as I was going off duty.'

'Did he say where he had been?'

'He did not.'

'I believe he did not have breakfast here.'

'I would not expect he would. He looked worse for wear. He needed a porter to help him.'

'Is the porter here?'

'He is not. He worked the night shift. He went home after helping Herr Finkelstein to his room – and into his bed.'

Interesting, thought Clara. Merlette had told her that Benji and Hilda were already at the Spiegler Fabrik when she arrived there around half past eight. So Benji, arriving back at the hotel at seven o'clock, looking like he needed to sleep off a night of indulgence, and yet somehow managed to make it to Spieglers ahead of Merlette. Had he just been pretending to be worse for wear? Or had he indeed been under the influence but shaken it off? Perhaps he had had a shower to sober up, then left without breakfast. Clara wondered too if he had left at the same time as Hilda, who may or may not have spent the night with Danny. But, more importantly, where had Benji been between a quarter to two and seven o'clock? It was frustrating that he had left the hotel on foot so she couldn't question a taxi driver. Perhaps, though, he had come back in a taxi. She asked the receptionist.

'I do not know, Fräulein,' he said, in a tone suggesting his patience was running thin.

She would have liked to have probed further but she knew her window of opportunity was closing. And there was something else she needed to ask.

'You have been most helpful, *mein Herr*. But just one last thing.'

He looked relieved. 'Yes, Fräulein?'

'Did you call a taxi for Herr Treves?'

'The French gentleman?'

Clara nodded.

'I did.'

'Did he leave alone? I was told he was trying to catch up to someone.'

The receptionist nodded. 'Yes, it was an English gentleman. I heard them talking, briefly.'

'So, you called a taxi for them both?'

'I did.'

'At what time?'

'It was around one o'clock.'

Some guests were approaching across the lobby, the receptionist turned from her. She had to act quickly.

'And did you see the other Frenchman, Herr Dreyfus? The man with the scars on his face.'

'No, Fräulein, I did not.'

'Not at all? I was told he followed Herr Treves out of the party.'

'I did not see him,' he said tartly. The receptionist's patience was all but expired.

'All right,' said Clara, putting both hands on the desk and leaning right into the receptionist's personal space. 'Where did the taxi driver take Herr Treves and the Englishman?'

He leaned back. 'I cannot say more . . . now if you'll excuse me, Fräulein . . .' The window was about to slam shut and Clara had not yet got the most important piece of information. She stepped back and pulled herself up to her full height, channelling her mother in all her imperiousness.

'Yes, man, you can. *Where – did – they – go?*'

The receptionist looked startled. Then lowered his voice so the approaching guests would not hear.

'All right,' he said, 'but this is the last thing I am going to tell you. Besides, I have told the police already.' Then he smirked. 'It was the Eldorado.'

Chapter 20

***CABARETS** – performances generally from 8 p.m., wine compulsory . . . –* **from *Baedeker's Berlin and its Environs,* 1929**

'Are you sure you want to go to the Eldorado, Clara?'

'Yes, I do. That's where Hugo and Jonny went last night. Someone there, apart from the killer, will possibly have been the last person to see Hugo alive.'

Larry held out his hand and helped Clara into the taxi outside the Hotel Adlon. And not just any taxi. Clara had insisted on going down the line of taxis, parked in the alley beside the hotel, and speaking to each taxi driver in turn. As a result, she had in her handbag the address of the place Benji Finkelstein had been taken to last night. It turned out that Benji had indeed left the hotel at one o'clock and wandered off on foot, but he had returned an hour later and asked to be taken somewhere. The driver had been reluctant to divulge the information, but a crisp twenty Reichsmark banknote, worth around one British pound sterling, loosened his tongue.

Clara did not, however, want to be taken to that address just yet. First, she asked to go to the Eldorado. The taxi driver appeared slightly less uncomfortable at this request but still asked Larry if he was sure the lady knew where she was going.

'The lady knows exactly where she's going,' Larry snapped. But out of the driver's earshot he whispered: 'You do know what sort of place this is, don't you, Clara?'

She did not. But she was beginning to suspect.

Motzstrasse 15, the home of the Eldorado cabaret club, was in Schöneberg, just south of the vast central Berlin park known as the Tiergarten. It was now almost nine o'clock and the lights along Klingelhöferstrasse sparkled as the taxi worked its way through the night-time traffic. The streets were busy for a Sunday evening and Clara was surprised that the cabaret club she wanted to visit was even open. Larry told her that while Berlin had Sunday closing for retail shops, entertainment venues were open every day and night. 'Twenty-four-seven, as we say back in the States. That's how Berlin has come to have the best night-life in Europe! And the Eldorado is one of the most notorious.'

'Notorious?' asked Clara.

'I thought you knew what went on there?'

Clara just shrugged.

'Well,' said Larry, grinning, 'you're in for a treat – or perhaps a shock – Miss Vale!'

The taxi pulled up in front of an unassuming four-storey building whose frontage could have been that of a low-budget cinemascope or picture house. Painted above the door was a young woman, winking seductively over a fan, flanked on either side by a smiling man and woman who looked like they could both easily be seduced by the winker behind the fan. '*Hier ist's richtig!*' *It's right here!* declared a banner below the winking woman. Clara hoped it would be right here that she found a clue to Hugo's killer. She stepped aside as a gaggle of giggling patrons spilled out of the doorway onto the street. They were a mix of men dressed as women and women dressed as men with a sprinkle of androgynously ambiguous people in between.

When the revellers moved on, Larry pushed open the door and ushered Clara inside. They were greeted by the tallest transvestite Clara had ever seen. She was well over six and a half feet tall in heels. Her blonde curly wig cascaded over broad, satin-clad shoulders, onto a magnificent bosom and down to an impossibly tiny waste. Clara winced at the thought of the degree of corseting needed to cinch it in.

'Larry!' boomed the blonde in a rich bass voice, then fixed her scarlet lips into a petulant pout. 'You said you'd call! Am I not good enough to be introduced to the American ambassador?'

Larry tutted. 'Oh, Susie, I'm sorry, but the ambassador is happily married, there was nothing I could do.'

Susie threw back her head and guffawed, her Adam's apple bouncing up and down like an Indian rubber ball. Then she turned her attention to Clara and brazenly appraised her. She pouted again.

'Is this my replacement?'

Larry wagged his finger. 'Now, now, Susie, don't be rude. This is Fräulein Clara Vale. A lady from England whom I had the pleasure of meeting in Cairo. I heard she was in Berlin so naturally we have become reacquainted.'

Susie rolled her extravagantly made-up eyes. 'Naturally,' she said, her voice dripping with sarcasm. But then, in an instant, her face was transformed by the warmest smile. She reached out her hand – tipped with scarlet nails – and said in an unaffected voice: 'Welcome to Berlin, Fräulein Vale. And welcome to the Eldorado. But do be careful of this Yank. He's a keeper of secrets and a stealer of hearts.'

Clara shook Susie's hand appreciatively. 'Thank you for the welcome . . . and the warning. Tell me, Susie, were you here last night?'

'I was.'

'Oh, good. Would you mind answering a few questions?'

Susie's eyes narrowed. 'Why?'

'Fräulein Vale is a private detective,' said Larry. 'She is investigating a murder.'

Clara pursed her lips. She wished Larry had *not* said that. The words 'detective' and 'murder' often scared people. She would have told Susie her reasons – or amended reasons – when she had assessed her for longer. She would need to have a word with Larry . . . but for now, she must deal with Susie. As she feared, Susie's previously open face was a mask of suspicion.

'I have work to do, Fräulein, I do not have time to talk.' Then she turned to greet the next customers as they stepped through the door.

'Sorry,' whispered Larry to Clara.

Clara sighed. 'Please leave future conversations to me.'

'All right,' he said, chastened. 'I'll follow your lead.'

Then he pushed open the door to the main club. Clara was struck by three things: a fug of smoke, a cacophony of jazz and the most daring on-stage performance she had ever seen. Men dressed in leotards, silk stockings and high heel shoes, performed in a chorus line of synchronised high kicking while a naked woman, painted from head to toe in gold, was carried on a platter around the room. The guests, fizzing with alcohol and the effects of cocaine, screeched their appreciation.

'Golly,' said Clara.

'Good golly or bad golly?' Larry peered at her.

'Just golly,' said Clara.

'Do you want to leave?' he asked, touching her elbow to suggest he would guide her out.

'Of course not,' she said, shrugging free, 'I have work to do.'

'Then jolly good golly it will be,' said Larry and smiled broadly. 'Would you like a drink?'

'Yes, please. I'll have a Bee's Knees.'

Larry led her to the bar. The barman – a surprisingly ordinary-looking young man – took the order. As he slid the two cocktails across the bar, Clara caught his eye and smiled.

'*Danke, mein Herr*. What is your name?'

'Hektor, Fräulein.'

'Thank you, Hektor. May I ask if you were working last night?'

'I was,' he said as he took a banknote from Larry and returned with some change which he pushed across the bar.

Clara reached out before Larry could take the change and slid it back to Hektor.

'My friend meant for you to keep this.'

Hektor looked to Larry who nodded. Hektor scooped the change into his pocket.

'Is there something you want to know, Fräulein?'

'Just a few questions, if that's all right?'

'Of course.'

She smiled and sat on a bar stool. Larry remained standing beside her. She turned her attention to Hektor. 'Sometime after midnight two gentlemen came here. One tall, slim and blond, the other short, plump and bald – with a black moustache. Both were wearing tuxedos. One was French and the other English. But they both spoke German well. Do you recall seeing them?'

'I think so. Both Jews?' asked the barman.

'Yes. But only the short one looks what you might call "obviously" Jewish.'

The barman snorted. 'All Jews look obviously Jewish, Fräulein. And if they don't look it, they smell it.'

Clara was very glad none of her Jewish friends were here to hear that. And if she didn't need to get more information from the young man, she would have put him in his place. Instead, she gave a tight smile and said: 'Did you see these gentlemen?'

'I did.'

'Good. How long did they stay?'

'In here or in one of the back rooms?'

'The back rooms?'

'We have small back rooms that can be rented by the hour. And another room – upstairs – for private parties.'

'Ah, I see,' said Clara. 'Well, I'm not really interested in which rooms they went to, just the time they left and whether they left together, alone or with someone else.'

'They left together. Around half past three.'

'You are certain of the time?'

'It was on my break. I was outside. Having a cigarette. I saw them leave.'

'Just the two of them?'

He shook his head. 'No. Another man got into the taxi with them.'

'Could you describe this man?'

He shrugged. 'Not really. He wore an overcoat and a hat.'

'And could you see his face? Did he have any kind of scarring?'

'He wore a hat. It was dark. I can't tell you more.' He took out a coin from his pocket and spun it on the bar.

Larry took the hint and matched the coin with another.

'Tell the lady everything you know, and I will double this.'

The bartender reached for the coin. Larry covered it with his hand.

The young man shrugged and said to Clara: 'There is one more thing. Someone followed them.'

'What do you mean? Someone got in the next taxi?'

Hektor shook his head. 'No. A car came out of the alley and followed the taxi. A black BMW. With a red-and-black flag tied to the side mirror.' He gave first Clara and then Larry a meaningful look. Clara did not understand. What was she supposed to infer from that?

'Did the flag have a swastika on it?' asked Larry.

Hektor shrugged. 'It might have. It might not have.'

Larry rolled his palm off the coin so the young man could see it. 'Did it, or didn't it?'

'It did.'

Now Clara understood. She had heard of the swastika. She felt a cold chill at the base of her neck. 'Do you mean they were followed by Nazis?'

'Yes, Fräulein, that's exactly what I mean.'

Chapter 21

Bella wished Miss Vale was home. There was a strange atmosphere in the Spiegler house. Dinner had been served but no one had much of an appetite. Mr Spiegler had come home late. He'd had to stay at the factory while first the police then Miss Vale did their investigations in the laboratory. And then the police had gone to speak to the security guard who had been the night watchman. But Mr Spiegler was not allowed to speak to anyone. So, when his wife asked him what the police had discovered, he was unable to tell her. She seemed to take this as a personal failing on his part, and she berated him for allowing the authorities to bully him into putting Fashion Week on hold. He tried to explain that he didn't have a choice, but she did not accept that. They then took their argument into a private room.

Bella had not understood the German, but Juju translated for her. She also translated when they overheard the younger Spieglers arguing too.

'So how did they get into your laboratory?' asked Mitzi. 'Did you leave it open?'

'I did not.'

'And that's what you told the police?'

'Yes, because it's true.'

'So they had keys?'

'Obviously!' Karl snapped.

'Well, there's no need to be so snippy. I'm just trying to find out what happened. Because unlike you, I am not a murder suspect.'

'I am *not* a murder suspect either!'

'Of course you are!'

'Well, I didn't do it. And I have an alibi. Which I expect the police have now confirmed.'

'Which is?'

'None of your business.'

Mitzi gave a sarcastic laugh. 'So it's that Arab girl.'

'*That Arab girl* is a lady. And you – as a Jew – should know better than to insult someone because of their race or religion.'

'I did not insult her.'

'Oh yes you did!'

And so the argument went on. The only useful thing that came out of it, for Bella, was to hear that Mitzi and her gentleman friend, Mr Isherwood, had gone to a cabaret club last night, called the Eldorado. And when they were there, they saw Hugo and Jonny. Just in passing. This, Bella realised, did not look good for Jonny. She remembered the conversation she'd had with Miss Vale in the café. That Miss Vale feared the police considered Jonny a suspect. It did not help that he had not come home last night. This had been confirmed by the Spiegler butler who had been interviewed by a policeman. However, when Mrs Spiegler had asked Jonny where he had been, he said he had already informed the police of that, and it was no one else's business. But now Mitzi, it seemed, had seen him with Hugo at the cabaret club. Had he been there all night? If so, at what point had they left? When did Jonny and Hugo part company? Or did they?

Bella did not feel she had enough authority to question Jonny. Then when Juju had tried to speak to her brother, he had told her he had nothing to say and shut himself in his room.

'Why do you think he's being so secretive about it, Miss Levine?' asked Bella.

Juju, fraught with worry, just shook her head. 'I don't know, Bella. I suspect it's because he and Hugo had become intimate, and he doesn't want that to be known, but in the process, he's making himself look guilty of something much worse! Or am I overreacting?'

Bella shook her head. 'No, I don't think you're overreacting. It's best he makes a clean breast of it all. You should tell him that.'

Juju flung her hands in the air. 'I've tried! Maybe Clara can talk some sense into him. Do you know when she's coming back?'

'I don't know,' said Bella. 'She rang earlier to say she's going from the laboratory to the Hotel Adlon. To do some more investigating. I offered to meet her there, but she said it's best she does it alone and she'll fill me in on everything when she gets back.' She let out a long sigh. 'I'm not used to sitting on me backside doing nowt!'

Juju bit her lip. 'Neither am I. I wonder if there's something we can do. Some investigating of our own.'

Bella thought about this a minute, then grinned. 'Aye, there is. Do you think we could use the telephone?'

'I don't see why not.'

A few minutes later and Juju had spoken to the operator in German and then passed the telephone to Bella.

'Rudy, it's Bella,' she said in English. 'You know I said last night I didn't think I could go out two nights in a row? Well, I've changed me mind. If that party's still on, I'd like to go with you. But on the way, I need you to take me somewhere else first. Is that all right?'

Rudy replied, bringing a broad smile to Bella's face.

'Aye, that'll be grand. I'll see you in half an hour.'

* * *

'Bleedin' Nora!' Bella gaped at the onstage entertainment at the Eldorado cabaret club. A naked woman, painted head to toe in gold, was being sawn in two by a female magician dressed as a man, assisted by a male cross-dressed assistant, teetering around in heels. The golden woman emitted mock screams each time the saw supposedly touched her. The audience roared with laughter at the comic routine.

'I warned you it was – how do you say in English – a risqué establishment,' said Rudy. 'Are you sure you want to stay?'

'Aye, I do,' said Bella. 'I want to help Miss Vale as much as I can. Following this lead might give us a breakthrough on the case.'

Rudy nodded. 'All right, how do you want to proceed?'

Bella scanned the audience. 'We need to find someone who saw Hugo and Jonny last night.'

Rudy looked towards the bar. 'There's someone there I recognise. He might be able to help.'

Rudy offered his arm and led Bella to the bar where a young man was working as bartender. He appeared to recognise Rudy.

'*Guten Abend*, Herr Dr Werner.'

'*Guten Abend*, Hendrik.'

And that's as much as Bella understood. She waited as the two men spoke, then Rudy paid for two cocktails and escorted her to a vacant table.

She took a sip of the cocktail. 'It's delicious!'

Rudy smiled. 'It's called a Berlin Sunset. Tequila and lime juice. Cigarette?'

'Yes, please.'

When both cigarettes were lit Bella said: 'So, what did the bartender say?'

'Well, we're not the first to question him. Miss Vale and Larry Winter beat us to it.'

'They're here?' Bella looked around, eagerly.

'No, they left. It was about half an hour ago.'

'Oh. We've just missed them then.' Her face dropped. 'I was hoping to help Miss Vale by finding out something she doesn't, not doubling up.'

Rudy smiled at her affectionately. 'Don't worry about that. I don't think Miss Vale knows what I know.'

'And what's that?'

'Well, Hendrik there told Larry and Miss Vale that the two Jews they asked about – Hugo and Jonny – were at the club until around three o'clock. They left – with a third man who no one can yet identify – and were then followed by someone else in a car. The thing is, I might be able to find out who the someone else in the car was. And I don't think Larry and Miss Vale will have access to the same information.'

'How do you know that?'

'Because I think the car belongs to someone in the group I belong to.'

'From the museum?'

'No. A political group. I told you about them last night. The National Socialists.'

Bella nodded, remembering the brief conversation they'd had in between their sessions on the dance floor. 'The group who want to encourage pride in Germany again.'

Rudy smiled. 'That's right. And by pure coincidence it is one of their social get-togethers that I wanted to take you to this evening. If you still want to come, that is . . .'

'Oh, aye, I do,' said Bella. 'Let me just finish me drink.'

'No need to rush,' said Rudy, and took a long drag on his cigarette.

Chapter 22

Clara decided not to tarry for too long after receiving the information from the bartender. She and Larry had their drinks, accompanied, thankfully, not by the chorus line dancers, but by a more sedate female singer who announced that she was doing a song recently made famous by Marlene Dietrich: '*Ich Bin Die Fesche Lola*' (I'm the fetching Lola). As the singer was launching into her next number, '*Adieu, Mein Kleiner Gardeoffizier*' (goodbye, my young guard officer) by Liane Haid, Clara nodded towards the exit.

'Shall we go? I have a few other leads I'd like to follow this evening. If you're still up for it?'

Larry's eyes twinkled. 'Oh yes, I'm still up for it. This detection business gives one quite the thrill.'

Clara chuckled. 'As much a thrill as flying above the clouds?'

Larry cocked an eyebrow. 'Well, not quite as thrilling as that. But I'm still game. Shall we?' He stood and pulled out her chair then together they headed to the exit. Susie, the tall blonde, was not there. In her place was a gorilla-like man, who looked as though he could double as a strong man in a circus.

He grunted at them something to the effect of 'hope to see you again' and they stepped out onto the street. Clara noticed a line of four taxis. 'I wonder if one of them took Jonny and Hugo last night. And if so, where?' said Clara.

'Well, there's only one way to find out . . .' said Larry.

'You're a quick learner,' she said and headed to the first taxi. It didn't take them long to ascertain than none of the drivers took Jonny and Hugo – or anyone meeting their description – last night. The last driver told Clara that there were two drivers that weren't there this evening. 'Sunday is always quieter than Saturday,' he explained. But then, when questioned further, said he could not give them any contact details for the two missing drivers. *Could not or would not?* wondered Clara.

As there was no further information she asked if he could take them to another address. Just as she was about to tell him the address she'd received from the driver at the Adlon she heard sounds of a commotion behind her. She spun around and saw the shadows of some men having a scuffle in the alley down the side of the building. And then, as her eyes focused more clearly, she saw it was far more than a scuffle. One person was on the ground and two people were kicking him.

'Larry!' she cried, pulled at his arm and pointed down the alley. Then she ran towards the altercation.

As Larry drew level with her, Clara realised the person on the ground was Susie. Her blonde wig had been pulled from her head by one of the thugs who now wore it himself. He also wore a brown uniform with a black, red and white armband – a swastika. 'Stop it!' she screamed. 'Leave her alone! Leave *him* alone!' She didn't care if Susie was really a man or a woman, she just wanted it to stop.

The Nazi with the wig froze with his foot in the air, ready to kick poor Susie, who lay on the ground with her hands over her bald head. The other Nazi stopped too and turned to Clara.

'Go away, Fräulein, this is not your business. The deviant has broken the law.'

'What law is that?' asked Clara.

But before she could receive an answer, Larry stepped forward. He had a gun in his hand and pointed it at the thugs. 'The lady said stop. So stop. Get out of here now.'

The Nazis stood their ground.

Larry pulled back the safety catch on his revolver. The thugs exchanged a glance then sauntered off down the alley.

'Don't let them go!' said Clara. 'They need to be held until the police get here.'

'The police will not come, Fräulein,' said a croaky voice from the ground. Susie pulled herself to her knees and wiped the blood from her face with the back of her hand, like red lipstick smeared across her cheek.

'But they must come!' said Clara. 'We'll call them. Those men ought to be arrested.'

'Susie's right,' said Larry. 'The police won't come. The Brown Shirts are a law unto themselves these days. And many of the police are on their side. They are the militia of the National Socialists and, when they need to be, are better armed than the police themselves. I'm sorry, Clara, but letting them go is the right thing to do.'

'But—'

'But he's right,' said Susie, clambering unsteadily to her feet. One of her high heels was broken, giving her a lopsided gait. She pulled off her other shoe and stood in her stockings. 'Thank you for your help.' She turned and opened the side door of the club.

'Do you need medical treatment?' asked Clara, desperate to do more.

Susie clutched at her ribs and winced. 'I've survived worse.' And with that she stepped through the door and closed it behind her, leaving Clara and Larry in the alley.

Larry pocketed his gun and reached out his hand. 'Come, Clara, there's nothing more we can do.'

* * *

***KREUZBERG** – the highest hill on the S. margin of the Spree Valley. The Tempelhofer Field, which lies S. of the Kreuzberg, has been partly built over and partly used as an aerodrome. In the industrial district to the E., in the Oberland-Str. are the premises of the Union Co' the largest German film factory.* – **from *Baedeker's Berlin and its Environs,* 1929**

Just south of the Mitte – the central part of Berlin housing the government buildings, the main tourist spots and the Hotel Adlon – Kreuzberg was a world away from the historic tree-lined boulevards diverging from the Brandenburg Gate. South of the river Spree, it was the most densely populated area of Berlin, hosting factories and warehouses and the housing that accommodated the people who worked there. Despite also boasting an aerodrome, a film studio and the press quarter of the city, most of the inhabitants of Kreuzberg worked in the textile and heavy machinery factories. Clara only knew this because Larry told her, but his focus was the aerodrome.

'Once we're through this investigation, I'll have to take you flying again! I don't have my own airplane here, but I can borrow one. I have good friends at that aerodrome.'

Clara nodded as the taxi wove its way through the narrow streets, hemmed in on either side by tall tenement slums, with washing lines strung between the buildings. 'Yes, I wondered why you had travelled here by train not plane,' she observed. 'Why is that?'

Larry shrugged. 'I don't take my airplane everywhere. Only when I've been contracted to do a flying job or—' he turned his head and smiled at her '—I'm on a vacation adventure.'

'And are you on vacation now?'

'Now? As in this exact moment?'

'No, now as in this week in Berlin. You're not on holiday, are you?'

'I'm not.'

Clara nodded. 'All right then. So what exactly are you doing if you're not working?'

'Who said I'm not working?'

'Oh? So you are working then. Doing what?'

'Does it matter?'

Clara sighed. 'Well, no, I suppose it shouldn't, but, Larry, I have to be honest with you, I'm a little put out by how secretive you've been. You weren't like this in Cairo.'

He raised an eyebrow. 'Wasn't I? What did I say about where I was going after I left you at Shepheard's Hotel when we first arrived in Egypt?'

'That you had work to do.'

'And I did. But did I tell you what that work was?'

'Well, no . . .'

'And did that bother you then?'

'Not really. Although you did say afterwards that you'd taken someone to an archaeological dig in Jordon.'

'Yes, afterwards. I wasn't at liberty to say before.'

'And why is that?'

He shrugged. 'Client confidentiality, Clara. I'm sure you know about that in your business too.'

'I do,' she agreed, 'but then I'm a private detective. You're a pilot.'

'I'm not just a pilot . . . I told you; I don't have my plane here.'

She pursed her lips. 'Then what else do you do? Why are you here?'

He laughed, but there was no humour in it. 'Why does it matter?'

Indeed, why did it matter? Clara couldn't put her finger on it, but there was something worrying her about Larry's secrecy. On the other hand, he and his gun had proven to be very useful this evening, and she didn't want to antagonise him, so she fixed a smile on her face and said: 'Sorry, it's been a long day and I'm tired. It doesn't matter. Your business is your business.'

The taxi slowed in front of a tall, soot-smeared building, with the flickering of gas light behind a handful of windows.

'Do you want me to wait for you?' asked the taxi driver.

'Yes, please,' said Clara and Larry in unison.

They picked their way through a poorly lit yard, stepping around bins and barrels, to a narrow staircase. There was no light, so Larry struck a match giving them just enough illumination to make their way safely to the door at the top.

Clara knocked on the door. They waited, but there was no answer.

'I wonder if the driver brought us to the right place?' mused Larry.

'Yes, it does seem a bit down at heel,' observed Clara. 'I wonder why Benji would have come here?' She knocked again. And this time, the door opened. A large woman wearing a dressing gown and with curling rags in her hair looked at them suspiciously.

'What do you want?'

Clara smiled and said: 'We're sorry to bother you, Fräulein, but we were told that a friend of ours came here last night. We were wondering if you could tell us anything about that.'

'I don't talk to foreigners,' she said flatly, and moved to shut the door.

Larry put his foot in the way. Clara reached into her bag and took out some money. 'For your time,' she said.

The woman looked at the coins suspiciously then snatched at them. 'What do you want to know.'

'Well,' said Clara, wondering how much goodwill the marks had bought her, got straight to the point. 'A young American man was here last night. Is that correct?'

The woman's eyes narrowed, but she nodded.

'Do you know him?'

She shook her head.

'Then what was he doing here?'

The woman curled back her lips into what might have been a smile or a snarl. 'You do not know? Then why should I tell you?'

Clara sighed and reached into her purse again. This did the trick.

'He was visiting my daughter.'

'And is your daughter here?'

'No. She's at work.' She did not say what or where that work was, but as it was now after ten o'clock Clara had a suspicion.

She cleared her throat. 'I see. And was she working when the American man came.'

The half-smile-half-snarl appeared again.

'I assume that means she was. Can you tell me what time the young American man left?'

The woman pulled her dressing gown tighter over her bosom. 'He stayed all night. He picked my daughter up near the Adlon at around two o'clock. They came home. He stayed a few hours.'

'How many hours?'

The eyes narrowed again. 'He left about half past six.'

'Are you sure?'

'Yes,' she said flatly.

'And what is your daughter's name?'

'Edith.'

And with that the door slammed shut.

'So,' said Larry, as they got back into the taxi. 'Does that clear young Benji of Hugo's murder?'

Clara nodded. 'I think it probably does. My estimation is that Hugo was killed between half past four and half past six. It's a rough estimation but if Benji was here from say half past two until half past six and then seen back at the hotel at seven, he simply could not have got to the Spiegler Fabrik in time.'

'So that's him off the suspect list?'

'Yes. I expect he's already told the police where he was too. So Strauss will have the same information as us.'

'Who's next then?' asked Larry, relishing the adventure.

'I'm not sure,' said Clara. But as she settled down into the back seat she knew that wasn't true. She knew exactly who she would be investigating next. However, her suspicions about Pierre Dreyfus and the evidence of the morphine vial she'd found in the laboratory would have to wait until the morning. She gave the taxi driver the address of the Spiegler residence and asked to be taken home.

Chapter 23

The taxi dropped Rudy and Bella off in front of a five-storey building on Prinz-Albrecht Strasse in Kreuzberg. The ground floor was fronted by a series of arches and from each arch – bar the middle one which covered the entrance – was a black, red and white flag emblazoned with a crooked-shaped cross. Rudy told Bella it was called a swastika and was the symbol of the new, nationalist movement that sought to bring pride back to Germany. 'It's actually an ancient symbol from India,' he explained. 'But a German archaeologist found hundreds of them when he unearthed the remains of the city of Troy – so it was clearly used here in Europe too. As the story goes, the symbol was used by an ancient white master race known as the Aryans. Some National Socialists – like our leader Adolf Hitler – believe we Germans, and the Germanic Austrians, are descended from them. Of course, there's very little historical evidence that that's true, but it's a harmless myth. And it helps to build pride in our country, so I don't mind fudging the history a little.' He smiled at Bella.

Bella smiled back. She didn't think there was any problem with having pride in a country either. She and her family had enjoyed street parties under the Union Flag to celebrate King George's twentieth year on the throne just a few months earlier.

The arched building was the headquarters of the National Socialist German Workers' Party in Berlin. The Berlin branch was headed up by a man called Hermann Göring. 'He is a very interesting gentleman,' said Rudy. 'A pilot, like our friend Larry, and he lived for a number of years in Sweden. His wife is a Swedish aristocrat. I believe, though, that she's been ill lately, so might not be here tonight. Göring speaks English quite well so he'll be charmed to meet you, Bella. He's the one hosting this little party, as a thank you for all the volunteers who have helped with canvassing for the Reichstag elections next week. That's like your General Elections for parliament.'

'Oh aye,' said Bella. 'I voted for the Labour Party. Me and Miss Vale met the MP for Newcastle on our last case. A fella called Sir Charles Trevelyan.'

Rudy tensed. 'The *communist* Trevelyan?'

'Dunno if he's a commie,' said Clara, 'I think he might just be a socialist. Good fella, he is. And you've got nowt against socialists have you? It's in your name.'

Rudy exhaled slowly. 'Well, yes, it is in our name. But we're not really socialists. The party started out that way, but we're not anymore. The left wingers were too sympathetic to communism. And with that comes the danger of Russian influence. So, we moved away from that. We're now a right-wing nationalist party. Trying to distance ourselves from the far left.' He smiled. 'Just like your Liberal Party is no longer very liberal. But don't worry about it. We certainly won't be talking about it tonight. However, best not mention your MP to Herr Göring – or anyone else here – because the Nazis and the communists don't get on. Is that all right?'

Bella shrugged. 'Fine by me. I'm not much interested in politics anyway.'

'Oh, and perhaps you'd also not mention you're staying with a Jewish family?'

This surprised Bella. 'Why not? The Spieglers are good folk. Just like the Levines.'

Rudy gave her an indulgent smile. 'You and I know that, Bella, but not everyone here will. It will just be easier if we avoid the subject. All right?'

Bella frowned. No, it was not all right. She didn't care two hoots about not mentioning a politician she'd only met once, but to pretend she didn't have Jewish friends, or that she was staying with a charming Jewish family, was a bit much to ask. But seeing she barely spoke more than six words of German, she didn't expect she'd have to say much tonight. She was really only there to find out who might have followed Hugo and Jonny from the Eldorado Club. And Rudy had promised he'd find out for her. She trusted that he would.

* * *

It was a very posh affair for a party that called itself the Workers' Party – socialist or not. The men were dashingly dressed in tuxedos or very smart military-style uniform. The women wore gorgeous silk gowns that wouldn't look out of place at Berlin Fashion Week. Bella was glad she'd worn her best dress: the emerald-green crêpe georgette that Juju had made for her.

'You look ravishing, by the way,' Rudy whispered in her ear as they checked their coats into the cloakroom and made their way into the room reserved for the party.

Bella flushed with pleasure. She was glad Rudy had noticed. She'd noticed him with his well-muscled frame impeccably presented in a black dinner suit, with white shirt and a white bow tie. What a treat it was to meet him again on this trip. They'd spent a few heady days on the cruise ship to Cairo, but she'd thought it would be no more than a brief holiday romance. And now here they were again . . . might there be more to come?

There was only one complication. Bella had still not told him she was married. There had been no need to when it was likely they would not meet again. But meet again they had. Was Cupid behind it all? Bella decided to see how things progressed this evening – and perhaps over the next few days – and then she would tell him about her confusing marital status: that she was officially Mrs Paul Plumber, not Miss Bella Cuddy. If it scared him off, well so be it. But she would also tell him that her marriage was something that could be legally ended. The only reason she hadn't was to spite her devious, philandering ex-husband who had allowed her to believe he was dead so he could shack up with another woman and start a family. When she'd found out and tracked him down, he'd said he would accept fault in the divorce. But she'd said she would only sue for divorce when it suited her. Up until now it had not suited her.

As she caught a glimpse of the handsome German man beside her, she was beginning to change her mind . . .

Rudy acquired drinks for them both – sparkling Sekt, a type of champagne – as she listened to the string quartet and the animated conversations in German. She understood the music better than the words, and allowed herself to gently sway to the rhythm.

Rudy returned and smiled. 'I don't think there'll be dancing tonight, but we can kick up our heels another evening if you'd like.'

'I would,' she said, 'but I'll need to see what's happening with the Fashion Week first, and what Miss Vale's plans are.'

'What *is* happening with Fashion Week? Is it off now?'

Bella shrugged. 'I hope not. I think that Mr Spiegler wants it to go ahead. It was supposed to start tomorrow afternoon at Hertzog's Department Store. Apparently there are buyers from around the world who are going to be there. But they need to get the go-ahead from the police first. Not really sure why. Mr Spiegler was talking to people about it this evening. So hopefully a decision will be made soon. Miss Levine will be very upset if it doesn't go ahead. She's had her heart set on showing her designs here for so long.'

'And her brother? Jonny, is it?'

'Aye, Jonny. He's her business partner. They own the building where Miss Vale's office is housed. They have a costume shop downstairs and Miss Vale's office is upstairs. That's where I work too.'

'And now you're working here.'

'Well, not really working. We came here to support Miss Levine. As a friend. And now this murder has happened and Miss Vale is doing a bit of detecting. I'm helping her as much I can but it's not a proper case. No one's hired us.'

'But you are still investigating.'

Bella nodded. 'Oh aye, we're still investigating. Mr Treves, the man who died, was an old friend of Juju and Jonny's. Poor Mr Levine is heartbroken.'

'Heartbroken?' asked Rudy. 'That's a curious word to use.'

'What's wrong with it?'

'Nothing,' said Rudy, 'it's just that it suggests intimacy. A romantic relationship, perhaps . . .'

Bella's eyes narrowed. What was Rudy getting at? She knew that homosexual friendships were not legal. Not in England and not in Germany, but from what she'd seen tonight they seemed to be more tolerated here in Berlin than at home. Nonetheless, she didn't think it was her place to discuss Jonny Levine's private affairs, so she just shrugged and said: 'Sorry, wrong word. I just meant he's very upset. Everyone who knew Hugo Treves is.'

'Not everyone . . .' said Rudy and gestured to a beautiful blonde woman wearing a floor-length gold satin gown, talking to a handsome dark-haired man, resplendent in a military uniform.

'Hilda Markwald!' said Bella. 'What's she doing here?'

'She's a member of the Nazi Party in New York.'

'There's a Nazi Party in New York?' asked Bella, very surprised. 'I thought it was a German thing.'

'Well, it's not called the Nazi Party there. It's the Friends of New Germany. Formed by German immigrants and people sympathetic to our way of thinking. They represent our views to the American government. They're trying to get the Americans to put pressure on the Europeans – particularly the French – to lift the economic sanctions against us. Those sanctions have brought great suffering to the German people.'

Bella nodded. The detail of what Rudy had said was lost to her. But she understood the notion that poor people were having difficulties. They were in her own country too. And even more since the financial problems from America. The Wall

Street Crash, she thought it was called. She'd heard Miss Vale talking about it with Jonny Levine.

'Well,' she said, eventually, 'if your Nazi Party can help the poor people then I think it's a good thing.'

Rudy smiled at her. Her heart did a little flutter.

Rudy finished his drink. 'I'll see what I can find out about that car for you, shall I?'

'That'd be grand,' she said. 'Thank you.'

Rudy nodded. 'See that fellow over there behind the piano?'

'Aye.'

'He's the one I need to speak to. But it's best if I speak to him alone. He's not too fond of foreigners and he might clam up.'

'Where should I go then?'

Rudy looked around and then pointed to Hilda Markwald and the gentleman in the military uniform. 'Miss Markwald can keep you company. And it will be a good chance for me to introduce you to Herr Göring.'

'That's Mr Göring?' asked Bella. 'The big boss?' She was surprised at how young and handsome he was.

'Not the big big boss, that's Herr Hitler. We call him the Führer. But Herr Göring is the big boss in Berlin. Would you like to meet him?'

Bella was nervous about being in the vicinity of Hilda Markwald. The woman had a vicious tongue. But Rudy seemed very keen on introducing her to the Göring fella, and she wanted to please Rudy. 'Aye,' she said. 'That'll be grand.'

Rudy put out his arm and she slipped hers through it. He guided her across the floor. Bella noted that some of the guests gave her an appreciative glance. *Good*, she thought, *they think I look the part.* But looking the part, she knew, was not the problem. It was *sounding* the part that she was more worried about. Rudy was an educated man. She was not an educated woman. She hoped she would not embarrass him.

Herr Göring smiled as they approached and greeted Rudy in German. Bella heard her name and the phrase *Englisch bitte.* The German man immediately switched languages and said: 'Miss Cuddy, it is an honour to meet you.' Then gave a curt bow.

'You know Miss Markwald,' said Rudy. Then turned to the blonde woman and said: 'A pleasure to see you again, Miss Markwald. Now, if you'll excuse me, I have to slip out for a moment. Would you and Herr Göring mind keeping Miss Cuddy company for a few minutes? I shan't be long.'

'Not at all,' said Göring.

'I suppose,' said Hilda.

Bella considered her tone offensive but chose to reply politely. 'Good evening, Miss Markwald. Mr Göring. Or is that Flight Lieutenant Göring? Dr Werner told me you were a pilot.'

Göring nodded approvingly. 'It is actually Flight Commander, but I am impressed at your knowledge of air force ranks, Miss Cuddy.'

Out of the corner of her eye Bella caught Hilda scowling. *Good. That'll show her*. But Bella knew she couldn't keep up the facade long. Best to come clean.

She chuckled. Charmingly. At least she hoped it had been charming. 'I'm afraid that's about as much as I know. I know a pilot. Just the one. And he's a flight lieutenant. Maybe you know him. He's a friend of Dr Werner. Larry Winter.'

Göring smiled. 'I do indeed.' He looked around the room. 'Is Winter here this evening, Miss Markwald?'

'He is not,' she said coolly.

'You should have invited him! It's been a while since I've seen old Larry. Pity I've missed him.'

'Well, he is still in Berlin,' said Bella, helpfully. 'As Miss Markwald knows. We were all at a party together last night.'

'Was that the dinner at the Adlon?' asked Göring.

'That's the one.'

Göring's eyebrows raised in affected shock. 'Miss Markwald has just been telling me about it. Apparently, it's the last time anyone saw that French fashion designer alive. And now there's been a murder. A cold-blooded murder!'

'You heard about Mr Treves then?'

'It was in the evening papers! He was a Jewish fellow, wasn't he?'

'I think so,' said Bella, wary of where the conversation might go.

'But you're not,' said Göring, examining her closely.

'No.'

'Good. Most of them are though. The fashion lot.'

'I'm not,' said Hilda, tartly.

Göring laughed. 'Indeed, you are not! But you do keep odd company, my dear.'

Hilda shrugged. 'I cannot choose my work colleagues.'

Göring gave a tight smile. 'So, what are you ladies going to do now? Will the Fashion Week go ahead?'

'The last I heard from Mr Spiegler,' said Bella, 'is that they're waiting for permission from the police.'

'That's what I heard too,' said Hilda. 'I'll be furious if it doesn't go ahead. I travelled all this way . . .'

'Can it go ahead with one of the designers dead?' asked Göring.

'I don't see why not,' Hilda replied. 'Despite what he believed himself, Hugo Treves was not indispensable in life, and he certainly is not in death!'

Göring laughed then turned to Bella. 'What do you think, Miss Cuddy? Can the shows go ahead without him?'

Bella thought for a moment then said: 'Well, I'm not an expert, this is the first fashion thing I've been involved in, but I think it could. The French model is still with us – as well as Mr Treves's business partner. But they might not be ready for it. It's been quite a shock for them.'

'Then we can do it without them!' declared Hilda. 'The French are not the be all and end all of everything!'

'Hear, hear!' said Göring, raising his glass. 'And if you think it will help, I'll have a word with the police commissioner. I have some – how should I say? – some *influence* with him.'

'Oh, will you?' asked Hilda, suddenly coquettish.

'For you, my dear, anything,' said Göring. 'And of course for you, Miss Cuddy. Any friend of Dr Werner is a friend of mine. May I ask where you first met him?'

'Aye,' said Bella. 'You may. It was in Cairo.' Bella tried to keep the pride out of her voice, but she was very pleased that she sounded like a well-travelled lady.

'Cairo! Of course! I thought I recognised your name.'

'You were in Cairo?'

'No. But I read all about it in the papers. And I got a briefing from the German embassy there. You were one of the two English lady detectives who cracked that international smuggling case, weren't you?'

Bella almost preened. 'Aye, that was me and Miss Vale. And there were some murders too.'

Göring laughed. 'Well, you do seem to attract them!' Then he lowered his voice to a conspiratorial whisper. 'Tell me the truth, Miss Cuddy, is that why you're really here?'

She shook her head. 'No. We're really here for the Fashion Week. We were supposed to be having a break from all the detective work!'

Göring laughed again. 'No rest for the wicked, eh?'

'Seems not,' said Bella. And at that moment Rudy rejoined them.

Bella looked over to the piano. The man was no longer there. Then she returned her attention to the group she was with. Rudy and Göring chatted for a while – in English – about German plans to send another archaeological expedition to Egypt which Göring suggested Rudy might lead. Then he was called away to meet some other guests.

'Well, ladies,' said Rudy, 'can I get you both another drink?'

'Yes, please,' said Bella.

'No, thank you,' said Hilda and cast her gaze around the room. She spotted someone and with a brusque 'If you'll excuse me . . .' wandered off.

'Someone higher up the pecking order?' asked Bella.

Rudy laughed. 'Oh, without a doubt.'

'So,' said Bella, glad they were alone, 'did you get the information we need? About the car?'

'I did,' said Rudy. 'Let me get those drinks, then I'll tell you all about it.'

Chapter 24

Clara waved goodbye to Larry with a sense of mild relief. She enjoyed his company – as she had done in Cairo – and the physical attraction was still there, but she couldn't shake the feeling that something was amiss. He was a little too keen to help her in her investigation, and he still hadn't come clean about his encounter with Hilda Markwald on the train. Of course, there could be perfectly innocent explanations for both of those things. Why couldn't he just be excited to do a bit of detective work? Was it unfair of her to compare him to the police detective with whom she had recently been involved? Of course, Sandy Hawkes wasn't mawkish about detection, it was his job. Larry was a pilot and . . . something else. Yes, that was another thing that was bothering her. Why wouldn't he tell her what other business had brought him to Berlin? What was the big secret? To be fair, Sandy Hawkes had kept secrets from her too. So why hadn't it bothered her so much with him? As the Spiegler butler let her in and locked the door behind her, it was Sandy, not Larry, she thought of as she climbed the stairs to her room, imagining how delighted she would be if she opened her bedroom door to find him waiting for her . . . She sighed, wistfully, knowing she would be going to bed alone. But on the other hand, she *was* dreadfully tired.

She glanced at her watch as she walked along the landing towards her room. It was approaching half past eleven. The butler had informed her that Herr and Frau Spiegler had already retired to bed, but that Herr Spiegler had requested to meet with her in the morning. That was fine by Clara. She was looking forward to a good night's sleep. The younger Spieglers were in the drawing room, listening to records on the gramophone, but Clara did not have the energy to deal with them.

As she passed Juju Levine's door it suddenly opened and a tear-stained woman, dressed in a flamboyant kimono-style dressing gown, whispered: 'Oh, Clara! I'm so glad you're home. Can you pop in here a minute?'

Clara had as much energy for Juju as she had for the Spiegler children, but she didn't have the heart to say no to her friend. 'Of course,' she said and followed Juju into the room.

'Asbach?' asked Juju and poured two glasses of the German brandy before Clara could reply.

'Thank you,' said Clara and took the glass from her. She then kicked off her shoes and the two women settled down together onto Juju's bed.

'I see you've been raiding my collection,' said Juju, indicating Clara's sea-themed gown.

'Oh, I'm sorry! I didn't have time to ask you. But I needed something to wear.' She pulled off her turban and shook out her hair. 'I hope you don't mind.' She then went on to tell Juju as much as she thought wise about what she'd discovered this evening.

'So, in short, I've managed to follow Hugo's movements last night up until he left the Eldorado Club.'

'And he left with Jonny?'

Clara nodded. 'Yes. Has he said anything to you about it? Has he told you where he was last night?'

Juju bit her lip. 'No. And that's what I want to talk to you about. Jonny has not come out of his room since he returned from being interviewed by the police. He hasn't eaten anything, and he refuses to speak to anyone. Including me. Even Bella tried . . .'

'Bella? Oh, is she in bed already? I was going to speak to her tomorrow, but as I'm already talking to you, perhaps we should ask her to join us.'

Juju shook her head. 'No. She's out. With Dr Werner. She's following up a lead on the case. She said she'd tell you about it when she gets back.'

'Hmmm,' said Clara, pursing her lips. 'We're not doing very well coordinating our efforts, are we?'

Juju stretched out and crossed her ankles. 'I'm sure you'll get everything in order soon, Clara. You always do.' She took a sip of her brandy then said, 'Do you want to try your luck with Jonny?'

'Well, I do need to speak to him.'

Juju blinked her large brown eyes. 'You don't think he's got anything to do with it, do you? I mean, you don't think he *really* knows anything about Hugo's death? Not Jonny, surely.'

Clara resolved to sound as calm as she could as she replied: 'I honestly don't know, Juju. Like you, I don't believe for a minute that he hurt Hugo, but I do think he may know something that could help us make sense of it. Do you know what he might have been talking about with Hugo last night? From what you've told me already, I'm assuming they had been – well, let me just be blunt here – I'm assuming they were lovers in Berlin but that they had a falling-out.'

Juju sighed and settled back on her pillow. 'That's right. They were. But Hugo hurt Jonny dreadfully. You see, Hugo had an insatiable sexual appetite. Although he loved Jonny, I have no doubt about that, he was unable to be faithful to him – with men or women. Whereas for Jonny, Hugo was his one and only love. But it just became too much for him. The humiliation. The jealousy, the betrayal . . . The final straw was when he and Hugo had arranged to spend a weekend away together, on the Baltic Sea. Hugo went ahead of him by motor and Jonny, who had to work late, caught the train the next morning. When he got there, there was another man in the cottage who Hugo had invited to join them for the weekend. Hugo thought Jonny wouldn't mind. But he did. They had the most dreadful row, and Hugo said some cruel things. It cut Jonny to his core. We left Berlin soon after that and returned to England. Hugo wrote, repentant, but Jonny never wrote back. But I think now, seeing Hugo again in the flesh, might have stirred something. I expect that's what they were talking about last night. I think Jonny might have been trying to reconcile with Hugo. I don't know if he has told the police any of this. Do you think they will hold it against him if he did?'

'I don't know,' said Clara, her heart aching for poor Jonny. 'But as it stands, he was very possibly the last person to see Hugo alive.'

'You mean apart from the murderer,' said Juju quickly, her voice bordering on panic.

Clara reached out and took her friend's hand, holding it firmly. 'Yes, of course, that's what I meant. But he could know something or have seen something that could help us find out who did it. I expect the police have already asked him that. Did he tell you anything about what happened in the interview with DI Strauss?'

Juju sniffed, suppressing tears. 'No, not a word. Do you have any clues, Clara?'

Clara thought about everything she had discovered in the laboratory – the gas, the cufflink and the morphine vial. The cufflink – and its partner in Juju's haberdashery box – was the most worrying as far as Jonny was concerned, if, as she suspected, it was his. But she hoped the morphine vial might implicate an alternative suspect. 'Yes, I do,' she said, 'but I need to speak to the police and the police doctor about it first. I hope you understand.'

'Yes, of course. Will you do that tomorrow?' A tear ran down Juju's cheek.

Clara wiped it away with her thumb. 'Oh, my dearest, don't worry. We'll get all of this sorted out. After I speak to Herr Spiegler tomorrow morning I'll head over to the police station. Perhaps young Karl can drive me.' She drained her glass. 'Are you all right?' She held both Juju's hands in her own.

Juju nodded. 'I am. As long as you're on the case, Clara, I know everything will be fine.'

Clara smiled reassuringly, hiding her true worries from her friend. 'Everything *will* be fine. But I'd better get off to bed or I won't be fit for purpose in the morning.' She swung her legs off the bed and picked up her bag. As she rose to go, she could not get the cufflink out of her mind. *Best ask her now.* Clara reached into her bag and retrieved it. 'Do you know who this belongs to?' she said, casually.

Juju was startled. 'You've found it! Jonny didn't know where it had gone. He asked me to keep the other one safe for him. I popped it into the haberdashery. Where did you find this one?'

Clara's throat tightened. 'I . . . well . . .' Then she smiled at her friend. 'It was on the floor just outside the door of the work-room.' It was a blatant lie, but the last thing she wanted to do tonight was tell Juju where she had really found its mate – and that the police were examining it as evidence. Nor did she want to tell Juju that she'd taken this one from the haberdashery box. As Juju would rightly wonder why she'd taken it. But she wanted to see what Jonny's reaction would be when he saw it. She would then tell him about the one she'd found in the laboratory, proof that he'd been there, and hopefully he would tell her the truth – before the police discovered that the cufflink was his. If she knew what had happened between him and Hugo last night, perhaps she could help him – and then they could both help the police find the real killer. She clenched the cufflink into her fist. 'I'll return it to Jonny, shall I?'

'If he'll see you,' said Juju glumly and poured herself another glass of brandy.

Jonny did not want to see her. Clara knocked and called out his name but there was no answer. She tried the door, but it was locked. 'You can't stay in there forever,' she whispered.

Chapter 25

Monday 8th September 1930

Clara was awoken by a gentle shake of her shoulder. She stirred and through bleary eyes saw Bella hovering over her: fully dressed and holding a tray.

'Morning, Miss Vale. I took the liberty of getting us both some breakfast on a tray. Mrs Spiegler said she doesn't mind. It's just I've got some things to talk to you about. In private, if that's all right.'

Clara shook her head, clearing away the cobwebs. She yawned and stretched. 'Morning, Bella. Breakfast. Yes. Good idea. Just give me a minute and I'll go to the bathroom . . .'

Five minutes later, Clara and Bella were seated back on the now-made bed, propped up against pillows, with the breakfast tray between them. Bella poured them both a cup of coffee from the pot.

'They didn't have any English tea,' she said, with a note of disapproval.

'No,' said Clara, 'coffee's the thing here. Make mine sweet, will you, I need a boost.'

'Aye,' said Bella, 'you had a long hard day yesterday. You were sound asleep by the time I got back last night.'

'What time was that?' asked Clara, spreading butter on her toast.

'Around one o'clock.'

'Juju said you were with Rudy.'

Bella flushed. 'Aye, I was.'

Clara smiled. 'Is that a flush of romance I detect?'

Bella bit her lip then gave a naughty little smile.

Clara chuckled. 'Well, I'm happy for you, Bella. I, on the other hand, was working last night . . .'

'Oh, I was working too!' said Bella quickly. 'Which is what I wanted to talk to you about.'

She proceeded to tell Clara what happened last night at the Nazi headquarters and what she'd found out.

'Golly,' said Clara. 'Sounds like we just missed each other at the Eldorado. But I'm glad Rudy had some connections. I didn't know how to proceed after that. But,' she said, then sighed, 'it's not looking too good for poor Jonny, is it? Are you sure that's what this Nazi fellow said?'

'Aye, that's what Rudy told me. Seems like the Nazis – for some reason Rudy wasn't very clear about – put a tab on Hugo Treves as soon as he arrived in Berlin.'

'I wonder why?' asked Clara.

Bella shrugged. 'I don't know. But I can try to find out . . .'

Clara nodded. 'Yes, please. But do be careful, Bella, those Nazis can be a nasty lot.'

'Really? They all seemed nice enough last night. And Rudy's a good bloke.'

Clara pursed her lips. She didn't have time to give Bella a lecture on the more nefarious side of the National Socialists, but she would do so at another time. For now, she just said: 'Well, they're not very fond of the Jews. And as our friends are Jews . . .'

Bella nodded. 'Aye, that I know about. And I've told Rudy that I'm not happy about it. But other than that, they seem harmless enough.'

Clara shrugged. 'Perhaps. Perhaps not. Time will tell. For now, it's useful that you've got connections there. So, the Nazi driver followed Hugo and Jonny to the Eldorado after they left the Adlon. Then he followed them as they left the Eldorado.'

'Aye, that's right. And there was another fella in the taxi with them.'

'Yes, I heard that already,' said Clara. 'Did the Nazi driver say who it was?'

Bella shook her head. 'Rudy didn't say. I don't think he thought to ask. If I'd been with him I would have. But he said this fella didn't like foreigners much so best I stayed away.'

Clara sipped her coffee. 'Hmm, doesn't like Jews, doesn't like foreigners . . . I'm seeing a pattern here.'

Bella frowned then said tartly. 'Aye, you might be, Miss Vale. But Rudy isn't like that. And he's the one I'm interested in. Not the rest of them.'

Clara lowered her cup. 'Yes, you are. And I'm sorry. So, he didn't see who the third man was. But he did see where the taxi dropped them. The three of them together?'

'That's right. It was at the Spiegler factory. At four o'clock. He said he watched them knock on the door and the security guard opened it and let them in.'

'They didn't force themselves in? The security guard didn't try to stop them?'

Bella shook her head. 'No, the Nazi driver said it looked like the guard was happy to let them in. Then he waited outside for about half an hour, but no one came out. He decided to leave then.'

Clara leaned back on the pillows and closed her eyes. Then rubbed her temples. 'So, now we have Hugo – and Jonny – at the Spiegler Modefabrik during the time frame we have already established for Hugo's death. Which means that Jonny may have been with him when he died. Or at least in the vicinity.'

Bella shook her head, vigorously. 'But he can't have done it! Not Mr Levine. It must have been the other fella. Whoever it was.'

Clara nodded. 'I certainly hope so. But the chances are very high that if Jonny wasn't involved, he at least knows who is. So why hasn't he said so?'

'Maybe he has,' said Bella. 'He has already talked to the police. Maybe he has told them.'

'Then why hasn't he told us? Or his sister?'

'I don't know, Miss Vale, I really don't. It's all a mystery.'

Clara had lost her appetite. She pushed the breakfast tray away then sat quietly for a while, thinking.

'All right,' she said, eventually. 'Here's what I think we should do. I'll speak to Mr Spiegler then try to get him to make Jonny talk. He is our host, after all. And if he insists on speaking to Jonny, surely Jonny can't refuse. Then when we've done that, I need to get to the police station. I have to give Detective Inspector Strauss and Dr Ritter the results of my experiment yesterday. I'll try to find out from Strauss what his thinking is on all this and whether or not Jonny is still a suspect. If he had any firm evidence against him,' she said, thinking, with trepidation, about the jet cufflink, 'then surely they would have arrested him already. So, for now, I think we can assume they don't have any evidence. That they are still considering other suspects. As am I . . .'

She then told Bella about her investigations last evening at the hotel, her clearing of Karl Spiegler and her subsequent clearing of Benji Finkelstein. 'But the rest are still in the frame. And I'd like you to follow up on that.'

'How can I do that?' asked Bella.

'Well,' said Clara. 'You might not have liked it, but you did a grand job on our last case working undercover as a maid. How do you feel about going to the hotel and pretending to be a maid again?'

Bella contemplated this for a moment and said: 'Aye, I see where you're going with this. I can get into rooms, talk to the hotel staff, find out everyone's comings and goings on the night of the murder.'

Clara smiled. 'Exactly that!'

Bella wagged her finger. 'Oh, Miss Vale, it would be a brilliant plan, but you're forgetting one thing.'

'And what's that?'

'That I don't speak German.'

'Damn!'

'But . . .' Bella grinned. 'I know someone who does.'

'Rudy?'

Bella laughed. 'Can you imagine him pretending to be maid? No, I was thinking of Miss Levine. Her German's excellent. And I think she'd welcome the chance to do something to help her brother.'

Clara nodded. 'You're so right. Juju would be. But she'll need careful handling. Do you think you can do that, Bella?'

Bella eased herself off the bed and picked up the tray. 'Leave it to me, Miss Vale, leave it to me.'

Chapter 26

Jakob Spiegler looked like he had the weight of all Berlin on his shoulders. He was cooped up in his study, chain smoking and already on the second pot of coffee of the day. When Clara knocked on the door and entered, he was on the telephone. He gestured for her to sit down while he finished the conversation.

'I'm sorry, Herr Hertzog, but there is nothing more I can do about this. I did not plan for a murder at the very start of Fashion Week! . . . Yes, I know the buyers are already here . . . Yes, I know they are expecting a show today . . . but . . . but . . .'

Jakob clutched the phone, his knuckles white. 'What's that? The *Nazi* Göring? And you actually took his call? What did he say? . . . You can't be serious! I hope you said no. Why should you put a – what did he call it – an *Aryan* in charge of the department store? . . . He said *what*? . . . Well, I hope you put him in his place . . . Ah, good, good. But you're right, we could use his influence with the police. Today is probably a lost cause. But tomorrow? Then the buyers are only waiting one day. But I'm not sure what we can offer him in return . . . Yes . . . Yes . . . Of course you can't do that! Let me think . . .'

Jakob ran his finger along the inside of his shirt collar. And then his shrewd eyes lit up. 'He has a wife, doesn't he? That Swedish aristocrat. Why don't we offer her a year's worth of free dress designs. Not our off-the-peg range. We can do couture, just for her . . . I could do the designs myself. Or . . .' he smiled as though he were a spider about to catch a fly '. . . if she comes to one of the shows this week, she can see which designer's collection she likes and we can pair them up . . . Yes, I'm sure whomever it is will agree. Other than Hugo Treves, of course . . .' He sighed, sadly. 'Yes, it's a tragedy. Hugo was temperamental, but he was still an old friend. I'm devastated by his loss. But listen, Herr Hertzog, I will come see you later.' He caught Clara's eye and gave her an apologetic shrug. 'I have someone here to see me. Good luck speaking to Göring. Let me know what he says. Good day to you.' He put the phone down and stared at it a moment, his brows furrowed. Then he turned to Clara and switched to English.

'I'm sorry to keep you waiting, Miss Vale.'

'Not a problem at all, Herr Spiegler. You've obviously got a lot to worry about. Do you think the Fashion Week will go ahead?'

Jakob shrugged. 'I hope so. You heard the plan. Let's see if it works. This Göring fellow is very influential.'

'But distasteful,' added Clara.

'Indeed,' said Jakob. 'Distasteful and dangerous. I fear this might be a deal with the devil. But what choice do we have . . .'

Clara did not reply. It was clearly a rhetorical question.

After a moment, Jakob smiled. 'Coffee, Miss Vale? And then I'd like you to bring me up to date on everything you know. And be assured I will compensate you for your time.'

Clara shook her head firmly. 'Oh, there's no need for that. My friends are involved and I am happy to help.'

'That may be the case,' said Jakob. 'But you are a professional detective. I would like to hire you accordingly. Is that acceptable to you?'

Clara thought about this a moment. Even though she had already toyed with the idea that Jakob could hire her, it wouldn't just be a straightforward business deal. There was a personal dimension to it. If Jakob was to become a client, she would have to tell him all she knew. All of it, including her fears about Jonny. However, on the plus side, it would give her more authority in the case. She had already intimated at the hotel that she was representing Jakob Spiegler. Now she could make it official. And, of course, it would be nice to be paid. She did have a business to run, and a full-time employee to pay . . .

'Yes,' she said, with a smile. 'That is acceptable.'

* * *

Fifteen minutes later and Clara had finished her report with: 'So, I think the next thing to do is speak to Jonny. He cannot keep himself locked in his room forever. Too many fingers are pointing at him and the longer he stays quiet the more guilty he looks. And from what you tell me – that he was waiting for you outside the factory at seven o'clock yesterday morning – his activities between four o'clock and then are unaccounted for.'

'You don't think he *is* guilty?' asked Jakob. 'I've known him all my life! Jonny is such a gentle soul. He couldn't have killed Hugo, could he?'

Clara shook her head sadly. 'Even the gentlest of souls can be provoked, Herr Spiegler. However, to answer your question, no, I don't *think* he did it. But I need to prove that he didn't, and the best way to do that is to prove what he was doing between four and seven o'clock. That he has a confirmable alibi. But an even better way to help him is to prove who the murderer *really* is. However, he needs to help me to do that. I believe he knows a lot more about this than anyone else. So, will you prevail upon him to speak to me? He can't refuse to come out of his room for his host.'

'No,' said Jakob, standing. 'He can't.'

But five minutes later, with Jakob and Clara standing outside Jonny's door, there was still no answer, and the door was still locked.

'Wait here,' said Jakob. 'I'm going to get the spare key.'

Jakob returned with a bunch of keys. He found the correct one and inserted it into the lock. 'There's a key in the other side. But . . . yes . . . I can push it out . . . there we go.' He turned the key and opened the door.

Jakob gasped. 'He's not here!'

Clara rushed past Jakob and searched the room, desperately hoping not to find Jonny's body lying out of sight. But, to her relief, Jakob was right. 'He's not here,' she agreed. 'But the window's open . . .'

Jakob and Clara walked to the open window. They were on the second floor. Below them was the well-kept lawn of the town house's back garden.

'Could he have jumped?' asked Jakob.

Clara leaned out and saw a trellis woven with clematis on the wall below. 'Or climbed.'

Jakob shook his head. 'Oh, Jonny. Why have you run? It doesn't look good for him, Miss Vale, does it?'

Clara bit her lip. 'No,' she said quietly, 'it doesn't.' Then she looked at Jakob earnestly. 'But please, keep this between us for now. If the police hear about it, they will be certain to think it's an admission of guilt. I need time to find out who really did it. So don't tell anyone else. Fortunately, Juju has left the house with Bella. I've asked them to follow up everyone's alibis at the hotel. And I've got to get to the police station. I'll try to find out from Strauss who else is in the frame, and whether or not he is about to move in on Jonny. In the meantime, do you think you can go look for him?'

'Where?'

Clara sighed. 'I have no idea. But you know Berlin better than I do. And Jonny is your cousin – you've known him a lot longer than I have. Have a think. Where might he have gone?'

Jakob thought for a moment and nodded. 'Yes, I've got a few ideas. I'll take the car and drive around. Can I drop you at the police station first, Miss Vale?'

'Yes, please,' said Clara. 'I'll just get my coat.'

Chapter 27

DI Strauss looked at Clara over the round spectacles that had slipped down his nose. He pushed them back up with his finger. 'So, Fräulein Vale, I believe you have been questioning staff at the Hotel Adlon.'

'I have.'

'Under what authority?'

Clara had expected this question but chose to feign surprise. 'My own, of course. And that of my client.'

'You have a client now?'

Clara smiled sweetly. 'I do. Jakob Spiegler. And that, as you no doubt know, was exactly what I told the receptionist at the Adlon.'

'That was quick. You didn't have a client when I saw you yesterday.'

'Well, I do now,' she said matter-of-factly. She tried very hard not to sound smug.

'All right,' said Strauss, 'but my jurisdiction in this matter remains the same. You cannot get in the way of my investigation, and if you find anything incriminating or pertinent to the case you need to tell me.'

'I am aware of my rights and responsibilities,' she said, hoping they were the same here in Germany as they were in England. She always handed over her evidence to the police if criminality was discovered, but *when* she turned it over was a bit more ambiguous. If she handed it over too early her case could be shut down. If too late, she was in danger of hindering a police investigation. So far in her new career as a private investigator she had managed to walk that fine line.

'Well, Miss Vale,' he said, switching to English, 'out of respect for the way you have helped me so far, I shall – how do the Americans say? – cut you some slack. My sergeant tells me you spent a few hours in the laboratory yesterday. Do you have some results for us?'

'I do,' she said.

'Good, let's go see Dr Ritter. I believe he's about to start the post-mortem. You're not squeamish, are you?'

'Not at all,' she said.

As he led her out of the office she considered how she could get the information she needed out of him without him thinking she was milking him. In the short time she'd known him she'd come to realise he could not be fooled. Perhaps the direct approach was best.

'So,' she said, as he led her through a maze of corridors and down stairs, 'have you figured out who that cufflink belongs to?'

'Not yet,' he said. 'But I believe it is jet. My sergeant is speaking to a jeweller this morning to see if there is anything significant about it – origin, styling and so on. If it's distinctive that might help narrow it down.'

'Did any of the men you interviewed yesterday have a missing cufflink?'

'None. They either had both cufflinks or didn't wear any. Just buttoned cuffs.'

Quick thinking, Jonny, to remove the second cufflink and pretend you weren't wearing any.

'But,' Strauss continued, 'that was just my observation. I will specifically ask everyone about it when I re-interview them. Perhaps someone saw someone else wearing the cufflinks.'

Clara's heart sank, but she maintained her calm. 'Good idea. When are you doing the second round of interviews?'

Strauss stopped and turned to her. 'My timetable is my business, Fräulein Vale.'

'Of course,' she said.

They carried on walking. A few minutes later, they were outside a door that said: *Leichenhalle*. Mortuary. Strauss pushed open the door.

Dr Ritter, wearing a rubberised apron and elbow-length gloves, was standing beside the naked body of Hugo Treves. Rigor had now eased and the corpse was ready for surgical investigation. The doctor had not started cutting, but Clara noted that the tools of the trade – the saw, the chest expander, the scalpels – were laid out on a tray.

'Ah, Strauss. Fräulein Vale. Just in time. What can you tell me before I dive in here? Did you test the canister?'

'I did,' said Clara, and went on to describe the process and findings. 'So, you see,' she concluded, 'I don't think the hydrogen sulphide killed him. The canister was opened after half past seven, and he was already dead then. You haven't done an internal investigation yet, Herr Doctor, but would you concur with that timing?'

'I would,' said the doctor, brusquely.

'All right,' said Strauss, 'we'll await the results of the post-mortem, Herr Doctor, on what *did* kill him, but that now leaves the question of why the canister was opened after he was already dead.'

Clara thought about this a moment, remembering her response when she first smelled the gas outside the laboratory. 'The smell,' she said. 'It was released because of its strong smell.'

'But why?' asked Strauss.

'To cover something else.'

Dr Ritter nodded. 'Yes, Fräulein Vale, I think you're right. It was an attempt to cover evidence of the real cause of death. Or at least to try to misdirect us. But I won't be fooled. And by the sound of it, you won't be either.'

Clara was surprised at the compliment from the caustic medic, who up until now had exuded an air of disapproval whenever she was in his vicinity. Perhaps her work on the hydrogen sulphide had won him over.

'Look here,' said Ritter, pointing to a rash on the back of Hugo's left hand. 'What does that look like to you, Fräulein?' He passed her a magnifying glass. She took it and examined the reddened derma.

After a moment, she glanced up and said: 'It looks like a chemical burn.'

'Indeed, it does,' said Ritter. 'Have you seen something like this before?'

She shook her head.

'Well, I have. It's a cyanide burn.'

Clara gasped. 'Yes! The almond smell! That's what the rotten egg sulphide was supposed to disguise.'

Ritter nodded.

Strauss grunted. 'So, he's been poisoned with cyanide?'

'I think so,' said Ritter. 'The symptoms are indicative. I found vomit on his chin, neck and clothing. And the likely cause of death is pulmonary cardiac arrest – which I'll confirm when I cut him open. But these are all symptoms of cyanide poisoning. Of course they're indicative of other things too, but the rash on the hand is very suggestive.'

'And cyanide, applied dermally, can be fatal in just a few minutes,' added Clara.

'Agreed,' said Ritter.

'So,' said Strauss, tapping the arm of his spectacles with his forefinger, 'Hugo was handcuffed to the pipe and the cyanide poured onto his hand.'

'Or dripped,' said Clara. 'Just a drop will be needed.'

Ritter nodded. 'And the killer hoped the fume hood would take the almond smell away, but when he returned later, the smell was still there . . .'

'Because the hood wasn't working properly due to the dress blocking the pipe,' Clara finished.

'Where did the killer get the cyanide?' asked Strauss.

Ritter shrugged. 'It's available at any chemist shop. It's used for many things. Mainly pesticides in the domestic market. But also for photography, jewellery manufacture and so on.'

'And could it be found in the Spiegler laboratory?' asked Strauss.

'Quite likely,' said Ritter.

Very likely, thought Clara. In fact, while she had been waiting for her hydrogen sulphide test to run its course, she had read about it in Karl's notes on textile manufacture. Cyanide was used in the production of rayon. She mentioned this to the doctor and the policeman.

'So,' continued Strauss, 'whoever had access to the spare keys to the laboratory would have been able to access the cyanide.'

Ritter nodded. 'It would likely have been in a locked cupboard. But yes, if the killer had keys, then that wouldn't be a problem. Have you matched those fingerprints from the fume cabinet yet, Herr Inspector? It might also be worthwhile seeing if there are prints on the poison cabinet too, if you haven't already.'

'We've already done that. Only young Spiegler's, I'm afraid. And also Hugo's on the fume hood.'

'The killer could have worn gloves,' said the doctor.

Strauss nodded. 'Yes, that's true. And while Karl Spiegler has a confirmed alibi for the time, there are others who don't . . .'

Clara wondered immediately about Jonny. Could he have known where to find the cyanide? And how to use it to kill? Not to mention what hydrogen sulphide could do. Jonny was a clever man. She wouldn't put it past him if he knew some basic chemistry – or at least how it was used in the textile industry. And she knew he had been at the Spiegler factory shortly before Hugo's death. But did Strauss know that yet?

'Have you spoken to the security guard?' she asked, quickly.

Strauss frowned. 'I have tried. But unfortunately, he was not at his lodgings. In fact, it looks like he might have fled. I have men out looking for him now.'

Ritter grunted. 'Well, he'd have keys. And access to the laboratory. And why flee unless he's guilty of something?'

And not just him, thought Clara, *Jonny, too . . .* She was relieved for now that Strauss didn't appear to be following that train of thought. It was all focused on the security guard. Who, until he was found, could not reveal that Jonny and the mysterious third man were at the factory with Hugo. So, she had a little bit of time still. But not long.

She would have loved to have stayed for the actual post-mortem – she found them fascinating – but time was of the essence. Ritter would just be aiming to confirm his theory of cause of death, which was already sound in her mind. And, unless there was a huge surprise waiting for them inside Hugo's corpse, Clara knew her time would be better spent elsewhere.

'Well, gentlemen,' she said, 'if you have no further need for me, I shall be off. I promised I'd help Miss Levine with some dress fittings.'

Strauss chuckled and then said in English. 'From forensic scientist to fashion model all in one morning. You lead a very varied life, Miss Vale. Thank you for your help. I'll let you know if I need to speak to you again.'

* * *

THE ELECTRIC ELEVATED AND UNDER-GROUND RAILWAY *– the regulations are similar to those of the Stadtbahn. There are two classes, second and third; fares vary in accordance with the fluctuation of the mark; special through-tickets are issued for combined train and tram journeys. Trains run between Alexander-Platz and Wittenberg-Platz every 5, on other portions every 10–20 minutes. On Sundays and, during the 'rush hours', on week-*

days the trains are extremely crowded. – **from *Baedeker's Berlin and its Environs*, 1929**

Clara bought a second-class train ticket from Alexanderplatz to Hausvogteiplatz, and was crammed cheek-by-jowl with other commuters on the over-packed train. But Clara was not distracted by the woman bouncing the fractious baby on her lap, or the businessman reading a newspaper with headlines speculating the outcome of the upcoming Reichstag election, or even the scowling youth wearing a brown shirt and a swastika on his arm. She had far too much to think about.

So, cyanide poisoning. Who would know how to kill someone with cyanide? A trained chemist such as herself and Karl. But Karl had been cleared, hadn't he? Yes, the timings he gave from when he left the Adlon to when he got home would not allow it. The butler had confirmed he was home before three o'clock. Unless the butler was lying. But why would he? Could Karl have slipped out after Bella got home? Either through the front or back doors – after the butler had gone to bed – or down the trellis as Jonny had done. Karl's bedroom was on the same side of the house as Jonny's, so he too would have access to the trellis route. And he was a fit young man. Clara imagined the rotund middle-aged Jonny might have had some difficulty in his descent. But could Karl have slipped out of the house, got to the factory, killed Hugo and then returned home in time for breakfast? It was certainly possible, but what might his motive have been?

What no one – including Strauss – had yet raised (at least not in her presence) was the missing notebook with the formula for Karl's new fabric. The forced-open drawer and the missing book certainly suggested it was linked to the murder. Why would Karl steal his own book? Unless it was to direct people away from himself . . . But surely he'd already done that with his alibi . . . Could that just have been belt and braces? Clara shook her head. No, it was far too tenuous.

And thinking about it, one did not need to have any training in chemistry to know about cyanide as a method of murder. During the last decades there had been a number of high-profile murder cases that had made international news. Just last year, fourteen women in Hungary were convicted of murdering their husbands or other relatives with cyanide, over a period of eighteen years. The gruesome details could be read in newspapers around the world – including those in Berlin. And moving from fact to fiction, one just had to read the murder mysteries of Agatha Christie or Dorothy L. Sayers to get an idea of how to kill with cyanide. Clara expected Germany had its own murder mystery novelists too . . . as did France. No, a specialist knowledge of chemicals was not needed. But . . . what about covering their tracks with hydrogen sulphide? Now, that would require more knowledge. Who might know more about chemicals?

Her thoughts moved to the suspects – other than Jonny – whose alibis had not yet been confirmed: Hilda Markwald, Danny Cohen and Pierre Dreyfus. It had been strongly suggested by the hotel receptionist that Hilda and Danny might have spent the night together. That was one of the lines of enquiry Clara had asked Bella and Juju to follow at the Adlon. She would be interested to hear what they had found out. Could it be confirmed that they were at the hotel all night? And if not, what might their respective motives be and might they know enough about chemicals to commit the crime? Danny was certainly angry enough at Hugo and had even threatened to kill him, but whether he knew about cyanide and hydrogen sulphide – and how to use them – she didn't know. As for Karl's new fabric formula – yes, he had motive for wanting that. A new fabric that could put him ahead of his rivals. But would he be prepared to kill to get it? Clara didn't know. Until she knew more about Danny's means and opportunity the motive would not come into play.

The same with Hilda. The woman was spiteful and shrewd. Although she had been a fashion model most of her adult life – not a career that required a formal education – Clara sensed Hilda was endowed with a sharp intelligence. Yes, Clara did not doubt she was clever enough to research how to kill someone with poison – and to cover her tracks. Could she have physically manhandled Hugo into the fume hood cabinet and handcuffed him? Possibly. She was tall and robust. Or had she forced Hugo to do it . . . at gunpoint. Clara had no idea if Hilda had a gun. Perhaps Bella and Juju would find one when they searched the suspects' rooms. As for the motive . . . she hated Hugo. She had not even tried to keep that a secret. As to the fabric formula . . . well, she was in the industry. Perhaps she intended to sell it to someone. Or set herself up in business. Or, and this was a more plausible scenario, perhaps Danny and Hilda were working together? That way they were each other's alibi. Now that would make sense . . . *Clever, very clever,* thought Clara. However, they were not the only suspects . . .

What about the security guard? He certainly had the opportunity to get the keys and let himself into the laboratory. And now he'd disappeared. However, Clara knew absolutely nothing more about the man so could not speculate any further. She would, however, speak to Jakob Spiegler about him.

But for now, she allowed her thoughts to settle on the man she had first suspected and so far, had no reason to cross off her list: Pierre Dreyfus. Although no one had been able to formally identify him as the third man in the taxi – she had hoped Jonny would do that – she believed it was indeed Pierre. She had also found the morphine vial under the laboratory bench. Of course it *was* a laboratory, so there might have been morphine there already, but it was unlikely. It was not an apothecary and morphine had nothing to do with textile manufacture. From her experience working in the military hospital pharmacy during the war, she knew the vial was the type prescribed for medicinal purposes. And, from what she'd seen of Pierre's dilated pupils on the train, he was a regular user.

Clara called to mind what she knew of the Frenchman. He came across as a calm, reasonable man, but she knew that morphine addiction could lead to an altered personality and bouts of rage. She realised, with a brief pang of guilt, that she should have given the vial to Dr Ritter. It was possible that the morphine had been used in the murder, and had not just dropped from Pierre's hand after personal use . . . The vial wasn't enough to kill Hugo. The cyanide had done that. But perhaps the morphine had been used to sedate him? She really should have told Ritter before the post-mortem, then he could look for an injection site on the body. Although, if he was worth his salt as a pathologist, he would find it anyway. Still, she would turn it over to him as soon as she had a chance.

For now, as the train pulled into Hausvogteiplatz Station, she had other things to deal with.

Clara's mind was already ticking over what she would say to Jakob Spiegler as she stepped out of the carriage and onto the platform. So she did not notice the tall man in the black suit who had been watching her from the other end of the carriage. Nor did she notice as he slipped behind a group of passengers and followed her down the platform. And as she climbed the stairs out of the station and caught a glimpse of him as she turned onto the street, she did not consider that he was more than just a man in the crowd that she'd never seen before. But if Bella had been there, he might not have been so brazen. As she would have recognised him as the man behind the piano at last night's Nazi party.

Chapter 28

Bella was impressed with Juju. The two women had managed to slip into the hotel laundry undetected and stolen two maids' uniforms. They then slipped into a cleaners' cupboard and changed. So instead of the flamboyant, colourful costume designer with the wild hair, a demure, plain woman stood in front of Bella with her hair wound tightly into a bun under a white maid's cap. Her body language was as starched as the apron she wore over her black dress.

'Well done, Miss Levine, I didn't know you had it in you. You're a grand little actress.'

'Years in the theatre, my darling Bella!' she said, allowing the old Juju to surface for just a moment, her hands fluttering like the wings of a butterfly. 'I never had any big parts, but I was frequently called upon to be an extra for something or other. I never let it get in the way of my job as the wardrobe mistress, but it was jolly good fun when I had the chance.'

'Well, you've got the chance now, Miss Levine.'

'Juju, don't you think? I don't believe a maid would call another one Miss Levine.'

Bella nodded. 'You're right. And we should probably not use our real names either. Who should we be?'

Juju thought a moment. 'Let's keep the J and the B. I'll be Johanna – that's pronounced with a Y in German – and you can be Berta.'

'All right.' Bella nodded. 'They're as good as any. Hopefully we won't have to do much speaking though. Best we just slip in and out. Last time I went undercover as a maid I was surprised at how invisible I was. The posh folk just look through you if you're carrying a feather duster or a tray. They talk in front of you too, as if you're not there. I would normally take offence at that, but it's very useful in detection work.'

'That's good to know.' Juju looked around the cleaners' cupboard and found two feather dusters. 'Here you are.'

'Ta very much. Now Miss L—sorry, Johanna, you'll obviously have to do any talking if anyone speaks to us. But try not to say too much to the management or guests. Play stupid. They expect it of us anyway. Just say "I don't know, sir" or "Can't say, miss." That sort of thing. And as for me – well, perhaps I can be properly dumb. Let's pretend I can't speak at all. That I'm mute. Because why else would I be working here if I can't speak German? But, as I say, let's try not to get into a position of having to speak to the bigwigs in the first place. We will have to speak to the other maids, porters and bellboys though – to get information. You'll just have to claim it's our first day on the job. Do you think you can do that?'

Juju nodded enthusiastically. 'Yes, Berta, I can!'

'Calmer,' said Bella, gesturing with her hands. 'You need to be calmer.'

Juju's face settled into a dim-witted mask. 'Better?'

Bella chuckled. 'Aye. Much.'

* * *

Clara had given Bella a list of suspects whose alibis she wanted confirmed. To do that, Bella needed to find out where their rooms were. She had come up with the idea of having notes to deliver. Notes that would not go through the usual channels at hotel reception but be hand-delivered. She found some notepaper and a pen in the hotel lounge – where she and Juju pretended to dust – then they slipped back into the cleaners' cupboard and folded the blank pages in four. Juju, because Bella had difficulty with letters, wrote the name of each suspect on them: Fräulein Markwald, Herr Cohen, Herr Dreyfus and Fräulein Hassan. Merlette Hassan was not one of Miss Vale's suspects because of her timings for Saturday night and Sunday morning, but Bella wanted to confirm the alibi she had given. Besides, there was something about the young lass that Bella could not quite fathom. She wasn't quite as ready as Miss Vale to cross her off the list.

After an assessment of the amenability of the male staff – consisting of walking past them and smiling coyly to see who gave a flicker of interest – Juju and Bella determined that the senior porter, a man in his fifties, was the best target. Bella remained in earshot as Juju, in the role of the hapless first-day-on-the-job maid, with a hint that she might be open to a bit of fun after hours, spoke to the porter. Bella couldn't understand what was said, but she could certainly read the body language. *Well done, Miss Levine.*

It went even better than expected. Not only did the porter tell Juju which room each of the guests were in, but he offered to accompany her to deliver the notes which she slipped under each door. Of course, there was nothing written in them, but the porter didn't know that. Juju appeared to explain to him that Bella needed to stay with them – which she did, walking a few steps behind – and beyond an initial and overt appraisal of her body, the porter didn't give her a second glance. They then went room to room with Juju flirtatiously playing the innocent to perfection, with Bella the mute tag-along. Bella did wonder if she hadn't been there if the porter might have attempted to waylay Juju, but, as it turned out, Juju managed to get through the whole charade with nothing worse than a pat on her bottom and a promise that she would step out with the gentleman when they were both off duty. A promise she had no intention of keeping.

Back in the cleaners' cupboard, Juju let out a long sigh. 'Good grief, the man must be desperate. He told me everything I asked of him – without questioning why I wanted to know.'

Bella grinned. 'Well, why wouldn't he? If the prize is a night with the lovely Johanna?'

Juju giggled. 'Oh, I do like being naughty!' Then she bit her lip. 'But not that naughty.'

The two women erupted in laughter and when they recovered, Bella literally wiping tears from her eyes, she said: 'All right. Back to the job. What did he tell you?'

Juju slid down the wall and sat on the floor, patting the space beside her. When Bella had settled, her legs stretched out and feet crossed at the ankles, Juju gave her report.

'First, young Merlette. It looks like Clara's information is correct. My young cousin Karl did accompany her to her room at just after midnight and left a bit before two. And Benji Finkelstein did lurk outside looking – as Hans described it—'

'Hans?'

'Yes, Hans, my beau-to-be . . .' She giggled. 'Hans said the young American man looked like a lover scorned.'

'Interesting,' said Bella.

'I thought so too. But then Hans said he skulked off at the time the receptionist told Clara.'

'And Miss Vale followed that through and found out that he had later been with a prostitute – all night.'

'A prostitute? Sweet little Benji? Well! It's always the innocent-looking ones, isn't it.'

'Aye, it is,' said Bella. 'Did Hans say if Merlette came out of the room after that?'

'Apparently she didn't.'

'Apparently?'

Juju shrugged. 'He said no one told him that she had. And he does seem clued up on all the gossip. And of course she *was* seen at breakfast the following morning.'

Bella nodded. 'All right. Nowt more we can do with that. How about Pierre Dreyfus?'

Juju's eyes lit up. 'Oh, now *that's* interesting. Despite what the receptionist said, Pierre *did* leave the hotel after Jonny and Hugo – as Larry said. I wonder why the receptionist said he didn't?'

'Well, I don't think he did say that exactly,' Bella replied. 'He just said he hadn't seen him. Perhaps he'd been distracted. It's a busy desk that. But it does seem to confirm that Miss Vale's suspicion that Pierre was the third man in the taxi is correct and that Pierre followed them to the club from the hotel. We'd better let her know. But before we do, what about that Hilda woman? Did Hans have anything to say about her?'

'Well, Hilda . . . oh my . . . she certainly caught Hans's eye. I should be jealous if I cared.' Juju fluttered her eyelashes in mock flirtation. 'It seems Clara's suspicion about her was correct too. Danny Cohen *did* spend around an hour with her.'

'Just an hour?'

'Yes. But—' Juju's voice became serious '—here's the interesting thing, after Danny left, and was seen going back to his room, she *didn't* stay in hers . . .'

'Bingo! Where did she go?'

Juju pursed her lips and recrossed her legs. 'Well, she was seen leaving the hotel by one of the back doors – at around three o'clock. There's a garden out back and she went there to have a cigarette . . . and . . . here's the thing . . .' Juju could barely keep the excitement out of her voice '. . . she met a man. They sat together on a bench, had a cigarette together, and then she handed him an envelope.'

'How does Hans know this?'

'Because he was watching from one of the windows. He thought it odd that a lady would be out at that time of night. And that a guest had used the back door.'

'It is very peculiar. Did he describe the man?'

Juju nodded. 'He did. And I'm afraid Clara is not going to like it. He's a regular here at the Adlon when he's in town and Hans recognised him. It was Larry Winter.'

Chapter 29

Clara arrived at Spiegler's Modefabrik at around one o'clock. Her half-eaten breakfast seemed a long time ago now, but she tried to ignore her grumbling tummy for a little longer. She needed to speak to Jakob Spiegler urgently and would just have to eat later. She spoke first to the receptionist in the foyer, who assured her Herr Spiegler had just arrived, then, on the off-chance there might be some biscuits on the tea trolley in the workroom, she popped in there on the way up to see him.

Sure enough, there were a couple of biscuits to spare. There were also two people steaming garments and packing them in a trunk: Danny Cohen and Benji Finkelstein.

'Miss Vale!' said Danny. 'Oh, I'm so glad to see you.' He lowered his voice, conspiratorially. 'I believe you've got the inside track on the murder investigation. What can you tell us?'

Clara stood with the biscuit halfway to her mouth: desperate to eat but too polite to do so. She also knew she had to be very careful about how much information she divulged. Benji had an alibi for the time of Hugo's death, but, as yet, she was not aware if Danny did. Nonetheless, she smiled at the American men. 'Well, I'm not sure about the inside track but I have just been to the police station.'

'Oh, do tell, Miss Vale,' said Benji, pulling up a chair for her. She thanked the young American man, struggling to reconcile his innocent persona with a man who had spent the night with a prostitute. *Everyone has secrets*, she thought.

'And you'd better eat that cookie before you faint on us,' said Danny, benevolently.

Clara smiled her thanks and munched on the biscuit as Danny and Benji drew their own chairs into the huddle. 'I can't take too long,' said Clara, awkwardly aware that she was speaking with her mouth full, 'Mr Spiegler is expecting me.'

'Just a few minutes . . .' Benji pleaded. 'We're all totally shocked about poor Hugo.'

'Yes, we are,' said Danny, with an air of genuine sadness. 'We have had our battles over the years, but at the bottom of it all we were great friends. I've known him for decades.'

'I didn't know him as well,' added Benji, 'but I did spend some time with him in Paris last summer. Mr Cohen arranged a three-month internship for me to learn all about the Parisian fashion industry. And I can say for certain that Hugo Treves was a genius of design. He could have made it as an haute couturist if he'd wanted to.'

'Oh, he wanted to,' said Danny. 'But he made too many enemies. As a younger man he worked with all the greats: Patou, Doucet, Poiret, but he fell out with them all. So eventually, with Pierre's help, he set up his own house. Unfortunately, he'd burned so many bridges by then that his only outlet was the off-the-peg catalogue market.' Danny shrugged. 'Which is my outlet too, but I am not the genius Hugo was. I am a modest designer with modest ambitions. I am a businessman first and foremost. Profit should always come before art.'

Clara noted a flash of disappointment in young Benji's eyes. He blinked and it was gone. But it was enough to intrigue her. 'And you, Mr Finkelstein, are you a modest designer with modest ambitions?'

He shrugged. 'I would no longer be modest if I said so, would I? But I do not believe that art and profit are mutually exclusive.' He flashed a nervous look at his employer, wondering, it seemed, if he had overstepped the mark by contradicting him.

Danny guffawed and slapped his protégé on the back. 'No, Miss Vale, Benji is not such a modest designer. This boy has artistic talent. And a good head for business. I don't have a son of my own, but this kid's the closest to it.' He beamed proudly at Benji. 'He's still got a lot to learn, but one of these days he will outshine me. I have no doubt about that. Benji has helped me with all of the designs we're showing this week. Give him a few more years and he could have a solo show of his own . . . but not quite yet.'

Benji looked embarrassed but pleased.

'I'm sorry,' said Clara, swallowing the last of her biscuit. 'Time is running on, and Mr Spiegler is expecting me . . .'

'Of course,' said Danny. 'Perhaps you can fill us in later.' He leaned forward, his large belly straining at his waistcoat buttons, and lowered his voice once more. 'Do you know if the police are close to arresting anyone?'

This, Clara felt, she could say. 'They have a very strong lead and are searching for someone now.'

'One of us?' asked Danny, indicating the workroom.

'You can't think it's one of us, Mr Cohen,' said Benji. 'Why do you think that, sir?'

Danny shrugged. 'Well, it could be, couldn't it? What do you think, Miss Vale? Are the police looking to pin it on one of us?'

Clara glanced from one American man to the other. They both looked concerned. Did they have reason to be?

No more – or less – than the rest of them, she thought. But she sought instead to allay their fears. 'No. Not one of us. Someone connected with the Spiegler factory who was here on Saturday night and early Sunday morning, and possibly the last person to see Hugo alive.'

'Who's that?' asked Danny.

She stood up. 'I'm sorry, but I'm not at liberty to say more. I need to see Mr Spiegler.'

The two men stood and waited for her to leave the room.

* * *

Jakob Spiegler had the look of a man near the end of his tether. 'Ah, Miss Vale,' he said wearily, as his secretary announced her arrival, 'do come in.' He cleared some fashion magazines from a chair in his cluttered office and waited for her to settle before he sat in the opposite chair. He crossed his legs, uncrossed them, then crossed them again, while all the time his fingers drummed the arm of his chair.

'I assume you have not found Jonny,' said Clara, 'or you would have said so by now.'

Jakob's shoulders sagged. 'I have not. I drove to a few old haunts, from his time in Berlin, but no one had seen him. I did leave my telephone number though and asked people to ring me if they saw him. I did not, of course, tell them why I wanted to speak to him.'

'Wise,' said Clara. 'Hopefully he'll turn up. So far, the police don't seem to be pursuing him but I don't know how long that will last.' She went on to tell Jakob what had happened at the police mortuary and what she could fathom of DI Strauss's thinking.

'He thinks it's my man, Lederman? The security guard?'

'Well, he appears to have fled, suggesting he's got something to hide.'

'Good grief! He hid it well. He seemed perfectly calm when I relieved him yesterday morning.'

'Did he say anyone had been to the factory overnight?'

Jakob shook his head. 'Not a word. He said nothing unusual had happened at all. And that's what I told the police.'

'Well, that's a lie for a start. Bella has found out that he was seen – by the Nazi who followed Hugo, Jonny and the third man in the car – letting them into the factory. That he appeared happy to do so. So, whether he's involved in Hugo's murder or not, he's certainly covering something up. Which is obviously why he fled.'

Jakob clenched his jaw. 'And perhaps why my cousin fled, too.'

'Yes,' said Clara quietly. 'As much as we love Jonny and want to clear his name, we cannot – as yet – discount that he might be involved.'

They both sat quietly for a moment, contemplating the implications of this.

Eventually, Clara mustered as much optimism as she could and said: 'But there is still a way to go before we can say that for sure. The police need to find the guard. We need to find Jonny and we must – without delay – speak to the third man. As yet, Strauss doesn't seem to know about him, nor of Jonny's visit to the factory. We only know because Bella's Nazi friend unearthed information the police don't yet have. But I'm sure it won't be long until they know that too.'

'Yes,' agreed Jakob. 'Particularly now that Göring is being prevailed upon to ask the police to allow Fashion Week to go ahead. It looks like it might happen, by the way. Herr Hertzog is talking about tomorrow. A lunchtime start – if we can get everything together. That, of course, remains to be seen. Which I've told Hertzog. I've said I'll get back to him after I've spoken to everyone to see if they're up for it. I don't think I can push it much beyond six o'clock this evening, Miss Vale. Hertzog and I need to make a decision on this.'

Clara nodded. 'Yes, we have very little time. So, I need to speak to Pierre Dreyfus as soon as possible. I have a strong suspicion he is the missing link.'

Jakob was incredulous. 'You think the third man was Pierre?'

'I do,' said Clara, and went on to explain about the morphine vial.

Jakob shook his head. 'Good grief. First Jonny, now Pierre!'

'Will you be able to set up a meeting with him for me?' asked Clara. 'I don't know him well enough to approach him myself. But, if you were to ask him to meet for coffee at the Adlon, then I could accompany you and interview him there. Can you do that?'

'I can. I do need to speak to him anyway – about rescheduling Fashion Week and whether he is prepared to show Hugo's collection without him.' He looked at his watch. 'Shall I arrange something for three o'clock?'

Clara nodded. 'Yes, that will do. It will give me time to visit the laboratory first. There's something I need to check. And oh, Herr Spiegler, can someone make me a sandwich?'

* * *

Clara unlocked the laboratory with the set of keys she'd borrowed from Jakob. They were Karl's keys which he'd given to his father as the spare set were missing – presumably still in the hands of the killer. Karl, Jakob told her, was spending the day at the university, hoping to reconstruct his formula notes for the new fabric as much as he could from memory.

As far as Clara could tell, the laboratory was as she had left it yesterday afternoon after conducting the hydrogen sulphide experiment. After she'd left, Jakob told her, the police sergeant, with the permission of Strauss, had locked up the laboratory and given the keys back to Jakob on the understanding that no one else would be let in. Clara, Jakob decided, was an exception as she had already spent time in the laboratory and had the approval of Strauss.

Clara looked around until she spotted a small wooden cabinet, about fifty centimetres high and thirty deep and wide. Stencilled in red paint was the label: *Gift*. Poison. She was pleased to see that tied to the cabinet by a length of string was a well-thumbed volume of *Poisons, Their Effects & Detection* by Alexander Wynter Blyth. This was a German version. Clara had an English translation at home. It had proven invaluable in her second case which involved belladonna poisoning. She turned to the contents page and found the entry on cyanide. She translated it into English as she read.

> *The cyanides are very rarely used for the purpose of murder: a poison which has a strong smell and a perceptible taste and which also kills with a rapidity only equalled by deadly bullet or knife-wound, betrays its presence with too many circumstances of a tragic character to find favour in the dark and secret schemes of those who desire to take life by poison.*

Perhaps not as rare as you might think, Professor Blyth, thought Clara. She then proceeded to skim the more detailed contents on chemical composition, effects, antidotes and detection. This made such sobering reading that she decided to take extra precautions, just in case the killer had spilled any of the contents on or in the cupboard.

She put on a laboratory coat, gloves, mask and goggles before proceeding any further. The cabinet had both an ordinary lock and a padlock. Clara searched on her bunch of keys and after a few tries, found the correct ones. She opened the cupboard to see half-a-dozen bottles on two shelves, lined up in the same way they would be in a chemist shop. In England she knew these items would fall under the Pharmacy and Poisons Act of 1908 which dictated how certain dangerous drugs and chemicals were to be stored and regulated. She did not know the regulations that governed pharmaceuticals in Germany. However, as this was a private laboratory, she expected that the regulations might not be so stringently adhered to. Nonetheless, she was glad to see that Karl had taken reasonable precautions by keeping the potions under double lock and key. The hexagonal shaped poison bottles – holding such deadly concoctions as arsenic, strychnine, atropine and cyanide – were of distinctive green, blue or amber glass. The glass was ridged, the idea being that even in dim light or with poor vision the person holding the bottle would be alerted to its dangerous contents. They were also embossed with the raised lettering: poison (*Gift* in German). There were two cyanide bottles, both in cobalt blue: KCN and HCN. KCN, Clara knew, was potassium cyanide in powder form. HCN was hydrogen cyanide in liquid form, also known as prussic acid. KCN was used more in medicinal applications, HCN in industrial. Both she and Dr Ritter believed it had been the liquid form that was dropped on Hugo's hand.

She considered dusting the bottle for fingerprints but decided that she would rather leave that for Dr Ritter and Strauss to do if they chose to. Although, because of the ridged glass, it would be unlikely that there would be anything useful. The same with the wooden cabinet. It was not highly polished. The fume hood was made of burnished steel, so prints were easily detectable on that. And as no prints but Karl's and Hugo's had been detected, the chances were that the killer was wearing gloves. As she was now. So, once again, she considered that this was someone who had a level of awareness of how chemicals were to be engaged with. This did not have to be formal training in chemistry, but someone who perhaps might have worked in an environment where chemicals were used. This could be anywhere: a factory, a photographic studio, a workshop or even a science classroom.

Who among the suspects so far had that kind of background? It was something she needed to probe further. And she would have to tell Strauss – if Dr Ritter had not done so already.

There was also no way she could tell if the cyanide had indeed come from this bottle. Unlike with the gas canister yesterday, she did not know how much liquid was in the bottle in the first place. And besides, all it needed was a small drop. A drop . . . Had the killer used a dropper or a pipette? If so, where had they put it? The bottle had been carefully replaced in the cupboard and double locked, but where was the pipette?

Clara had checked the bins yesterday, but she had not checked the sink. When she came in today, she had noticed a few items in the sink – a couple of beakers and test tubes – but that was perfectly normal in a laboratory. She had not thought anything of it. She closed and double locked the poison cabinet but kept on her protective clothing. At the sink she picked out the items and put them on the drying rack: two beakers and a test tube and . . . *yes!* . . . a pipette! Very carefully she put the pipette on a metal tray, found a cotton bud and wiped the mouth of the pipette to retrieve any residue. Then, with the instructions of Professor Blyth fresh in her mind, she tested the cotton bud.

A very delicate test for prussic acid is as follows: about one-half centigram of ammonia, ferrous sulphate and the same quantity of uranic nitrate are dissolved in 50cc of water and 1cc of this test liquid is placed in a porcelain dish. On now adding the smallest quantity of prussic acid, a grey-purple colour, or a distinct purple precipitate is produced.

Clara watched with a mixture of horror and satisfaction as the liquid in the porcelain dish turned a greyish purple. She then searched the laboratory and found a sealable container and placed the dish and pipette within. She put the container in the lockable cupboard where she'd found the gas canisters yesterday. She would inform Dr Ritter of its location and he could collect it himself. She certainly wasn't going to be carrying cyanide around with her!

Or had she been . . .

She nervously retrieved the small vial she had found yesterday and kept in her bag. *No, surely if there had been cyanide in there I would have fallen quite ill already . . . if not worse!* But just to make sure, she swabbed the vial for residue and tested it. She was enormously relieved that it did not turn any shade of purple. She then consulted Professor Blyth's book again:

> *. . . add an iodic acid solution to the liquid in which morphine is supposed to be dissolved, and then shake the liquid with a few drops of carbon disulphide. If morphine be present, the carbon disulphide floats to the top distinctly coloured pink.*

Clara nodded in satisfaction when the floating residue in the stoppered test tube turned a very clear pink. This too, along with the vial, she placed in another sealed container and put in the lockable cupboard. She would telephone Dr Ritter as soon as possible to tell him.

With her experiments completed and time ticking on, Clara took off her protective clothing. Then she collected her coat from where she had hung it on the clothes rail. It was only then that she noticed something was missing – the swatch of synthetic linen fabric that Karl had shown her on Saturday, the first experimental fabric that he had created She could have sworn it had still been there yesterday when she was conducting her experiments. She even remembered thinking to herself that if Karl could not remember the complete formula, he could analyse the fabric and recreate it. And now it was gone. But who had taken it and when? Hadn't Jakob said that no one else had been allowed in the laboratory after it was locked by the sergeant? Had Karl come to collect the fabric? Jakob had not said so. Clara shook her head. Perhaps her mind was playing tricks on her. Perhaps she hadn't seen the fabric there after all . . . But she was sure she had! Wasn't she . . .? And then she had an idea. She had taken photographs yesterday. And had not yet had the film developed. She would ask Jakob to take her to a photography shop as soon as they had finished talking to the morphine addict, Pierre Dreyfus.

Chapter 30

Jakob drove the motor west along Taubenstrasse from Hausvogteiplatz. The road was dappled with light as the afternoon sun filtered its way through the linden trees. An orange leaf – one of the first of the season – fell onto the windscreen before being blown away by a brisk September breeze. There was a sense that the weather was about to turn in Berlin, and Clara could not help but think that there was more to fear than a mere chilling of the air.

It was only a five-minute drive to the Hotel Adlon but the traffic was particularly heavy in the Mitte and took longer than expected. Jakob told her a story about the original owner of the Adlon, Lorenz Adlon, who was hit by a car in front of the Brandenburg Gate, just a stone's throw from his hotel. 'Old Lorenz was a staunch monarchist,' he explained. 'And in the kaiser's day no cars were allowed to drive through the gate – it was reserved for Wilhelm's car only. So even though the kaiser had abdicated three years earlier, Lorenz refused to acknowledge that we were now a republic. And that included refusing to accept that ordinary cars could now drive through the Brandenburg Gate. So, one day in 1921, he stepped out of the hotel for a morning walk and into the path of an oncoming vehicle. Which, he told his doctors in the hospital, had no right to be there – only the kaiser could drive through the gate!'

'Goodness me,' said Clara. 'That's foolhardy.'

'It was! And he was a fool who didn't learn from his mistakes. The same thing had happened three years earlier too! At the exact same spot!'

Clara laughed out loud. 'Well, I hope he learned his lesson after the second time! I don't imagine there was a third.'

Jakob gave her a sideways look.

'Oh, you can't be serious!'

He chuckled. 'No, there was no third time.' Then he shrugged. 'He died a few days later.'

'Oh,' said Clara, trying not to laugh again. 'That is tragic but . . . well . . .'

'Foolish,' Jakob finished for her.

'Quite.'

Jakob turned right onto Markgrafenstrasse, with the beautiful Gendarmenmarkt Square on the left. The paved square was overlooked, top and bottom, by the baroque Französischer Dom and the Deutscher Dom – the French Cathedral and the German Cathedral – with the exquisite neoclassical Konzerthaus in between.

'When all of this hoo-hah is over,' said Jakob, 'and before you all go home, I'd love to take you and my cousins to a concert there.'

Clara sighed. 'We're a fair way from this hoo-hah being over, I'm afraid. The case is getting more complicated. Can you tell me, Herr Spiegler, if anyone went into the laboratory between when the sergeant locked it yesterday and me going in today? Did Karl?'

Jakob shook his head. 'No. It remained locked and I had the only keys.'

'The only keys apart from the ones Hugo's killer has, you mean.'

'Yes, that's what I mean. Why, Miss Vale? What's happened?'

Clara went on to tell him about the missing fabric.

'And you're sure it was there yesterday when you left the laboratory? That the killer didn't take it at the same time he took Karl's notebook?'

Clara shook her head. 'No, I'm not completely sure. But I'm fairly sure. Is there a photography shop nearby? I took some shots yesterday. If I get those developed that will confirm it one way or another.'

Jakob nodded. 'Yes, there's one on Friederichstrasse. We can go there after we speak to Pierre. But you say you are *fairly* sure already . . . I trust your judgement, Miss Vale. So, if the fabric was there yesterday but not today that only means one thing . . .'

'The killer returned to get it.'

Jakob tightened his grip on the steering wheel. 'I don't know how that is possible. I posted a new night watchman to replace the fellow who has gone missing – who by the sound of it might be the killer! No one could have got into the building without the new watchman knowing. Surely, I can't have the misfortune of having two untrustworthy watchmen in a row, can I?'

Clara shook her head in sympathy. 'That would be a misfortune. But there's another possibility . . . what if the person who let themselves in was supposed to be at the factory? That the watchman would not think it unusual that they were there?'

Jakob shook his head. 'No. I gave instructions that *no one* was to be allowed in overnight. No one at all.'

'Then,' said Clara, as the motor turned left onto Behrenstrasse, and the Brandenburg Gate edged into view, 'the killer must have sneaked in. And out again. Is there a back door to the factory?'

'Of course. That's where deliveries come and go.'

'And the keys for that door are on the missing ring too?'

Jakob pursed his lips into a tight line. 'Yes.'

Clara nodded. 'I think, Herr Spiegler, it's time you had your locks changed.'

* * *

Pierre Dreyfus was nursing a drink in the Elephant Bar, his scarred face in the shadow of an exuberant potted palm tree.

'Pierre,' said Jakob in German as he pulled out a chair for Clara, 'I hope you don't mind but I asked Fräulein Vale to join us.'

Pierre looked up, startled, his dilated pupils staring at Clara.

He's been on the morphine, she thought.

'Why did you do that?' he asked. 'No offence, Miss Vale,' he added in English, 'but Mr Spiegler and I have things to talk about.'

'I shan't keep you long,' said Clara, 'but Mr Spiegler, as he'll confirm, has formally hired me to investigate Hugo Treves's murder.'

'I thought the police were doing that,' muttered Pierre.

'They are,' said Clara, 'and I shan't get in their way, but Mr Spiegler considered it prudent to hire an investigator who keeps the interests of Spiegler Fashion in mind. Isn't that correct, Mr Spiegler?'

'It is, Miss Vale. Come on, Pierre, she's on our side. Please try to cooperate.'

Pierre sighed and downed the last of his drink. A cognac by the look and smell of it. 'Would you like a drink, Miss Vale?'

'I think just coffee,' said Clara, knowing she had to keep a clear head.

'And one for me,' added Jakob.

Pierre shrugged and called over the waiter.

As they waited for the drinks, Clara fixed her eyes on the Frenchman. 'Can you tell me, Monsieur Dreyfus, where you were between the hours of one and seven o'clock on Sunday morning?'

Pierre, his hands shaking, opened a cigarette case. 'I expect your friend Jonny has already told you that, Miss Vale.'

Clara, who did not want to let it be known that she had not spoken to Jonny, or worse, that he was on the run, kept her face as calm as she could. 'He has,' she answered phlegmatically. 'But I would like to hear it from you please. There are a few details I need to clarify.'

Pierre picked out a cigarette. 'All right, well then you know that I met Jonny and Hugo outside the Eldorado Club.'

'At around three o'clock?'

'Yes.'

'You got into a taxi together.'

'Yes.'

'Did you see anyone following you?'

Pierre paused, the cigarette pincered between two fingers. 'Someone followed us?'

'Yes. Did you see anyone. A black car that followed the taxi.'

Pierre shrugged. 'I can't say I did. We were having an animated conversation. The three of us. I didn't notice anything else.'

'Oh?' said Clara. 'What were you animated about?'

Pierre sighed and lit his cigarette. He inhaled deeply and then exhaled. 'Sorry,' he said, pushing the cigarette case across the table. 'I should have offered.'

'Thank you, but no,' said Clara.

'I'll have one,' said Jakob and helped himself.

'So,' prompted Clara, 'what was the conversation about?'

'Jonny would have told you.'

'Yes, but I'd like to hear it from you. Jonny, it seemed, was rather drunk, so his recollection was impaired.' This was a guess by Clara, but an educated one. It proved to be correct.

'Yes, he was. As was Hugo. They'd been having a whale of a time in the Eldorado.'

'But not you. You didn't go in?'

Pierre shook his head. 'No. I waited for them outside.'

'For two hours?'

Pierre shrugged. 'I stayed as long as I needed to. There is a small bar over the road from the Eldorado frequented by local people who don't go in for the shenanigans in the other joint. I sat at a window table with a view of the Eldorado's entrance. So I could see when Jonny and Hugo came out.'

'Why were you concerned about when they came out, Monsieur Dreyfus?'

'I wanted to speak to Hugo. And also to make sure he didn't move on to any casinos. I believe—' he smiled tightly '—that you've been speaking to Larry Winter. So, I expect he has told you about my concerns regarding Hugo's gambling habits.'

'He did,' she said simply. 'So, you wanted to stop Hugo from gambling. You were acting as his nursemaid.'

Pierre's eyes narrowed. 'Not as his nursemaid, Miss Vale, but as a protector of the company's finances. We can't afford to lose any more money. And we need the new business that will come from Fashion Week.' He turned to Jakob. 'Is it going ahead?'

Jakob nodded. 'Yes, I heard from the police just before Miss Vale and I left to come here. Hertzog has agreed to have a lunch-time launch tomorrow. That's what I wanted to speak to you about, Pierre. Will you show Hugo's collection without him?'

Pierre nodded firmly. 'We can't afford not to.'

Clara wanted to get back to the events of Saturday night and Sunday morning, but she decided to do a quick detour first.

'What happens to the business now that Hugo is dead? Will it continue? I mean beyond Berlin Fashion Week.'

Pierre sucked hungrily on his cigarette and then exhaled. 'I hope so. We had 50/50 shares and I, of course, still have mine. But I need to see what happens to Hugo's shares. Who inherits them. He never told me. I've been in touch with the company lawyer, and he said Hugo had named a beneficiary.'

'Who's that?' asked Jakob.

Pierre tapped a nub of ash into an ash tray. 'He wouldn't tell me. He said he needed to wait for the outcome of the police investigation, and then he would contact the beneficiary and see if they accepted the inheritance. Only then will he tell me who it is.'

'So not you then,' observed Jakob.

Pierre shrugged. 'I'd be surprised if it was. But I have no idea who else it could be. As you know, Hugo didn't have any living family, so I have no idea who he would leave it to.'

Clara pondered this for a moment and then asked: 'Who would have inherited the shares if he hadn't made a will and named a beneficiary?'

'I suppose they would just have been absorbed back into the company.'

'So technically you would then have been the beneficiary?'

'I suppose so.'

Clara nodded. This was very useful information. She wondered if DI Strauss was aware of it yet. She would ask Pierre that shortly. For now, she wanted to return to the events leading up to Hugo's death.

'Would you mind if we went back to the taxi. You didn't say what the animated conversation was about. Can you now?'

Pierre shrugged. 'Everyone was cross. Hugo was cross that I'd followed him. Jonny was cross that I'd butted in on his and Hugo's evening together. I was cross that I couldn't trust Hugo to not gamble away the business.'

The waiter arrived with their drinks. Clara paused a moment in her questioning to have a sip of coffee.

Pierre, hand shaking, had a stiff drink of cognac.

'So,' said Clara eventually, 'why did you all end up at the Spiegler Factory?'

'That was Hugo's idea.'

'What did he intend to do there?'

Pierre put down his glass and wiped his mouth with the back of his hand. 'He said he had something to do. He didn't say what – at first.'

Jakob interjected. 'Did he have keys? Keys to the factory?'

Pierre shook his head. 'No. Your security guard let us in. Didn't he tell you?'

'My security guard has gone missing,' said Jakob bitterly.

'Really? Since when?'

'Since I last saw him at seven o'clock on Sunday morning. The police are looking for him now.'

Pierre paled. 'Oh no.'

'What's wrong?' asked Clara.

Pierre lowered his head. Without raising it, he said: 'The police won't believe me now.'

'About what?'

'The time I left.'

'Which was?'

'Four o'clock. The guard saw me leave. I spoke to him. He asked if the other two gentlemen would be leaving soon too. I said I had no idea. But I did leave. I swear. And when I left Jonny was still with Hugo and Hugo was still alive.'

'Where did you leave them?' asked Clara. 'Where in the building?'

'In the laboratory.'

'All right,' she said, 'I'll get to the events in the lab in a moment. For now, can you tell me what time you believe Jonny left?'

Pierre raised his head. 'He hasn't told you?'

'He has,' said Clara quickly, 'I just need to confirm timings. And now that the guard is missing that is more difficult to do.'

Pierre seemed to take this at face value. 'All right,' he said stubbing out his cigarette. 'On Sunday morning – after we heard what had happened to Hugo – Jonny told me he'd left not long after me. About a quarter past four.'

'Did he say where he went after that?'

Pierre nodded. 'Yes. He said he went walking along the River Spree. He wanted to sober up.'

'Did he return to the hotel?'

'No. And that's the problem. He had no one to vouch for his whereabouts between then and when he arrived back at the factory at just after seven. That's why he asked me to lie for him.'

Clara was startled. 'What did he ask you to say?'

'That he caught up with me walking back to the hotel. That he came in with me.'

'And that's what you told the police yesterday morning?'

Pierre nodded, glumly. 'Yes. But now I expect they know it's not true. I don't think anyone else at the hotel could tell them he came back with me.'

'Did anyone see you come in?'

He shrugged. 'The doorman, I suppose.'

'And the receptionist?'

'No, I don't think he saw me. But if the police interview the doorman he will tell them Jonny wasn't with me. And as the security guard at Spiegler's is missing, there is no confirmation about when either of us left.'

'But the doorman saw you here,' said Clara. 'So, there's no need to worry about yourself, is there?'

Pierre tapped the cigarette case with his fingernail. 'Well, there's an hour missing. I also went for a walk. To clear my head. I only got to the hotel at five o'clock. So, I expect if the police don't know I left the factory at four, they might think I had plenty of time to kill Hugo. Or that Jonny and I might have done it together.'

Clara leaned forward. 'Why do you think they'll think that, Monsieur Dreyfus?'

Pierre let out a long sigh. 'Because of my knowledge of gas.'

Chapter 31

Clara endeavoured to remain calm in the wake of Pierre's revelation. Was he just about to implicate himself in Hugo's murder? 'I see,' she said, after a nervous sip of coffee. 'And how did you acquire your knowledge of gas?'

Jakob, she noticed, did not look surprised. She wondered why he hadn't mentioned this to her before.

Pierre's hand touched his scarred cheek. 'After this. When I recovered I was no longer fit for frontline service. But I was not offered a discharge. The military thought I was well enough to serve in another capacity. So, I was sent to look after the stores.' He gave a hollow laugh. 'Stores of gas. The powers-that-be never considered the irony of that. Putting a man who had nearly died from poison gas in charge of poison gas. It was not just the Germans who indulged in chemical warfare, Miss Vale. We French did too – and the Americans and you Brits, although that information seems to have been kept from the public.'

Clara nodded. It didn't surprise her in the least. She was well aware that no country came out of the last war beyond reproach. 'I see,' she said. 'And have you told the police this? About your knowledge of gas?'

He shook his head, glumly. 'No. But it is on my service record. All the police have to do is request it from Paris. But that's not the worst of it. You see, I didn't just lie to the police about the time Jonny left, I also lied to them about being in the laboratory. The security guard didn't see where we went after we got through the foyer. We told him we were just going to the workroom. Which, at first, I thought we were.'

'What were you going to do in the workroom?' asked Clara.

'It was Hugo, not me. Hugo wanted to go there to pick something up. What neither Jonny nor I realised was that what he wanted to pick up was the dress Hilda wore. The near-duplicate of the garment he had designed. He was still furious with Danny – and Hilda – about the dress. Even though he had agreed with Jakob and Danny that neither dress would be shown at the New Museum, he had changed his mind. And believed he had a right to. He contended that his design was the original so why should he not be able to show it? And he was outraged that Danny and Hilda had taken umbrage about it. Hugo took it as a personal humiliation and insult. He said he wanted to teach them both a lesson.'

'What did he plan to do with the dress?' asked Clara.

Pierre shrugged. 'I thought he was just going to take it. He said he wanted them to not be able to find it, and he'd enjoy seeing them looking for it. But then he decided he would take more drastic action. He announced that he wanted to burn it. Jonny said he didn't think that was a good idea, that it could be dangerous and a fire might spread. He tried to talk him out of it. As did I. But Hugo wouldn't be deterred. He claimed to have an idea of how to do it safely. Remember, Jakob, when you gave us the tour of the building?'

Jakob nodded. 'Before you and my cousins arrived at the factory on Friday, Miss Vale, I took the French and American teams for a tour.'

'Including the laboratory?'

'Yes.' Jakob sighed. 'I probably shouldn't have, Karl always wanted to keep people out – for safety reasons, he said. But forgive me, I'm a proud father, and wanted to show off a bit. I told everyone that Karl was developing a revolutionary new fabric.'

'And the fume hood?' asked Clara. 'Did you point that out too?'

'He didn't. But I did,' said Pierre. 'I pointed it out because I've seen one before. I explained to everyone that it was used to get rid of noxious fumes.'

Clara nodded. 'I see. And who was there? Hilda, Hugo, Benji, Danny and Merlette?'

'Yes,' said Jakob. 'All of them. And Pierre. But not Jonny. He was with you and Juju registering at the police station.'

'Did you tell the police about the tour?' asked Clara.

'No, they didn't ask about anything that happened on Friday. Their questions were about the tensions at the show on Saturday night, who was at the party at the hotel and when they left, and then who was here on Sunday morning, and also what time. I didn't deliberately not tell them about the Friday tour; the questioning just took us in a different direction. Besides, I had no idea it might be significant. Is it?'

'It might be,' said Clara, considering that it could, possibly, clear Jonny and point the finger at someone else. 'And you?' she said, turning to Pierre. 'Did you tell them about the tour?'

Pierre shook his head. 'No. Again, it didn't come up. But they did ask me where I'd been in the early hours of Sunday morning. I told them I was in the workroom and only there. And that I left at four o'clock with Jonny close behind.'

'I see,' said Clara, wondering why Strauss had not arrested Pierre there and then. Perhaps the DI was waiting for the likely time of death to be confirmed to match the suspect's alleged timelines. Yes, she thought, that was most likely. She checked her watch. It was now almost half past three. Dr Ritter's post-mortem would now be complete. She expected Strauss would be making decisions right now on who to bring in for further questioning. She did not have much time. 'All right,' she said. 'You'll have to tell the police about it all now. It will be best to be as truthful as you can, Monsieur Dreyfus. So please tell me, what happened in the laboratory?'

Pierre picked up the cigarette case and tapped it repeatedly on the table.

Jakob snatched it from him. 'For heaven's sake, man, just come clean with it.'

Pierre glared at Jakob then growled: 'All right. I will. Hugo remembered what I'd told him about the fume hood. And he knew that Jakob kept spare keys in his office. The office wasn't locked – stupid of you to leave it open, Jakob – so Hugo got hold of the bunch and let himself into the lab. All the time Jonny and I were trying to talk him out of it. Then when he got to the lab, he shoved the dress into the fume hood cabinet and said he was going to set it alight. I tried again to talk him out of it. He told me in no uncertain terms to get lost. Bar physically restraining him I had no option but to just leave him to it. Danny and Hilda did deserve it. And it wasn't worth getting into a brawl about. So, I left him and Jonny to it.'

'What was Jonny doing?' asked Clara.

'He was trying the softer approach. He was trying to soothe him. Like – well, Miss Vale – like a lover might do. And that's another reason I left. I thought Jonny might have a better chance without me. But now it looks like it was Hugo who didn't have a chance. My God, why did Jonny do it?'

Jakob slammed his hand down on the table. 'Shut up, man! Jonny did no such thing.'

Pierre shrugged sadly. 'But it looks like he did.'

Something caught Clara's eye: DI Strauss and his sergeant had entered the bar.

'Oh no. Stay calm,' she whispered.

Strauss approached the table. 'Fräulein Vale, Herr Spiegler, will you excuse us please?'

'What's this about?' asked Jakob.

'It's police business. So, if you and the lady don't mind, please leave.'

'But—'

'Now!' barked Strauss. 'Or I'll have the sergeant remove you.'

Jakob and Clara got up.

'And oh, Miss Vale,' Strauss added in English, 'we've identified that cufflink. It is made of a very distinctive Whitby jet. That's from England, I believe. Thank you for handing it in to us. I wonder if your friend Jonny still has its mate?'

* * *

Jakob demanded to use the telephone at the hotel desk. A few minutes later, his face ashen, he reported to Clara: 'The police have already been. They asked to speak to Jonny. My wife said he hadn't come out of his room yet. She couldn't find the spare key – I still have it – so they forced in the door. And then saw the room was empty and the window slightly open. They assume Jonny has fled.'

'They assume he's *just* fled? As the police came to get him?'

'Yes, that's what my wife said.'

'Good,' said Clara. 'That will buy us a bit of time. You didn't tell anyone that Jonny was gone earlier, did you?'

Jakob shook his head. 'No. But I probably should now.'

'Yes, you should,' said Clara, looking over her shoulder to see if Strauss was emerging from the Elephant Bar. He wasn't. 'But not just yet.'

'All right. I'll take your advice on this, Miss Vale. But we should probably get home. My wife is very upset.'

'Yes, let's do that,' agreed Clara. 'Bella and Juju should be back there now too. But first we need to pick up those photographs from the shop. And, if possible, Karl from the university. I think the new fabric formula might be the key to all this, Herr Spiegler. And I don't think Strauss is following that line of enquiry just yet.'

Chapter 32

Juju was reluctant to leave Bella at the hotel. 'But you can't speak German,' said Juju.

'I know,' Bella replied, as Juju removed her maid's uniform in the cleaning cupboard. 'But I hopefully won't need to. I need to search some rooms, Miss Levine, and it's best if I do it alone. I can slip in and out more easily if it's just me. If I'm challenged, I'll play the deaf-mute card. You have already told Hans that I'm unable to talk. I'll play that up. But, if all goes to plan, no one will challenge me. Besides, I need you to go back to the Spiegler house and tell Miss Vale everything we've discovered so far. I'll join you as soon as I can.' She smiled sympathetically. 'You've done a grand job, Miss Levine, but this part of the job could be dangerous.'

'But if it's dangerous you shouldn't be alone!'

Bella shook her head. 'No, Miss Levine, it's best that I am. Don't worry.' She grinned. 'I do this for a living.'

'All right,' said Juju, handing Bella her feather duster. 'But do be careful.'

'Aye, I will.'

* * *

Bella was experienced in surveillance and undercover detection. Even though she was a physically striking woman – tall, strongly built and with bright ginger hair – she had learned over the years that if one falsely adopted a quiet, unobtrusive demeanour, didn't project any kind of self-confidence, or for that matter awkward self-consciousness, one could become almost invisible. Add to that her maid's uniform with her hair hidden under a cap, and the obliviousness with which most people treated those of the serving classes, she found she could slip through the halls of the Adlon unchallenged. She had hoped to find some keys with which she could gain entry to the various rooms she needed to search, but she had been unable to find any that could easily be 'borrowed'. And she could not risk being caught in the act of trying to steal them. So instead, she resorted to one of the first skills she'd learned working for Vale Investigations: lock picking.

She had a list of rooms, discussed with Miss Vale, that she needed to search: Hugo Treves's, Danny Cohen's, Pierre Dreyfus's, Merlette Hassan's, then Hilda Markwald's. Although Miss Vale had not specifically asked her to, she thought she'd also give Benji Finkelstein's room a once-over, just to be thorough, and Larry Winter's. The latter was not just to be thorough. She was seriously suspicious of the man now that he'd been spotted meeting clandestinely with Hilda Markwald, not once, but twice – and then lying about it. What were they trying to hide? Did Hugo know what it was? Is that why he'd been killed? She blanched at the thought that the friendly American pilot who had helped save Miss Vale's life in Cairo could be a bad egg, but she'd had enough experience with charming men in her life to know that they weren't always what they seemed.

Bella had memorised the numbers of all the rooms that Hans had led Juju to when they delivered the fake notes.

Unfortunately, Larry Winter was not on that list. She would have to find out his room number another way. She'd think about that later. For now, she had enough to go on, and she started with the room of the dead man.

It was clear that the police had already been there. The room had been turned upside down. Drawers and wardrobes had been emptied, and Hugo's suitcase was missing. Bella had no idea what the police had taken with them in the suitcase, but she expected that if there had been anything of interest, it would have been removed. Still, she searched the place from top to bottom just in case there was anything the police might have overlooked. There wasn't.

Next on the list was Danny Cohen. She had timed her search to coincide with lunch, so the chances of anyone being in were slim. Still, she knocked on the door. She waited and knocked again. Silence. Good. She looked left and right down the corridor to make sure she wasn't seen and then slipped the two picking tools into the lock – a hook-shaped wire and a skeleton key. It was a standard pin tumbler mechanism, and it only took a minute for Bella to manipulate the component parts, click open the lock and open the door. Once inside, she was relieved to see Danny Cohen's room was tidy and orderly. It was easier to search than if items were strewn everywhere, but on the downside, she would need to be extra careful to replace everything where she found it. She did not want it to be known that she had been here.

There were the usual clothing and personal toiletries, a document case, a sketchbook filled with rudimentary outlines for women's clothes using just a few lines, and then a folder filled with more sophisticated drawings and watercolour paintings. She noted the initials on the paintings differed from that on the sketches: BF and DC. It looked like DC – Danny Cohen – came up with basic ideas and then BF – Benji Finkelstein developed them. She paged through the book and the paintings, recognising various outfits that were now in the American collection, but could not see the design for Hilda Markwald's controversial dress. She remembered what Danny had said on Friday: he did not have his sketches there to show Jakob. He was right, they weren't here. But they might be somewhere else . . . She searched but could find nothing else, other than a display book of fabric, similar to ones she'd seen in the soft furnishing department of Fenwick. Placed inside the front cover, but not properly attached, was a folded swatch of white fabric that felt like linen. She fingered the swatch and placed it back in the book. *Nothing out of the ordinary*, she thought and moved onto the next room.

Merlette Hassan's room was chaotic. *What a messy young lass*, thought Bella. It was not what she'd expected at all. On the one hand, Merlette was quietly elegant and youthfully endearing. She was always impeccably presented – as a model should be. But did this messy room suggest there was something bubbling under the surface? Something Merlette struggled to contain? Bella couldn't put a finger on it, but there was something . . . well, something she couldn't quite fathom about Merlette Hassan.

Bella decided she would speak to Miss Vale about it when she had a chance. For now, she dutifully set to work, raking through the model's belongings. The only thing of significance she found – or at least she thought might be significant – was an old photograph, about five by three inches and on stiff card. By the look of the clothing, it was taken in around 1910. A beautiful young couple looked straight into the camera lens – neither smiling, as was the style of the time. Bella wasn't entirely sure, but the man looked like a young Hugo Treves. And the woman . . . well, she bore a strong resemblance to Merlette. Bella looked on the back of the print and saw the stamp of the photographic studio. She recognised the word Paris, but as she could not read French she could not figure out anything else. She slipped it under her skirt and into the waistband of her bloomers. If she was caught and questioned, she did not want it to be easily found. And anyone – man or woman – who tried to get into Bella Cuddy's bloomers would not live to tell the tale!

Hilda Markwald's room was next on the list. Hilda's belongings were as rigidly arranged as the woman herself, so it did not take Bella long to find a dossier of documents. They looked like they were written in German. The dossier was too big to fit into her bloomers, so she paged through, trying to figure out which single page she could take for Miss Vale to read. There were documents, letters, a couple of maps and something with dates and times that could possibly be an itinerary. The names of Göring and another name she recognised from the party at the Nazi headquarters last night caught her attention: Hitler. Hadn't Rudy said something about the leader of his party being called Herr Hitler? This page was as good as any to take. She removed it from the dossier, folded into a square, and had just lowered her skirt when the door to the room opened. Hilda Markwald stood there, taking in the scene. 'What the hell are you doing here?' she demanded in English.

'I'm working as a maid, obviously,' said Bella, with a hard stare.

'But why?'

'Thought I'd earn a bit extra while I'm here. Miss Vale doesn't pay me that much, you know.'

Hilda matched her hard stare. 'Rubbish. You're searching my things. Have you found anything interesting?' She took a menacing step forward.

Bella shrugged. 'Nowt of any style. So, I'll be on me way then.' She headed for the door.

Hilda slammed it shut. 'Oh no you don't.'

Bella carried on regardless.

Hilda grabbed her arm and dug her inch-long nails into the flesh.

This was all Bella needed to snap into battle readiness. She clutched Hilda's forearm, twisted it around, and as the blonde woman was off balance Bella kicked at her ankles and Hilda tumbled to the floor. She lay there for a moment, looking stunned. Bella prepared to step over her, but as she did Hilda rolled out of the way, pulled out a revolver and rose to her knees. The gun was trained on Bella. 'Touch that door and I'll shoot. And don't think I'll miss. I'm a trained markswoman. *Bitch.*'

Bella was as impressed as she was shocked. Hilda clearly had had some kind of training. Not just in weaponry, but the roll and recovery too. She contemplated for an instant kicking the gun out of Hilda's hand, but when she saw the woman's ice blue eyes anticipating her next movement, she considered it too much of a risk. She put her hands in the air.

'Right,' said Hilda, 'I'll ask the question again: what have you seen?'

Seen, thought Bella, *not found. She didn't see me put the page in me bloomers.* 'Nowt,' she said. 'I've just got here. You interrupted me before I could search properly. Just that pile of papers but I couldn't read anything. It's all in German. So, I'll just be on me way then.'

Hilda cocked her weapon and curled her painted lips into a red-rimmed snarl. 'Correction, Miss Cuddy, *we'll* be on our way. And we're going out the back entrance. There's someone waiting for me with a car. I'm sure we can find room for you too.'

Chapter 33

The sound of weeping greeted Clara, Jakob and Karl as they arrived back at the Spiegler house. In the drawing room, Juju Levine was draped across a chaise longue while Stella Spiegler perched on a footstool trying to console her. Karl rushed to his wife and knelt beside her, Clara approached Juju and young Karl stood watching awkwardly from the doorway.

'Juju, are you all right?' Clara asked in English.

Juju raised her tear-stained face at the sound of Clara's voice. 'Oh, Clara! The police have been here trying to arrest Jonny. But he must have heard or seen them from his window, because he's escaped!'

'Escaped?' Clara managed to feign shock.

'Yes, it looks like he jumped from his window and has done a runner. He was on the second floor! Oh, Clara! I hope he's all right! I don't know why he ran, I really don't! He's got nothing to hide, so why run?'

'Perhaps he thinks the police might have some evidence against him,' offered Karl from the doorway.

Juju swallowed hard. 'Do you think they have?' Then she turned to Clara. 'You've seen the police today, Clara, what did they say?'

Clara nodded and took a seat beside Juju. Everyone in the room turned to listen to Clara's reply. She explained what had happened at the post-mortem, that the gas had likely been a distraction, and that the cause of death was cyanide poisoning.

'Cyanide? Who would know how to administer that?' asked Karl.

'That's the question I'm asking too,' said Clara. She went on to explain how she'd found traces of cyanide in the pipette and how she'd already telephoned Dr Ritter to tell him. 'So,' she concluded, it looks like it was taken from the cyanide bottle in your poison cupboard, Karl.'

'But it's kept double locked!'

'Are the keys on the spare bunch kept in your father's office?'

'Well, yes . . . Oh God, that wasn't very sensible of me to put all the duplicated keys on there, was it?'

Clara gave him a sympathetic look. 'Not really. But it could have happened to anyone. Were all the keys on there? Including the one to your desk drawer where the notebook was kept?'

Karl shook his head. 'No, that one is usually just left in the drawer. I haven't had a duplicate made of it because I don't usually keep anything important in there. The notebook was only going to be there temporarily until I took it to the university.' He reached into his pocket and withdrew an ordinary drawer key. 'See, I still have it.'

Clara nodded. 'That's why the drawer was forced then. But nothing else in the laboratory was.'

'So, whoever has the keys is likely the killer,' observed Stella. 'I heard the police sergeant tell his constable to look for keys in Jonny's room.'

'Did they find them?' asked Karl.

'Of course not!' said Juju. 'Jonny had nothing to do with this!'

Jakob gave Clara a meaningful look. It could either have meant: *you'd better not tell her what Pierre said*, or it could have meant the opposite. Clara decided it was the opposite. Best the truth come out and they all work together.

'Well,' said Clara, 'it turns out Hugo was the one who stole the keys in the first place. But the keys were not on Hugo or anywhere in the laboratory when his body was found. So the assumption is whoever killed him took the keys away.' She went on to explain what Pierre had revealed about the three men being in the laboratory soon before Hugo died. And the alleged timing of each of them leaving.

'But we only have Pierre's word that he left at the time he did,' observed Juju, gathering herself. She took a handkerchief from Stella and wiped her face.

'Yes, we do,' said Clara. 'Apart from the security guard. Pierre said he could confirm the time he left. And, for that matter, the time Jonny supposedly left too.'

'But the security guard is missing,' interjected Jakob.

'Who is that? Lederman?' asked Karl.

'Yes. I saw him at seven o'clock on Sunday morning to relieve him. He seemed perfectly normal. He said nothing out of the ordinary had happened overnight.'

'Well, he was obviously lying,' said Stella.

'Yes,' said Clara. 'He was. The question is why. Was he lying because he had been asked to – or paid to – by someone, or because he was covering his own crimes.'

'Well, then the police should be looking for him!' said Juju.

'They have been,' said Clara. 'But he's also gone missing. I'm sorry, Juju, but I think they are working on the theory that Jonny and the security guard are in cahoots. And now that they're both missing at the same time, it reinforces that theory.'

She went on to tell the group about the cufflink. 'That's concrete evidence that Jonny was in the laboratory. And I expect Pierre has now come clean on that too. He lied at first, to protect Jonny, but I don't think he will any longer. Not when he's got to save his own skin.'

'But he could be lying about that too!' said Juju. 'How do we know he was not the one to kill Hugo?'

Clara nodded and then looked at Karl. 'We don't know that. And, as Karl has already pointed out, whoever killed Hugo had to have some knowledge of cyanide, how to extract it from the bottle and administer it. And also the fact that hydrogen sulphide could be used to mask the smell. Pierre told Herr Spiegler and I that the reason he lied to the police in the first place was that he feared his knowledge of poison gas from the war would count against him. He didn't specifically mention cyanide, but I know that cyanide was used in chemical warfare in the trenches.'

'Then everything points to him!' said Juju.

Clara shrugged. 'A lot certainly does. But the fact that Jonny has run does not look good for him. I'm afraid, Juju, the police will take that as tantamount to a confession of guilt.'

Juju shook her head. 'No, I don't believe it. And who says he actually *has* run away? He could have been kidnapped!'

Jakob put his hand on his cousin's shoulder. 'The room was locked, Juju, no one could have got to him.'

'But they could have come through the window! And forced him to leave with them the same way. That's possible, isn't it, Clara?'

It was an implausible scenario, but the whole case was built on implausibility. 'Yes, it's possible,' Clara conceded.

Juju jumped to her feet. 'Then what are you waiting for? Can't you do your forensic stuff and find some evidence of it? You can search the room and the garden! You can take fingerprints from the window! You've done it before on other cases.'

Clara did not believe Jonny had been kidnapped, and that this would be a waste of time. But Juju's face was so desperate, and she had no other ideas of how to proceed with the investigation until Bella came back from the hotel and they'd had a chance to discuss her findings, so she reluctantly agreed. 'All right,' she said. 'Karl, you can help me outside. Juju and Frau Spiegler, you search Jonny's room and see if there's anything there that doesn't belong to him – or the house – and Herr Spiegler, perhaps you can talk to your neighbours up and down the street, and the ones that back onto your garden, to see if anyone spotted anybody leaving the house, or in the grounds.'

* * *

Clara and Karl looked up at Jonny's bedroom window.

'Can you shimmy up that trellis, Karl? I want to see how easy – or otherwise – it would be for someone to get up.'

'All right.' He took off his jacket and passed it to Clara.

Clara was aware that Karl's youthful physique was quite different to Jonny's portly middle-aged build, but the young chemist, although fit, was not particularly athletic. So, if he could do it, then Jonny would have a chance too. As, of course, would anyone climbing *up* to Jonny's room.

The clematis was old and well-established with strong woody stems intertwined with a solid trellis that appeared to be firmly bolted to the wall. It certainly looked safe enough. And it was only a single storey. Karl slowly climbed the trellis, carefully picking his hand and footholds.

'How does it feel?' shouted Clara.

'Quite secure,' he said. 'And if I fall, the lawn will soften the blow.'

'So you reckon it's easily climbable?'

Karl had by now reached the top and was heaving himself up onto the windowsill. 'I wouldn't say *easy*, but it's doable.'

'Even for Jonny?'

Karl grinned down at her. 'I'll let you know what it's like after the descent.'

The descent, with Karl working backwards and having to feel for footholds without the benefit of sight, looked trickier. But he made it to the bottom with only a couple of slips. He brushed the loose foliage off his trousers and shirt and took the jacket back from Clara. 'Yes, I think Cousin Jonny could have done that. Particularly if he felt he didn't have any other choice.'

Clara shook her head. 'The kidnapping theory is quite a stretch, you know. I'm still going with the idea that he left of his own volition.'

'But why?' asked Karl. 'If he's not guilty of killing Hugo, why would he go on the run?'

Clara sighed. 'I honestly don't know.' She looked around. 'Let's see if we can find any clues.'

'What are we looking for?'

'Something that looks out of place. For instance, when we first arrived here, I noticed some clematis buds and soft stems and leaves on the lawn. They'd been broken off. We haven't had strong winds or rain for the last few days so it's not likely they've naturally fallen. So that supports the theory that the plant on the trellis has been disturbed. And look here,' she said, pointing to the flower bed at the bottom of the trellis. 'That's your footprint there, but over there and there are two other prints. Not full prints, unfortunately, so I can't take a casting, but clearly a disturbance by a shoe.'

'Two prints?' Karl noted. 'From the same person or two different ones?'

'I think the same person. They're about the same size and depth of indentation. That's the left foot there then the right foot came down afterwards.'

'So that scuppers the kidnapper theory then.'

'Not necessarily,' said Clara. 'It just shows that one person stood on the soil. It's possible that Jonny jumped the last few feet onto the lawn and didn't stand on the flower bed. Can you climb up again and do that?'

Karl obliged and, as Clara had suspected, it was possible to jump the last few feet without touching the flower bed. But would the tubby Jonny with his short legs do so? Possibly not. She needed to check with Juju if he had left a pair of shoes in the room. Then she could see if they fitted the partial prints. But for now, she was certain that someone *had* come down the trellis. Whether one, two, or even more people, she could not say for sure.

She wondered if there might be fingerprints on the outside window – as Juju had suggested. However, dusting and photographing them would take time and they wouldn't mean anything until she could match them to someone. And she would have to have the photographs developed. Which reminded her . . .

'Karl, I want to talk to you about something. I borrowed your camera yesterday and photographed the laboratory. If you don't mind, I'd like you to look at the prints. They're inside the house. The main thing I would like you to confirm is whether what I think is your hybrid linen rayon fabric – the white cloth you showed me – is in fact in the photograph. Because I think it was there when we discovered the body yesterday morning, but it was *not* there when I was in the laboratory this morning. Your father says you haven't been back to the laboratory since Sunday. Is that correct?'

Karl nodded. 'It is. I haven't been there. But you're right, the fabric *was* there when we found the body. I checked because when my notebook was missing I wanted to see if the fabric was too.'

'But you didn't take it yourself?'

Karl shook his head. 'No. The police told me not to touch anything. So I didn't.'

'Well,' said Clara, 'if that's the case, then the killer, with the keys, has returned to the laboratory and taken it.'

Karl growled. 'This is all to do with the fabric, isn't it? Someone wants my formula. And now someone has it – and the sample fabric.'

'I think so, yes. Your father told me that he took the French and American teams for a tour of your laboratory on Friday. Before we got there.'

'He did *what*?'

'I know. He admitted that you didn't want anyone in the lab, but said he was so proud of you that he wanted to tell his friends. And let's not forget Hugo and Danny *were* his friends. They go back many, many years.'

'He had no right!' Karl looked furious.

'Calm down,' said Clara. 'It won't help anyone if you two get into an argument about this. But it *does* actually help Jonny's case.'

'How's that?' asked the young man, his face still taut with anger.

'Because Jonny wasn't on that tour. He was with us – you, me and Juju – at the police station. So, he didn't see the fabric. He wouldn't have known what to take. And from what I can see – and you'll have to confirm when you look at the photograph – it was only that fabric that was stolen.'

Karl nodded, calming down a little. 'Yes, I see. But I wonder why the killer didn't just take it on Sunday morning after they killed Hugo.'

'Perhaps they were interrupted . . .'

'Perhaps. But they managed to take my notebook. Oh, hang on . . .' Karl looked startled. 'How did they know that the notebook was there? I had the only key. I don't think my father even knew where I kept my notebook. Unless . . .' He paled, his eyes widening with realisation.

'What is it, Karl?'

He swallowed hard. 'Oh, Miss Vale. It's not just my father who has made a mistake. I think I might have mentioned that I keep some things in my desk drawer when I really should keep them in a safer place.'

'And who did you mention it to?'

'It was on Saturday night. At the party. There was a table full of people. Someone . . . it was Hilda Markwald . . . was telling a story about when her diary was left in her dressing table drawer in Paris. That a maid found it, read it and then proposed to blackmail her because it listed a number of famous lovers. Miss Markwald just laughed at her and said she didn't care who knew who her lovers had been. And then I said, "Well, I hope no one finds my notebook. I keep it in a drawer too – in my laboratory." It was just said in jest and Miss Markwald then teased me about it possibly containing a list of lovers. I got embarrassed because Merlette was there and I said, "No, nothing like that. Just some boring old formulas" and everybody laughed.'

'Everybody? Who else was at the table?'

Karl thought for a moment and said: 'Me, Merlette, Miss Markwald, Hugo, Danny, Benji and . . . Pierre. Oh, and that American pilot.'

'Larry Winter?'

'Yes. But not Jonny. He had gone to the cloakroom, I think. But Pierre and Hugo *were* there. And we now know that Pierre was on the tour of the laboratory *and* he has a knowledge of chemicals.'

'And his and Hugo's company is in financial difficulties,' added Clara. 'Having a revolutionary fabric could be a game changer for them, couldn't it?'

Karl nodded. 'Yes. But if they go into production with it, surely we'll know it was them who stole it. Or Pierre, seeing he's the only one of the two still alive.'

Clara pondered this. 'Yes. But what if they sold it, anonymously. Is that possible?'

'Oh yes. The textile industry is not immune to industrial espionage.'

'Right,' said Clara. 'I think we've got something here we can take to DI Strauss – it could further implicate Pierre and possibly help clear Jonny. But let's look at the photograph first to confirm it.'

As the two turned to go back into the house, something on the edge of the flower bed caught Clara's eye. It was a stub of a cigarette. She picked it up and examined it. Her heart skipped a beat. 'Karl, does anyone in this house – family or staff – smoke Lucky Strike cigarettes?'

He thought a moment and then shook his head. 'No. We only smoke German brands here. Lucky Strike is American, isn't it?'

'Yes, it is,' she said, carefully folding the butt into a handkerchief. 'I think we might have found a clue.'

Chapter 34

Clara and Karl returned to the drawing room and waited for Juju, Stella and Jakob to return. Clara took the photographs from her satchel and laid them out on a coffee table.

'These were taken when I returned to the laboratory on Sunday afternoon to conduct the hydrogen sulphide canister test. Apart from Hugo's body not being there, is there anything different from the last time you saw the laboratory?'

Karl looked closely at the three photographs showing different parts of the laboratory. 'No,' he said eventually, 'they look the same. I can't see inside the cupboards, of course, but the benches, the shelves and the rail look the same.' He pointed to the swatch of white fabric hanging form pegs. 'There's the linen rayon hybrid. Just where I hung it up after showing you on Friday.'

Clara was relieved. Her memory hadn't been playing tricks on her. 'Yes, that's what I thought. And that's what's missing now. It was there yesterday but it wasn't there at lunchtime today when I popped in to check on the cyanide. Your father said the police sergeant locked up the laboratory and handed him the keys at five o'clock. They are *your* keys; the only set, other than the missing ones. So that means someone came in and took the fabric between five o'clock yesterday and one o'clock today. Your father said he had let no one in and the receptionist said that no one who didn't work there had come in.'

'At least through the front door,' Karl clarified.

'Yes,' agreed Clara. 'Your father suggested that too. Apparently, there's a back entrance for deliveries and such.'

'That's right. But . . .' Karl was thoughtful. 'We're assuming it was someone who didn't work there. What if it was an employee?'

Clara nodded. 'Yes, I think the police will be conducting interviews with everyone who works there. How many people is that?'

Karl considered this a moment. 'Apart from my father and I, there are twenty employees, that includes seamstresses, packers, some admin staff, the receptionist and two security guards – one for the day shift and one for the night shift. And now a temporary night-shift guard that my father has had to hire. Do you think we should be interviewing all of them too?'

Clara pondered the scale of the task then shook her head. 'No. Not yet. We have not yet cleared the immediate suspect list. And so far, Pierre Dreyfus is looking highly likely – but I'm no longer quite as sure.'

'And why's that?'

Clara shrugged. 'I don't really know. I got the sense he was telling the truth when he said he left Hugo and Jonny in the lab. And that his reason for being evasive was his fear that the police would find out about his chemical knowledge and hold it against him. Which is exactly what they have done. I don't blame them for that, it was my line of reasoning too, but there's something else here, something I can't quite put my finger on . . . What would be helpful is if we can find out if any of the staff saw Pierre on the premises between those hours. I'm sure the police will be asking that very question. And, of course, if anyone has seen Jonny.'

'Or the security guard,' added Karl.

'Him too. Actually,' said Clara, 'do you know where he lives? It might be useful to interview his neighbours – and perhaps search his house.'

Karl's eyes widened. 'Is that legal?'

Clara shrugged. 'No. But private investigators do it all the time. That's exactly what Bella is doing at the hotel now. I'll be interested to hear what she's found.'

'All right, I can get his address and take you there. But what about the cigarette, Miss Vale? You said it's a clue. Does Pierre smoke Lucky Strike?'

'No,' said Clara. 'I saw him smoking just a couple of hours ago. It was a French cigarette.'

'Oh,' said Karl, disappointed. 'I thought it might point to the killer.'

'It might still,' said Clara. 'Firstly, we don't know if Pierre *is* the killer – for the reasons I've mentioned. But if he is, we don't know whether he acted alone. He might have had a partner.'

'An American partner?'

'Or someone who smokes American cigarettes. But yes, an American is most likely. So, in the immediate group that's Danny, Benji and Hilda. Do you recall what they smoke? Did you notice on Saturday night?'

'I can't say I did. But we can find out, can't we?'

'Yes, we can. And it's also worth noting that Danny and Benji were at the factory this morning. One of them could have slipped into the laboratory and taken the fabric.'

'But Benji has an alibi for Sunday morning, doesn't he?'

Clara nodded. 'He does. But Danny doesn't. Last he was seen on Saturday night, Sunday morning, it was assumed he was accompanying Hilda to her room. Juju and Bella were hopefully going to confirm that. And the time he left. But for now, he's still very much in the frame.'

'So, Pierre and Danny could have been working together?'

'It's possible. Or Danny on his own. Or with the security guard. But we need more proof. And we also need to find Jonny. I have a feeling he might know a lot more about this than we do.'

Karl's eyebrows knitted together. 'Oh, I hope he's not been hurt, Miss Vale. I really do.'

Clara sighed. 'So do I, Karl.'

Juju and Stella Spiegler entered the drawing room.

'What have you found?' asked Clara quickly, hoping Juju had not heard the final musing about Jonny's wellbeing.

'Well,' said Juju, flushed with excitement. 'We searched the room as you asked. The police had already made a bit of a mess, but I was still able to remember what Jonny packed and brought with him. All his clothes are there apart from one suit, a coat and his hat.'

'So, he left in a hurry but still had time to put on his coat and hat?' mused Clara. The kidnapping theory was becoming increasingly unlikely. 'Did he have another pair of shoes? Are they in the room?'

'Yes,' said Juju. 'His dress shoes that he wore on Saturday.'

'Good,' said Clara. 'I'll need to look at those. But for now, carry on, what else did you find – or not find?'

'His briefcase is gone.'

'Did the police leave with that earlier?' asked Clara.

Stella shook her head. 'No. I watched them leave. No briefcase.'

'So that means he took it with him too. Out of the window . . .'

'The window with the mud splatter,' finished Juju.

'Mud splatter?' asked Clara.

'Yes! There is mud on the window! As if someone had thrown a clod at it.'

'I noticed that too,' said Karl. 'When I climbed up.'

'But the windows were cleaned on Thursday,' added Stella. 'I instructed the maid to do so.'

'So, the kidnapper must have thrown mud at Jonny's window!' Juju chipped in.

'Show me,' said Clara.

A few minutes later, they were all in Jonny's bedroom. As Juju had already said, it was in disarray. Stella pointed out the dried mud splatter on the window and Clara had to agree that it looked like someone had thrown a clod at the glass. She peered down to the lawn below.

'Do you have those shoes, please Juju?'

Juju extracted them from where they had been neatly placed under the bed, set apart from the chaos of the rest of the room.

'Why do you need them?'

'I'll tell you in a minute,' said Clara. The curious group followed her down the stairs and out into the garden where she positioned the shoes in the indentations of the flower bed. They fitted.

'Yes,' she said, 'I think these are Jonny's footprints. 'Juju, do you know if Danny or Hilda smoke Lucky Strike cigarettes? Danny particularly?'

Juju squinted curiously. 'I have no idea, why?'

'Because I think one of them was here last night or in the early hours of the morning and took Jonny with them.'

Stella gave an indelicate snort. 'I can't imagine Hilda Markwald throwing mud at a window, can you?'

'No,' said Clara. 'I can't.'

'Neither can I,' said Jakob, joining the group. 'But I can imagine Danny doing that. And, guess what? The nanny from the Wittgensteins' – they overlook our back garden, Miss Vale – said she was up early at five o'clock with the new baby and was looking out of the window. She said she saw two men, a short one and a tall one, leaving through our back garden gate and getting into a car at the bottom of the lane.'

Everyone gasped. 'The short one must be Jonny!' Juju exclaimed. 'Did she say if he looked under duress?'

'She said they both looked calm. The short one was carrying a briefcase, and they were talking to each other.'

'Do you think the tall one was Danny?' Juju asked.

'It's possible,' said Jakob. 'But lots of men are tall.'

'That's true,' said Clara. 'But do lots of men smoke Lucky Strike cigarettes?'

Jakob's face settled into a satisfied smile. 'Not lots of men in Berlin, Miss Vale. But Danny Cohen does.'

Chapter 35

Clara gathered the photographs from the coffee table. She was just waiting for Jakob to finish talking on the telephone to Hertzog, the department store owner, before they, accompanied by Karl, would head out together to follow up the latest leads. Jakob insisted he make the telephone call first, as it was now touch and go that they *would* be able to go ahead with the show tomorrow. News had just arrived that Pierre had been arrested at the Adlon. Without him, the French team would not be able to do a showing. And with Jonny missing, Juju said she did not want to participate. So, of the foreign teams, that just left the Americans: and Danny might be implicated too. If he was also arrested, young Benji and Hilda were not likely to proceed on their own. If Clara were honest, she'd be relieved if it didn't. She didn't think she could turn her attention to modelling with an unsolved murder investigation demanding her attention. But she also knew the cancellation of Fashion Week would have financial consequences for everyone involved. Jakob was discussing this all now with Hertzog.

'Oh, Clara, please can I come with you?' beseeched Juju as they waited for Jakob to finish his call. 'I can't abide not doing anything. Bella will tell you – I did a good job with her at the hotel.'

'I'm sorry, Juju, I need you to stay here to wait for Bella. I'm not sure what's taking her so long. But when she does get here, tell her what's happened and then both of you can go back to the Adlon to wait for me there. I really need to hear what Bella's discovered.'

'I can tell you what I heard this morning,' offered Juju.

'Yes, please,' said Clara. 'If it hadn't been for everything else going on I would have asked you before.' She looked to Jakob's study. The door was still closed. 'But go on, tell me now.'

'All right,' said Juju and went on to give a breathless overview of her adventure masquerading as Johanna the chambermaid and her flirtation with Hans the head porter. Clara chuckled but there was serious business afoot, so she pressed Juju to get to the crux of the report.

'Well,' said Juju, 'Merlette apparently remained in her room all night after Karl left. And the timing is what they have claimed.'

'Good,' said Clara. 'What about Benji?'

'Well, Benji is interesting, but perhaps not relating to the murder investigation.' She told Clara about him sitting outside Merlette's room like a lovelorn puppy.

'That is interesting,' said Clara. 'I wonder if they have previously had a relationship or if Benji is just hopeful. An interesting piece of gossip but not really the evidence we're looking for here.'

'No, it's not. But I think you'll be interested in Pierre. Hans confirmed that Pierre *had* been seen leaving the hotel so he very much could have been the third man in the taxi at the Eldorado Club.'

Clara nodded. 'Yes, he confessed that he was earlier this afternoon. So that leaves Danny. Did you find out anything about him?'

'Only that he left Hilda's room after an hour and returned to his own. No one saw him leave again. But that doesn't mean he didn't . . .'

'No,' said Clara, 'it doesn't. But if he was working with someone else, it doesn't really matter if he left the hotel or not. They could have killed Hugo without Danny being there and Danny could then have retrieved the fabric this morning if the killer forgot about it. But this is still all speculation. We need evidence. And we need to know who else was involved. It could of course be Pierre, but as I've said, I'm not fully convinced of that. So, who else is not yet in the clear? Hilda. What did you find out about her?'

Juju lowered her eyes.

'What?' asked Clara. 'What's wrong?'

'Well,' said Juju, shifting uncomfortably. 'She *was* seen leaving her room. At around three o'clock.'

'Aha!'

'Yes, but perhaps not aha in the way you think. Or want.'

'Oh? What's wrong, Juju. Spit it out.'

'All right. But you're not going to like it. Hilda was seen meeting someone in the hotel garden. A man. She gave him an envelope and they sat together talking and smoking.'

Clara's heart sank. 'Was it Larry?'

Juju nodded. 'Oh, Clara, I'm sorry.'

Clara swallowed hard. 'That's all right, Juju. Thanks for letting me know.'

As Clara finished packing the photographs in her satchel and saw Jakob emerging from his office, she remembered that she did know someone else who smoked Lucky Strike cigarettes. Larry Winter.

* * *

It was approaching five o'clock by the time Clara, Karl and Jakob got to Spiegler's Modefabrik. The receptionist – a gentleman called Herr Schmidt – was preparing to shut the office for the day.

'Ah, Herr Spiegler, I'm glad you're here, I wasn't sure what to do with the keys. Do I give them to the new guard?'

'There is another set of keys?' Clara whispered to Karl.

'Only for the front and back doors,' he replied. 'Not for the interior doors.'

Clara nodded and turned her attention to the conversation between Jakob and the receptionist.

'Give the keys to me and I'll pass them on to the guard. I want to talk to him anyway. But before you go, Schmidt, Fräulein Vale here has a few questions for you. She is a detective from England, and I have hired her to help get to the bottom of things. So please, be as helpful as you can.'

Schmidt turned to Clara, suitably impressed. He bowed. 'Of course, Fräulein Vale, how may I help you.'

'Thank you,' she said. 'I would like to clarify the comings and goings of some people today. You were not at work yesterday, I believe.'

'No, Fräulein, it was Sunday. I am Christian, not Jewish, and Herr Spiegler did not expect me to come in, even though there were people in the building.'

Jakob nodded. 'That's right. I tend to keep the factory shut on Sundays anyway. It's just easier. Not all my staff are Jewish – and for those that are, they can take the Shabbat off if they choose to. We only worked yesterday because of Fashion

Week. And it was only the foreign teams. None of the factory staff were here.'

'Apart from the guard who left at seven o'clock in the morning. Is that correct?' asked Clara.

'It is,' Jakob agreed. 'So, Schmidt here cannot contribute anything in that regard. But as of today, he may be of more help.'

'Thank you,' said Clara and turned back to the receptionist. The man chewed his lip, obviously nervous. Clara smiled, hoping to settle him. 'Herr Schmidt,' she said, gently, 'did you see Herr Cohen and Herr Finkelstein arrive today?'

'The American gentlemen?'

'That's correct. One older one, and a younger one.'

'Yes, they arrived at around ten o'clock.'

'Did you see where they went in the building?'

Schmidt shook his head. 'I did not follow them, no. They said they were going to the workroom. I had no reason to think they were not.' He looked to his employer.

'That's all right, Schmidt. You were not expected to follow them.'

Schmidt cleared his throat and nodded. He looked nervously to Clara again.

Clara kept her tone friendly. 'That is very helpful to know, thank you. Now, did anyone else arrive? Such as Herr Dreyfus. That's the French gentleman with the scarred face.'

Schmidt shook his head. 'I did not see him, Fräulein.'

'What about another American man? Although you might not know he is American as he speaks excellent German. Herr Winter. A tall, blond man in his thirties. Older than Finkelstein, younger than Cohen.'

Schmidt shook his head again. 'No, Fräulein, he did not come this morning. However . . .' He looked again to his employer. 'I'm sorry, Herr Spiegler, I did not think it was important to mention.'

'What is it, man? Spit it out.'

The receptionist bit his lip and replied. 'That American gentleman *was* here on Friday. It was after Fräulein Vale and her English friends had gone home. That gentleman arrived and asked if Fräulein Vale was here. I said she wasn't. I asked if I should call you, Herr Spiegler, but he said no. He asked instead if the other lady was here. The American lady, Fräulein Markwald.'

Clara's eyes narrowed. She had ceased to be upset by the repeated mentions of Hilda and Larry together. She was just becoming angry. However, she quelled her temper and remained calm. It was as clear as day that Larry had lied to her about his and Hilda's relationship – whatever it entailed.

'I see,' she said, her voice devoid of emotion. 'And did you let him go to the workroom alone? Or anywhere else in the building?'

The receptionist bristled. 'I did not, Fräulein! Herr Spiegler told me I should allow the foreign teams to come and go as they would be working here for the next week. But that gentleman was not on the list. I did my job properly, Herr Spiegler, I promise you.'

'I'm sure you did, Schmidt,' said Jakob soothingly. 'But just answer Fräulein Vale's questions, please.'

Schmidt nodded. 'All right. But I did not let him in. I was going to send the messenger boy to call Fräulein Markwald when I caught sight of the large American gentleman, Herr Cohen. I asked him to fetch the Fräulein instead.'

'Herr Cohen? And where did you catch sight of him?' asked Clara.

Schmidt pointed. 'On the first-floor landing.'

Clara looked up and saw the landing to which he referred. To the left of the landing was a door leading to the workroom. To the right a door that led to the offices and the lavatories. And then there was a staircase that led upwards to subsequent floors. That was the way to the laboratory.

She nodded. 'Did you see where Herr Cohen had just come from when he was on the landing? Had he just come down the stairs or through one of the doors?'

Schmidt bit his lip again. 'I'm sorry, Fräulein, I did not. My attention was all on the visiting American gentleman, Herr Winter. I just happened to glance up and see Herr Cohen at the top of the stairs. So I called to him and asked if he would request Fräulein Markwald to come to reception as she had a visitor.'

'Did he?'

'Yes. After first greeting Herr Winter.'

'Oh? Did they appear to know one another?'

'They did. They were very friendly. Although they spoke in English so I did not understand what they were saying.'

'Interesting,' said Clara. 'This was Friday, wasn't it?'

'Yes, Fräulein.'

'Is that important, Miss Vale?' asked Jakob in English.

Clara shrugged. 'Well, I wasn't aware that Lieutenant Winter and Danny Cohen were acquainted before Saturday night at the Adlon. Were you?'

'I wasn't aware, no. I had never met Winter before Saturday night, but there's no reason Danny wouldn't know him. They are both German / American. They might very well know each other Stateside. And if they both know Hilda . . . Did *you* know that Winter and Hilda were previously acquainted?'

'Yes,' she said, without going into any detail of what she'd seen and heard on the train. She turned back to the receptionist and switched to German. 'Thank you, Herr Schmidt, this is very useful information. Now if you don't mind, just a few more questions. Did Herr Cohen summon Fräulein Markwald when you asked him to?'

'He did. And she came quite promptly.'

'Did Herr Cohen return with her?'

'He did not. Fräulein Markwald was unaccompanied.'

'I see, thank you. And how would you describe the Fräulein's demeanour when she saw Herr Winter?'

The receptionist thought for a moment and said: 'Cool. But no more or less than how I have always seen her.'

'The ice maiden,' chipped in Karl.

'Yes,' said Schmidt. 'Very cool and calm. She did not smile but she did not appear to be upset either. She and the visitor took a seat in the corner over there . . .' He pointed to a cluster of armchairs. 'They spoke for about five minutes and then the gentleman left. The lady went back upstairs without saying anything further to me.'

Schmidt waited for his information to be received then asked, nervously, 'Is there anything else I can tell you, Fräulein Vale?'

Clara shook her head. 'No. That's all I need, thank you. But if you do think of anything else – like for instance if anyone else visited, then please let Herr Spiegler – senior or junior – know. Or if any of the other staff see anyone who they don't know please ask them to tell you.'

Schmidt's eyes widened. 'Inside or outside the building?'

'Both,' said Clara. 'Why do you say that?'

'Because,' said Schmidt, walking to one of the long window slits that flanked the front door, 'that gentleman over there – see him standing on the edge of the park – well, he followed you here at lunchtime, Fräulein Vale, and now he's back again. He just stands there, smoking. And watching.'

Clara felt a shiver run up her spine. Who had been following her, and why? She, Jakob and Karl peered through the window at the tall blond man in the dark suit. He was indeed smoking and staring at the front door of the building. If he noticed the four people spying on him through the slit window, he gave no indication.

'Do you recognise him?' asked Jakob.

Clara did not but she had a sense that she might have seen him before. Then she had a flash of a memory of a man she'd seen following her up the steps from the U-Bahn station. She had thought nothing of it at the time, but she had briefly noticed him as he was quite handsome. 'I can't say I recognise him, but I think he might have followed me here from Alexanderplatz this morning. Have you seen him before?'

'No,' said Schmidt. 'Not before today, Fräulein.'

'I have,' said Karl, a tremor of fear in his voice.

'Where?' asked his father.

'At the university. He's a Nazi bodyguard. He was with Göring when he came to give a talk to the student union last week.'

'And what was the talk on?' asked Clara.

'The Jewish Problem,' said Karl, between clenched teeth.

Chapter 36

Karl drove over the Oberbaumbrücke, the bridge that was slung between two mock medieval towers and spanned the River Spree. Karl and Clara were heading south to Kreuzberg after having left Jakob at the Adlon, with the instruction to find Danny Cohen and keep him there until Clara returned.

It was half past six, an hour before sunset, and the Berliners were either making their way home after work or enjoying the late summer sun on the banks of the river. Clara noticed lovers walking hand in hand, young children feeding the swans and dog walkers strolling the towpath as their charges jumped in and out of the river. Unfortunately, the riverbank would have been deserted between four and six in the morning on Sunday, the time when Jonny had allegedly gone for a walk to clear his head, at the same time that Hugo Treves was handcuffed in the laboratory and poisoned with cyanide. The handcuffs . . . those were still a mystery. Who had handcuffs? Police officers? Security guards?

'Karl,' she asked, as he manoeuvred the car down Friedrichstrasse, 'do the security guards at the factory carry handcuffs?'

'Yes, I think so,' he said.

'And do you know if the guard – this Lederman fellow who has gone missing – had his on Sunday morning?'

Karl turned to look at her briefly before turning his attention back to the road. 'I have no idea.'

'Do you think the handcuffs would have been visible? Did he wear them on his belt? Or were they kept in a pocket?'

'Hmmm,' said Karl, 'I can't say I've ever noticed. You should ask my father.'

'I will. And I expect the police already have. But if you add the handcuffs into the mix, that gives added reason to suggest the guard was in on it. He lied to the police and to your father, saying he didn't see anyone at the factory, when Pierre admitted to me that the guard actually let them in.'

'Yes,' said Karl, 'but you need to add to that Pierre's knowledge of poison gas. So, at the moment, it looks like Pierre might have done it with the assistance of the guard.'

'Agreed,' said Clara, 'that *is* what it looks like, but appearances are sometimes deceptive. On the other hand—' she shrugged '—sometimes they are exactly as they seem. And this does look quite damning. I asked your father about the guard. He said he couldn't tell me much about him. He's single, unmarried. Lives on his own. He's worked at the factory for about six months. Before that he'd worked at the Tempelhof Aerodrome.'

'Pierre must have met him before if they worked together to kill Hugo,' offered Karl.

'Possibly, or he might simply have been bribed into silence – and for the use of his handcuffs, if they were his,' mused Clara. 'I wonder if Pierre has ever flown into Berlin rather than taking the train. He is a frequent visitor, isn't he?'

'Well, he's not here every month, but I have met him a few times before. He's accompanied Hugo. They've even stayed at the house. Why do you ask about Tempelhof? Do you think he might have met the security guard there?'

'It's possible,' said Clara, 'I'm really just trying to find connections. Because it's in those connections, who is connected to whom, and the nature of that connection, that the answer will lie. And the more I think of it, the more I believe we are dealing with multiple connections. So, if Pierre was connected to both Hugo and the guard then it doesn't matter if the guard wasn't connected to Hugo. And if Jonny is connected to Hugo and Danny, or perhaps someone else, then it might be someone else's connection to Hugo that is pertinent, not Jonny's alone. And there may be other connections – other people – that we haven't yet considered. You see, Karl, I think of murder investigations like Bohr's theory of the atom. You know what I'm talking about, don't you?'

Karl nodded and smiled. 'Yes, Miss Vale, I do. That's a very apt theory. Do you know that Niels Bohr is half Jewish? He gave a lecture at my university once.'

'He gave one at mine too,' said Clara. 'Just after he won the Nobel Prize. So, you understand my analogy then?'

'Yes, I do,' said Karl, thoughtfully. 'Every atom has a positively charged nucleus, made up of protons, and is encircled by orbiting electrons, which are negatively charged particles. The protons in the nucleus and the electrons are held in atomic tension through their opposite charges of energy. So, you're saying, Miss Vale, that Hugo is the nucleus and the suspects – the people who were connected to him – are like the electrons, circling him.'

Clara smiled, appreciatively. 'Yes, I am. But the analogy goes further than that. How many electrons are there in an atom?'

'Well, that varies from atom to atom. A hydrogen atom has one electron, carbon has six, oxygen has eight . . .'

'That's right,' said Clara. 'But what I'm getting at is that the number of electrons is equal to the number of protons. That is the atomic number. Isn't that correct?'

Karl nodded.

'So, each electron,' Clara continued, 'is held in tension by an opposing proton. Now, this has not been scientifically proven yet, far greater minds than mine are currently working on it, but to me that suggests that each specific electron – each suspect in our analogy – is held in tension by a specific proton. Everyone circling Hugo had their own issue with him. In Pierre's case it was their financial problems. As long as that was in balance the orbit continued uninterrupted. With Hilda, it was their past relationship – both personal and professional. With Danny, it was the creative rivalry, symbolised by the dress. With Jonny it was their past, and perhaps recently revived, love affair. With all of them their orbit around Hugo continued uninterrupted until . . . well, what has Bohr suggested happens to electrons when they get a sudden additional charge?'

Karl turned the car off Friedrichstrasse into a side street lined with soot-stained tenements. 'Ah, you're talking about his quantum leap theory, aren't you? But that's still under dispute.'

'It is under dispute,' agreed Clara, 'but it's useful to think about with this case. A quantum leap is the abrupt transition of a quantum system – in this case an atom – from one quantum state to another. Or from one energy level to another. When the system is exposed to a sudden burst of energy, the system absorbs the energy and there is a sudden transition to a higher energy level. That's known as excitation. But when the system loses the energy, it transitions back to its previous state.'

Karl nodded vigorously. 'Yes! That's what's happened here. One of the electrons has become excited or agitated, there's been an explosion of energy, but now they appear to have returned to their previous state.'

Clara smiled at Karl. 'That's exactly what I'm contemplating. You know, I wouldn't be talking like this to anyone else but you. What a relief it is to have someone who understands how I think! So, where this points, I think, is to the someone else. We have the obvious suspects, and they may very much be involved, but I strongly suspect there is someone else too. And that is the person who *appears* to have returned to their normal state. Has Pierre?'

'No, he's still agitated.'

'That's right. And the guard has disappeared. That's not a normal state either. And so has Jonny.'

'Hmmm,' said Karl. 'But isn't that the opposite of what the police are thinking? Aren't they looking for people acting out of the ordinary?'

Clara nodded. 'Yes, and there is something in that. And that's why they're looking for the guard and Jonny. And why they've arrested Pierre. But, like Bohr's quantum leap theory has not been proven, because it's not the accepted way of thinking about things, I think we need to be looking at who *doesn't* seem to have changed. Who seems perfectly as they were before?'

'Danny?'

'Yes, he's one of them. Who else?'

'Hilda?'

'Oh yes, she's practically glacial in how little she's changed.'

Karl slowed down in front of a tenement building.

'What about the connection to my fabric formula?' asked Karl. 'Using the same metaphor, do you think that's a separate atom with separate connections or part of the same atom?'

Clara contemplated this. 'Perhaps we're dealing with a molecule then. More than one atom combined. Or a compound, with different types of atoms that have joined to form a specific relationship. Or . . .' she chuckled '. . . we might simply be stretching the metaphor too far. But let's pick this up again later. There are other suspects I'm thinking about too and I'm not sure yet how they fit into all this. For now, let's see if Lederman's neighbours have anything to tell us. Perhaps he has a connection with Hugo – or someone else – that we don't yet know about.'

* * *

Herr Lederman lived in an attic apartment at the top of a four-storey tenement building. The landlord was reluctant, at first, to allow them in, but a few marks offered by Karl, soon changed his mind. The landlord also confirmed – for a few more marks – that the police had been in the apartment on Sunday afternoon and again at lunchtime today. And no, just like he'd told the police, he had not seen Herr Lederman since Friday when he had collected the rent. Although he had heard him return home at about eight o'clock on Sunday morning. No, he had not heard his tenant leave again. What did they think he was, his tenant's keeper? As long as Herr Lederman paid his rent, kept the noise down and disposed of his rubbish in the communal bins then he had no reason to involve himself in the man's business. But the recent police interest was not very welcome, not welcome at all. Did the gentleman and lady know why they were interested in Herr Lederman?

The gentleman and lady said they did not.

'Then why are you here?' asked the landlord.

'Herr Lederman works at my father's factory,' explained Karl. 'And he hasn't been in to work today. We are concerned that he might be ill.'

The landlord smirked. 'Does the esteemed Herr Spiegler always send his son to visit when his workers catch a cold?'

'Only on days when the police have been concerned for his health too,' said Karl. 'Now, can you let us in please?'

The landlord shrugged, pocketed the marks and turned the key in the lock.

'That's all,' said Karl and shut the door in the man's face.

'Well, that's saved me picking the lock,' said Clara. 'Although I doubt I could have done it without Herr Nosey Parker noticing.'

They turned to examine Lederman's room. It was a small bedsit with a bed, table and single chair. There was a small kitchen area but no ablution facilities. Lederman shared a bathroom with his neighbours on the floor below.

The room, like that of Jonny's at the Spiegler house, showed signs of recently being searched. There were also signs that fingerprints had been found and dusted on some cooking utensils and a glass. A chest of drawers had been emptied, with just a single sock remaining. 'I wonder if Lederman emptied that before the police came and that's what made them think he'd fled,' mused Clara. She looked to the top of the wardrobe and under the bed – the usual place where people kept their suitcases – to see there were none. There was no coat and hat on the peg on the back of the door either. And no shoes, besides a pair of slippers, under the bed. She expected that if she went downstairs and questioned the neighbours, they would tell her his shaving equipment was gone from the bathroom too. There certainly wasn't any here. No, it looked like Herr Lederman had indeed packed and left in a hurry.

She searched for any papers – or any clue at all – as to where he might have gone. There was nothing. She was just readying herself to suggest to Karl that they go downstairs to speak to the neighbours when the door to the attic room was flung open.

'What the hell are you doing here?'

Clara spun around to see DI Strauss with his trusty sergeant hovering at his shoulder. Strauss's eyes narrowed. His sergeant's widened. One was angry, the other surprised.

It was the angry one Clara was most concerned about.

'DI Strauss! I'm so glad you're here. It saves me popping into Alexanderplatz! I have a lot to tell you.'

'Do you now?' growled Strauss. 'Well, you can start by telling me why you are snooping around a crime scene without permission.'

Clara fixed a smile on her face, aware that poor Karl was starting to quiver. 'Crime scene? I had no idea it was a crime scene, Inspector. I was just accompanying Herr Spiegler here to check on the welfare of his employee who did not come into work today. The landlord very kindly let us in.'

'So, no picking of locks then? I'm surprised at your restraint, Fräulein Vale,' he said caustically. Clara did not know him well enough to determine if he was genuinely angry or just pretending to be. She decided to assume the latter and keep the conversation light.

'Ah,' she said, 'just as well. I've heard German locks are a tad more challenging than English ones.'

This seemed to elicit a twitch of amusement from Strauss, but his face soon settled into a practised mask of disapproval. Clara didn't mind. She was used to that from Inspector Sandy Hawkes in England. She hoped she could weave the same charm she had with him on his German counterpart.

'Well, Inspector,' she said, pointing to the fingerprint dust on the glass, 'did that reveal anything? Is it linked to the prints in the laboratory?'

Strauss shook his head. 'No. The only prints we could find in the laboratory are those of Hugo Treves and Herr Spiegler here.' He pinned Karl with an intimidating stare.

'But . . . but . . . I didn't do anything!'

Karl was visibly shaking now. Clara reached out her hand and squeezed his forearm. 'It's all right, Karl, the Inspector is not accusing you of anything, are you, Inspector? It's perfectly normal for your prints to appear in your own laboratory. Isn't that correct, Inspector?'

She stepped in front of Karl, protectively. Strauss noticed and his tone softened. 'Yes, Herr Spiegler, it is what we expected. We have no evidence to suggest you were involved in Herr Treves's death.'

Clara nodded and let out the breath she had taken preparing to defend Karl further. 'But do you have evidence that Lederman was involved, Inspector? The handcuffs, for instance . . .'

Strauss gestured to the room. 'Well, I expect you know by now, Fräulein Vale, that the cuffs are not here, so either Lederman took them with him when he fled, or they were the cuffs used on Herr Treves. Oh, and I don't know if you've had a chance to speak to the downstairs neighbour yet, a Frau Hoffmann, but Lederman *was* seen leaving with a suitcase at lunchtime on Sunday, before we had a chance to get here, and that he was picked up by a taxi. We have traced the taxi and we know where he was dropped.'

'Oh?' said Clara. 'Where was that?'

'Why on earth do you need to know that?'

'Because I'm investigating the case on behalf of my client?'

'Then get the information yourself!'

'I will,' said Clara, squaring up to him.

'I have no doubt about it,' said Strauss, not backing down. 'But it won't do you any good.'

'And why's that?'

'Because Lederman's handcuffs have now been found, Fräulein Vale. So, they were *not* the ones used on Herr Treves.'

'All right,' said Clara, absorbing the information. 'That's helpful to know. So, the guard's cuffs were *not* used in the murder. But that doesn't mean he didn't see anything – or know anything. Otherwise, why would he have left so suddenly?'

Strauss nodded. 'Yes, that's what we're wondering too. But unfortunately, we may never know.'

'And why's that?' asked Clara.

'Because,' said Strauss, nodding to his sergeant, 'he won't be doing any more talking. We have just found Herr Lederman washed up on the banks of the Spree – wearing a pair of handcuffs.'

'Dead?' gasped Karl.

'Very,' said the inspector.

Chapter 37

Anders Lederman was laid out on the table. The handcuffs had been removed and lay in a metal tray. It did not require the police pathologist Dr Ritter to point out the glaringly obvious: there was a stab wound directly into Lederman's heart. Clara and Strauss put on aprons, gloves and masks. The masks were needed for the stench: Herr Lederman's bloated body showed signs of being submerged in water for a good while. Ritter had not yet opened the chest, but Clara knew that he would be looking for signs of drowning. This would consist of pinkish foam in the mouth that had come up from the lungs, and in the lungs themselves, bubbles and black marks known as Paltauf's spots. These were caused by bleeding due to increased pressure on the lungs during asphyxiation. If these signs were not present it would indicate that the victim had died from the stab wound to the chest *before* he was thrown into the water. She mentioned this to Ritter who looked begrudgingly impressed. 'I see you've attended a drowning post-mortem before.'

'Two, actually. I assisted the police pathologist in Newcastle upon Tyne in two previous cases. One turned out that the victim had died before going in the water, the other died of drowning, but the body was moved elsewhere, post-mortem. In each case the location of the corpse was an attempt to obfuscate the cause of death which took a while to determine. I think in this one it's quite clear,' she said, pointing to the stab wound. 'What can you tell me about that?'

Ritter peered at her over his mask. 'Why should I tell you *anything*, Fräulein Vale?'

'It's all right,' said Strauss, wiping his spectacles that were beginning to steam up over his mask, 'I have an agreement with Fräulein Vale that I will allow her into the post-mortem in return for some information.'

Ritter growled. 'You did not ask me, Herr Inspector.'

'No,' said Strauss, brusquely.

The two men stared at one another for a few moments, the corpse of Anders Lederman between them. Clara wondered if she might be booted out. But eventually Ritter backed down, with very little grace. 'Bloody woman,' he muttered.

Strauss nodded to Clara. 'Go on, Fräulein Vale, ask your questions.'

'Thank you, Inspector. So, Dr Ritter, can you tell yet what was used to stab him?'

Ritter motioned her towards the body. He picked up a pair of callipers, measured the diameter of the wound and placed the callipers against a metal rule. 'It was quite a thick blade. Two inches wide at the hilt. I will have to confirm the degree of penetration when I open him up, but it looks like quite a lot of force was needed. By the angle of the wound it appears that the blow was delivered almost horizontally, that is the blade entered perpendicular to the chest – straight in. So, someone standing directly in front of him. As to the height, well, Lederman was a tall man, six feet from head to foot. So, to have a perpendicular entrance wound to the chest, the killer, standing in front of him, would have to be around one to two inches taller than him. So, I think we're looking for a tall man of around six feet two.'

'Well, that eliminates Jonny Levine, doesn't it?' she said. 'Jonny is a short man. Around five feet seven.'

'Not so quickly, Fräulein Vale,' said Strauss. 'Herr Doctor, could the victim have been kneeling or sitting when he received the fatal blow?'

'He could,' said Ritter. 'Or even lying on the floor. I have taken a blood sample and there was chloroform present. Enough to subdue, not kill him. So, he could have been prostrate or slumped on a chair when he received the fatal blow. In which case a stab wound directed from above could be perpendicular.'

'And what height would the killer be if there was a perpendicular entrance wound to the body of a seated or kneeling victim?' asked Clara.

The doctor considered this a moment and said: 'If the victim was kneeling and the killer was the same height, he too would have to kneel for the entrance wound to be perpendicular. If the killer was a shorter man, he could have the knife at thigh height and still achieve a perpendicular wound, or if the victim was seated on a chair, then either a short or tall man could have delivered a perpendicular blow. A tall man would just have to raise his elbow to waist height before the thrust.' He looked at Clara and Strauss. 'I think a demonstration is needed. Fräulein Vale, you are about five feet seven, are you not?'

'Five feet six,' she said.

'Close enough. Herr Inspector you are six feet, the same height as the victim.'

'That is correct.'

Ritter handed Clara the metal rule. 'If you don't mind, Fräulein, you can play the part of the killer. Herr Inspector, you will be the victim. Firstly, stand in front of the Fräulein. Now, Fräulein, raise your elbow into your armpit and thrust from there.'

Clara did, gently, stopping the rule as it touched Strauss's body. It was in the vicinity of his navel.

'You see,' said Ritter. You are six inches shorter than the Inspector and the victim, and your horizontal thrust would only penetrate his abdomen, not his chest. I on the other hand—' he took the rule from Clara and thrusted again at Strauss, this time making contact at heart-height. '—am an inch taller than the Inspector and my horizontal thrust is to his chest. But, if the Inspector were to be seated—' he nodded to a chair and Strauss duly sat '—I can hold my elbow at my thigh and thrust from there to inflict a perpendicular entrance wound.' He handed the rule back to Clara. 'Now you try.'

Clara estimated the angle required and held her elbow at her waist. This gave the required thrust.

'Now, Inspector, if you would be kind enough to kneel . . .' said Ritter.

'It's all right,' said Clara. 'I get your point. If the victim was standing when he was stabbed, it could only have been a tall man who did it. But if seated or kneeling or even lying on his back, a taller or shorter man – or indeed woman – could have done it. And if the victim was on his back, less force would have been required to penetrate the chest.'

'That is correct,' said Ritter. 'So, your friend Levine is not off the hook.'

Clara sighed inwardly. She could no more see Jonny stabbing someone to death than she could imagine him capable of poisoning them with cyanide. But if she'd hoped this post-mortem would exonerate him, she was disappointed.

'Thank you for clarifying that,' she said coolly. 'Do you know how tall Pierre Dreyfus is?'

'He is five feet eleven.'

'And you have him in custody?'

'We do,' said Strauss. 'But we have not formally charged him. He is blaming Jonny Levine. When we find your friend, we will then interview them both and see whose story holds up.'

'You do know that Dreyfus has experience with poison gas,' said Clara.

'We do indeed. But Jonny Levine has experience with something else.'

'What do you mean?' asked Clara.

'Herr Doctor,' said Strauss, 'please continue.'

Ritter grunted his assent, then pointed again to the corpse. 'We have not yet finished discussing the wound, Fräulein Vale, nor the murder weapon. As I said, it's a thick blade. And if you look here and here—' he pointed to the bloodied entrance '—that suggests there was no external sharp edge, other than the initial point. I have seen this before. Tell me, Fräulein, when is a blade blunt on both outer edges but sharp at the point?'

Clara realised what he was getting at. 'When it's not a knife but a pair of closed scissors.'

Ritter nodded. 'Quite. And large scissors at that. Like those used for dressmaking.'

'But that's hardly conclusive!' said Clara. 'And even if it were, anyone has access to dressmaking scissors. Including Pierre Dreyfus.'

'Anyone does,' agreed Strauss. 'But fashion designers have easier access. I have sent my sergeant to search the equipment of all the teams at the Spiegler Modefabrik to see if anyone's scissors are missing. And if not, we'll confiscate them all and see which scissors might match this wound.'

'That's a bit of a stretch, don't you think?'

'I'd call it inventive. And if this does not result in any further physical evidence, the search might fluster the killer. And a flustered killer might make a mistake and reveal themselves. It's elementary police procedure. Now, Fräulein Vale, what can you tell me in return? A deal's a deal.'

'It is,' said Clara, 'and I have some very useful information for you. But there's one more thing I need to clarify with the doctor as it will have an impact on the pertinence of what I'm going to tell you.'

Strauss sighed. 'You're already pushing my patience, Fräulein Vale. And as for the Herr Doctor here, I think you are already way beyond it.'

Ritter growled in agreement.

'All right, this will be the last thing. I promise. Can you tell, Herr Doctor, how long the body was in the water before it was found?'

Ritter nodded. 'Yes. That's easy enough. It appears to be around twenty-four hours.'

'And when was the body found, Inspector?'

'It was pulled from the water at four o'clock today.'

'So that means it went into the water around four o'clock in the afternoon yesterday, is that correct?'

Both men agreed. 'Well, then that exonerates Jonny Levine. He was at the Spiegler house at that time. He went home after you interviewed him at the factory, Inspector. You can check with the Spieglers and their servants. He was home at four o'clock on Sunday. In fact, he was home a couple of hours before that.'

Strauss nodded. 'All right, I'll check on that. But he wasn't home today, was he? In fact, he has fled. An innocent man doesn't flee, Miss Vale,' he added in English.

'No, but one who fears he will be falsely implicated in a murder might. Or one who fears for his own life might too.'

'Is that the information you have for us? Evidence that he was in fear of his life?'

Clara shook her head. 'No, not exactly. But I do have evidence of the time he fled the Spiegler house.' She reached into her pocket and withdrew an envelope. Inside the envelope was the Lucky Strike cigarette butt. She explained exactly how and where she had found it and the information that Jakob Spiegler had gleaned from his neighbour's nanny. 'So, we have strong evidence that Jonny climbed out of the window and left the Spiegler house in the company of a tall man who smokes Lucky Strike cigarettes at five o'clock this morning. Which means he was not out and about at the time of the security guard's death.'

'If I believe the evidence of the Spieglers and their servants,' said Strauss.

'And why wouldn't you?' asked Clara.

'Because Jonny Levine is their cousin and they are trying to protect him. As are you. I believe he is your landlord in England. And a close friend, isn't that correct?'

'It is,' said Clara. 'But if you honestly believed I was trying to cover for him, then why did you allow me access to the case? You obviously heard enough about me from the German Embassy in Cairo to suggest I was trustworthy, didn't you?'

Strauss nodded. 'Yes, I did. And in addition, our mutual friend Larry Winter vouched for you too. In fact, it was *his* recommendation that swung it for you, Miss Vale. But, unless you can provide something more tangible to identify the culprit – or culprits – then I'm not sure what more you can offer us on this investigation. So, thank you for your help to this point, but I think this is as far as we will take our collaboration. Good day to you.'

He gestured to the door. Clara looked one more time at the body, expressed her thanks to Dr Ritter and left.

Chapter 38

It was nearly eight o'clock when Clara and Karl arrived at the Adlon. Clara sincerely hoped Juju would be there with Bella. She had so much to discuss with her assistant. The case was showing some promising leads, but she needed Bella's help to follow them all up. And she was very interested to hear what Bella's search of the hotel rooms had unearthed. But Bella wasn't there.

'Oh, Clara!' said Juju, clearly beside herself with worry. 'Bella didn't come home! I waited as long as I could then I came here to tell you.'

'When did you last see her?' asked Clara.

'Just before one o'clock. She said she was going to search the rooms while the guests were at lunch and then come straight home afterwards. But that was *hours* ago! Oh, Clara, you don't think anything's happened to her, do you?'

Clara's stomach clenched. This was so out of character for Bella. She was a quick worker and would have been in and out of those rooms within the hour. She really *should* have been home by mid-afternoon at the latest. Perhaps, with her lack of German, she had struggled to make her way home. But she had assured Juju and Clara that she had memorised the train route and would know where to get on and off. And if she had made a mistake and got a little lost, she was a very resourceful woman. No, something might very well have happened to her. But Clara did not want to worry Juju.

'I'm sure she's fine, Juju. She might have discovered something and decided to follow it up before reporting back. She's a very experienced investigator. I'll tell you what, can you find that porter fellow who you wooed earlier and ask him if he's seen her?' She gestured to a table in the Elephant Bar. 'I have to speak to Danny and Jakob. But as soon as I've finished, I'll help you ask around for Bella. Meet you back here in about half an hour. Is that all right?'

Juju nodded. 'All right.'

'And don't go out of the hotel,' added Clara. 'Whatever the porter tells you, come back and tell me first. Promise?'

'Yes, I promise.'

Clara approached the table, and both Jakob and Danny stood to greet her. Meanwhile, Karl went to sit with Merlette and Benji who were having a drink at another table. Clara warned him to play dumb about the investigation. She did not want any gossip spreading around until she'd had a chance to question Danny.

'Good evening, gentlemen,' she said in English.

'Evening, Miss Vale,' said Danny and pulled out a chair.

She sat with thanks. She caught Jakob's gaze. It was calm and steady. She took that to mean the conversation with Danny had been low-key, as she'd requested it to be, and that no information about the case, other than Pierre's arrest, had been communicated. Jakob was of a similar temperament to his cousin, Jonny: thoughtful, intelligent and trustworthy. She had previously depended on Jonny's discretion, while knowing at the same time she could not always depend on Juju's. She looked over her shoulder towards the fountain in the hotel foyer.

She really hoped Juju was not blurting out any more information than she needed to. But there was nothing she could do about that now.

She smiled at Jakob and Danny. 'Thank you.'

'A drink?' asked Jakob, standing up.

'Yes, please,' said Clara. 'Can I have a Martini? Oh, and some canapés too. Whatever you can get. I skipped dinner.'

'Would you like a proper meal?' asked Danny. 'We can move to the restaurant if you like.' He patted his large belly. 'I've eaten but I won't say no to another round.'

'No, thank you,' said Clara. Then to Jakob, with a smile: 'Perhaps some extra canapés for Danny too.'

Jakob nodded and retreated to the bar, leaving Clara and Danny alone.

'So, has Jakob told you about Pierre's arrest?'

Danny shook his head, setting his jowls aquiver. 'He didn't need to. It was all over the hotel. Apparently that cop Strauss handcuffed and dragged him off not long after you and Jakob left earlier this afternoon.'

Clara looked suitably concerned. 'Yes, that's what I heard too. Dreadful business.'

'What do you think they've got on him?' asked Danny, his eyes alight with curiosity.

Good, thought Clara, *I don't have to lead him too much.*

'I believe it's been discovered that Pierre is knowledgeable in poison gases and that a poison gas was used in Hugo's murder. That, and the fact that he has admitted to being at the Spiegler Fabrik in the early hours of Sunday morning.'

'As was Jonny,' said Danny.

Clara wondered how that was known. Was that also hotel gossip? Or had Danny spoken to Jonny about it. *After* he'd left the Spiegler house. She did not, however, want to allow the conversation to veer towards Jonny just yet. So, she just nodded. 'Yes. But I was wondering, Mr Cohen—'

'Please, call me Danny . . .'

Clara smiled. 'All right, I was wondering, Danny, what you know about Pierre's interest in gases and chemicals. Were you aware of it before this weekend?'

Danny nodded and then waited as Jakob placed three glasses on the table followed by a waiter who placed two platters of canapés in the middle. Both Clara and Danny tucked in.

'So,' she said, holding a cracker with cream cheese and salmon, 'you were about to tell me about Pierre's interest in gases and chemicals.'

Jakob slid into his seat, his face a mask of neutrality, and picked up his drink.

Danny touched the side of his face. 'I expect you know about how Pierre got that scarring.'

'I do.'

'And that Hugo saved his life during the war.'

'I know that too.' And so as to hurry things along, she added: 'He also told me that he was assigned to the chemical stores after he was released from hospital and spent the rest of the war there. But what I don't know is whether his interest or involvement continued *after* the war. To your knowledge, has Pierre been involved with chemicals at all in the twelve years since Armistice?'

Danny nodded. 'He has. I didn't know him before Hugo introduced me to him in around 'twenty-six, but by then they'd been in business together for two years. Hugo, as I think you know, studied art here in Berlin after the war and the four of us, Jonny, Juju, me and Hugo, worked for Jakob. Then when inflation here went mad and it looked like the Weimar Republic might fall – that was back in 'twenty-three with that Hitler fella and his failed coup – the four of us left. Jonny and Juju back to England, Hugo back to Paris and me – well—' he grinned '—I decided to try my luck in the Big Apple. And lucky it's been.'

'That's all very interesting,' said Clara, 'but how does this tie into Pierre and his interest in chemicals?'

'Well,' said Danny, 'I don't know if you know this, Jakob, but Pierre tried to set up a laboratory like the one your son has to develop new fabrics, dyes and so on.'

'I had absolutely no idea!' said Jakob. 'When was this?'

'Not that long ago. I think he started it in 'twenty-eight but it cost a lot of money to set up. He's not a trained chemist like your son, so he had to hire in staff. The overheads were high. Then came the crash at the end of 'twenty-nine and money got even tighter. And it didn't help that Hugo went on one of his gambling sprees again. The net result was that the lab had to close. And Pierre wasn't happy. Not one bit. It had been his dream. He never just wanted to be an accountant.'

'Good Lord!' said Jakob. 'Why didn't they tell me?'

Danny shrugged. 'I don't know. It wasn't a secret. But maybe Pierre was just a bit embarrassed that it had failed. And Hugo, well, we know how vain he was; if he wasn't at the centre of it, he had zero interest. The lab was very much Pierre's baby.'

Clara was stunned. This put Pierre's potential involvement in Hugo's murder in a new light. And him, very much in the picture again. She had been leaning towards ruling him out, but this information changed things. The motive might now be, not some bizarre recreation of the world war chemical attack, but an act of bitterness for Pierre's failed business venture that Hugo either did not support enough or might even have destroyed due to his gambling. So, how must Pierre have felt on Friday when Jakob proudly gave him a tour of his son's laboratory? How jealous and resentful? And who better to blame it all on but the self-absorbed Hugo Treves.

But how was Jonny involved in it all? Why had he disappeared? And how was Danny – who was just this moment lighting up a Lucky Strike – implicated? If indeed he was at all.

She finished her salmon cracker and had a sip of her Martini. She glanced at Jakob, and then said, casually, 'By any chance, Danny, have you seen Jonny?'

She watched his reaction carefully. He looked mildly surprised, nothing more. 'Why? Has he been looking for me?'

'He might have been,' said Clara, not wanting to alarm him. 'It's just that he went for a walk earlier and he's not home yet.'

'Oh, I wouldn't worry about him,' said Danny. 'Jonny likes to walk when he's got something on his mind.'

'What might he have on his mind?' she asked.

'Well, you tell me, Miss Vale. One of his oldest friends has been murdered. I expect that would be enough to concern him, don't you think?'

There was a slight edge to Danny's tone. Up until now he had passed Clara's questioning with flying colours. Nothing he had said suggested he knew any more than he was letting on.

His answers had been honest and credulous. But now this . . . barbed sarcasm. Why?

She took a sip of Martini. Jakob raised an eyebrow. *So he picked it up too . . .*

'Well,' she said, 'yes, I expect that *is* what he's thinking about. But it's getting a little late and the family might soon start to worry about him. I was just wondering if you'd seen him.'

'And if you do,' added Jakob, 'ask him to call, please. Stella needs to know how many people to cater for for breakfast tomorrow.'

'Will do,' said Danny and helped himself to another handful of canapés.

At that moment, Juju came into the bar. She waved to Clara, her face fraught with worry.

'Excuse me,' said Clara, 'I need to speak to someone. Thank you for talking to me, Danny. I'll leave you to your food. Just one more thing: do you know where your dressmaking scissors are?'

Now this did surprise him. And Jakob, who she had not yet had a chance to speak to about the death of his security guard.

'Why on earth do you want to know that, Miss Vale? Do you want to borrow them?'

Clara smiled. 'No, I was just wondering. Now, if you'll excuse me, gentlemen . . .'

Danny and Jakob stood, both of them looking perplexed. She'd tell Jakob everything later – for now, she needed to speak to Juju. And by the look on her friend's face, it was urgent.

'Oh, Clara,' said Juju as Clara ushered her out of the bar and into the relative privacy of the foyer, 'I've spoken to Hans. He *has* seen Bella. It was at lunchtime. She was leaving the hotel.'

'Then I wonder where she's got to now?' said Clara, with deepening worry.

'That's not all,' said Juju. 'He said she did not leave alone. She was with Hilda Markwald. They left, arm in arm.'

'Arm in arm? That doesn't sound like Bella! She and Hilda are hardly chums.'

'That's what I thought too. And he also said they went out the *back* door, not the front. And there was a car waiting for them. They got in the back seat and it drove away.'

'Oh no,' said Clara. 'What's happened to our Bella?'

Chapter 39

Bella clawed her way to consciousness. She'd been drifting in and out of a thick cloud for an incalculable time – mentally and physically. It was only when she realised the cloud was in fact a plump feather pillow that she started to focus on her surroundings. She was on a bed. She felt like the day after a night on the drink: dry mouth, bleary vision, queasiness in her belly. She was uninjured, as far as she could tell, but her limbs felt heavy. She could not muster up the energy to lift either her arms or legs. So instead, she rummaged around in her addled memories to bring some sort of order to the jumble of mental images: a hotel room, a blonde woman, a fight, a gun, a forced walk downstairs, an alley, a car, a man . . . and then? She couldn't remember anything beyond then.

She shook her head and tried to focus on what she could see now. Yes, she was on a bed. In a strange room. Was it a hotel room? It wasn't the Adlon. The carpet there was royal blue with gold fleur-de-lys. This was a more modern, art deco style: geometric shapes in orange, green and bronze with black outlines. On the side of the room to which she was facing there was a black lacquer dresser in oriental style, with a desk lamp in brushed chrome – the light was on. Then there was a door, and beyond that, two black leather armchairs in chrome frames. It seemed like a modern house. Not like the old style of the Spieglers with its heavy mahogany furniture. Her attention returned to the door. It was a normal door. Nothing remarkable. Other than it didn't have a peephole. Most hotel rooms she'd been in had peepholes. This suggested to her that it might be a private residence. In the crack under the door, she could see the shadow of someone walking past. Not just once, either. There were people out there. Friend or foe? Until she knew for certain otherwise, Bella would assume they were foe.

She turned her thoughts again to the events at the Adlon. She remembered now who the blonde woman was: Hilda Markwald. Hilda had forced her to walk, arm in arm, out of the hotel through one of the back doors. Hilda's gun had been pointed at Bella's ribs, hidden by her coat. Anyone who had seen them would just have thought they were two women walking. Although she wondered if anyone had questioned why a guest was walking arm in arm with a maid. Because Bella was still now wearing her maid's uniform. Her cap was gone, and her ginger hair was spread across the white pillow, but she was in the black dress and apron. As she considered this she remembered what was in her bloomers. She pulled herself up to a seated position, shaking her head to clear the cobwebs, then felt up her skirt and into her underwear. Yes, the photograph and the papers were still there. She thought of taking them out to look at them, but then remembered that they were written in German. As for the photograph – the woman who looked like Merlette and a young Hugo Treves – she needed to get them to Miss Vale, but first she needed to figure out how to get out of this room.

Bella had realised by now that she'd been drugged. She remembered getting to the car, and a man who opened the back door. Bella had recognised him: she'd seen him at the Nazi party. She'd started to ask what the Nazis wanted with her, when

Hilda had poked her in the ribs with the gun and told her to lie down on the back seat. Hilda spoke to the man in German and then he'd reached into his inside jacket pocket and produced a syringe from a small leather case. With the threat of being shot by Hilda, or injected by the Nazi man, Bella had braced herself and then . . . she remembered no more until she woke.

Her head was a lot clearer now. She swung her legs off the bed and realised she was still wearing her shoes. She walked to the door – feeling steadier with each step – and tried the handle. As expected, it was locked. She touched her hair, expecting to find hairpins, but could feel nothing. The pins had been removed with her cap. There was nothing she could make into a pick. She searched the room but could find no substitute. She'd at least hoped there was a wire coat hanger in the wardrobe, but they were all wood – even the carved hooks. And there were no clothes either. So, if this was a private residence, then perhaps she was in a guest room.

She spotted a washstand with a pitcher of water. She poured a glass and drank fully, then she splashed some on her face and neck. She was beginning to feel better; she'd worked through worse hangovers than this, although the mirror above the washstand revealed that she looked far worse than she hoped she'd soon feel. She smoothed down her hair with damp hands, but there was not much more she could do about it. It was not for vanity's sake, but rather the need not to stand out if seen by people out there. And she did hope to get out there.

With the door not a viable escape route Bella turned to the window. The curtains were not closed and moonlight flooded into the room. She checked her watch – it was eight o'clock.

She'd been here for how long? Six, seven hours? The view from the window revealed that she was on the third floor of a large house – possibly a private residence, or a former house used by an organisation for offices. Was she in the Nazi headquarters Rudy had taken her to last night? No, she couldn't be. That was on a busy Berlin street. She opened the window and listened, but could hear no traffic. Below was a gravel drive and beyond that, lawns and a tree line. The house was well illuminated and light spread across the surrounding grounds. It was either a very large back garden in the middle of the city or they were on the edge of the city. There were two cars on the driveway below them.

As she leaned out of the window she heard the roar of an engine. She pulled back, not wanting someone starting one of the cars to see her, but soon realised the sound was not coming from below but above. She looked up and saw the lights of an aeroplane ascending at a steep angle from beyond the tree line, as though it was just taking off. She gasped; could she be near an aerodrome?

The sight of the aeroplane reminded her of the one and only time she had been in one: with Larry Winter in Cairo. And then she remembered what the porter at the Adlon had told Juju: Hilda and Larry had met in the early hours of Sunday morning in the garden of the hotel. That was the second time they had been seen together in the dead of night. Bella tried to recall what Miss Vale had told her she'd overheard them saying on the train: it was something about it being too soon to say or do something. 'We don't want to reveal our hand and raise too much suspicion.' Was that what Hilda had said? And then she'd accused Larry of being stupid and said he was going to 'give the game away'.

What game were they involved in? If Hilda Markwald was prepared to abduct her at gunpoint, it must be a dangerous one. Hilda, she knew, was a Nazi. Rudy had told her as much. But Rudy was a Nazi too – and he was a good man. *Wasn't he?* Were there good Nazis and bad Nazis? Bella had never even heard of Nazis before Saturday night so had no idea. Miss Vale, the Levines and the Spieglers didn't think much of them, but perhaps they only knew the bad sort. She had no doubt that Hilda was a bad sort. But what about Larry Winter? He had seemed like such a nice man in Cairo. He'd helped save Miss Vale's life. Was he a Nazi too? His father was German. He came here a lot. Hilda was also German, although she lived in America. Bella shook her head. She really didn't know enough about it all. But she did know that Hilda, at least, was a bad egg. She looked up, hearing another aeroplane taking off: yes, they were near an aerodrome.

Could she try to get there and ask for help? It was a public place. She'd just need to get beyond those trees . . .

Below her window, a ledge ran around the outside of the building. It was a narrow ledge, but just wide enough to stand on. She was an expert in jiu-jitsu and balance was part of her training. She looked along the ledge: she was only one room from the corner and there was a drainpipe there. If she could shuffle along to the drainpipe, she could lower herself down to the ground. She looked over her shoulder to see that no one was about to come through the door, then she hoisted herself up and over the windowsill. If she kept her left fingers on the window frame she could shuffle along and reach the next window. There would only be about a foot of wall where she had no handhold. But if she kept her weight leaning forward, she would be all right.

Bella checked that the drive below was clear of people, took a deep breath and stepped out onto the ledge. She took a moment to feel the air. There was no wind, all was still. She wedged her fingers into the window frame and edged along, inch by inch. Then she came to the bit where she would need to let go with her left hand and have no hold for a while. She kept her hands, and her forehead, flat against the wall and continued her shuffle. A few breathless moments later and she could feel the wood of the next window frame with the fingers of her right hand. She was safe. Now to move past the next window to get to the drain-pipe beyond. But before she did, she cautiously peered into the window in case there was anyone there who would see her.

And there was.

A bedside light was on, and she could see someone was lying on the bed. A man. A short, plump man that looked very much like Jonny Levine.

Chapter 40

Bella gasped. *Jonny!* She looked closer and noted that he was asleep. *Asleep or unconscious? Has Jonny been drugged too?* She tapped on the window. Jonny didn't stir. She tapped louder . . .

Then the door opened. Bella quickly pulled back, out of sight. But she was desperate to see who was entering the room. She peeked around the edge of the window frame and was just able to see into the room. *Please, God, don't let him see me!* But the blond man – the same one who had injected her in the back seat of the car – came into the room carrying a tray of food. He placed it on the dresser and then leaned over Jonny. He shook him, quite gently, but Jonny didn't stir. The man frowned and checked Jonny's breathing and pulse. Satisfied, he patted Jonny's shoulder and withdrew from the room, leaving the tray of food.

Then the door was locked again.

Bella knocked again. This time Jonny did stir a little. But settled down without responding.

She was too scared to knock any louder in case it drew attention. But even if it didn't, and Jonny woke up, what was she to do then? He had been drugged too. He would be unsteady as she had been. Also, as he had disappeared a good few hours before her abduction, there was a chance that he might have had a second dose of the drug. She did not know what shape he would be in. Certainly not well enough to clamber along a narrow ledge and shimmy down a drainpipe for three floors with only hard gravel to fall upon. And the tubby Jonny was not the fittest of specimens to start with. No, thought Bella, if Jonny was going to escape it would have to be through the door.

He stirred again. She tapped again. He didn't respond. She thought for a moment of leaving him, going for help and then returning with the police, but what if he was moved in that time? Or if he came to harm? No, she couldn't leave him. But what could she do . . . And then, as he turned on the bed and repositioned himself, she had an idea: bed springs. She could try to prise a bed spring from her bed and use that to pick the lock of her door. It was a crazy idea, but the only one she had. It was at least worth a try . . .

She shimmied back to her room, clambered through the window and heaved the mattress from the bedstead. Yes, there were bed springs, but how would she manage to prise one loose . . . she had no pliers, and she could see nothing she could use as a tool. Perhaps the bed springs were not such a good idea after all.

'There must be something I can use . . .' she muttered as she searched the room again, this time examining the lamp to see if there was anything useful she could salvage from it. But as she did, she heard a key turn in the lock. For a split second she thought of pretending she was still unconscious, but the mattress was off the bed and the room was in chaos. She scampered to the other side of the door so she would be behind it when it opened . . .

'*Gott im Himmel!*'

Bella shoved the man carrying a tray, he stumbled, she leaped over him and tried to get out the open door. He spun around and grabbed her ankle, pulling her to the ground. It was a repeat of the scuffle with Hilda. Bella's opponent this time was a well-built young man, but one who hopefully did not have a gun. Bella was trained for this. She barrel-rolled, straddled her legs, then pincered them around his neck. And then she squeezed. He grabbed at her ankles, trying to prise them apart, but Bella was strong enough to keep up the pressure. All his attention was focused on trying to get her legs from his throat which left her arms free to reach for the cord of the lamp. She pulled it off the table, clutched it around the neck, and as the man managed to wrench himself free of her legs, she swung the lamp and connected with his skull.

He crumpled.

Bella jumped to her feet and adopted a defensive pose, ready to kick out. But the man did not move. Cautiously, she approached him. He was out cold, but still alive. Bella was relieved that she hadn't killed him, although she would have been prepared to do so in self-defence. No, he was just unconscious, with an already visible lump on his forehead. She hoped he would wake up with no more than a headache, but she didn't have time to mollycoddle him. She dragged him to the mattress on the floor, took the tie from his neck and bound his hands to the bedpost. Then she ripped a curtain tie from the window and tied his feet. Finally, she shredded a pillowcase and used it to gag him. With a last pat to his shoulder, as she'd seen him do to Jonny, she left him. The key to the room, attached to a ring with some others, was still in the door. She checked the corridor outside the room was clear, locked the door then walked one door down to Jonny's. She tried a few keys until the right one clicked and turned, and she stepped into Jonny's room.

She locked the door behind her and then rushed to the bed.

'Jonny! Mr Levine! It's Bella Cuddy. Oh, Mr Levine, are you all right?'

Jonny snorted, started and stirred. Then his eyes gradually opened. 'B-Bella?'

'Yes, Mr Levine! It's me! Here, let me get you some water.' She went to the washstand – the same as in her room – and poured a glass of water. She returned as Jonny was struggling to pull himself up with the pillow supporting his back. She passed him the water but held the glass as he drank.

'Thank you.' His voice was weak, but his eyes were coming into focus. 'What are you doing here?' he asked.

'The same as you, I think,' said Bella. 'I believe we've both been drugged, Mr Levine. I woke up a while ago.'

Jonny shook his head, trying to clear the cobwebs. 'I think I woke up before. But then someone – a man – gave me an injection of something . . . again . . .'

'A blond man?'

'Yes, I think so.'

'He's a Nazi.'

'Oh,' said Jonny, not looking too surprised. 'Where's Larry?'

'Larry Winter?'

'The very one. He picked me up at the Spieglers at the crack of dawn and said he'd take me somewhere safe.' Jonny looked around the room, his eyes focusing finally on Bella. 'Did he fool you too?'

Bella shook her head. 'No. It was Hilda Markwald who brought me here. But she didn't fool me. She forced me into a car at gunpoint. Then that Nazi fella jabbed me with his needle.'

Jonny, suddenly startled, looked to the door.

'It's all right. He's tied up in my room. Gagged too. But we don't have much time. Someone will come looking for him. I've got to get you out of here, but you'll need a few minutes for your arms and legs to start working again, if you're anything like me. So, in the meantime, tell me about Larry. How did he fool you?'

Jonny explained how he'd returned home to the Spieglers after being interviewed by the police on Sunday morning. He had been devastated at the news of Hugo's death. He admitted that he *had* been with him at the laboratory and tried to talk him out of burning Hilda's dress, but he finally gave up and left. He went to walk off his frustration along the river and then returned to the Spiegler Fabrik at opening time. He only learned later, after Karl and Clara found the body, that Hugo was dead. After the interview with Strauss, he realised he was the main suspect and he didn't have a verifiable alibi. He asked Pierre to say they'd left at the same time, but he wasn't sure if Pierre had done that. But even if he had, he didn't think it would be long until the police concluded that as the last person to see Hugo alive, he was the main suspect. They hadn't arrested him, but he reckoned it was just a matter of time.

'But you weren't the last person to see him alive,' said Bella. 'That'd be the murderer.'

Jonny nodded. 'Yes, I know. But so far, it looks like the murderer is me. Unless they've come up with another suspect?'

'Yes,' said Bella, 'that's what Miss Vale is working on now. So far, the security guard and Pierre are looking like strong candidates.'

'Pierre? But he left the laboratory before me.'

'He could have come back. After you left.'

Jonny agreed. 'Yes, that's possible.'

Bella sighed. 'But you didn't do yourself any favours by hiding away and then disappearing, Mr Levine.'

'I know. I'm sorry I locked myself away, I didn't know what else to do. I was devastated to hear that Hugo died. He was the love . . . well . . . he was one of my closest friends, Bella. I was awash with grief. Then to think I might be blamed for it. I just needed to think it all through. I was going to talk about it to Jakob, Juju and Clara in the morning, but then, around dawn, there was a bang on my window. I looked out, and there was Larry Winter on the lawn. Just standing there, smoking a cigarette. I opened the window. He told me that he had it on good authority that the police would be there soon to arrest me. He said that he believed Hugo had been killed by someone for political reasons, but that the blame would be put on me. He said he needed time to piece it all together. He said if I left with him then he would take me to a safe place, to hide me from the police, until it could all be worked out. I'm sorry, Bella, I shouldn't have listened to him, but I did. I had no reason to distrust him. He is a friend of Miss Vale's after all . . .'

Bella growled. 'Yes, it seems all of us have been fooled by the charming Lieutenant Winter. So what happened then?'

'Well,' said Jonny, 'I asked him if I could tell someone where I was going so they didn't worry about me. He said that would put my friends and family in danger and it was best if you didn't know. He said he'd explain everything later, but there was something political happening, and it was bigger than any of us. Bigger than even Hugo's murder. So, I trusted him. I got dressed, put on my hat and coat, threw down my briefcase to him, then climbed down the trellis. It sounds crazy now, even to me, but you have to remember the emotional state I was in, Bella, with Hugo dead . . .' Jonny paused, before continuing. 'I haven't done anything like that since I was a lad, and I was sure I'd fall. But I managed. Then Larry took me through the garden. There was a car waiting for us in the back lane. I got in, there was that Nazi fella waiting, then he pulled something from his pocket and jabbed me. That's the last I remember.'

Bella nodded. 'Yes, that was the drug. And it looks like they drugged you a second time. So best we get away before they try to do it again.'

'What's your plan?' asked Jonny.

Bella sighed. 'I have absolutely no idea.'

Chapter 41

'Is Fräulein Markwald in?' Clara asked at the reception desk.

'She is not,' said the receptionist, the same man whom Clara had spoken to previously.

'Do you know when she will be back?'

'Is this part of your *investigation*, Fräulein?' The receptionist clearly did not appreciate her treating his guests as suspects. Clara did not give two hoots about what he thought of her. Bella was missing.

'It is. So, when will she be back?'

'I do not know. And if I did, I would not tell you. Our guests' privacy is paramount at the Adlon, and the last I checked, Fräulein, *you* are not a guest.'

Clara was just about to reply when the desk telephone rang. The receptionist answered. 'Yes, Inspector, I shall tell him immediately.' He looked at Clara and smirked. 'Of course, Inspector, I shall tell the Fräulein too.' He put the telephone down.

'Are Herr Spiegler and his son still in the Elephant Bar?' he asked a bellboy.

'I think so, sir.'

'Please ask them – and the lady, Miss Levine, if she's there – to come to the desk at once. It's urgent.'

Clara leaned in. 'Was that DI Strauss? What is so urgent?'

'That is not your business, Fräulein.' He pointedly turned his back.

Clara's fists clenched. But she might as well wait for the Spieglers and Juju. A few moments later they arrived. The receptionist called Jakob aside and whispered to him. Jakob nodded gravely.

He then turned to the group. 'Strauss wants us all back at the house. He's there now, interviewing Stella, Mitzi and the servants. We'd better go.'

'All of us?' asked Juju.

Jakob cleared his throat. 'All of us *except* Miss Vale,' he said in English. 'He specifically asked that she *not* attend. According to the receptionist his exact words were: *I do not want that woman anywhere near my investigation.* Sorry, Clara.'

'That's all right,' said Clara, 'it serves my purposes better this way. I need to find Bella and Jonny, and being waylaid by Strauss would just be more hinderance than help. Off you all go,' she said.

Juju tarried, near to tears.

'You too, Juju. I promise I'll find them. And I'll bring them home.'

Juju nodded and left with her cousins.

Clara turned back to speak to the smirking receptionist.

'Can you at least tell me if Fräulein Markwald has checked out of the hotel?'

He gave a blank stare and looked over her shoulder. Then his face erupted into a smile. 'Ah, Ambassador! Herr Wels! Your table is waiting for you! Let me take you myself.'

He slipped around the desk, skimmed past Clara and bowed ingratiatingly to two distinguished-looking gentlemen.

'Miss Vale!' said one of them. 'What a surprise to see you here!' He stepped past the bowing receptionist and greeted Clara.

'Sir Horace!' said Clara.

'Your father did not tell me you were in Berlin,' said the British ambassador.

Clara smiled, trying not to gloat at how uncomfortable the receptionist looked.

'I'm not sure I mentioned it to my father, Sir Horace. I trust you and Lady Rumbold are well.'

'Splendid! And we would be delighted to host you for tea at the embassy if you have time on your visit. Unfortunately, this evening I have a prior appointment. Well, not unfortunately,' he said, turning to the German gentleman behind him. 'Of course, I am very much looking forward to our dinner, Herr Wels. Miss Vale, may I introduce Herr Otto Wels, the leader of the Social Democratic Party of Germany. Herr Wels, this is Miss Clara Vale. I know her father, Sir Randolph Vale, the banker.'

Wels bowed. 'Good evening, Miss Vale,' he said in impeccable English. 'I hope you are enjoying your visit to Berlin.'

Well, thought Clara, *I would be enjoying it if Jonny and Bella had not disappeared!* She was just about to ask for a private conversation with the diplomat and the politician when she spotted Larry Winter walking into the foyer.

She knew exactly where to find Sir Horace and Wels. But she did not know if she'd be able to catch Larry again.

She assured Wels she was enjoying Berlin, told Sir Horace she'd be delighted to accept his invitation to tea then wished them a good evening. A moment later, she was striding across the foyer with the wind speed of a full-force hurricane and grabbed Larry's arm. 'I need to speak to you. Now!'

* * *

Larry and Clara found a quiet corner in the lounge and sat down. Clara dismissed a hovering waiter, announcing they didn't have time for drinks.

'No time for drinks?' said Larry, teasingly. 'This must be serious. What has England's premier lady detective discovered now?'

Clara glared at him. 'This is serious, Larry. Very serious.'

'All right then,' he said, 'but can I at least have a cigarette?'

She nodded. He extracted his cigarette case and lit up a Lucky Strike, before crossing his legs and exhaling slowly. 'How can I help you, Clara?'

'You can tell me what you have done with Jonny and Bella.'

'Jonny and Bella? What in the world are you talking about?'

Clara slammed her hand down on the table. The ashtray clattered. 'For crying out loud, Larry! I know you're involved in this. Hilda was seen leaving the hotel with Bella at lunchtime today. And I don't think Bella went willingly. *You* were seen leaving the Spiegler garden with Jonny at five o'clock this morning. I don't know if he went willingly. But I do know that you and Hilda are in cahoots. I overheard you talking on the train about a plan you had that Hilda did not want you to reveal too soon. And you were seen again, in the early hours of Sunday morning, meeting with her in the hotel garden. Despite your protestations that there is nothing going on between you, the evidence suggests there is. So, tell me, where are Jonny and Bella?'

Clara was taking a chance accusing him of abducting Jonny. She did not know for sure that the Lucky Strike man was him and not Danny, but her gut told her it was. Add to that Larry's suspicious behaviour with Hilda, and evasive conversation whenever Clara had tried to question him, and she believed Larry was at the centre of all this. That he was Hugo's murderer she doubted, but he definitely knew more than he was letting on.

She waited for him to play coy and try to charm her as he always did, but to her relief, he put the cigarette in the ashtray and said seriously, 'All right, I'll tell you. But not here, let's go for a walk.'

Clara leaned back, crossed her arms over her chest and shook her head. 'I am not leaving this hotel with you, Larry, not until Jonny and Bella are returned – uninjured and safe. Now *what* have you done with them?'

Larry sighed and lowered his voice. His tone was hypnotic and soothing. 'Don't worry, Clara, they're safe. And will remain so.'

'So, you have taken them?'

'Yes.'

'For heaven's sake, why?'

'Well,' said Larry, picking up his cigarette again, then putting it back down, 'I suppose I'd better come clean with it. Did you notice that I came into the hotel just a few minutes after Herr Wels, the politician your ambassador introduced you to?'

'I did.'

'It wasn't a coincidence. I, and my colleagues, have been keeping an eye on Wels. For his own safety.'

'Your colleagues?'

'German and American. The truth is, Clara, I work for American Intelligence as a German liaison officer. I have done so since before I met you. I was not just in Cairo to fly people around. My trip from there to Jordan was part of my intelligence work. And that's what I'm doing here too.'

'You're a *spy*?'

'An intelligence agent. I can't say more. But what I can tell you is that we have information that there might be an attempt on the life of the leader of the Social Democrats before the election next Sunday. The Nazis are behind it, and they were planning on using the Fashion Week as a cover for the assassination.'

'My God!'

'Yes, it's serious.' Larry picked up the cigarette and took a long drag, giving him time to order his thoughts. Eventually, he said, 'But I'm afraid there's more, Clara. We suspect that the Nazis have a mole in one of the foreign fashion teams – the French, British or American – who will facilitate the attack from the inside, ensuring the assassin has full access. Herr Wels and his wife will be in attendance at one of the shows this week. His wife, apparently, is one of Hertzog Department Store's best customers. And from what I've heard, the shows have now been given the go-ahead to resume.'

'Yes, they have,' said Clara. 'They were hoping to start again tomorrow. But can we get back to the notion that a member of one of the foreign teams is here as an agent for the Nazis?'

'Of course,' said Larry. 'It's shocking, I know, but that's what our intelligence suggests.'

Clara shook her head firmly. 'I don't know what information you have, Larry, whether it's credible or not, but I can tell you that it's absolutely *not* the British! That's just Juju and Jonny. And of course Bella and I.' Then she paused, mid-thought. 'Oh no, you're not telling me you think Jonny is a Nazi agent . . .'

'No,' said Larry, 'I'm not, but my colleagues, particularly my German colleagues, are not as convinced by his innocence. Particularly after Hugo's murder. On the surface, it looks like he did that, Clara, and my colleagues think he might have done it to keep Hugo quiet. They were lovers, you know . . .'

'I know.'

'And it's been suggested that there was some pillow talk. That Hugo might have discovered Jonny's involvement with the Nazis and that he threatened to expose him.'

Clara shook her head vigorously. 'But he's *Jewish*.'

Larry shrugged. 'So is everyone on the foreign teams, apart from you, Bella, Merlette and Hilda.'

'Then it must be Hilda! She's been acting very oddly. Is that who you suspect?'

Larry gave an ironic laugh. 'No, I don't suspect Hilda. She's an agent too. We're working the case together.'

Clara was incredulous. 'Hilda's a *spy*?'

'Yes. And a very good one. That's what you heard us talking about on the train, Clara. I'm sorry I lied to you about that. But I needed to keep our association a secret. Both of us were working hard to try to find out the identity of the mole. That's what you overheard. I wanted to question the team members more directly; Hilda thought that would reveal our hand too soon. And she was right. As I said, she's an excellent spy.'

'Well, you're right there. I didn't for one minute think she wasn't a Nazi.'

'That's because she actually *was* one. But she had a change of heart when her younger brother was killed by Nazi thugs. He was a communist student agitator, the black sheep of the family. Hilda's German family are Prussian aristocrats. Old money. Keen Nazi supporters. But her brother had other ideas. When he was killed, she moved to New York. It was there that I met her. I knew about her brother and that she was angry with the Nazis about it, and I used it to recruit her as a double agent. She has the ear of Göring and so is one of our most important assets. We can't afford for her to be exposed. So, when she found Bella searching her things . . .'

'Bella? What did Hilda do to her?'

'It's all right, Clara, she's fine. Hilda found her searching her room. She wasn't sure if Bella had seen something that could expose her, so she brought her in for her own protection. Just like I brought Jonny in.'

'Brought them in *where*?'

'I can't tell you that. But I can assure you they are safe. And when this is all over, I will fly them out of the country back to England. I promise you that.'

'You will do no such thing! I want them released now, Larry, or I'm going to the police.'

Larry laughed. 'The police? Who do you think I'm protecting Jonny from? The police are riddled with Nazis. They are just looking to pin Hugo's murder on his homosexual Jewish lover.'

'I never got the impression Strauss was prejudiced against Jews.'

'He isn't. He's one of the good guys. But he is under pressure from more senior officers to pin it on a Jew. And as that Jew – your Jonny – might also know something about the plot to kill Otto Wels, all the better.'

'Does he know anything about it?'

Larry shook his head. 'No. I questioned him about that, and I don't believe he does.'

'Good. I'm glad you're convinced of that. So do you believe the mole is still operational at Fashion Week?'

Larry nodded. 'Yes, I do. Because he – or she – did not stop at killing Hugo, who I believe discovered their identity. They have now killed the security guard too.'

'You know about that?'

'Strauss told me. He knew that the guard was working for us.'

Clara gasped. 'The aerodrome! Of course!'

Larry cocked his head. 'You know about the aerodrome?'

'I know the guard previously worked there. And you sometimes fly in and out of there. I felt there was a connection.'

'Then you were right. He was one of our agents at the aerodrome – he worked in the customs department – then we transferred him to the Spiegler Fabrik when we received the intelligence that it would be a front to bring in someone who would help the assassin.'

'Who do *you* think the mole is?'

Larry let out a long sigh. 'I wish I knew. It's not Jonny and I don't believe it was Hugo, although Hugo might have found out who it was and that's why he was killed. But it could be any of the others – apart from Hilda, of course.'

'Strauss has arrested Pierre Dreyfus.'

'I know. We have a man participating in his interrogation, but so far, he hasn't unearthed anything.'

'Because Pierre is innocent?'

Larry shrugged. 'Or just well trained.'

'But there's a chance it isn't him.'

'There is. Strauss is still under pressure to pin it on Jonny. Which is why he's re-interviewing the Spiegler household now.

I haven't told Strauss I have him. He'll be mad when he finds out, but I hoped that by now you would have found the real killer, Clara.'

'I beg your pardon?' Clara spluttered.

He chuckled. 'No pardon to be begged, ma'am. I respect your detection skills immensely. Which is why I prevailed upon Strauss to let you in on the case. So do you know who did it yet?'

Clara looked over her shoulder, back to the Elephant Bar where she'd last seen Danny, Benji and Merlette. Sweet, innocent Merlette. 'I have an idea,' she said. 'But I will not tell you until you return Jonny and Bella to me.'

'I can't do that, Clara, surely you know that.'

'Oh? Why should I know that? You can and you will. And if you don't, I have an invitation to tea with Sir Horace Rumbold. I'm sure he'd be very interested to know that the Americans and the Germans are unlawfully holding two British citizens against their will. So, Larry—' she smiled coolly '—I'll just wait here until you bring them back. And don't take too long about it.'

Larry shook his head. 'Oh, Clara, you don't know what you're asking. My colleagues will not just let them go. It was only because of *my* intervention, because I know how much they both mean to you, that they were not permanently silenced.'

Clara felt a cold shiver down her spine. 'What do you mean, permanently silenced?'

'You know what I mean. Some of my colleagues thought it would be more expedient to kill them. It's imperative that our operation is not prematurely exposed. But I convinced them just to safely abduct them instead.' He reached across the table and took her hand. 'I did it for you, Clara, because of how much

I care for you. You know that I'd like our friendship to be so much more . . .'

She snatched her hand away. 'You have kidnapped my friends and put their lives in danger! I will never forgive you if anything happens to them, Larry. Never!'

Larry swallowed hard. 'I know. I'll go and get them now. Will you wait here for me?'

Clara's eyes narrowed. 'I will wait here for *them*.'

Chapter 42

'What happens when he wakes up?' asked Jonny as he and Bella stood over the unconscious form of their Nazi captor.

'He'll try to alert someone. But hopefully we'll be out of the building by then,' said Bella.

But even as they spoke the man stirred. Bella and Jonny's eyes met. Jonny knelt down, reached into the man's inside jacket pocket and found a leather case. He opened it to reveal a hypodermic needle and glass vial. He read the label on the vial: 'It's morphine. My father was prescribed this in the weeks before he died. It's a strong painkiller and sedative.'

'Give him some,' said Bella.

'I don't know how much to give him.'

'How much did your dad get?'

'I can't remember. But I do know too much might kill him.'

'It's him or us,' said Bella. 'Just give him a little bit.'

Jonny nodded, held his breath and extracted a few millilitres into the syringe. He injected the fellow in the neck. 'Please, God, don't let me kill him.'

Bella's eyes narrowed. 'How do we know they weren't planning on killing us?'

Jonny shook his head. 'They would have done it by now. Why just sedate us, and—' he pointed to the food tray '—feed us too.'

'Aye, you're probably right. But what did they want with us? And who are they? This fella and Hilda are Nazis. Could Larry be one too?'

'I'd be surprised if he was. He was telling me that the Nazis were after me and he was trying to protect me from them.'

'Well, he obviously lied,' said Bella. She removed the man's belt and wrapped it around her fist.

'What's that for?'

She flicked out her hand the belt unwound, the buckle becoming a weapon. 'In case we meet another Nazi.' Then she weighed the bunch of keys in her hand. 'Don't suppose you know which way is out?'

Jonny shook his head. 'No. Let's try to find the stairs – and not be seen.'

Bella locked the bedroom door behind them and they gingerly made their way down the hall, towards what they thought was the centre of the house. There were six rooms on the floor. It was a big house. If she hadn't been in fear of her life – and Jonny's – she might have poked around in the rooms to see what she could find. She still had no idea how any of this fitted in with Hugo Treves's murder, and the clues might be here. They eventually reached a stairwell. The decor was sparse, more like an office building than a house, with plain stairs. The only marker of style was the art deco banister.

They waited, watched and listened. No one came up or down, so in silent agreement they took their chance. But as they reached the landing of the second floor, they heard a door open and shut. And voices. Bella jiggled the nearest door handle, willing it not to be locked. Relief flooded through her as it opened. She peered into the room to see an empty office, and quickly pulled Jonny inside.

As the voices came nearer it became clear that it was a man and a woman speaking German. Jonny leaned into the door to listen.

Bella was hoping for an immediate translation, but Jonny held up his hand, indicating that she wait. The people spoke for a couple of minutes and then moved on. Then Jonny turned to her, his eyes wide.

'You're not going to believe this, Bella.'

'Oh, Mr Levine, after what's happened today, I'll believe anything. Tell me.'

'That was Hilda Markwald.'

'I thought it was! Who was the man?'

'I don't know. But he was asking her if she'd seen Klaus.'

'Who's Klaus?'

'I think it's the Nazi upstairs. Only, I'm not sure he *is* a Nazi.'

'I saw him at the party. Rudy Werner was talking to him.'

'Yes,' said Jonny, 'and I saw him lurking around outside the Spiegler Fabrik, and I think he was the fella who followed me and Hugo there from the Eldorado Club. But I think he might be a plant. Or he's a double agent, or something . . . Hilda said something about hoping Göring hadn't noticed he's "playing for the other side" . . . I'm not sure what she meant but we can figure it out later. They're going upstairs to look for him now. And they were talking about moving us. They said they need to get us out of here before the pilot comes back.'

'Larry?'

'I assume so. I'm not going to wait around to see.' He walked over to the window and opened it. 'Let's go this way, Bella.'

'You can't!'

'Why can't I? I did it at the Spieglers'. It's only the second floor and there's a trellis here too.'

Bella peered out the window and saw that he was partially correct, but the trellis did not look as sturdy as the one at the Spiegler house and the potential fall was onto gravel, not lawn. But it was achievable. 'All right. But let me at least lower you some of the way. Give me your belt and tie.'

Jonny did as he was told and after Bella turned on a light so she could see better, she tied the belt and tie together, then took off her apron and added that to the makeshift rope and then finished it off with the belt she'd stripped from Klaus. She used that to brace it around the radiator under the windowsill. She then tossed the rope out and saw that it only dangled about five feet, but it was enough to reduce the potential height Jonny could fall from the trellis.

'Now,' she said, 'put your hand through the loop I've made with your belt. Use your other hand to grip the trellis. When you get to the end of the rope, take your hand out of the loop and make your way down. If you fall, don't straighten your legs. Try to go into a crouch position and then roll your body along the ground. It will absorb the fall. You might hurt an arm or shoulder, but you won't break your legs or back.'

Jonny's self-assurance was beginning to slip. 'Crikey, Bella, do you think I can do it?'

She held him by both shoulders and looked down into his face. 'I know you can. Off you go.'

So, with Bella hoping her faith in Jonny's physical ability had not been misplaced – particularly when he had difficulty even getting up onto the windowsill – they enacted their plan. And to their immense relief, it worked. Jonny got to the end of the rope, unhooked his hand and then cautiously picked his way down the trellis, jumping the last couple of feet onto the gravel. He bent his legs as he landed. He didn't roll but fell to his knees on all fours.

'Are you all right?' Bella whispered from above.

'I am,' said Jonny. 'Your turn.'

Bella was just about to climb onto the windowsill when the door suddenly opened behind her, and to her absolute shock Rudy Werner entered the room.

'*Gott im Himmel!* Bella! What are you doing here?' He shut the door behind him and stepped towards her.

She grabbed the belt, hoping to use it as a weapon, but realised it was tied to the radiator.

'What am *I* doing here? What are you doing here?'

'I'm working.'

'Nazi work? Like kidnapping people and drugging them?'

'*What* are you talking about?' He took another step towards her.

She lunged for the desk lamp, ripped the cord from its socket, and held it aloft. 'Back off, buster!'

'Bella? What's wrong? I have no idea why you're here, but I can assure you, you have nothing to fear from me.'

'Oh, aye? Then why did you drug me.'

'I did *not* drug you. In fact, I had no idea you were here.'

'And where is here?'

'That, I'm afraid, I can't tell you.'

'A Nazi building?'

'No. Quite the opposite.'

'What do you mean?'

'I mean I am working with people against the Nazis.'

'So, you're not a Nazi anymore?'

'Oh, I am, but . . . look, Bella, I'll explain if you put that lamp down. I have no idea why you think you were drugged . . .'

'Think? *Think?* I *know* I was drugged. And so was Jonny Levine.'

Rudy looked to the window.

'Don't worry, he's long gone. And he'll be calling the police.' Bella sincerely hoped Jonny was long gone. That he wasn't foolish enough to wait for her.

Rudy held out his hands placatingly, as if trying to calm a skittish horse. 'All right. I'll admit it. I did know you were here. It's thanks to me – and Larry Winter – that you and Jonny were not harmed. But I can't say how long I can protect you. If you've escaped from Klaus, it will soon be discovered. I'll buy you some time. Get out of the window, and I'll tell them I haven't seen you.'

Bella's eyes narrowed. 'You're just going to let me go? I don't believe it.'

Rudy sighed and took another step towards her. She braced, ready to swing the lamp. He stopped.

'Oh, Bella,' he said, shaking his head. 'You don't know what you've stumbled into here. But you need to leave, now. I *promise* I'll cover for you.'

'Why should I believe you?'

'Because I love you, Bella Cuddy, and when this is all over, I'll find you again and explain it all.'

There were voices from the corridor. Rudy ran to the door and locked it. 'Damn! It's too late.' Rudy looked around, frantically. Then he appeared to have an idea. 'Hit me with that lamp.'

'*What?*'

'Hit me. Make it look like you overpowered me and escaped.'

'I can't hit you!'

The door handle rattled. Someone called out in German.

'Do it!'

Bella, her emotions in turmoil, dropped the lamp to the floor, then pulled back her fist and socked Rudy on the nose. He yelled, fell to his knees and tried to staunch the blood.

'Go now!' he groaned.

Someone kicked the door.

'I'm sorry,' said Bella, then ran to the window to begin her hasty descent. With the cacophony of a door being kicked in above her, she reached the end of the makeshift rope, found hand and footholds on the trellis, and made her way to the ground. As she landed, crouched like a cat, Jonny grabbed her arm.

'Let's go!'

'It was Rudy!'

'I know, I heard everything. Let's get the hell out of here.'

They ran at Jonny's shuffling pace, along the side of the house and then down the driveway, trying to stay in the shadows. There were only a few feet to go until they reached the road, when suddenly they were pinned by car headlights, turning into the driveway. Bella and Jonny froze, then Bella grabbed his arm and pulled him into the garden, her earlier thought of getting to the treeline resurfacing.

'Stop! Now!' The voice was in English.

They kept on running.

Then a gunshot shattered the air.

'Stop or I'll shoot!'

First Jonny, then Bella stopped.

'Hands in the air.'

They obeyed.

'Now, turn around.'

And as they did, they came face to face with Larry Winter, holding a pistol trained directly at them.

Chapter 43

Clara was relieved to see Merlette and Benji were still in the bar. Danny had left. Merlette was looking as exquisite as ever in a dark green cocktail dress. Her lean body was draped across an armchair as casually as a silk shawl over bare shoulders. Her drink was as green as her dress, and she sipped it daintily while she and Benji talked. Clara did not know what they were talking about, but they appeared comfortable in one another's company.

Yes, she thought, *Merlette looks very relaxed for someone whose boss has just been murdered, and other boss arrested.* What was it she'd said to Karl earlier today? The ones we should be looking at are those who appear not to have changed at all. Those who have made the quantum leap to violence and then returned to placidity. She remembered too Dr Ritter's words at the post-mortem, that if the security guard had been seated or lying on the ground when he was stabbed through the heart with the scissors, the blow could have been delivered by either a short or tall man. Or even a woman.

Could Merlette really have killed the guard, and Hugo? What could her motive have been? Clara knew very little about her. She had lived with Hugo in Paris after her mother had died when she was still a child. Her mother had been a Tunisian seamstress who worked for Hugo. Why did Hugo take in the daughter of one of his deceased employees? Was it purely sexual on his part? No one had mentioned to her that Hugo's sexual appetites extended to children. If they did, she knew that Jonny would not have had anything to do with him. No, that couldn't have been it. But perhaps Hugo was more to her mother than merely her boss. Yes, that would better explain things. Clara remembered when she'd seen Hugo emerging from Merlette's compartment on the train, saying she'd had a nightmare. She'd thought at the time that they might have been having an affair. But on reflection, the way he'd said that Merlette had 'settled' had been almost paternal. Clara gasped. Could Hugo have been Merlette's father?

The more Clara thought about it, the more it made sense. Why then would she have killed him? Clara reminded herself, as shocking as it might be, that children did kill parents and parents killed children. Merlette may have been harbouring rage and resentment towards him. Clara had met people like that before. Seemingly placid on the outside, bubbling with rage on the inside. In fact, she herself harboured rage against her own brother due to the way he had bullied her when she was a child. And Hugo could be a bit of a bully. But this was all speculation. Clara needed proof. Proof that Merlette *had* actually killed Hugo.

Firstly, did she have the physical strength? Clara appraised the young woman's physique: her arms like flower stems, her wrists no thicker than a child's. It was doubtful. But not impossible. Particularly if she'd had help.

It was then that Clara noticed another woman: young, blonde and with a fulsome build. Her cheeks were rouged red, her creamy bosom accentuated by a low-cut neckline. She looked like a caricature of a milkmaid. A strong milkmaid. And she was staring intently at Merlette and Benji. Merlette looked up and caught her eye. She whispered something to Benji. Benji turned around and glanced at the woman. Merlette stood, about to walk over to the 'milkmaid', when Benji tugged her hand and pulled her back down.

'*Je vais aller*,' Clara saw him mouth. French for 'I will go'.

Merlette nodded.

Clara waited for Benji to stand. As he did, he spotted Clara and smiled. 'Ah, Miss Vale, care to join us? I've just got to speak to someone. Please, take a seat, I'll be back in a moment.'

Then Merlette acknowledged her too. On closer inspection, Merlette did not look quite so relaxed. Her eyes were anxious, possibly even fearful. In French, she said: 'Mademoiselle Vale! Please sit down. There is so much I want to ask you. I am so worried! What has happened to Monsieur Dreyfus?'

Clara sat down. As she did a waiter appeared, and she ordered a Martini. Not that she wanted a drink, she simply did not want Merlette to realise she was about to be interrogated.

'I'm afraid I don't know,' said Clara, truthfully. 'I saw him this afternoon with Monsieur Spiegler, but then we left. I believe he was arrested soon after that.'

'But *why* was he arrested? Surely the police don't think Monsieur Dreyfus killed Hugo!'

'I'm afraid that's exactly what they think. Were you aware that Monsieur Dreyfus – let's call him Pierre – had experience with chemicals and gas?'

'But of course! He has always been interested in that. Ever since I've known him. And he was trying to set up a laboratory in Paris too.'

'So, I heard,' said Clara. 'Tell me a bit more about that. Did you ever work there?'

'*Me?* No, Mademoiselle, I am merely a model. But Benji did. Perhaps he can tell you more about it.'

'Benji? Benji Finkelstein? *He* worked at the laboratory?'

'Yes, for a few months last year. But this is not important. Finding out who killed Hugo is.'

Clara looked intently at the young Frenchwoman. 'That's exactly what I'm trying to do.'

'I don't understand.'

'Just please answer my questions!' It came out sharper than Clara had anticipated.

Merlette flashed a wary look and drew back. *Oh no*, thought Clara, *I've scared her off.* She leaned forward. 'I'm sorry, Merlette, I did not mean to snap. I have just had a long, upsetting day. As have we all. I can't explain to you yet why this is important, but you said that Benji worked in a laboratory. Please tell me more about that.'

Merlette hesitated for a moment, then said: 'All right, Mademoiselle. If you think it will help. Benji came to Paris on an internship. Monsieur Cohen sent him from New York. He was to learn as much as he could about the fashion industry. So he did some work in the laboratory, and he learned about how to do accounts with Pierre, and he spent time watching Hugo do the design work. He even spent time with the dressmakers and pattern cutters. It's what my mother would have called a good all-round apprenticeship. But I'm afraid . . .' she looked to the doorway where Benji and the blonde woman had recently departed, then lowered her voice '. . . he has not been entirely honest with everyone. That dress, Mademoiselle Vale, the one that is the same as mine, he *did* steal the design from Hugo. And some others. He has admitted it to me and is very sorry. I told him that he must now confess to Monsieur Cohen. But he told me that Monsieur Cohen already knows!'

Clara was stunned but she remained calm. 'Is that all he has confessed to you, Merlette?'

Merlette's eyes widened in shock. 'What do you mean, Mademoiselle? Surely you don't think . . . oh no, Mademoiselle, he couldn't have, could he?'

'I don't know. But let's see if we can work some of this out, shall we?'

Merlette swallowed hard and nodded.

'Good girl. Let's start with Saturday. Did he tell you where he went after the party?'

Merlette lowered her eyes. 'He did. That lady he has gone to speak to. That blonde lady. He told me that he was with her. The whole night. It's my fault, really. He was jealous of me and Karl Spiegler. Karl and I – well, as you know, we spent some time together in my room on Saturday evening. And Benji was jealous. So, he sought out the company of another.'

'Were you and Benji ever lovers?'

Merlette nodded. 'Yes. Benji and I were romantically involved when he was in Paris. But he was always more serious about it than I was. I must admit, Mademoiselle, that I was quite relieved when he left. He wanted to marry me, you see. But I was worried that it was only because I told him . . .' She stopped, mid-sentence, and bit her lip.

'What did you tell him? Please, Merlette, it could be important.'

Merlette took a long shuddering breath and looked again to the door. Benji had not yet returned. 'It was our secret. Hugo's and mine. But I told Benji about it too.'

'Are you at liberty to tell *me* your secret? Now that Hugo has gone?'

Merlette nodded. 'Hugo Treves was my father,' she said, quietly. 'He did not admit it publicly – it still hurts me that he never did – but we both knew it to be true. It was this secret that I confided in Benji. And it was then that he asked me to marry him. But you see, Mademoiselle, that is what made me suspicious of him.'

'Suspicious? About him stealing designs from Hugo?'

Merlette shook her head. 'No. Suspicious that he only wanted to marry me because Hugo was my father. I believe he got it into his head that I would inherit Hugo's share of the company if he were to die. So, in the end I became worried that he was more in love with his career than me. I cannot have a man who loves something more than me.'

Clara's hand quivered, ever so slightly, as she put down her Martini. 'I see. Well, that makes sense now.'

'What does?'

'Something Pierre told me before he was arrested. He said he'd been in touch with the company lawyer in Paris. He assumed that as Hugo had no children that the shares in the company would pass to him. But the lawyer told him that Hugo *had* named someone in his will. That there was a beneficiary. I wonder if he meant you?'

Merlette's hand went to her mouth. She gasped. 'Oh, Mademoiselle, that would be wonderful if it were true. Not for the company, that I do not value so much. But that Hugo – my father – acknowledges me!' Her eyes welled with tears. 'Oh, Mademoiselle! I pray that this is true.'

Clara was touched by the young woman's response. Was this someone who could have killed her father? She didn't think so. But Benji certainly could have. To get Hugo out of the way perhaps, so Merlette could inherit the business . . . and he could then work on wooing Merlette back. If only he didn't have that alibi.

But his alibi was a prostitute and her mother. Two people that could have been paid to say whatever Benji wanted them to. Because, apart from the time he was said to have left the prostitute woman's house, everything else added up. The dress. The chemicals. Even stealing the formula. And Benji was there this morning. She had been so focused on Danny's whereabouts that she had not considered the man she had already thought was clear of suspicion. He could easily have slipped into the laboratory and taken the fabric. There was just one more piece of the puzzle she needed to figure out.

'Tell me, Merlette, when you say Benji loved his career more than you, do you mean that he loved money more than you? That he would do anything for money?'

Merlette considered this a moment and eventually said: 'Well, I don't know if he'd do *anything*, but money is very important to him. He does not want to be Monsieur Cohen's apprentice forever. He wants to start his own company and with his own laboratory. Just like the Spieglers have here. He is very jealous of Karl, Mademoiselle Vale. He even suggested to me that we should tell the police that Karl killed Hugo.

But of course, he didn't! And the police don't think so, either, do they?'

'No, they don't,' said Clara. 'So Benji wanted Karl to be blamed for Hugo's death, *and* he wanted money.'

'I think so,' said Merlette, the truth of what was unfolding dawning on her.

'All right,' said Clara. 'And do you think he might have been prepared to do something illegal to get it?'

Merlette pondered this a while. 'Well,' she said eventually, 'he's already done something illegal, hasn't he? He stole Hugo's designs. And I know he was desperate for money. He told me that he had got into some trouble back in New York. He said he's busy working on a deal here in Berlin that he hoped would sort it all out. Oh, Mademoiselle, do you think Benji has done something terrible?"

Clara appraised Merlette. It was clear she was seeing Benji in another light. 'I'm beginning to suspect he might have. Now, I know this is going to sound very shocking, but can I ask you one more thing?'

Merlette nodded, looking grave.

'Do you think Benji would take money from Nazis?'

Merlette gasped. 'Nazis? But Benji is Jewish!'

'Yes, I know. But do you think that would stop him from taking money from them? If he really needed it. Think carefully, Merlette. This is very important.'

Merlette's slender frame quivered. She looked to the door and then to Clara, her eyes wide with shock. 'No, Mademoiselle, I do not think that would stop him.'

Chapter 44

Clara left Merlette in the bar and went in search of Benji. She scanned the foyer: the guests and porters criss-crossing the floor, the children running their fingers through the Elephant Fountain while their parents were distracted, the piles of suitcases waiting to be transported upstairs or outside to waiting taxis, but no, she could not see the tall frame of Benji Finkelstein and his milkmaid companion. He had said that he wouldn't be long and that he would be returning to join her and Merlette soon, so he could not have gone too far.

She looked to the reception desk: dare she ask again? To her relief there was a different man on duty, a younger man, one she had not encountered before and so had not had a chance to offend. She hoped he had not been warned about her.

She adopted her most charming smile and approached him.

'*Guten Abend*,' she said in her best German.

'*Guten Abend, Fräulein*.'

'I was supposed to be meeting friends. I wonder if you have seen them. A Herr Finkelstein, a young American man who is a guest here, and a young lady. He is tall and slim, the lady short and fulsome with blonde hair. Fräulein Hassan said they were in the Elephant Bar about a quarter of an hour ago but then they left. Do you know if they are still in the hotel? I need to speak to Herr Finkelstein, and I cannot wait much longer.'

The young man's lips pursed as he blinked a few times, then he regained his composure. 'I have indeed, Fräulein. But Herr Finkelstein has asked not to be disturbed.'

'He is in his room?'

The man cleared his throat. 'Yes, Fräulein. I am sure he will be down shortly.'

'I'm afraid I can't wait that long.'

His hand reached for the telephone: 'I could call him . . .'

Clara considered this a moment and then decided that she did not want to alert Benji that she was looking for him. If he were guilty of what she suspected, then that might alarm him. But she had another idea . . .

'No, that's all right. Don't disturb him. But could you give him a note please? When he returns?'

'Of course, Fräulein.' He passed her a notepad and pen.

She wrote a few innocuous lines about letting him know that the fashion show might still be on tomorrow and asking him to call the Spiegler residence at his earliest convenience. It didn't really matter what she wrote, she didn't expect him to read it. But what she did expect was exactly what happened next. She folded the note, wrote his name on the outside, and then the receptionist placed it in one of the cubbyholes behind him. Number 347.

She thanked the receptionist, then furnished him with a suitable tip.

Smiling, she retreated and appeared to head towards the ladies' cloakroom but then diverted towards the lift and asked the bellboy to take her to the third floor.

* * *

Room 347 was next door to Larry Winter's room. Clara knew the pilot – and now-revealed spy – was in 346 as he had given her the room number on Saturday evening so she could telephone him to arrange to meet during her stay in Berlin. *Fancy that*, thought Clara, *Larry was next door to the mole he had been looking for all this time.*

Suspected mole, she reminded herself. And *suspected* murderer. While the evidence all now seemed to point to Benji, it was not yet confirmed. But she felt she was close, very close. By the process of elimination, and considering who had motive, means and opportunity, she had reached the conclusion that Benji was not only the Nazi mole who would give access to a political assassin at Fashion Week, but also the thief of Karl's formula *and* the murderer of Hugo and the security guard. She needed to search his room, to find the conclusive evidence: Karl's notebook and the stolen fabric, and perhaps the scissors used to kill the guard. But he was in there with the woman. Edith, if Clara recalled correctly. That's what her mother had called her. She wondered how long they would be. He had said he wouldn't be long. Surely there wouldn't be time for them to have intercourse . . . But perhaps it would be what she had heard referred to as a 'quickie'. She pressed her ear to the door and could hear the murmuring of voices – they did not appear to be in the throes of passion.

She would wait for them to leave, then go in. But waiting in the corridor would be conspicuous so she decided to pick the lock to Larry's room and wait there instead. She would then be able to hear when the next door opened and closed and slip in after they left.

She looked left and right, made sure the coast was clear, then picked the lock to room 346.

Once inside she had a quick look round. It did not look as though Larry had spent much time there. *Too busy spying!* she thought, tartly. She was tempted to have a good dig through his neatly packed belongings, but, when she spotted a drinking glass, she decided the time would be better spent eavesdropping on the couple next door. She shook off the fleeting thought that she was being a sexual voyeur and picked up the glass, placing it close to where she thought the bed might be situated on the other side of the wall.

The murmurings she'd heard earlier became more distinct – and more alarming.

'*Nein, mein Herr*, I promise you my mother told the English lady exactly what you said she should say.'

'I don't believe you.' Benji's voice was as cold as steel, so different from the amiable American drawl Clara was used to.

'But it's true! Please, don't hurt her. She did as you asked. I promise you!' Edith's voice was edging on panic.

'Perhaps this time she did. But I cannot trust she will continue to do so. And I cannot trust that you will too.'

'But you can trust me!'

'Really?' Benji's voice dripped disdain. 'I trusted you *not* to draw attention to me at all. And yet you came to the Elephant Bar. Both Fräulein Hassan *and* Fräulein Vale saw you. It is just a matter of time until Fräulein Vale puts two and two together. She is a clever woman. No, I'm sorry, *Mein Liebling*, we had fun, but it's over.'

'*Nein, nein, Mein Herr!* Please, no!' Edith's voice was shrill with terror.

What is he doing to her?

Clara threw the glass on the bed and ran out the door. She had no time to waste. She did not have time to pick the lock, so she pulled off her shoes, and used the heel of one to smash the glass casing over the fire axe near the lift. Axe in hand, she ran to Benji's door and rained blows on the lock, barely drowning out the screams from inside.

A few moments later, she was inside the room and Benji was kneeling on the bed with a pair of scissors, the blades open, poised above the writhing body of Edith whose bloodied hands had managed to fend him off – but not for long.

Clara launched herself at Benji with the axe, using the blunt edge to smash the scissors from his hands. He screamed in pain. Edith rolled off the bed and Clara leaped on it, standing above Benji who was reaching again for the scissors.

'Make one more move and I will chop your hand off!'

He paused. But Clara prepared for him to try again.

'I would do what the lady says,' said a voice in English from the door. 'And if she doesn't chop your hand off, I'll shoot it off. The game's up, Finkelstein.'

Clara, breathing heavily, remained where she was on the bed, standing over Benji, until she saw his hand withdraw and then his shoulders slump in defeat. She stepped off the bed, still holding the axe aloft.

It was then that she saw Larry holding a revolver, and at his shoulder was Bella, her face awash with worry.

'You all right, Miss Vale?' she asked.

'Yes, Bella, I am. Is Jonny with you?'

'Aye, miss, he's downstairs with Merlette. Safe and sound. Lieutenant Winter came to get us. Though we thought at first he was going to shoot us!'

'Sorry,' said Larry, 'I had to make it look convincing in case anyone was watching.'

Clara looked to Edith, quivering on the floor. Her bloodied hands and arms shielding her head. Clara put down the axe, reached for a towel on the washstand, and knelt beside the injured woman, assessing her wounds. 'Go to reception,' she said to Bella. 'Ask them to call an ambulance. This young lady needs help as quickly as possible. And then ask them to call the police. We've found Hugo's killer.'

'Benji bloody Finkelstein,' said Bella, 'it's always the quiet ones.' Then she ran off.

Larry stood his ground, the revolver still trained on Benji, who was clutching his wrist. 'Well done, Miss Vale.'

Clara nodded. 'And well done you. Thank you for fetching Bella and Jonny. In return I've found your mole. He was next door to you all the while.'

Chapter 45

Tuesday 9th September 1930

Jonny Levine sat hunched in a garden chair under an oak tree in his cousin's garden. He had a blanket over his shoulders and Clara could not help thinking that he looked decades older than his fifty years. There was a chill in the air, and the grand old oak, sensing autumn was coming, had begun to shed a few leaves. Clara, who had just arrived home from the police station, decided to keep her coat on and join him. It was not long after dawn and she was utterly exhausted after the many hours of questioning by Strauss, ready to fall into bed. But she needed to speak to Jonny.

With the sounds of the Spiegler household waking up behind her, she made her way down the steps and across the lawn, her shoes crunching on acorns. 'Mind if I join you?'

Jonny looked up, his face ashen. 'You're back.' He brushed some leaves off the chair next to him and Clara sat down.

'Where's Juju?' asked Clara.

'Still in bed, I think.'

Clara looked at her friend in his crumpled suit under the blanket. 'You look like you haven't been to bed.'

He gave a faint smile. 'So do you. Is Bella with you?'

Clara shook her head. 'No. She's at the hospital with Rudy.'

'She hit him that hard?'

'Broken nose. He'll be fine but they're doing some X-rays.'

'Do you know what he was doing there? There was a lot I wanted to find out last night, but Juju wouldn't let me out of her sight. Where were we being held . . . and why?'

Clara nodded. 'Yes. I do know. Larry told me some of it and Strauss filled in the rest. You were at a house near the aerodrome owned by Hilda Markwald's family.'

'The Markwalds? I thought they were all Nazis.'

'Not all of them,' said Clara. She went on to tell him what Larry had told her about Hilda's younger brother, the communist, being killed by Nazis and how she was now working with the Weimer Republic Intelligence with American support.

'So, she's a double agent?' Jonny said, visibly surprised.

'Yes, and so is her other brother. Bella told me you met him last night. Klaus.'

'The fella with the syringe, I suppose. Yes, there is a resemblance now that I think about it.'

'That's the one. Hilda recruited him to the anti-Nazi cause after she saw that socialists and communists were going to be targeted in a purge. The men who killed their brother had never been held to account. So, both of them are now working, under cover, to expose the Nazis' real plans.' She explained about the dossier Bella had found in Hilda's room. From the papers she had hidden in her bloomers, it was clear that Hilda was passing on detailed information of the inner workings of the Nazi Party to her spy masters. Larry had convinced Clara *not* to expose Hilda as, he said, the intelligence she had access to could prove very useful in the future. 'And Larry has also asked Strauss not to arrest anyone for your kidnapping.'

Jonny nodded. 'Yes. I suspected as much. I'll be going into the station today to give my statement, but I expect it will not make it into the official report.'

Clara nodded. 'I expect not.'

'And Rudy?' asked Jonny. 'What about him? Is he also a double agent?'

'Sort of,' said Clara. 'It's hard to understand, as he is still a believer in the Nazi cause. He thinks it's a just cause and that they can and will save Germany. But he has become increasingly concerned that the extremist wing of the party will take over. He heard rumours of the planned assassination of Wels, the Social Democrat leader, and told Larry about it, who then recruited him to help stop it.

'As you know there's an election on Sunday, and Rudy wants to give them a chance to clean up their act and go the democratic route. He told Bella the same. He doesn't approve of the violence, nor the persecution of communists, homosexuals and Jews, so he played a dangerous game from the inside this week. But he *does* approve of their ideas about providing jobs for Germans, not letting too many immigrants in, and building up pride in their country again. And Bella thinks there's nothing wrong with that too.'

Jonny sighed. 'And you, Clara? Do you think there's anything wrong with that?'

Clara picked up an acorn and pulled the little cap from the nut. 'On the surface, no, but I'm very worried about it. I've read in the papers what that Hitler fellow has said, in that book of his, *Mein Kampf.* It looks now that they are trying to go the democratic route, but I wonder if a leopard can really change its spots. Time will tell, I suppose. But if the assassination had gone ahead there would be no chance that the moderates would prevail.'

'Why's that?' asked Jonny.

'Because they would have blamed it on the Jews – and that would have justified further persecution. They already had a Jewish patsy lined up to blame.'

'Benji?'

'Yes. He thought he was only going to arrange for the assassin to get into the fashion show and orchestrate the seating arrangements to give the killer a clear shot, but from what Hilda has found out, he was going to get the blame for the whole thing.'

'So, Hilda knew he was the mole?'

Clara shook her head. 'No. She didn't know the mole's identity until last night. He had been given a code name in the dossier.' There was a suspicion that Hugo had discovered the identity of the mole. And we still don't know if he did. But the intelligence services thought that might have been why he had been killed. And that put you in the picture as the potential mole – or at least someone who now knew the mole's identity. But, of course, now we know that wasn't the case.'

Jonny shook his head and pulled the blanket tighter around his shoulders. 'But why Benji? How did they recruit him and why did he agree to do it? I mean, he's *Jewish*.'

'From what I can gather, it's to do with money. Turns out it was not just Hugo who had a gambling problem. Benji got into trouble with a casino boss in New York. He spent all his own money, borrowed more from his parents to pay it back, then gambled all that away too. He then went to a loan shark, who it turns out was working for the Nazis and had specifically targeted Benji because of his upcoming trip to Berlin.

'They threatened to break his kneecaps and shame him to his parents if he didn't pay back the loan with substantial interest, or . . . he could do them a "little favour" in Berlin.' Clara shrugged. 'Benji agreed.'

Jonny growled. 'Just a greedy little collaborator then.'

'A frightened, greedy little collaborator,' Clara added. 'And an ambitious one. The assassination might have gone ahead unhindered if Benji had not been tempted to steal Karl's formula. He realised its creative and monetary potential when Jakob spoke about it on the tour of the laboratory. So when Karl mentioned at the party that he kept his notebook in a desk drawer at the laboratory, Benji got the idea to steal it. And as if greed wasn't enough, jealousy was added to the mix.'

'Oh?'

Clara told Jonny about Benji's past affair with Merlette in Paris, and that he had arrived in Berlin intent on pursuing her. The fact that she was over him and instead, open to a romance with Karl, was no doubt a shock.

'When Karl and Merlette coupled up in her room that night, Benji was furious and left the hotel, intending to go to the Fabrik for Karl's notebook,' she explained. 'But as he left the Adlon – burning with envy, greed and unrequited desire – he met Edith who offered her sexual services. It turned out Edith's services could, upon request, include the use of handcuffs. Benji, it seems, decided they could be useful for his other plans. He paid her and her mother to lie about the time he left, just in case the robbery at the laboratory was discovered and investigated, left Edith around four o'clock and made his way to the Fabrik. The guard let him in, but it turned out he was not the first of the night. You and Pierre had just left.'

Clara searched Jonny's face. 'What happened there?' she asked gently. 'Pierre told me that you were trying to stop Hugo destroying the dress. Is that right?'

Jonny took off his glasses and rubbed his eyes. When he replaced them, Clara could see his cheeks were wet with tears.

'Yes, that's right. Juju told me that you know about what happened between me and Hugo and how we fell out. Well, we were trying to sort things out. That's why we went to the Eldorado. It looked like we were going to have a second chance.' He looked away and swallowed hard. 'For a while it was like having the old Hugo back. But then, when we left the club, Pierre appeared and got in the taxi with us. He thought Hugo was heading off to gamble again. Hugo was furious with him, and they had a blazing row in the cab. That got Hugo really worked up and he started dredging up old grievances. It didn't take long for his fury with Danny and Hilda to bubble back to the surface . . . So he asked the driver to take us to the Fabrik instead. And I think Pierre has told you what happened after that.'

Clara nodded. 'He has. He said he left hoping you could convince Hugo not to destroy the dress.'

'That's right. And I tried. But Hugo was too far gone. He was drunk – we both were – and full of spite. There was no reasoning with him. Eventually, I decided there was nothing more to do than leave him to his revenge. Oh Clara, if only I hadn't! If I'd stayed with him he would still be alive now!'

Jonny's shoulders began to shake.

Clara reached out her hand and clutched his. 'No, Jonny, no! If you'd stayed, you might have been killed too. This is all Benji's fault, not yours.' She held his cold hand. He looked desolate in the shadow of the old tree. 'I think we should go inside. Let's get a cup of tea and warm up.'

Jonny shook his head. 'No, not yet. I want to know what happened next. No one has told me that.'

'I don't think that's a good idea, Jonny.'

'Please, Clara.' He squeezed her hand, tightly. 'Tell me. I need to know.'

And so, as gently as she could, she told him the rest of the story.

Larry had told her that Benji confessed to going to the laboratory, expecting to be alone, and was shocked to find Hugo there, drunk and trying to burn Hilda's dress. Hugo confronted Benji about the dress, blaming him for stealing the design and threatening to tell Danny. When Benji said Danny already knew, Hugo was furious and said he would expose them both, ensuring they would never work in the fashion industry again. This enraged Benji, who attacked Hugo. They fought, but as Hugo was an older man, and already worse for wear, Benji quickly got the better of him and Hugo was knocked unconscious in the scuffle. Benji then handcuffed him inside the fume hood until he could decide what to do. There was no going back . . . he had come too far. If he let Hugo go he would expose him and Danny, and if they were exiled from Fashion Week Benji would not be able to fulfil his role in setting up the assassination. Which would mean he'd all but signed his own death warrant. He decided it was simply a matter of self-preservation. Hugo would have to die instead.

Benji found the keys Hugo had taken from Jakob's office then looked around the laboratory for a way to kill him, quickly realising that using chemicals would point the finger of blame at Karl the chemist – his love rival with Merlette.

When Benji saw the poison cupboard, he decided to use cyanide. He donned gloves and a gas mask and administered the cyanide.

Clara paused her story, searching her friend's stricken face. 'And that's all that happened.'

Jonny swallowed hard, his chin falling to his chest. He was silent for a moment. Then he looked up. 'That's not all that happened, Clara. I know you're trying to protect me, but I need to know it all. What happened after the cyanide? How did he die?'

Clara squeezed his hand. 'It would have been quick, I promise you. And as Hugo was already unconscious, painless. He wouldn't have felt a thing.'

'Are you sure?'

Clara nodded.

Jonny let out a long, painful breath. 'Thank you. That helps, a little. But I'd also like to know what happened after that. How Benji tried to get away with it. And how – thank God – he was caught. I'm so grateful that you caught him, Clara. I couldn't bear thinking Hugo's killer had got away with it. So, tell me, please, what happened then.'

Clara appraised her friend and saw that while he was wrapped in grief, he was not about to fall apart. 'All right,' she said, eventually. 'Here's what I've managed to piece together.'

As Jonny pulled the blanket tighter around his shoulders, Clara explained how, after Benji killed Hugo, he looked for the key to Karl's desk drawer but couldn't find it. Benji told Strauss that after killing Hugo he was frightened the guard would discover him. He was impatient to leave, so broke the drawer open and took the notebook. But he forgot about the fabric – which he would later come back to retrieve.

When he left the laboratory, the guard asked if he was alone or if Herr Treves would be leaving too. Benji thought of killing the guard there and then but decided instead to bribe him. He said Herr Treves was sleeping off the alcohol and Benji did not want it to be known he was there. He gave the man whatever money he had to say that he had seen *no one* that night and not to go into the laboratory, as that was where Herr Treves was and he did not want the poor man to be shamed any further. Benji took the guard's address and said he would be around later that morning to give him a considerable amount more. The guard agreed, not realising he had been given a stay of execution.

When Benji arrived back at the Fabrik later that morning, before Karl and Clara, he couldn't resist checking up on his handiwork. He could still smell a whiff of almonds, so he decided to release the foul-smelling hydrogen sulphide gas to cover it, but also to further implicate Karl who he hoped would be the prime suspect.

As the police investigation started, all seemed to be going well. Strauss told Clara that during his first interview on Sunday Benji had confessed, shamefaced, that he'd been with a prostitute all night. He gave the woman's address and urged the police to check. Once they did he was free to leave. He then headed to the guard's house. What Benji didn't know was that Lederman was working for Larry's spy agency and was just playing along, his suspicions raised. He was hoping Benji might be the mole, and would implicate himself in the Nazi assassination plot.

When Benji arrived at Lederman's house, with a large sum of money he had stolen from Hugo's room, he paid the guard to leave town. Benji wanted the police to think Lederman had something to hide and would divert their attention for a while so he could continue with his task of setting up the assassination of Wels. To Benji's relief, the guard took the bribe. Or so it appeared. Lederman left the house with his suitcase, but then sent word to Benji to meet near the river. It was there that the guard revealed he was working for the spy agency and asked for yet more money to turn a blind eye. But Benji had nothing left. He did, however, have chloroform which he had taken from the laboratory. He subdued Lederman, used the guard's handcuffs to restrain him, then stabbed him through the heart with the scissors and threw his body in the river. The scissors were Jonny and Juju's. Now that it had become clear that Karl had a confirmed alibi, Benji needed to divert the police to another suspect who was allegedly in cahoots with the guard. As Jonny was already acting suspiciously, Benji thought he was the best candidate. So, he stole the scissors from the workshop and took them with him to his riverside meeting with Lederman. By the end of Sunday, Benji thought he'd done enough to cover his tracks.

And on Monday, when Pierre was arrested and Jonny went on the run, Benji really believed he was in the clear. At least long enough to get back to the job he had been tasked to do in the first place. But he had not reckoned that Edith would come back, or that Clara would see her.

'And that, in the end, was his undoing.' Clara finished the sad tale, and waited in silence for Jonny to speak.

But all he could do was weep.

Chapter 46

Saturday 13th September 1930

Clara felt the now-familiar fear of falling flat on her face as she stepped onto the runway. She was wearing one of Juju's creations for office ladies: a navy-blue long-sleeved straight silhouette with a wide belt and a detachable peplum that gave the impression that a jacket was being worn over a skirt. Clara walked to the end of the runway, not meeting the eye of any audience members, and removed the peplum as Juju had instructed her, so the outfit could be converted into a sleek afternoon dress for after-work social events. Clara swore to herself that after this final show at Hertzog's Department Store, she would never again volunteer to be a model. Running a detective agency, unmasking murderers and tracking down international spies was easy-peasy in comparison.

She let out a long breath as she approached the end of her return walk, and made sure to give the next model enough room that she would not feel compelled to elbow Clara as she had done on the previous round. Although it had turned out that Hilda Markwald was no longer a Nazi, she was still a nasty piece of work – a spiteful, grieving woman who, conveniently for the intelligence services, held a powerful grudge against the National Socialists. She swanned past Clara, wearing one of Danny and Benji's creations. It was a stunning grey-and-green plaid skirt, jacket and matching cape, that could be worn for walking, bicycling, general outdoor pursuits or, thought Clara wryly, whatever other activities a conniving but stylish lady spy might get up to.

As she was thinking of spies, she looked ahead and saw Larry waiting for her at the end of her walk. She had not seen him since the night at the police station. He smiled at her and reached up his hand. She took it and smiled back as he helped her down the steps.

'You look devastatingly beautiful, Clara.'

'Devastatingly?'

'Devastatingly divine. A goddess. A queen.'

'Oh, do shut up, Larry.'

Larry laughed and stepped aside as Juju swooped in.

'Clara! That was wonderful! Oh, I can't tell you how wonderful that was. Can you hear the applause? They loved you!'

Clara smiled warmly at her friend. 'They loved your designs, Juju. Each and every one. That applause is for you and your creative vision.'

'Do you really think so?'

'I know so! You're a star. And finally, the world of fashion has seen it.'

'She's right,' said Jonny, putting his arm around Juju. Clara was glad to see him back on his feet: the show must go on, after all. 'I'm so proud of you. Now, let's get ready to meet the buyers.' Jonny steered his sister away, nodded to Larry and cast a knowing look over his shoulder to Clara.

Clara knew what it meant. Everyone was wondering what would now happen between her and Larry. She must confess, she'd been wondering the same herself.

Clara weaved around a bevy of German models and made her way to the bay window where the British team had set up camp. She caught Larry's eye, but he was now talking to Hilda. He indicated that he would join Clara shortly. She turned to look out of the window. Hertzog's Department Store was on Spree Island overlooking the grand museums and palaces of Berlin. Clara could see the magnificent Stadtschloss, the former palace of the kings of Prussia, which now, in the days of the Weimar Republic, housed the Palace Museum. Beyond the Stadtschloss, just out of sight, was the Neus Museum where the Fashion Week had launched a week ago. It seemed like another lifetime now, the night before the murder of Hugo Treves and Clara's whirlwind investigation that unearthed a Nazi plot to assassinate the leader of a rival political party.

But now, at this final show of Fashion Week, which had eventually got the go-ahead to start on Wednesday, Herr Wels, the leader of the Social Democrats, sat opposite Herr Göring of the National Socialist Party, as if nothing untoward had happened. The election was tomorrow – a civilised contest for civilised men. This evening, their wives jotted down the numbers of the creations they wanted to buy from mainly Jewish designers in a Jewish-owned store. Both women appeared entranced by Merlette's final walk in one of her father's greatest creations: the black evening dress that had caused all the problems in the first place. Danny, as an act of repentance, had helped repair the damage caused when Hilda had torn it from Merlette's body, and suggested to the young model that she wear it in honour of her father, his late friend. Merlette had shed a tear as she put it on, telling Clara that she had always worried about the colour and wanted him to do it in something less funereal. 'But he insisted, Mademoiselle Vale, so I shall wear it tonight in his honour. The colour is fitting,' she had said.

Clara watched as Pierre, released from custody, helped Merlette up the steps onto the walkway. He had been roughed up a little by the police, although his blackened eye was somewhat disguised by his scarred face. His lawyer had hurried to Berlin after hearing Pierre had been arrested and had managed to get him out – after Benji had been charged with the double murder of Hugo Treves and Anders Lederman, and the attempted murder of Edith Voster. The lawyer had also had a meeting with Merlette, and it was now acknowledged that Hugo had indeed named her as his daughter and heir in the will. Merlette and Pierre had agreed to run the company together – they just needed to find another designer.

In the American camp, Danny was stunned when Benji confessed everything to the police. He had had no idea his apprentice was working for the Nazis, nor that he'd stolen Karl's formula – although he did admit to knowing that Benji had stolen Hugo's design for the black dress. He apologised profusely. As this was the least of many crimes, no one laid any charges and it was left to Danny to sort it out with Pierre. Pierre had said he would let it go as long as Danny never did it again.

But as for Benji's crimes, no one was going to let that go, not least the Berlin police. Benji admitted trying to hide the stolen fabric in Danny's sample file, and Karl's notebook was found after Benji's room was searched. After first denying everything, despite literally being found red-handed wielding the very same scissors that had killed the guard, Benji finally admitted to it all.

So Danny, too, was in need of a new designer and assistant. He asked Juju if she would be willing to come to New York. She said she would think about it but needed to talk to Jonny first. Jonny, recovering from his ordeal and the grief of Hugo's death, was not in the mood to discuss intercontinental relocation just yet. Clara really hoped they would not move to the Big Apple. She'd miss them both far too much.

As for the Spieglers, Karl had reclaimed his notebook and the experimental fabric, and was now focused on finishing his PhD. After that, he had suggested he might go to Paris to help Pierre set up the laboratory. He blushed when his sister exclaimed that the real reason was to continue courting the lovely Merlette. Jakob was just pleased that all the distractions were now over, and Fashion Week was finally underway. His wife, Stella, was less phlegmatic.

'Oh, Miss Vale, I don't think Jakob sees the dangers for us here in Berlin. I fear that in the next few years Jews will no longer be welcome here. I hope he listens to me, sees sense and sells up.'

'Where will you go?' asked Clara.

Stella sighed. 'Cousin Juju and Jonny have offered for us to live with them for a while in England. Then perhaps we will move to New York. I might even suggest that Jakob goes into partnership with Danny. But first, he needs to be convinced that Germany cannot, for now, be saved.'

Can't it? thought Clara as she considered the well-heeled crowd attending Fashion Week. Although there were reports of political violence on the streets, growing lines of unemployed people and a worrying rise in attacks against Jews, socialists and anyone the Nazis considered sexually deviant, Berlin still seemed to be thriving.

'Penny for your thoughts, Fräulein,' said a voice at her shoulder. She turned to see DI Strauss peering at her from behind his round spectacles.

'Inspector! I didn't know you were here.'

'I got a free ticket, but I gave it to Dr Ritter and his wife. The fashion does not interest me.' Then he switched to English. 'But I do want to speak to you, Miss Vale. I know we did not always see eye to eye. Your help on this case sometimes hindered and sometimes helped. We were, already, closing in on Benji Finkelstein. A witness came forward to say they had seen him walking with Lederman down near the river – not long before Lederman was killed. But, I must confess, we would not have got to him in time to save the life of that girl, Edith Voster. So, I thank you for that. And also for providing much of the chemical evidence Ritter needs to write up his report. But I have one more favour to ask of you.'

'What is it, Inspector?'

'I need you to pass on some information to your friend Jonny Levine.'

'All right,' she said. 'What is it?'

'Tell him, he *must* convince his cousins to leave Germany. And the sooner the better.'

'And why is that?'

'Because, Miss Vale, I am part of a secret organisation set up to combat the influence of the National Socialists – the same one Hilda Markwald is working for. The Nazis might not win at the election tomorrow, Miss Vale, but there are now Nazis in every organ of state and industry. It will not be long until they *are* in power. We need friends in other countries. Friends who will not think that all Germans are Nazis.'

'Why don't you go?' asked Clara.

He shrugged. 'My talents are best used here. While I still can. I do not publicise it, Miss Vale, but my grandmother was Jewish. I believe one day that might be enough to have me thrown out of the police. But for now, I can still do my bit.'

'All right,' said Clara. 'I'll talk to him.'

At that moment Larry joined them, his conversation with Hilda concluded. Strauss withdrew, bidding farewell to Clara and reminding Larry he had something to pick up from the police station before he left town.

'So, you're leaving then,' said Clara.

'I am.'

'When?'

'First thing in the morning. I'll be flying out.'

'You're not waiting for the election to finish?'

Larry shook his head. 'No, there's nothing more I can do about that. Wels now has full protection, organised by Strauss. The Nazis are pretending there was no plot to kill him, so wouldn't dare try now. So now it's all down to the ballot box and the will of the German people. And I have some business to attend to that unfortunately cannot wait.'

'And where is that?'

Larry grinned. 'I'm afraid I can't tell you that, Clara. But I was wondering if before I go, we can have dinner together. After the show is over.'

Clara shook her head. 'I'm sorry, Larry, I already have plans. The Spieglers have invited us all to a concert and then dinner at their house.'

'Might you be able to arrange an invitation for me?'

Clara looked over to Jakob who was holding a clipboard. 'I don't think so,' she said. 'But if you were to delay your departure a day, I could see you tomorrow.'

'I can't do that,' said Larry, looking disappointed. 'I don't have a choice. I *must* leave first thing tomorrow. But please, Clara, I would like to talk to you. Privately. To get our relationship back on track. If you could meet me after dinner—'

Clara was startled. 'Relationship? I hadn't realised we were in a relationship, Larry.'

'Aren't we?' He leaned towards her. His face just a breath from hers.

She felt a stirring and let her lips brush his.

'Oh, Clara,' he whispered.

'Final positions! Get into your final positions!'

'I've got to go,' she whispered. She pulled away and took a step back.

'So, you'll see me tonight then?' He gave his most charming smile.

Clara shook her head, firmly. 'No. If you really want to see me, Larry, you can stay one more day. You know where to find me.'

Then she went back to the runway, took Juju's hand and together they walked with the other designers and models to a standing ovation from the people of Berlin.

Epilogue

Tuesday 16th September 1930

Bella did not care how scandalous it looked, she was going to enjoy her last, long, lingering kiss with Rudy – being careful not to hurt his nose. The commuters on the platform of the Lehrter Bahnhof, waiting to board the overnight train to Amsterdam, parted around the couple in their passionate embrace, like the sea around the keel of a boat. And like a boat, Bella had felt buoyed these last few days. While Berlin and the rest of Germany was going to the polls to elect their new political representatives, she and Rudy had spent every moment they had together.

'I'll come to England as soon as I can,' Rudy whispered for a brief moment when his lips were free from hers. 'There's a conference in Oxford next year. I'll arrange time away to see you.'

'And I'll talk to me ex-husband about getting that divorce finally done. I don't know how long it will take but he wants to be free as much as me.'

'Write to me!' he said, as the conductor called for the last of the passengers to board.

'I'm not very good at letters,' she said, picking up her suitcase, 'but I'll try me best.'

He cupped her face in his hands and gave her one final kiss. 'I love you, Bella Cuddy.'

'I love you too,' she said, then reluctantly turned and climbed onto the train.

Miss Vale was waiting for her.

'Are you all right, Bella?'

'Aye, I am. I'll be seeing him again. And you? I don't see Larry here. I thought he'd come to say goodbye.'

Clara smiled, wistfully. 'We said goodbye on Saturday. He had to leave, urgently.'

'Oh aye? To where?'

Clara laughed. 'He didn't say! But I suspect Flight Lieutenant Winter might not have flown out of my life forever.'

The two women walked to their compartment, deposited their cases, then joined Juju and Jonny in the dining car. Jonny was reading a newspaper.

'Are we still front-page news?' asked Clara.

Jonny shook his head. 'Not anymore. We're on page five. It's all about the election now. The Nazis haven't won but they've gained over a hundred seats.'

'But not enough to put them in power,' said Juju.

'Not yet,' said Jonny, and stared moodily out of the window.

Juju picked up the newspaper and flicked to page five, still basking in the glow of her Fashion Week triumph. With Bella opposite, Clara took her seat as the train pulled out of Berlin.

Historical notes

The idea for this story was sparked by my dual love of vintage guidebooks and vintage fashion. When I was writing *The Pyramid Murders* in 2024, I bought the 1929 first edition of *Cook's Traveller's Handbook for Egypt and the Sudan*. While searching for it, I also came across a 1929 first edition of *Baedeker's Berlin and its Environs*. Powerless to resist, I bought them both! I knew then that Clara would be visiting Berlin. I also felt that I had not quite finished with the characters of Larry Winter and Rudy Werner that Clara and Bella first meet in Cairo. I knew they would feature in the story, but I still had no idea what the book would be about.

However, when doing some research into 1930s vintage fashion for *The Penford Manor Murders* I spent time reading up about Berlin Chic and German fashion in the Weimar Republic. It was then that I found an incredible book by Uwe Westphal about the Jewish fashion industry in Berlin and how it was destroyed by the Nazis. (I mention it more fully in my acknowledgements below.) And that's when I knew what my story would be about: a murder mystery that takes place at the height of the Jewish-led German fashion industry, but with the growing threat of Nazism about to wipe it away.

As described in this book, the centre of the fashion industry was Hausvogteiplatz, with over two thousand thriving businesses, large and small, in 1933. But within a few years they were either bought out or forced out in the Nazi attempts to

'Aryanise' the fashion industry. If you travel to Hausvogteiplatz today, there is a memorial just outside the U-Bahn station entrance, with the names of people known to have worked in the square before the Nazi purge. There are names too of those who were known to have died. Spiegler's Modefabrik is a fictional building and business, and I imagined it could have been in any one of the beautiful buildings (largely undamaged in the war) that flank the square.

The department stores of Berlin were also mainly owned by Jews, and just like in this book, the fashion departments were stocked with 'off-the-peg' creations. Fashion Week was started by a consortium of department stores to showcase German-made fashion during and after World War I. Hertzog's, mentioned in this book, was one of the organisers. The store, known as Rudolph Hertzog Department Store on Breite Strasse, Museuminsel, was confiscated by the Nazis in 1934 and no longer exists. In its place is now an office building. Elsewhere on Museum Island, the Neues Museum (the New Museum), was severely damaged by Allied bombs, and only finally restored to its former glory in 2009. It is well worth a visit – not least for the bust of Nefertiti which is housed there. During the war she was looted by the Nazis and kept in a salt mine, along with other stolen treasures.

Olivaer Platz in Charlottenburg, where the Spieglers live, was also mostly undamaged, and many of the grand town houses still overlook the leafy square. Unfortunately, the same cannot be said for the Fasanenstrasse Synagogue. As in this book, it became the target of Nazi harassment from the early 1930s, shut down by order in 1936 and then burned down on Kristallnacht in 1938.

Today the synagogue site, with a few remaining walls, has been converted into a Jewish community centre, with a memorial to the named Holocaust victims who were once congregants.

The Eldorado Club was also a real place. It is featured in Christopher Isherwood's *Goodbye to Berlin* and the stage and film versions of *Cabaret*, where the fictional Isherwood meets the irrepressible Sally Bowls. Considered a nest of iniquity, it was shut down and seized by the Nazi Stormtroopers (SA) in 1933 and then became their headquarters. The building stands today. Now – still called the Eldorado – it houses an organic food market.

The Hotel Adlon is also a real place and is still one of Berlin's leading hotels. The story that Jakob recounts to Clara about Lorenz Adlon, the owner of the hotel, being knocked down by a car in front of the Brandenburg Gate, is true.

Hermann Göring, as most readers will know, was a real person. Handpicked by Hitler, he was elected to the Reichstag in 1928 and again in 1930 (in the elections featured in this book). The Nazis were later to sweep to power in the elections of 1932 and Göring was to become the Reichstag president. It is believed that he is the one who gave the order for the Reichstag to be burned down and the blame put on the communists, paving the way for Hitler to be appointed chancellor in 1933. As mentioned in this book, he was a pilot and war hero from World War I and was considered one of the Nazi golden boys. He was married to a Swedish aristocrat who died of tuberculosis in 1933. Göring then founded and headed up the Gestapo. After the war he was tried at Nuremberg. He spoke excellent English and frequently challenged the prosecutors and pointed out errors in the transcripts. Despite this, he was found guilty and sentenced to death. He killed himself with a cyanide capsule before the execution could be carried out.

The idea of a plot to assassinate the leader of the Social Democratic Party on the eve of the 1930 elections is made up for this story. But Otto Wels was a real man. He opposed Hitler in the Reichstag in 1933, pleading with his fellow lawmakers not to pass the act that would allow the dictator to come to power. His impassioned speech fell on deaf ears. His life in danger, he fled to Paris, where he died in 1939, two weeks after the war began. The British Ambassador Sir Horace Rumbold (who invites Clara to tea) was also a real man. From 1928–1933 he sent warning after warning to the British government about the dangers of Hitler and the National Socialists as well as German re-armament. But his warnings too were to fall on deaf ears. He was recalled to London in 1933. He retired and then died in 1941.

Finally, I would like to mention the Friends of Germany in New York of which Hilda Markwald was a member. In reality, this was only established in 1933, after the Nazis come to power. But before then, there were groups in the USA – and elsewhere – supportive of Nazi ideas. Sadly, there still are.

Acknowledgements

I am not Jewish nor German. I visited Berlin back in September 2024, travelling, like Clara, by ferry and then train. I stayed in Charlottenburg, not far from Olivaer Platz where the Spieglers live. My husband, Rod, accompanied me and together – with the help of my trusty Baedeker – we tried to find as many of the places I mention in this book as possible. Unfortunately, much of Berlin was bombed during World War II, so not everything that was there in 1930 is still there today. But then again, much is, and it was wonderful to roam the streets imagining what Clara might see, feel and think. I want to thank Rod for his patience with me when Herr Baedeker said one thing and Mr Google Maps said another. Naturally, I always sided with Herr Baedeker.

I would also like to thank Rabbi Sybil Sheridan and the congregation of the Reform Synagogue of Newcastle upon Tyne for their help and hospitality. Rabbi Sheridan's family owned a textile factory in Berlin in the early 1930s, and subsequently had to flee the Nazis, so her insight was very poignant. I am also grateful to Linda Scott and family who hosted me for a Shabbat meal. I drew on that experience to create the scene at Spiegler house.

Beyond one-to-one conversations, I am indebted to a number of authors whose work helped me recreate Berlin in the 1920s and early 1930s. Otto Friederich's *Before the Deluge: a portrait of Berlin in the 1920s* (Harper Perennial, 1995) was particularly informative, as were the latter chapters of Amos Elon's *The Pity of it All: a portrait of Jews in Germany 1743–1933* (Penguin, 2002).

Christopher Isherwood's *Goodbye to Berlin* (Hogarth Press, 1939), on which the film and stage play *Cabaret* was based, was most useful for giving me a sense of what it was like for a foreigner living in Berlin in this period. The author Isherwood based the story partly on his own experiences there in the early 1930s and the character Mr Isherwood is semi-autobiographical. As an homage to both the author and the character I have included Mr Isherwood as a character in this book as Mitzi's English tutor and 'gentleman friend'. The character of Mitzi is loosely based on Natalia Landauer in *Goodbye to Berlin*, whose family owned a department store.

As mentioned in my historical notes, the idea for this story emerged from my reading into the Jewish fashion industry in Berlin in the 1920s and '30s. I owe a particular debt to the fashion journalist Uwe Westphal and his book *Fashion Metropolis Berlin: the story of the rise and destruction of the Jewish fashion industry* (Henschel, 2019. Trans. Christine Jennings) as well as a number of his online talks.

Thanks too to the Art Deco Society of the UK who invited me to speak at their centenary celebrations in 2025 and to judge a vintage fashion competition. The task was to make an outfit from an original vintage design (1930–1934) that Miss Clara Vale would wear on her next adventure in Berlin. The winning design by Pandora Harrison is worn by Hilda Markwald in the final show at Hertzog's Department Store, and the runner-up design by Karen Harvey is worn by Clara, both featured in Chapter 46.

Finally, my thanks go to the team at Embla Books, particularly Jane Snelgrove, Martina Arzu and Emma Wilson, as well as my fabulous agent and friend, Sara Keane.

About the Author

Fiona Veitch Smith is a lover of Golden Age mysteries and historical fiction and has been shortlisted for the CWA Historical Dagger. She has worked as a journalist, a university lecturer and a communications manager, and mentors new novelists. She grew up in Northumberland, then spent her teens and twenties in South Africa. She now lives in Newcastle upon Tyne.

Visit http://www.claravalemysteries.com/ for information about the world of Miss Clara Vale.

Visit http://www.poppydenby.com/ for more information about the author, and about the world of Poppy Denby.

About Embla Books

Embla Books is a digital-first publisher of standout commercial adult fiction. Passionate about storytelling, the team at Embla believe our lives are built on stories – and publish books that will make you 'laugh, love, look over your shoulder and lose sleep'. Launched by Bonnier Books UK in 2021, the imprint is named after the first woman from the creation myth in Norse mythology. Embla was carved by the gods from a tree trunk found on the seashore; an image of the kind of creative work and crafting that writers do, and a symbol of how stories shape our lives.

Find out about some of our other books and stay in touch:

X, Facebook, Instagram: @emblabooks
Newsletter: https://bit.ly/emblanewsletter